WILD IN DEADWOOD

WILD DEADWOOD READS ANTHOLOGY VOLUME 2

CHARLES LEMAR BROWN

LARAMIE CUMMINGS

LYNN DONOVAN

LOUISE FOSTER   SAVANA JADE

V.J. LEE   AMANDA REID

HALEY RHOADES   R WEIR

TWISTED TEACUP PUBLISHING

TAKE A WALK ON THE WILD SIDE OF DEADWOOD...

One Shot by Charles Lemar Brown
    Retired Oklahoma Bureau of Investigation Agent, Noble Harris, has been called to Deadwood, South Dakota in hopes that his expertise will help solve the case of a murdered model. The annual Wild Deadwood Reads book fair is in full swing, and once it is over, chances are the murderer will be leaving town. With the clock ticking, Harris must narrow down the suspect list and attempt to uncover the motive behind the model's demise. Will his skills be enough or will a killer go free?

Deadwood Dynasty by Laramie Cummings
    Returning to her hometown of Deadwood, South Dakota, for her uncle's funeral, Oakley Foster is thrust into truths she never expected to face. As buried family secrets begin to surface, she must confront her cold and ruthless father in a battle for her family's legacy and inheritance.

Echoes of Love at Mt. Moriah by Lynn Donovan
    When ethereal violin music draws Brian Rourke deeper into Mt. Moriah Cemetery, he discovers a mysterious green-eyed performer whose century-old melodies lead him toward an unexpected connection with a local historian who shares her striking emerald eyes.

Deadwood's Deadly Puzzle by Louise Foster

PI Tracy Belden's fraud investigation in Deadwood, SD turns tragic when she discovers the body of a suspect. Now, to solve her puzzle and her case, she must uncover the secrets his death was meant to hide.

When Enemies Collide by Savana Jade

In the town of Deadwood, two rival pranksters find themselves reluctantly sharing a vacation. What begins as a battle of wits quickly turns into an unexpected romance as they navigate their differences and discover the thrill of love amidst their playful rivalry. Will their antics draw them closer together or tear them apart? Join them on a journey where enemies become lovers in the most unexpected of ways.

Forgetting Dakota by V.J. Lee

Dakota promised he would always find her. However, after suffering a traumatic brain injury, he can't seem to remember her. Hadley promised always to love him, but he chose his ex, the one who made him feel comfortable—the one he remembered—the same woman who would do anything to get him back. They both promised to create heaven for one another, but now she's living in hell. Dakota may have forgotten her, but for her, there will be no forgetting Dakota.

The Wolf's Gamble by Amanda Reid

Ossory wolf Aaron Monaghan travels to Deadwood after he receives word his cousin was murdered, only to find a beautiful psychic confounding his every turn with a secret of her own. When he realizes she's his mate, will it be too late to protect her and her incredible secret from the killer's crosshairs?

Grace. by Haley Rhoades

Fresh from her divorce, Morgan Merrifield escapes with her gossip-obsessed country club friends, only to catch the eye of musician Derek Fox at his comeback concert. With explosive secrets on both sides and the ruthless rumor mill always hungry, their unexpected connection might be worth risking it all—if they're finally ready to play.

Adrift and Out of Time in Deadwood by R. Weir

Private Eye Jarvis Mann is hired to find a runaway girl in Deadwood. The wild west town being wilder than he bargained for...or ever imagined.

ONE SHOT

CHARLES LEMAR BROWN

1

"One shot." Noble Harris mumbled to himself as he pinched the bridge of his nose and stared down at the body.

A tiny bit of blood-matted blonde hair covered the entry wound in the woman's head. The white pillow beneath her face was a pool of crimson. Normally, he would have already turned the scene over to one of the forensics crews from the Oklahoma Bureau of Investigation's lab, but there was nothing normal about this case. To begin with, he was retired and had been for just over a year. Add to that the fact that he was on a very short clock, and the timer had already started, and end with the reality that he was hell and gone from Oklahoma, clear up in South Dakota, and one might begin to understand why he seemed to be in a bit of a foul mood.

Noble looked across the bed at the only other living person in the room, shook his head, and confessed, "Kent, I'm good, but this might be stretchin' even my abilities a bit thin."

Kent was Sheriff Kent Davenport of the Lawrence County Sheriff's Department, located in Deadwood, South Dakota, and a long-time friend of Noble Harris. Except for their chosen profession, the two were as different as night and day. Noble stood at an even six feet, while Kent Davenport might top five-foot-eight if he wore the right shoes. Noble's hair now displayed more gray than black, a stark contrast to the natural dark black mop atop Kent's head. Kent loved riding his Harley Davidson and did so every time the opportunity presented itself. Noble was more comfortable in the rocking chair on his front porch, sipping bourbon and watching squirrels chase one another around the trees in the yard.

It was only because of their long-time friendship that Noble had agreed to fly into Rapid City and take a look at the case. Davenport had picked him up at the airport and explained how time-sensitive it was during the drive to the lodge.

Now standing over the body of Lysa Lynn, Noble found himself wishing he was back in Love County, Oklahoma, sitting on the front porch of his little ranch, sipping Jim Beam from a jelly glass and watching the sun creep higher into the eastern sky.

Why the hell did I let myself get talked into this? he thought to himself.

It almost seemed as if Davenport had read his mind and was answering his question when he spoke the words, "You're the best I've ever seen."

"Ain't no one this good, partner," Noble declared.

"Well, before you throw in the towel..." Davenport extended his arm across the body and offered Noble a dark brown file folder, "at least take a look at the report."

Noble accepted it and took two steps back away from the body before opening it. Inside was a preliminary report with three Polaroid photographs paperclipped to it. The first photo had been taken from the doorway and showed the entire crime scene. The other two were of the victim: one of her entire body across the bed and the other, a close-up of her head showing the entry wound. The report itself was half a page and included the caliber of the bullet, the name of the person who found Lysa Lynn, and the name of a possible witness.

The report stated that the bullet that had done the damage had passed through the head, the pillow, and the mattress, embedding itself in the wooden framework of the bed. It was badly mangled but had most likely been fired from a .38 caliber handgun.

Ginger Ring was the name of the person who found the body. Ginger was herself a cover model, author, and co-host of the Wild Deadwood Reads Event that Lysa had modeled at before her untimely demise. Noble took a notepad from the pocket of his pearl-snap western shirt and made a note to question Ginger himself.

The possible witness's name was Dan Frisbee. Scribbled beside his name was a room number. Noble stepped past Davenport, opened the door of the deceased's room, and glanced down the hall. Dan's room was two doors down on the opposite side of the corridor. Ginger would have to wait; Dan would have to be questioned first.

Davenport stepped up behind Noble and asked, "What are you thinking?"

Noble turned to look at him. "I'm thinkin' I'm a durn fool for lettin' you talk me into this," he answered, then added, "I need a few more minutes in the room, and then I want to talk to Dan myself."

"So, you're on board?" Davenport asked.

"Let's just say I'm standin' on the dock lookin' at the boat, and I'm intrigued," Noble answered with a half-grin.

Davenport slapped him on the back. "I knew it." He laughed, then in a more serious tone added, "The event is over at three o'clock. Some of these folks will be flying out shortly after the event ends. I figure if we don't have this wrapped up by then, the killer might never be caught."

"So, you mentioned in the truck on the drive from the airport," Noble sighed. "Ain't never easy with you, is it?"

Davenport grinned, "If it were easy, everyone could do it, and we wouldn't need folks like you."

Noble suppressed a smile as Davenport turned and left the room. The file in his hand felt good. He had known when he handed over his badge and gun it wasn't going to be easy to let the chase go, but he had never imagined it would be as difficult as it had been. He could not remember a longer year than the one he had just lived.

One last look at the dead model stretched out on the bed, and Noble shut the folder. With a half-smile, he left the room. *How hard could it be?* he thought to himself. *It was writers and models after all. Not the usual unsavory criminal masterminds he was used to investigating.*

"Any preliminary thoughts?" Davenport asked as he stepped out into the corridor.

"Yeah," Noble nodded and grinned at his friend, "I need a drink."

"You're joking, right?" Davenport gave him a questioning side-eyed look.

"I never joke about alcohol." The grin faded from Noble's face, and he drew his eyebrows down hard as he spoke. "I need to see the layout of this place, and I need a drink. I figure we can kill two birds with one stone, as the saying goes."

"Two birds, huh?" Davenport snorted. "I always heard it was a bird in the hand is worth two in the bush."

"Same old Davenport," Noble chided.

"What?" Davenport raised his hands and feigned ignorance. "What'd I say?"

Noble laughed. "Bush, boobies, bottoms, and any variation of the three, and you're all eyes and ears."

"Well, now, partner, can you think of three more lovely things to be all eyes and ears about?" Davenport asked defensively.

Noble rolled his eyes. *The more things change, the more they stay the same*, he thought.

~

The nameplate pinned to the front of the bartender's shirt read Sam. Noble figured it was short for Samantha. It was only a few minutes after eight o'clock when he sat down at the bar. He had not missed the questioning look she had given him when he had asked for a double shot of Jim Beam Devil's Cut.

"We don't carry the Devil's Cut," Sam shrugged as she pushed a strand of her long blonde hair out of her face.

"Then I guess it'll be just plain ole Jim Beam," he smiled back.

Davenport had been called away as soon as they stepped off the elevator, leaving Noble to find his own way back through the hotel lobby and into the casino. Although the casino was small, it had all the bells and whistles that accompany such gambling establishments. As he passed through it, he noticed that there were very few patrons. He figured it must be a bit early for gambling. He laughed to himself. *Too early to gamble, but never too early for a drink.*

Just past the casino, he found the restaurant. The bar he had been searching for was situated in the restaurant's center. Like the rest of the Lodge at Deadwood, the bar was magnificent indeed. The minute Noble had stepped out of Davenport's truck, it was as if he had been transported back in time a hundred years. With its massive wood beams and natural rock façade, the place screamed American frontier, and while he loved stories of the old days, he was sure glad to find modern toilets and electricity inside.

6

He took a sip of the whiskey from the glass Sam had poured for him. As he watched her move around behind the bar, getting things ready for the lunch crowd, he pondered what he knew and what he didn't know about the case. Lysa Lynn was a model. She had been shot in the head at close range with what appeared to be a thirty-eight-caliber handgun. Dan Frisbee was an eyewitness of sorts. Ginger Ring had found the body.

What he did not know would fill up the rest of the notepad in his pocket. He shook his head. How many cases had he solved with less to go on? He took another sip from his glass. Davenport had once asked him how he did it. At first, Noble had simply shrugged, unsure of the answer himself, but Davenport had pressed him.

"It's like I'm holding a ball of twine, and the truth is hidden deep within its core." Noble remembered the look of confusion on Davenport's face as he continued, "The twine is tight, really tight, but I study it until I find a single loose string. It might take me a while, but if I work on that one piece long enough, another strand will loosen up, and before you know it, the whole thing starts to unwind."

"What if you never find that first loose string?" Davenport asked.

"I guess I'll let you know when and if that ever happens," Noble laughed.

Noble shook his head and drained the last bit of amber liquid from his glass. As he set the glass back on the bar, he thought, *time to start looking for that first loose string.*

2

Three people can keep a secret if two are dead. The quote from
Benjamin Franklin ran through Noble's head as he navigated along
the wide corridor that led to the conference room where the book
signing was being held. Nobody except Davenport knew him here,
and Davenport was elsewhere. He figured he might as well take
advantage of his anonymity for the time being.

The doors to the signing opened, and Noble fell into the
haphazard line that had formed. A bearded man with an easy smile
was handing out canvas bags to the people before they entered the
room. The line moved steadily, and Noble soon found himself taking
a bag from the man. As he did so, he read the name printed on the
badge hanging from the man's lanyard—Dan Frisbee.

Noble nodded at Dan, glad to have a face to associate with the
name and then followed along with others headed into the signing.
The excited buzz of fans and readers meeting authors filled the room.
The atmosphere in the room seemed familiar to him even though he
had never been to a book event. He searched his memory bank, trying
to figure out where he had felt this way in the past. Still unable to
locate the similar sensation, he began to move along the aisles of
tables, carefully studying the names of the authors and the genres of
books they had available.

As he wandered through the venue, he heard several people

asking the authors to sign their memory books. A rather attractive young woman with pink hair retrieved hers from the table of an author who had a series of what Noble figured were adult motorcycle club romance books. Each of the books in the series had a man dressed in black, and most of them were shirtless beneath their leather vests.

"Excuse me, ma'am, where can I get one of those books?" Noble asked the young woman as she started for the next author's table.

The woman's eyes narrowed in confusion until Noble pointed at the book in her hand. Then with a shrug, she pointed at the canvas bag in his hand before moving away. Noble shook his head as he opened the bag; perhaps in the year off since his retirement, he had lost a step.

Inside his bag, he found a copy of the memory book. Further digging yielded a layout of the venue with tables and author locations, several bookmarks, a couple of pens, a tube of Chapstick, three magnets, and a paperback novel. The book's cover depicted an oriental woman against a Chinese temple and identified the author as Jade Lee. Curious to see if the novel was signed, Noble flipped through the first few pages. It was not.

Using the venue layout map, he located Jade Lee's table and made his way to it. A trio of middle-aged women was clustered around the table. He listened to their conversation while he waited patiently.

"I loved your last book," one of the women said as Jade Lee signed a book and handed it to her.

"I haven't read any of yours yet," the next woman confessed as she pushed her book toward the author, "but I'm really looking forward to starting this series."

Once all three women had their novels and their memory books signed, they moved on, leaving Noble alone in front of the author with no idea what to say. Mentally, he chided himself. Goodness, he really *had* lost a step.

"Would you like me to sign that for you?" Jade Lee smiled and asked, pointing at the novel in his hand.

Noble nodded as he stepped forward and handed her the book. "Please and thank you, ma'am."

Jade found the page she was looking for and signed her name at the bottom of it. "Would you like me to personalize it?" She looked up, still smiling.

"Yeah, I think so," Noble nodded. He had never been one for autographs or signed works—at least he had never thought he was—but standing here, knowing this lady was going to sign her work to him, gave him a weird fuzzy, feeling in his chest.

"And your name is?" Jade's smile grew wider.

"Oh, I'm sorry. I guess you'd be needin' that," Noble chuckled. "Noble Harris, ma'am."

He watched as Jade wrote to and his name across the top of the page, closed the book, and handed it back to him. "I would not have pegged you for a historical romance reader, Noble," she pointed at the memory book as she spoke. "Would you like me to sign that as well?"

Noble chuckled. "You're right. I'm more of a Louis L'Amour or John D. MacDonald kind of fella, and no, I don't think I need this one signed but thank you."

"That accent sounds awful familiar," she nodded across the room. "Sounds an awful lot like the Brown family. Are you from Oklahoma, by chance?"

"Yes, ma'am, I am," Noble responded.

"Really? So do you know the Browns, then?" Jade asked.

"Can't say as I do," Noble answered, looking over his shoulder in the direction Jade had indicated.

"You should stop by their tables and introduce yourself," Jade suggested.

Noble nodded, "I just might do that, but first I need to talk to the ladies that organized this event. Any chance you could point me in the right direction?"

Jade stood up from her seat and looked around the venue. Noble watched her search the room. After a few seconds, she pointed back towards the door he had come through, "The lady with the long red hair is Ginger Ring."

Noble nodded.

"And the lady across the aisle from her with the short curly red hair and the glasses is Linda Rae Sande," Jade pointed once more before returning to her seat. "They are the two you are looking for."

"Thanks again, ma'am," Noble nodded and touched the brim of his Stetson hat, "It was nice to meet ya."

As Noble turned to go, a voice amplified by a sound system, resonated through the room, "Hello everyone, I'm Robert Kelly. I'm your M.C. for the day. Let me start off by introducing all of you to the two ladies responsible for putting the event together."

By the time Noble located the owner of the voice, Robert had already made his way to Ginger Ring's table. Noble watched him make the introduction and then move to the table occupied by Linda Rae Sande. Robert, whom Noble guessed at about five-foot-ten and a hundred and seventy pounds, seemed to be completely comfortable working the crowded room. Ginger, on the other hand, seemed a bit reserved, almost shy.

As Robert finished introducing Linda Rae Sande and began making a series of announcements, Noble worked his way through the rows of tables. Ginger Ring's attention was still focused on Robert as Noble stepped up to her table.

"Excuse me, Miz Ring," he spoke just loud enough to get her attention.

Ginger turned at the sound of her name and looked up at him. For the briefest instant, he found himself lost in her hazel eyes; then she spoke, "Yes, what can I do for you?" Noble was not sure where her accent was from, but he knew it was not from any of the southern states.

"I'm Noble Harris," he offered his hand as he introduced himself. "Kent Davenport told me to check with you about the murder case."

Ginger reached across the table and shook his hand, "Yeah, no for sure," she smiled, and Noble noticed an almost eerie twinkle in her eyes. "So how long have yuz two been friends?" she asked.

Noble thought about it for a moment then answered, "Over twenty years, I reckon."

"That's a long while," Ginger stated, then asked, "How can we help you with the case?"

Right to the point, Noble thought to himself, before saying, "I need to interview a few people, yourself included, so I need a place with fewer distractions." With a wave of his hand, he indicated the hustle and bustle of the crowded room.

He watched Ginger's eyes follow the wave of his hand. In that moment he realized why the book signing felt so familiar. In his younger years his Granny had dragged him annually to the holiday craft fair in Ardmore, Oklahoma. When he was older, he often visited the same building for the annual gun show. Although the book signing was not either of those, there were a lot of similarities.

Ginger's eyes met his again, "Give me a sec to let Tina know, and I'll show you to the studio. I think that would be the quietest place for you to interview people."

Turning to the lady whose table backed up to hers, Ginger explained what was going on. When the two turned back to Noble, Ginger made introductions, "Mr. Harris, this is Tina Susedik. Tina, Mr. Harris."

"Nice to meet ya," Tina nodded.

"Nice to meet ya," Noble tipped his hat, "Please call me Noble."

"Noble it is then," Tina agreed, then to Ginger, "I'll hold down the fort while you get Noble here organized."

"Alrighty then," Ginger moved around the table and motioned for Noble to follow her back out into the foyer. As they passed through the double doors leaving the conference room, Ginger asked, "Do you know who you're gonna interview first?"

"Dan Frisbee," Noble answered.

"In that case, let me grab Tony to cover the front table, and we'll get Dan on our way to the studio." Ginger held up a finger to indicate that Noble should give her a second before turning to reenter the conference room.

In less than a minute, she was back with a stocky, dark-haired young man dressed in a western shirt with the sleeves removed. The bulging biceps and shoulders left no doubt in Noble's mind that Tony lifted weights.

"Noble, this is Tony Brettman," Ginger introduced them, "Tony, this is Noble Harris. Noble is helping Sheriff Davenport investigate a murder."

Tony offered Noble his hand, "Anything I can do to help, please let me know."

Noble shook the young man's hand and nodded. Ginger stepped past them and started along the foyer to where Dan was still handing bags out to new arrivals. She briefly explained to Dan what was going on. Dan nodded and handed the bags he had been holding over to Tony. Without another word, Ginger and Dan walked away, heading for the other end of the foyer.

And so it begins, Noble thought as he started after them.

3

And so it begins, the Guardian thought, *and so it begins.*

The Guardian—the name had seemed appropriate. After all, what did a good guardian do? They protected those in their care and shooting Lysa had assured those in the Guardian's care were protected.

The death of Lysa Lynn was both necessary and justified as far as the Guardian was concerned. There had been no regret, no remorse, not even a momentary pause to consider whether or not to pull the trigger.

It was done. The kingdom was secure. All within the kingdom were safe. The Guardian would lose no sleep over Lysa Lynn.

Tomorrow, all would leave this place and travel home to continue their lives, and the death of Lysa Lynn would fade into history. The Guardian smiled.

The room Noble was led to turned out to be a small conference room that had been transformed into a makeshift photography studio. A solid black backdrop affixed to a metal rack spanned the largest part of the back wall. Noble could see the edges of two windows peeking around both ends of the cloth. A rolling coat rack that partitioned off one corner of the room held a variety of clothing, most of it western in nature. Western hats, guns, knives, and chaps lined up along the edge of one wall caught Noble's attention. He did a quick check to see if there was a .38 caliber pistol but did not see one.

"Will this work, or no?" Ginger asked as she motioned to a set of tables just to the left of the door.

"It'll work fine," Noble assured her, continuing his mental inventory of the room.

"Alrighty then," Ginger said, and as she walked away, added over her shoulder, "Guess I'll get back to the signing. Holler if ya need anything."

"Should I sit here?" Dan asked, pointing to one of the three chairs in the room.

Noble nodded, and once Dan was seated, he took the notepad from his shirt pocket and flipped it open. Normally, Noble would have chosen to sit across the table from the person he was interviewing, but both tables in the room were pushed up against the wall and covered with various costume accessories and camera equipment. After a moment of consideration, he simply pulled one of the other chairs around to face Dan and cleared a small section of one of the tables, so he had a place to write.

"Dan Frisbee, I'm Noble Harris," Noble introduced himself. "I don't believe we've actually been introduced."

"Nice to meet ya," Dan nodded. "Sheriff Davenport says you're really good at solving cases."

"I guess we'll see," Noble shrugged. "Not much to go on so far. I'm hopin' maybe you can help me."

Dan's eyebrows furrowed. "Be more than happy to, but I'm not sure how helpful I'll be."

Noble flipped the notepad to the page where he had previously taken notes and briefly studied what he had written before saying, "Sheriff Davenport told me you may have witnessed the alleged killer gettin' into the elevator after the shootin' last night."

"Yes." Dan nodded.

Noble waited for him to elaborate. When it became clear that Dan would not, he turned to the first empty page in his notepad and suggested, "Why don't we back up a bit? Perhaps to dinner last night and go from there?"

Dan nodded again. "Okay."

Once more, Noble waited. Once more, Dan sat as if he were waiting for the next question.

Holy shit, Noble thought, *it's like pullin' teeth with a paper clip*.

"So, where did you have dinner?" Noble asked.

"At Oggie's," Dan answered, nodding towards the other end of the lodge.

"Oggie's?" Noble inquired.

"Yeah," Dan replied this time pointing in the same direction he had nodded earlier, "You know, the sports bar here in the lodge?"

Noble jotted the name down, figuring Dan's question was rhetorical. He wondered if all of his interviews today were going to be similar to this one. If so, it was going to be a long day.

"Did you dine alone, or were you with someone?" Noble asked his next question.

"I was with a group," Dan answered.

Noble waited, then raised an eyebrow. "Could I get the names of the others who dined with you?"

"Sure," Dan nodded. "Let's see. There was me, and Linda Rae, then Jean." Noble could tell from the way he pointed in a circular motion that he was mentally making his way around a table. "Then Robert and Tony, then Tina and Jane, and finally Ginger." He nodded to his right as he spoke the last name.

Noble, who had been jotting down the names, began at the top of his list, "That would be Linda Rae Sande?"

Dan nodded his agreement.

"And Jean," Noble looked up from his list, "who would that be?"

"That would be Jean Woodfin," Dan clarified. "She is the event photographer."

Noble wrote her last name and the word "photo" out to the side before moving to the next name. "Robert would be Robert Kelly, and Tony would be Tony Brettman, the models?"

"Correct." Dan agreed.

"And Tina and Jane?" Noble asked, pencil poised to write.

"Tina Susedik. She's an author," Dan clarified, "and Jane Yunker. She's also an author."

Noble filled in the two women's last names and placed the word "author" beside their names before saying, "And Ginger, I'm guessin' that would be Ginger Ring."

"And you would be guessing correctly," Dan grinned.

"So, authors, models, and a photographer," Noble tapped the point of his pencil against the bottom of his notepad as he asked, "where do you fit into the picture?"

Dan laughed, "Me? Well, let's just say I'm a volunteer. I've been helping my good friend Linda Rae with this event since the start."

"Helpin' how?" Noble's eyes narrowed as he asked.

Dan looked at the floor and tugged at his beard as if he was thinking about how to answer the question. When he looked back up, he said, "I help move things around and assist with the setup. Really, anything that needs to be done, if I can help with it, I do."

"Got it," Noble jotted the word "help" out beside Dan's name in his notepad, then asked, "So what did you do after dinner?"

Dan answered quickly, almost as if he had rehearsed the response, "Me and Linda Rae opened up the conference room for the authors who hadn't gotten their tables set up yet."

"If I'm not mistaken, Ginger Ring is a co-host of the event," Noble reached over and tapped the memory book on the table as he spoke, "so would it be correct to assume that she went with y'all?"

Dan shook his head. "No, she went with the models to do an all-models shoot down at the rodeo arena."

"And when you say all of the models?" Noble turned his attention back to his notepad.

Dan leaned his head back and squinted one eye in thought, then tapped his right index finger on his leg as he spoke each name, "Ginger and Lysa, Rob, Tony, and Lemar." When he finished the list, he raised an eyebrow and nodded at Noble.

"Lysa and Lemar," Noble repeated the two names back, then asked, "Lemar would be Charles Lemar Brown?"

"Yes, but mostly we just call him Lemar," Dan clarified.

"Why is that?" Noble asked.

"Have to asked him," Dan shrugged.

"Fair enough," Noble half-grinned. "So, Davenport tells me you told him you saw Lysa and Lemar comin' down the hall together last night, headed to her room."

"Yes, I did," Dan half-mumbled.

"Something wrong?" Noble asked.

Dan looked down at his hands as if he was unsure whether he wanted to answer the question. When he finally raised his head, he shrugged. "I don't know Lemar all that well, but he just doesn't seem like the kind of guy who would kill someone, especially another model."

"I guess you're figuring he must be pretty high on the suspect list to already be worryin' 'bout his welfare," Noble laid his notepad down.

Dan shrugged again. "He was the last one to be seen with her alive, and it would be my dumb luck to be the person who saw them together."

"Make you a might uncomfortable, huh?" Noble asked and watched as Dan nodded.

The sound of movement behind him and the way Dan's eyes moved to the door, let Noble know someone else had entered the room. Before he could turn to see who it was, a female voice began to apologize. "Oh my, I'm sorry. The door was open, and I didn't realize there was anyone in here."

Noble rose and turned. Dan introduced the new arrival from his seat. "Noble Harris, this is Jean Woodfin, the photographer. Jean, this is Noble Harris, he's investigating Lysa's murder."

Noble watched as Jean's face flushed. "I'm sorry to interrupt. I just need another battery for my camera."

"No problem, ma'am," Noble said as he offered his hand.

Jean shook it quickly before turning and starting for a large back-pack in the far corner of the room. Noble had noticed her small stature, but when she picked up the pack, he realized she was only half as big as it was and shook his head. Jean failed to find the battery needed in the first compartment she opened. Flipping the pack around, she opened a second one, found it, and switched it out for the dead battery. She apologized again as she turned and started back toward the door.

"Really, ma'am, it's no problem," Noble reiterated as Jean all but sprinted out of the room.

Jumpy or just in a hurry to get back, Noble wondered to himself. Whichever it was, only time would tell, but the idea of someone else coming into the room behind him unannounced did not sit well in his mind. He stepped to the door and pushed it shut.

As Noble turned back to Dan, "Now, where were we?"

"You were asking me about seeing Lysa and Lemar in the hall-way," Dan reminded him.

"Ah yes, that's right." Noble shook his head in agreement and then asked, "And what time was it you saw them?"

Dan tugged at his beard before answering, "Just after ten o'clock."

Noble eased himself back into his seat, picked up his notepad, and wrote down the time Dan had given him in it. "And how can you be sure of the time?" he asked.

"Because I had just come from the conference room where me and Linda Rae and Ginger had finished stuffing the giveaway bags," Dan explained, "as Ginger was locking the doors, she said, 'We did good this year. Finished before ten o'clock.' Linda Rae looked at her watch and said, 'Just barely. It's four minutes 'til.' I went straight from there to my room. Can't be exact, but it doesn't take that long to get from one end of the lodge to the other, then ride an elevator to the fourth floor, so I'd say just after ten o'clock."

"Fair enough," Noble wrote in his notepad as he spoke, then asked, "And exactly what were the two of them doin'?"

"Lemar was helping her down the hallway toward her room," Dan answered.

"Helpin' her?" Noble looked up from taking notes. "Helpin' her why?"

Dan looked down at the floor and sighed deeply before looking back up at Noble and answering, "I believe she was intoxicated."

"And why did you believe she was intoxicated?" Noble asked the question quickly and studied Dan's eyes as he waited for the answer.

Once again, Dan looked down before meeting Noble's eyes and answering, "A couple of things, actually. The smell. The whole corridor reeked of alcohol. Then, the way Lemar was having to hold her up to keep her from falling on her face right there in the hallway."

"Did either of them see you?" Noble asked his next question.

"I don't think so," came Dan's response. "I was a good ten feet behind them, and because they were moving slow, I made it to my door and let myself in just about the same time they reached her door."

"So, you didn't actually see Lemar go into the room then?" Noble's brow raised as he asked.

"Yes, and no," Dan maintained eye contact with Noble as he spoke. "As I stepped into my room, I took one last glance down at the two of them. Lemar had a keycard for the door. The last thing I saw was him swinging the door open and Lysa pulling on him. I did not see him enter the room; I just figured he probably did since she was. . . well, you know, it's the old two consenting adults kind of thing."

Noble shook his head. The idea of two adults consenting when one of them was too intoxicated to stand upright had always seemed a bit off to him. He saw no sense in voicing this opinion or getting into an ethological discussion on the matter at that moment, so instead, he studied Dan as he asked, "So you called it a night then?"

"I did," Dan nodded in agreement.

"And you were in your room all night from then until this mornin' when?" Noble asked.

"Well, this morning I left my room a few minutes before seven o'clock to meet the girls for breakfast," Dan looked past Noble, and for a moment, Noble thought someone was at the door.

"But I wasn't exactly in my room all night." Dan's eyes met Noble's as he finished the statement.

"You left your room during the night?" Noble's eyes narrowed.

"I did," Dan nodded, then added, "I was just drifting off to sleep when I heard what sounded like a shot. At first, it didn't register, and I thought I might have dreamed it. You know that crazy kind of feeling when you're coming out of sleep and not sure what is real and what was a dream."

Noble nodded.

Dan continued, "Something didn't feel right, so I got up, pulled on my pants, eased the room door open, and stepped out into the hall-way." Dan closed his eyes as if he was trying to better visualize what he was about to say, then continued once more, "The corridor was empty, but there was someone getting into the elevator at the end of the hall. All I saw was a black bag, maybe leather, it could have even been a purse, and then the doors closed."

Noble made an entry in his notepad before asking, "Do you know 'bout what time this happened?"

"Eleven fifty-six," Dan answered, "at least close to that time. I looked at the clock on the nightstand as I was getting back into bed."

"So, you didn't investigate further?" Noble asked.

"No." Dan gave him a confused look.

"If you thought a shot had been fired, why not?" Noble asked.

Dan nodded his head slightly as if to indicate he understood before he went on. "I figured whoever it was getting on the elevator had probably dropped something or banged into a wall or the elevator door. I guess the image of Lysa and Lemar staggering down the hallway sort of took my mind in that direction."

"I can see how that could happen," Noble nodded, "so after that, you didn't leave the room until this mornin' around seven?"

"Correct," Dan nodded.

"Anything else you can think of that might help the case?" Noble asked.

Dan shook his head.

"If you think of anything else, please let me know," Noble stood and offered Dan his hand, "I'll be around all day."

Dan stood, and as they shook, he said, "If I think of anything else, you'll be the first to know."

As Dan stepped around him, Noble returned to his seat and began to go back over his notes. At the door, Dan asked, "Open or shut?"

Over his shoulder, Noble answered, "Open is fine."

"Want me to send anyone else in?" Dan asked.

Noble looked up from his notepad as he answered, "No, thank ya. I need a minute to figure out who that will be."

Noble listened to the sound of Dan's footsteps fading and then turned his attention back to his notes. Somewhere among the scribbles on the paper in front of him was a piece of twine for him to pull at; he could feel it. It was too early to be certain, but there was already a part of him that was sure he could solve this one.

At the bottom of the page of notes he had taken, he wrote. . .

Dan Frisbee: Do not rule out as a suspect yet.

May be inserting himself into the case to keep tabs on its progress.

4

It was still early, but the preliminary information seemed to point straight at Charles Lemar Brown. Noble mentally warned himself not to be led by circumstantial evidence. He rose from his seat; his intention was to find Lemar.

"Would it be alright if I grabbed my camera bag?" Noble turned at the sound of Jean Woodfin's voice.

"Yes, Ma'am," Noble answered. "I was just fixin' to step out for a minute, so the room's all yours."

Jean started across the room toward her bag in the corner. Noble started out the door but turned at the last second and asked, "Miz Woodfin, how does this modelin' stuff work?"

Camera bag in hand, Jean turned around and gave him a questioning look but did not answer. Noble thought for a second. "That was kind of a broad question, I suppose. What I meant was, when do the models use this room? I see the backdrop and the light things, but no models so far."

Noble watched as Jean's eyes narrowed and she looked past him, as if she was needed elsewhere. For a long moment, he thought perhaps she might not answer his question, but then she eased the bag to the floor, and explained, "It gets heavy fast."

Crossing the room, Jean eased herself into the seat Dan had

vacated, before saying, "I've been on my feet a lot the last couple of days, so if it's okay with you, I think I'll sit while we talk."

"Perfectly fine with me, Ma'am," Noble stepped away from the doorway and leaned against the wall.

Jean took a deep breath and let it out slowly before beginning. "Some of the models get here on Wednesdays, but most don't come in until Thursday sometime. The first sets—that's a loose term we use for a group of photos—start sometime Thursday, usually late afternoon or early evening. Those are taken here. Then late in the evening, during the golden hour—that's just before sunset and right after—we do a set outside. Then we shoot all day Friday, sometimes in here and sometimes outside at different locations."

"I see," Noble pushed himself off the wall as he spoke. "Mind if I ask you a few more questions?"

Jean smiled. "I figured you might want to. That's why I took a seat."

Noble instantly decided he liked her. Her spunky attitude reminded him a bit of his late Granny. He slid into the chair across from her and pulled out his notepad, "Okay then, can you tell me who all came in on Wednesday?"

Jean shook her head. "Not really," she answered. "There was a problem with my flight, so I didn't get here until mid-afternoon on Thursday. The only two people I know for sure who were here Wednesday are Ginger and Linda Rae."

Noble wrote Jean's name at the top of a new page and made an entry below it of the day she arrived. Below that, he listed the names of Ginger Ring and Linda Rae Sande, placing the word Wednesday and a question mark at the end of each of their names. When he looked back at Jean, she was studying him intently.

"Everything okay?" he asked.

"Yes," Jean answered, then asked, "Why shouldn't it be?"

Noble gave her a one-shoulder shrug and a half grin. "No reason, I guess. It's just you were lookin' at me...well, kinda strange."

Jean laughed. The laugh shocked Noble even more than the look he had seen on her face when he had looked up. It was one of those pure laughs, the kind that most people grow out of before they reach their teenage years. It was real, refreshingly so, and his half grin grew until it spread across his entire face.

"Did I say something funny?" he asked.

Jean waved a hand at him as she spoke. "Not at all. I was laughing at myself more than you. You're not the first person to accuse me of lookin' at 'em kinda strange." She did a fairly accurate Oklahoma accent for the last part of her sentence before switching back to her normal way of speaking. "It's the photographer in me. I was studying your features and wondering if images of you might sell. With that scar along your jawline, I see cowboy or maybe even MC."

Noble felt the heat trying to crawl out from beneath the collar of his shirt. "MC? What is that?" he asked in an attempt to cover it up.

"MC is short for motorcycle club. It's a whole genre. The guys usually wear black leather," Jean explained.

Noble laughed at the idea of himself in a black leather biker's vest and riding chaps. Not just a mere chuckle, but a deep laugh that originated from somewhere deep. It was a short burst, mere seconds, but it felt good. He tried to remember the last time he had laughed, really laughed, and could not.

"I guess I said something funny." Jean raised one eyebrow and grinned.

Noble quickly composed himself. "I was just picturin' myself in black leather."

Jean gave him a sidelong glance and continued to grin. "So, you're saying you don't think you could pull MC off?"

Noble shook his head. "No ma'am, I don't think so. That would be more of a Davenport kind of thing."

"Davenport?" Jean asked, and then quickly added, "Oh, you mean Kent. Yeah, I can see him on a MC cover."

"So, you know Kent Davenport?" Noble asked. He wondered if the suggestion of his modeling had been real or a way to distract him from the case. He found it hard to believe that the sweet little lady sitting in front of him would try to manipulate him but then reminded himself that this was a murder investigation, and he needed to stay focused.

"I do," Jean answered. "I met him last year here at the conference."

Noble made a short notation that Davenport had made an appearance at the previous year's book signing, not because he felt it would help with the case but more as a reminder to harass Davenport about it. Finished writing, he let his mind wander briefly back to the first time he had met Davenport in the parking lot of the Oklahoma Bureau of Investigation building in Oklahoma City.

"You can't park there," Noble had told Davenport when he pulled his Harley Davidson to a stop in the space next to Noble's truck.

Davenport revved the engine and gave Noble a confused look.

"Hey, you can't park there," Noble shouted, and flashed his badge.

With one final rev, Davenport shut the engine off and flashed a badge of his own. "You were saying? Looks like it's a case of you show me yours and I'll show you mine," he grinned and wiggled his eyebrows.

"So, you're the new asshole on board?" Noble had turned to walk away.

"Don't be mad because mine is bigger than yours," Davenport shot back as he stepped off his motorcycle. "It's not your fault; it's genetic."

Noble stopped and turned around, "What the hell are you talkin' about? What's bigger than mine?"

Davenport stepped up on the curb, and with a confused look on his face answered, "Well, assholes of course. I thought that was what we were talking about. Seems to me you actually brought it up, and since you seemed to be quite the tight-ass, I just figured mine must be bigger than yours."

Noble shook his head, "Really?"

"Yes, really," Davenport answered. Then his eyes widened, and he added, "Oh shit, you thought I was talking about our dicks, didn't you? Well, since you brought it up, mine is most definitely bigger than yours. Like at least three inches bigger."

"Mr. Harris," Jean's voice snapped Noble back to the present. "Did you have any more questions for me?"

Noble fought back a rare blush as he answered. "You said earlier that you and the models...let me get this right," he looked down at his notepad, "did sets, yes, sets on Thursday and then all day on Friday."

"That's correct," Jean nodded as he looked up from his notes. "But that was more of a statement than a question, now, wasn't it?"

"You got me there," Noble smiled, then asked. "During the sets, was there anything out of the ordinary?"

Jean chuckled, "You mean like an argument, or a fistfight, or someone threatening to kill someone else?"

Noble grinned, "Yes, any of those, although they all seem a bit obvious. I guess what I'm really tryin' to get at is, were there any problems? Did everyone work well together?"

Jean folded her hands together in her lap and leaned slightly forward as she answered, "Mr. Harris, I've been doing this for a while now, and while I won't say there are never any problems, this group of models always works very well together."

"So that's a no, then?" Noble asked.

"A solid no," Jean answered.

"One last question," Noble flipped to the next page in his notepad before asking. "You said the models have always worked well together, so have all of the models here worked with Lysa Lynn before?"

"No, sir," Jean shook her head, then after a brief pause, "This was Lysa's first time modeling."

"I see," Noble stood as he spoke and offered Jean his hand. "Well, Miz Jean, I think I've kept you from your duties long enough. Thank you for visitin' with me, and it was nice to meet you."

Jean took his hand as she rose from her seat and, with a smile, "You are very welcome, and it was nice to meet you as well. I hope you find who did this awful thing."

Noble watched as she crossed the room and retrieved her camera case. As she left, he scratched a few last notes onto his pad:

Miz Jean Woodfin: Unlikely suspect.

However, questioning her on Friday's sets seemed to bother her for some reason.

Also, showed pause when admitting this was Lysa Lynn's first time working with the other models.

5

You may be good, but I'm better, the Guardian thought as Noble stepped through the doors of the conference room and scanned the space. It felt good to be in the same room as Noble. It felt exhilarating.

~

Noble spotted Jean as soon as he returned to the conference room. She was standing with Tony and Robert. Noble tried to tell himself there was nothing unusual about the three of them grouped together so soon after he had questioned Jean, but his cop instincts figured it was doubtful.

Stay on task, he thought, *you're on the clock and time is already runnin' short.* With a shake of his head, he turned and began to make his way through the rows of tables. He had checked the layout on the map he had found in the canvas bag before leaving the modeling room, but now that he was back in the conference room, all the tables seemed to run together. It took him a moment to find Charles Lemar Brown in the crowd. Thankfully, the picture he had found of the author in the conference memory book had been taken recently enough for him to be easily identified.

The long silver hair was the first thing that caught Noble's eye.

As he got closer, a well-kept beard of the same color became visible along with a pair of large, round glasses with black metal frames. The author had not been wearing these in his headshot, and Noble wondered if they were for reading.

"What kind of books do you read?" Charles asked him as he stepped in front of the author's table. The Oklahoma twang in his voice was unmistakable.

Caught off guard by the question, Noble answered without thinking, "Louis L'Amour mostly."

"He was one of the first authors I fell in love with," Charles remarked.

"I see," Noble nodded. "Actually, I'm not here about books." Getting straight to the point, he added, "My name is Noble Harris, and I'm helpin' the Sheriff's office with a case. I need to ask you some questions."

"If this is about Lysa, I've already told Sheriff Davenport everything I know," the frustration in the author's voice did not go unnoticed.

Noble shrugged. "I'm sorry to have to put you through this again, but it really is important to the case."

Charles's shoulders slumped as he removed his glasses, folded them up, and slid them into the breast pocket of his western-print, pearl-snap shirt. "Okay, go ahead and ask your questions."

"What questions?" the woman seated to Charles's left asked as she turned back around from the conversation she was having with an author behind her. Her hair was the same color as Charles's only a bit shorter, but the family resemblance was obvious.

Before Noble could answer, Charles spoke up, "Amy, this is Noble Harris. He's helpin' with the murder investigation, and Mr. Harris, this is Amy. She's my sister and assistant."

"What's this about questions?" Amy asked, adding, "Haven't you already given a statement?"

"It's okay, Sis," Charles looked from her to Noble as he spoke. "Mr. Harris is only tryin' to get to the bottom of things. If answerin' some questions helps him catch Lysa's killer, then I'm happy to do it."

Amy shrugged but did not look happy at all. Noble made a mental note of her demeanor.

"I think it would be best if we went somewhere quieter," Noble leaned forward a bit, hoping to draw less attention. "They have given me a corner of a conference room to conduct interviews."

"I see," Charles responded with a frown, then turned to Amy. "I guess you'll need to hold down the fort for a few. Just tell anyone who comes by I'll be back soon."

"Okay," Amy pulled her chair closer to the table as she spoke.

Charles made his way around the table, and he and Noble started for the door. The two had barely gone six feet when the little grey-haired author at the table next to Charles's table spoke up. "Lemar, where are you goin', son?"

Noble stopped and waited as Charles, or Lemar, began to explain that he was going to answer some questions in another room. When he finished, he turned to Noble and made introductions. "Noble, this is my mother, Carolyn Brown, but most folks just call her Momma Carol. Momma, this is Noble Harris."

Momma Carol extended her hand with a smile, "Nice to meet you, Mr. Harris. I hope you catch whoever did this awful thing."

Noble shook her hand and could not help but smile back. The handshake was warm but firm. The twinkle in her grey-blue eyes spoke of mischief.

"Who is this?" a woman asked as she stepped up to the table and handed Momma Carol a bottle of water. To Noble, the new arrival looked like a shorter version of Amy and had the same mischievous twinkle in her eyes as Momma Carol.

"This is Noble Harris," Momma Carol made the introduction. "Mr. Harris, this is my youngest, Ginny Rucker, and the fella behind her is her husband, Bobby Rucker."

A round of handshakes and more questions ensued. Momma Carol recognized Noble's accent and wanted to know where he lived in Oklahoma. Ginny wanted to know why Lemar, as she also called Charles, was being questioned again.

Charles finally spoke up, "Sorry to rush, but the longer I'm away from my table, the less books I sell."

"You're right," Momma Carol agreed. "Y'all get on, but Noble you stop back by when you're done, and we'll have a visit."

Charles stepped back and allowed Noble to take the lead. As the two made their way across the room, Noble noticed the heads turning and caught short bits of murmured conversations. It would not take long before everyone in the room knew who he was and that he was helping with the investigation.

The noise of the conference room dulled but did not disappear as Noble and Charles stepped into the corridor that separated the book signing from the makeshift photography studio. Noble strolled the short distance to the studio door, stepped back, and allowed Charles to enter the room first, then followed him in and closed the door.

"Before we get into questions about Lysa," Noble began as he motioned for Charles to have a seat, "do you prefer Charles or Lemar? I ask because I noticed your family calls you Lemar, but your books have your full name on them."

"I'd say Lemar," Lemar answered as he eased into the chair Noble had indicated. "Most folks who know me call me Lemar. Charles was my dad's name, so from an early age, I was called by my middle name."

"Then why not just go by Lemar Brown as an author?" Noble asked.

"Some folks know me as Charles," Lemar looked a bit sheepish as he answered. "Ya see, during an interview some years back, the fella who was conducting the interview kept referring to me as Charles because I had given my full name on the application. The application did not have a preferred name, and he never asked which name I preferred. When the interview was over, he took me around to meet the other employees and introduced me as Charles. Not wanting to say anything to my new boss, I just went along. Now the folks from that era of my life know me as Charles or Charlie. Anyway, that's probably more information than you needed."

"Not at all," Noble slid into the chair opposite Lemar and took out his notepad. "Information is why I'm here, and I've found that sometimes the most unlikely tidbit of information can be the exact thing that breaks an investigation wide open."

Noble opened his notepad to an empty page and held the page with his index finger as he flipped back through his notes from Jean and Dan. From the corner of his eye he observed Lemar, who watched patiently with each page flip. Lemar's only movement was a steady, rhythmic bouncing of his right leg. Early in his career, Noble would have immediately suspected nervousness brought on by guilt. However, somewhere along the way, he had learned that just as often it was a sign of ADHD or sometimes just HD.

Flipping back to the empty page, Noble looked up at Lemar and asked, "So how long had you known Lysa?"

"Since Thursday afternoon," Lemar answered immediately.

Noble made a note on his pad and then asked, "So, you arrived here on Thursday?"

"No, sir," Lemar replied, "We got here Wednesday evenin', but Lysa didn't arrive until Thursday afternoon."

"How 'bout the other models? How long have you known them?" Noble inquired.

"I met them a year ago," Lemar smiled, "right here in Deadwood."

Noble remarked, "Seems to be a good memory."

"Yes, it is," Lemar nodded and continued, "I crossed off a couple of firsts. It was my first time to sign books at a big conference and it was my first time modelin'. Kind of a milestone in my life."

"Congratulations," Noble said, "So this is kind of an anniversary for you, huh?"

Lemar's smile broadened, "Most definitely."

Noble looked down at his notes. "So, tell me how you ended up bein' the one who saw Lysa to her room last night," he instructed when he looked up again.

The smile vanished from Lemar's face, and he looked down at the floor for a long moment. When his eyes met Noble's once again, he spoke, "Yesterday, Friday, we modeled all day. We started at ten o'clock and worked in here most of the day." Lemar gestured around the room with his left hand. "We only broke for lunch about noon and dinner around five. After dinner, we caravanned to the rodeo grounds to take outside pictures and some group photos. On the trip over to the rodeo grounds, Lysa's demeanor had changed. Throughout the day, she had been Miz Energetic just a movin' ball of joy and positivity, but she was anything but when we met up after dinner. I thought maybe she had been cryin' so I asked her if every-thing was okay. I think I expected her to tell me she was just tired, but instead she broke down. It turned out that when she went up to her room to freshen up for the evening photoshoot, her fiancé had called and...well, there's really no easy way to say it. He dumped her for another woman. I think it was someone she knew."

Lemar paused.

Noble waited for him to continue. When it became clear that

Lemar was finished, he said, "Lysa opened up to you after a bad breakup. That still doesn't explain how it was that you ended up bein' the last one to see her alive."

Noble watched as Lemar stared at the floor and massaged his forehead with his right hand. Without looking up, Lemar continued, "While Lysa was gettin' herself back together, in my truck... you know, fixin' her makeup and whatnot...I told Rob and Tony what had happened. The three of us decided it would be good for her if we took her to the festivities in town after the shoot. Maybe get her mind off everything."

With a sigh, Lemar looked up from the floor and lowered his hand away from his forehead. "We had a really good time in town. None of us guys are drinkers, but Lysa...well let's just say she wasn't shy about tossin' em back. She was pretty wasted by the time we found our way to the lodge parkin' lot."

Lemar paused and shook his head. "Rob and Tony actually had to help her walk from my truck to the elevator. Rob remembered he had left his toiletry bag with his toothbrush in here, so I took over for him so he could come get it. Tony's room was on the second floor, mine was on the third, and Lysa's was on the fourth. Without thinkin', Tony hit all of the buttons, and about the time the door opened on the second floor, he got a phone call. I told him I had it. He asked me if I was sure, and I told him yes. If it hadn't been for a toothbrush and a phone call, we would have probably all seen her to her room. As it turned out, I helped her get into her room and made sure she was on the bed before leavin'. The last time I saw her, she was passed out, lyin' on her stomach. I even moved the trashcan beside the bed in case she woke up and had to vomit."

Noble scratched several lines of notes, then flipped back to the page with Dan's notes before asking, "A witness puts you at Lysa's door a little after ten o'clock. Says you had the keycard. How did that come to be?"

"Lysa gave it to me," Lemar's eyes narrowed.

Noble shrugged. "Just askin'. Got to cross all the T's and dot all the I's."

"She was drunk," Lemar shrugged. "I asked her if she had a key. I was afraid I was gonna have to carry her back downstairs if she didn't have one."

"But she did," Noble nodded.

"Yes," Lemar replied, "she gave it to me and..."

Something in the movement of Lemar's eyes caught Noble's attention, and he asked quickly, "And what?"

Once again, Lemar shrugged. "I let her in."

Noble leaned forward, "I can't help Lysa, and I can't help you if you're not honest with me. There's something you're not tellin' me, so I'll asked again: and what?"

A flush of red flashed across Lemar's face, but he did not look away. "She was drunk," he repeated, then added, "and when I opened the door, she pulled me close and whispered, 'Wanna screw?'"

"Did you?" Noble asked.

"Good Lord," Lemar flushed red again, "She's closer to my kids' age than mine, and she was drunk."

"That doesn't answer my question," Noble stated.

"No, I did not," Lemar's eyes narrowed, "and before you ask, no, we did not."

"Because she was drunk?" Noble pressed.

"And because she was too young," Lemar shot back.

"One last question," Noble said and waited for Lemar's response.

After several seconds, Lemar responded, "So, ask."

"Did you shoot Lysa Lynn?"

Lemar was shaking his head before Noble finished asking the question.

"I did not."

After informing Lemar that discussing his interview with anyone else could be construed as tampering with an investigation, Noble made it clear that he might have some follow-up questions and let him return to signing books. Once Lemar left, Noble made several additional entries into his notepad. The last set of entries read. . .

Lemar Brown: Most likely not the killer.

Body language is wrong. Either he is innocent or one hell of an actor.

6

The Guardian sneered and looked around the room. Noble would return, that was a sure thing. Had he found a clue yet? Doubtful. Suppressing a laugh, the Guardian rose and stretched. The atmosphere of the conference was amazing, but the exhilaration that came from the hunt made it so much more glorious. It was like playing hide and seek, only the Guardian was in plain sight, and Noble could not, would not find...ah, Noble's back. The Guardian sat and watched him move across the room. It took all the Guardian's resolve not to scream 'Marco'.

～

"Excuse me, Robert," Noble stepped up beside the model as he spoke, "but I need to ask you a few questions. Would you come with me to the conference room across the hall?"

Robert nodded but did not speak. He turned and started across the room. At first, Noble thought perhaps he had misunderstood or was simply choosing to ignore his request for an interview. Feeling irritation beginning to seep in, Noble followed after him, unsure how to handle the situation if Robert decided to refuse his request.

Robert stopped at the table Tony was manning long enough to hand him the microphone he carried to emcee the event. As Noble neared the two, he heard Tony say to Robert, "No problem, brother, I've got you covered."

As Noble stepped up, Robert turned, "All yours, sir."

The feeling of irritation that had begun did not fade but rather switched gears. Noble had been annoyed when he thought Robert was going to refuse to cooperate, now he found Robert's nonchalant, businesslike demeanor irked him as much, if not more, than the initial aggravation.

Noble argued with himself as he led the way through the maze of tables. He had always prided himself on being able to keep an open mind both in an investigations as well as life in general. That he found himself already harboring prejudice towards Robert was not fair to Robert or to the investigation.

Noble stepped out of the conference room and into the corridor. The volume of noise decreased significantly. Noble turned and offered Robert his hand. "Noble Harris."

"Robert Kelly," Robert shook the offered hand. "I didn't see the sense in trying to communicate in there," he motioned towards the book signing with a nod of his head, "we would have been shouting the whole time."

Noble nodded and chided himself for jumping to conclusions. He motioned Robert toward the studio and followed him in. Robert did not wait but dropped into the seat Noble had been using. Noble wondered if he was being baited or if Robert was really this accustomed to being in charge. He closed the door, stepped around Robert, and settled into the chair Robert had left for him.

"When did you arrive in Deadwood?" Noble got straight to the first question.

"Thursday afternoon," Robert responded but did not offer anything further.

"Why not Wednesday evening?" Noble asked.

"Flight delays," Robert answered. "I was supposed to be here Wednesday, but two delays, a reroute with an extra-long layover, and it was late Thursday before I made it to the Lodge."

Noble took out his notepad and made a note of when Robert arrived. Years of investigation had taught him that slow, meticulous fact-gathering usually led to a clue, but those same years had taught him that it was more likely to take weeks than days, and in all of his years he had never solved a murder in hours. Except in those rare cases where someone confessed, and that did not seem likely in this case.

"I understand you and the rest of the models spent the better part of the day yesterday in here with Jean," Noble studied Robert's eyes as he spoke.

Robert nodded but did not speak. His eyes stared straight into Noble's. Noble broke eye contact first and made a notation before asking, "How does the modeling work? I mean, as far as who is paired with who?"

Continuing to stare straight at Noble, Robert answered, "That depends. Most of the time, couples are paired up for the duration of the event because it saves time. Other times, they may switch in and out. If there is a specific request from an author, that can cause some changes, too."

Noble nodded and then asked, "Who was Lysa paired with at this event?"

Without taking his eyes off Noble and with no noticeable emotion, Robert answered, "Me."

"Had the two of you worked together before?" Noble asked.

"Nope," Robert shook his head as he spoke, then added, "I think this was her first time modeling."

Noble scribbled a quick line and then laid the notepad aside before asking, "And the other models, had you worked with any of them?"

"Yes, all of them," Robert answered but did not give any further details.

Noble decided to switch gears. "After the last shoot, I understand you and Tony and Lemar took Lysa out drinkin'. Whose idea was that?"

A slight twitch of Robert's left eye indicated to Noble that Robert did not like the question. If Noble had not been studying him closely, he would have missed it.

"I believe I suggested it, but all three of us were in agreement," Robert's tone was flat, not cold or belligerent, more matter-of-fact, he added, "and the plan was never to take her out drinking. The plan was to take her to town to get her mind off her breakup."

"So, none of you guys bought her alcohol?" Noble watched Robert carefully as he asked the question.

Stone-faced, Robert answered, "Actually, both Lemar and I did."

"A lot?" Noble pushed the issue.

"A couple each," Robert answered.

Noble noticed a bit of red creep from under the collar of Robert's shirt. "Why not Tony?" Noble asked.

The staring match between the two reached new heights with each question and answer. Noble could feel his heartbeat quicken and wondered how Robert's vital signs would register on a polygraph.

"Tony's in a relationship," Robert stated, emotionless once again, "he's not the kind of guy to buy other women drinks, plus he'd forgotten his wallet in the pants he wore during our last shoot."

"So, then, just you and Lemar got Lysa drunk?" Noble had to admit to himself he was enjoying this interview more than he had thought he would. Robert's jaw tightened ever so slightly at the question. He smiled to cover it.

"No one got Lysa drunk," he continued to smile as he spoke, "Lemar bought the first round, I bought the next two, and then Lemar may have bought one more, of that I can't be positive. After that, Lysa switched from beer to shots and bought her own."

"Everyone had three or four beers before switching to shots?" Noble picked up his notepad and pencil as if to make a notation.

Robert raised a hand to stop him, "No. Not at all. Neither Lemar nor I drink alcohol, and Tony only had one beer then switched to water. Lysa was the only one drinking."

Noble laid the notepad down on the table and twirled the pencil in his fingers, "What did you do after you retrieved your toiletry bag from in here?"

Robert's jaw tightened and his eyes narrowed. Whether it was the sudden realization that Noble knew what he had done the night before or the sudden shift in questioning that caused Robert to react, Noble did not know and did not care. The fact that he had elicited a reaction was enough.

After composing himself once again, Robert answered, "I went to my room, changed into gym clothes, and went to the workout room on the first floor."

"How long were you there?" Noble asked.

"Half an hour," Robert replied,

"Then?" Noble leaned forward.

"Then I went back to my room, took a shower, and went to bed," Robert stared hard, then added, "and that's where I was until seven o'clock this morning when I got up and came down to have breakfast with Ginger and Tina."

Watching Robert carefully, Noble asked, "So, the last contact you had with Lysa was when you left her with Tony and Lemar at the elevator?"

"Yes," Robert nodded as he answered. Even with the movement of Robert's head, Noble caught the quick double blink followed by another solitary one.

Noble wondered if he was trying too hard to find a reason to doubt Robert or if the man's physical reactions truly indicated an attempt at deceit. Noble knew that body language interpretation during an interview was not an exact science, but experience and his gut told him that Robert was hiding something.

"I think that will be all for now," Noble picked up his notepad as he spoke. "I may need to ask you more questions later."

As Robert rose, he said, "I'll be around."

Noble remained seated as Robert crossed the room and opened the door. Before Robert stepped into the corridor, Noble said, "Thanks for your cooperation."

Robert turned his head long enough to respond with a "you're welcome" and then stepped out, and pulled the door shut behind him.

Noble leaned back in his chair. Robert reminded him of someone, but he could not put his finger on who that person was.

Picking up his notepad, he scribbled a few more notes, finishing with:

Robert Kelly: Not a strong suspect, but possible. Body language indicates Robert is hiding something. Find out what!

7

The Guardian listened to the chatter. Laughter and excitement filled the room. Authors, cover models, and readers, mixed and mingled. It was a book lover's dream. Lysa's demise had only made the dream better. It could not have gone any better even if the death had been planned.

Tony Brettman was all smiles as he signed book covers and the various odds and ends scattered across his table. The sleeves of the shirt his removed allowed the bulging muscles of his upper arms to show. Leaving the top three buttons on the front of his shirt unbuttoned provided just enough of a view of his pecs to let people know that he had not missed many days at the gym. Add to the muscles, a full black beard and an energetic personality, and it was not hard for Noble to see why he seemed to be so well-liked.

For several minutes, Noble stood just inside the doors of the book signing and watched as the readers moved from one table to another. Not looking for anything in particular, he was simply allowing his mind to settle between interviews. It had been well over a year since his last interview, and he had forgotten how hard doing them back-to-back could be on a person physically and mentally. Once again, he cursed himself for allowing Davenport to talk him into taking on the case.

He had almost decided to wait until after lunch to interview Tony, but then he checked the time on his phone and mumbled an obscenity under his breath. There was still plenty of time before lunch to do one more. Reluctantly, he slid his phone back into his pants pocket and started across the room toward Tony's table.

As Noble made his way past the last couple of tables, he overheard two ladies discussing lunch. Thinking it had nothing to do with him, he was almost out of earshot when one of the ladies said, "There is still a half of a sandwich in the refrigerator in my room. If you don't mind taking my key and grabbing it for me, I think that's all I want for lunch."

The key!

Noble made a mental note to check the photographs of the room when he returned to the studio. He told himself it was probably nothing, a dead end, but the tingle in his gut gave him the first inkling of hope he had felt all morning.

"Tony Brettman, I'm Noble Harris," Noble introduced himself as he offered the model his hand.

Tony shook it. "Nice to meet you, Mr. Harris. I guess it's my turn to be questioned?"

"That's a pretty good guess," Noble answered. "Do you need to get someone to man your table?"

Tony shrugged. "Nah, it'll be okay."

Noble turned and started toward the door. Tony made his way down the row of tables and caught up to Noble. The two exited the conference room together. The corridor was empty, and it took only a few seconds to reach the studio. Once both men were inside, Noble closed the door behind them.

Tony waited patiently until Noble indicated which seat he should take and then sat down. Noble smiled inwardly at the difference in the way this interview was beginning compared to the last one.

"Let's start with an easy one," Noble said, not even bothering to take out his notepad. "When did you arrive at the lodge?"

Tony nodded, "Early Thursday morning."

"I understand Lysa was paired up with Robert yesterday," Noble watched Tony for any reaction, and when there was none, he asked, "Who were you paired up with?"

Tony chuckled, "No one. I'm flying solo this weekend. Lysa was paired with Robert, and Ginger and Lemar were paired up."

"Since I've already heard from others about the events of the photoshoot yesterday and the festivities in town," Noble leaned back in his chair and ran his finger along the scar on his jaw, "I think, perhaps it would be better, if instead of askin' a bunch of questions, I let you tell me your version of how things went."

Again, Tony nodded, then asked, "Where should I start?"

"How about when Lemar told you and Robert that Lysa was upset," Noble suggested.

Tony took a deep breath, looked up at the ceiling for a minute as if gathering his thoughts and then began. Noble listened as Tony walked him through the photoshoot at the rodeo arena and then step by step took him through the evening's events, finishing with the moment he left Lemar in the elevator holding up Lysa.

When he finished, Noble picked up his notepad, flipped it open, and asked, "Any reason why Robert would be uptight about answerin' my questions?"

Tony looked stunned and shook his head as he answered, "I don't quite catch your meaning, sir."

Noble shrugged, "Well, I asked you to tell me about yesterday, and you just spent twenty minutes giving me a whole lot of details about what happened. Your buddy, well... let's just say he was less givin'. Kind of answered the questions in as few words as possible and then waited for the next one. Any idea why?"

Tony laughed, "I'd say that's just Business Rob. When he's modeling or working at an event, he's all business. Now, Fun Rob, he's, well... he's Fun Rob. I'm sure since we are technically at this event to work, you got Business Rob."

"And Fun Rob," Noble used his fingers to do air quotes as he asked, "was he the one with y'all when Lysa was gettin' plastered?"

The smile that had been on Tony's face faded, and a bit of red crept up his neck toward his beard. "I'm not sure what you're getting at, but Rob, Lemar, and I were all there, and we were all watching over her to make sure she was okay."

Noble changed his hands from finger quotes to palms out. "I see. Just askin' questions here. I didn't mean to rile ya."

"Rob's a good guy," the flush that had colored his neck faded as he spoke. "He's always helping someone: Momma J with setup, all of us models with posing and outfits. Heck, I even saw him at one event helping Dan stuff giveaway bags. So, if you're trying to get me to say something bad about Rob, sir, you're out of luck. He's one of the good ones."

"Just askin' questions," Noble repeated. "One never knows when the right question will blow a case wide open."

"With all due respect, sir," Tony raised one eyebrow, "I think that was the wrong question."

"Perhaps," Noble nodded in agreement. There was something about this kid he liked. Something about the way he carried himself and his demeanor. A bit cocky but with a dash of humility added. Enough self-confidence to be going places but not so much as to be unwilling to ask for help or take constructive criticism. Tony reminded him of someone. It took him several seconds before it finally dawned on him, Tony was Kent Davenport twenty years ago.

Wow! Noble thought when the realization hit him. Unable to push past the resemblance, he studied and analyzed the similarities and differences between him and Davenport. At Tony's current age, Davenport had stayed in the weight room and so was muscular, much like Tony. Noble was not sure if Davenport had ever been quite as shredded as Tony. Of course, Davenport had loved his beer and strippers back then; had he been able to leave the first alone, perhaps he would have been as big as Tony.

Of course, Davenport had always preferred a clean-shaven look. It was hard to match the facial features since most of Tony's were hidden under his thick black beard, but the eyes...now those definitely reminded him of a younger Davenport.

"Any more questions, sir?" Tony's voice brought Nobel back to the present.

Noble shook his head, "Not at the moment. Thank you for your time."

"So, I'm good to go then?" Tony shifted to the front of the chair he was seated in.

"You are," Noble nodded.

As Tony made his way out of the room, Noble put his notepad down and reached for the file Davenport had given him. He needed to look at the pictures of Lysa's motel room.

Flipping the file open, he took the pictures from it and spread them out across the table. He pushed aside the close-up of her head. The one of her full length on the bed included one of the bedside tables. He checked it, did not see what he was looking for, and pushed it aside. Carefully, he studied the last photograph, the one of the entire crime scene. Still, he did not find it. Lysa's keycard should have been somewhere in one of the photographs, or so he thought.

Still staring at the Polaroid, Noble fished his phone out of the front pocket of his jeans. He laid the photograph aside and dialed Davenport's number.

"Got it solved already, huh?" Davenport asked with a half chuckle when he answered.

Noble ignored him and asked, "Did you happen to find the keycard for Lysa's room?"

"Come to think of it, I don't recall seeing it on the inventory sheet," Davenport answered.

"Be nice to know for sure if it was in the room, don't ya think?" Noble said, his tone a bit icy.

After a brief pause, Noble heard the static of a police radio and Davenport said, "Gotta run to the station. I'll check on the room key while I'm there, and then I thought I'd head over your way, and we'd grab a bite of lunch. How's that sound?"

"Sounds fine," Noble answered, realizing suddenly that he was hungry.

"Good. See you soon." Davenport said and broke the connection.

Noble checked the time on his phone, put the Polaroids back in the file, and picked up his notepad. He decided he would ask Lemar about the keycard on his way through the book signing room on his way to the restaurant. Rising from his chair, Noble grinned. For the first time since he had agreed to this case, he had a good feeling. This might well be the loose string that would start the proverbial ball of twine unwinding.

He crossed the room, let himself out, and pulled the door shut. A quick trip across the corridor and he made his way through the tables of the book signing until he reached Lemar's table.

Lemar was signing a book for a young lady, so Noble waited until he was finished and then said, "I was wondering what happened to the key to Lysa's room."

A look of confusion was followed by a flush of red on Lemar's cheeks. "Mr. Harris, I think I may have taken it with me when I left the room, but I'm not sure."

"How can you not be sure?" Noble asked.

Lemar stood, came around the table, and motioned toward nearest door, "Maybe we could discuss this somewhere a bit more private."

Noble followed him toward the main entrance of the conference room and then out into the lobby. Lemar led him over to a quiet place near the large windows that looked out across the parking area.

When Lemar turned around, he spoke in a low voice, "Mr. Harris, to say last night's events flustered me would be an understatement. You see, I've been divorced for several years now and... well, let's say I live a pretty quiet life when I'm not modeling or signing books."

"Okay," Noble shrugged, not sure where the conversation was going.

Lemar visibly blushed. "I am closer to sixty now than fifty, and to say the least, I am not used to beautiful women asking me to have sex with them. As I told you before, I was flustered and may have walked out of the room with the key. I really don't remember."

"I see," Noble nodded. "Thanks for your honesty. I'm meeting the sheriff for lunch, and after that, I may need to ask you a few more questions in the studio."

"Yes, sir," Lemar looked around the lobby as he spoke, "let me know when you need me, and I'll be there. I'd much prefer the studio."

Noble nodded again, and Lemar started back to his table. Noble watched him until he disappeared from sight and then took out his notepad. He made a few notes about the keycard and the conversation with Lemar and then flipped back to the page of notes from Tony's interview. Only half a page, mostly verification of what he had already been told, but in the space at the bottom of the page, he wrote:

Tony Brettman: Not a suspect.
Body language indicates to me, if he had done it, he would not be able to hide it, emotionally or physically.

8

Asshole. The Guardian watched Noble through the double doors of the book signing. Watched as Noble scribbled in his little notepad. Searching, prying, trying to make sense of something that made no sense. This was not some premeditated crime. As far as the Guardian was concerned, it was no crime at all. Ha! Let him scribble and scratch, he was outmatched, outclassed, and way out of his league.

Noble watched Davenport scan the restaurant. When his friend's eyes finally located him, Noble raised his hand as if to say, "I'm here, you found me." With his usual grin, Davenport crossed the room and slid into the seat opposite Noble.

"You order yet?" Davenport asked.

"Nope, I waited on you," Noble answered.

The lunch crowd had arrived twenty minutes earlier, and Noble had noticed the steady increase in volume as more and more customers filtered in. From time to time, a laugh would ring out then fade away. The smell of food wafted through the air, and Noble's waitress had made two trips to his table before Davenport had shown up. If Noble had been hungry earlier, now he was famished.

Davenport motioned to a waitress. She gave him the universal one-fingered "just-one-second" sign and headed back towards the kitchen. Noble did not bother to tell Davenport that she was not their waitress. She disappeared through the kitchen doors, and seconds later, the young woman who had visited Noble earlier came bustling through and headed straight for their table.

"Trinity tells me you're ready to order," she said as she approached, "so what can I get you gentlemen?"

Davenport chuckled, "Darlin', I'm afraid you've come to the wrong table. There are no gentlemen here."

"Is that so?" she played along. "I suppose I could take your orders anyway. That is as long as neither of you two are total scoundrels."

It was Noble's turn to chuckle. "I guess you'll have to take my order and leave him to fend for himself."

Davenport shook his head, but he was all smiles when he looked up at the waitress and asked, "See what I have to put up with here?"

"I do indeed," the waitress agreed.

"And do you have a name, little darlin'?" Davenport wiggled his eyebrows as he asked.

"Her name is Val," Noble answered for her. "Most likely short for Valerie, and you, my friend, are happily married."

Davenport looked from Val to Noble and, with a glare of feigned disgust, joked, "Some friend you are."

Noble raised an eyebrow. "You let Mary find out you're flirtin' with a pretty lady half your age and then tell me what a good a friend I am. Partner, as I see it, I just saved your life again."

"Again?" Davenport started to argue but Val cut him off.

"Gentlemen, or scoundrels, or whatever you two prefer to be called, as much as I'm enjoyin' the banter, I have other tables. So how about I take your orders and then see if I'm needed elsewhere while you two settle this little dispute?" Val suggested, her eyes filled with amusement.

Noble ordered the whiskey sirloin steak, and Davenport opted for the Bangkok shrimp. As Val made her way across the room, headed for the kitchen, Davenport chuckled. "You know, partner, you were right about Mary. She would have pulled that poor girl's hair out."

"Before or after she castrated you?" Noble asked with a grin.

"Who knows?" Davenport shrugged, "Speaking of wives, how's Carla doin'?"

Noble gave him a side-eyed look and pursed his lips. "Had to go there, didn't ya? You know she's not my wife."

"Might as well be," Davenport shrugged again.

"Well, she ain't," Noble's eyebrows raised as he spoke, "so let's just drop it."

"You should ask her to marry you," Davenport gave a sharp nod as if he had just arrived at the perfect solution, "yeah, that's what you should do."

Noble refused to be drawn in. He stared at the table and busied himself rearranging the silverware.

"Oh, my...oh, my, holy shit," Davenport's eyes widened, and he slapped the table with enough force to make both his and Noble's silverware jump. "You have asked her. You asked her, and she turned you down."

Noble shot Davenport his best shut-the-hell-up glare, "You wanna shout that a little louder? I think maybe the folks out in the parking lot didn't hear ya."

Davenport raised both hands and hung his head. "Sorry, partner. Kinda caught me off guard with that one."

"It happens," Noble shrugged.

"Not to you, Casanova," Davenport shook his head. "What happened?"

Noble shrugged again. "The past, that's what happened. You of all people should know how complicated me and Carla's relationship was...is, oh hell, you know what I mean."

"Yeah, you're right," Davenport admitted. "Still gotta sting. I'm sorry, partner."

Noble waved his hand as if to push the conversation away, "Let's move on to more pressing matters. I asked Lemar about the key, and he couldn't remember if he had it with him when he left the room or not. I checked the Polaroids, and it's not in any of them. Did you find it in any of the stuff forensics inventoried?"

"Nope," Davenport answered, then asked, "Do you think you need to question Lemar again? I mean, he's looking more and more like the prime suspect."

"Seems like most of the evidence points his way, that's for sure," Noble admitted, "but my gut's tellin' me he didn't do it."

Davenport snorted as if to say, yeah, right, then asked, "Is this the same gut that's been sitting around on the porch drinking whiskey and sulking for the past year?"

"I have not been sulkin'," Noble's response was a little too quick. "Besides, what else was I supposed to do after I retired? You know that's kind of what retirement means."

"There's a difference between retirement and quitting on life," Davenport's tone grew serious. "Yeah, that chapter of your life is over. Being the bad-ass, no-case-I-can't-solve OSBI agent is now in the past. That doesn't mean you have to sit around drinking whiskey waiting for death to show up. Hell, look at me; I moved north, found myself another job, even got married and settled down. If I can do it, so can you, partner."

Noble gave him a questioning look before asking, "Are you offering me a job?"

Davenport laughed. "If I thought you'd take it, I'd offer you one, but no, I'm simply saying, you aren't dead yet, so quit acting like it."

"Piss off," Noble half-glared at his friend. "I came up here to see you, didn't I?"

"Yes, you did," Davenport nodded in agreement, "but if it hadn't been for a call from Carla, I wouldn't have even known you were in a funk."

"So, this was a you and Carla plan?" Noble squinted and shook a finger at Davenport.

"Absolutely," Davenport grinned.

"I ought to call a cab and catch the next flight back to Oklahoma," both eyes narrowed as Noble spoke.

"But you won't," Davenport continued to grin.

"And why is that?" Noble asked, already knowing Davenport's answer would frustrate him further.

"Two reasons," Davenport held up two fingers as he spoke, "First, because you're already invested in the case and you've never left a case unsolved; and second, because if you go home now, I'll call Carla and tell on you... and, well, we both know you don't want to face that wildcat and tell her you ruined her plan."

Noble expressed his frustration in his usual way by saying, "Piss off."

"Two piss offs in less than ten minutes. Man, I'm on a roll today," Davenport chuckled.

Noble decided it was time to change the subject. "What's your take on Robert Kelly?" he asked.

"How do you mean?" Davenport gave him a look of confusion as he spoke.

"I don't know exactly," Noble responded. "I get the feelin' he's way too sure of himself. It could be that it's his nature, but there's something about him that...hell, I don't know. I can't seem to put a finger on it."

"A bit too sure of himself, huh?" Davenport ran his thumb along his chin as he mused, "All businesslike and such, dedicated to his work. Hell, I think I knew a guy like that once."

"What the hell are you tryin' to say?" Noble's eyes narrowed.

"Just that the reason you find Robert abrasive is that it's like looking in the mirror and seeing yourself staring back," Davenport raised an eyebrow.

"Robert Kelly doesn't look anything like me," Noble shook his head in disagreement.

"Maybe not physically," Davenport agreed, "but everything about him matches you to a T, oh, I don't know, say fifteen years ago."

Noble took a moment to think about what his friend had suggested, and even though he knew Davenport was probably right, he shook his head. "I'm not seein' it."

Davenport responded with a chuckle and then pointed towards the kitchen doors. "Looks like Val is headed this way with your steak."

"First positive thing I've heard come out of your mouth since I stepped off the plane," Noble grumbled, which brought another chuckle from his friend.

Val slid the plate with Noble's steak onto the table in front of him and then did the same with Davenport's shrimp. "Can I get anything for either of you? Maybe some steak sauce for you, sir?"

Noble looked up at her and shook his head in disgust, "Darlin', the only thing one should put on a steak is a little salt and maybe a pat of butter."

"If you say so, sir," Val shrugged, refusing to argue with him.

"How 'bout you?" Val turned to Davenport. "You need anything, hun?"

"A new dinner date," Davenport grinned up at her, then indicated Noble with a nod of his head. "The one I've got seems to have soured."

Val and Davenport both laughed. Val winked at him and said, "Sorry, hun, I've got to work, and I think we already clarified that you're married."

Davenport feigned a pout. As Val walked away, he picked up his fork and speared a shrimp from his plate. Noble had already cut into his steak and was happily chewing. The char on the medium-well meat paired nicely with the flavor of the whiskey, producing the perfect harmony in his mouth.

Neither Noble nor Davenport spoke for the next fifteen minutes. Each of them ate, lost in their own thoughts. When Noble finished the last bite of his steak, he pushed his plate away, and asked, "Did you know Lysa Lynn before she was killed?"

The fork holding the last of Davenport's shrimp stopped halfway to his mouth, and he looked across the table at Noble. For a long second, neither of them moved, and then Davenport raised the fork to his mouth, removed the shrimp, and began to chew. Noble waited until he was sure Davenport had swallowed, then repeated the question.

"Am I on the suspect list?" Davenport asked.

"Should you be?" Noble shrugged as he asked.

Davenport laid his fork down across his plate and leaned back. After rubbing his chin for several seconds, he answered, "You know me, partner. You know I've always liked living out on the edge. Some might even say I was cocky, arrogant, or egotistical, but nobody who knows me would ever call me stupid."

Noble waited for him to elaborate, when he didn't, Noble asked, "Is that supposed to be an answer?"

Davenport shook his head, "What I'm saying is that I would have to be a complete idiot to murder someone and then call you in to do the investigation."

"That *would* be pretty stupid, wouldn't it?" Noble agreed, then carefully studied his friend as he added, "Still, I'm gonna need a yes or no."

Davenport laughed, "You know what I should do? I should leave you wondering, but because you're my friend, I'll give you this one. No, I did not know Lysa Lynn before she was murdered, and no, I did not murder her. Satisfied?"

"Depends," Noble stared hard into Davenport's eyes. "Who's payin' for lunch?"

Davenport laughed and motioned to Val that they were ready for the check.

9

The Guardian's eyes followed Noble as he entered the conference room through the main double doors. So, you figured out the key, the Guardian's mind whirled; bet you think you've got it all figured out now. Well, Mr. Harris, retired OSBI, I left a present for you in the studio.

Noble looked across the rows of tables until his gaze found Lemar's. He stepped inside and to the left of the conference room's double doors and stood quietly, observing Lemar. The author visited with several readers who stopped in front of his table. Once they had moved on, he turned and said something to his sister, Amy. Both then turned to look at their mother, Momma Carol, who was deep in a discussion with the third sister, Ginny, and the author on the other side of Momma Carol.

Noble's gaze had followed the flow of events, now his eyes returned to Lemar. As he watched, Lemar stood up, stretched his head from side to side, then ran his hands down the front of his shirt as if straightening it. Noble mentally noted each motion. After a couple of minutes, Lemar made a quick scan around the room and returned to his seat. Noble was fairly certain that Lemar had not seen him standing there in the shadow, but he decided it was time to move anyway.

His first thought had been to question immediately Lemar again upon returning from lunch, but after watching him, Noble decided to give him more time to stew, encase he was indeed nervous. To Noble's gut, Lemar still seemed innocent, but his body language and much of the evidence were sure starting to point in his direction.

As Noble moved out of the shadow, he decided to interview Ginger next. He told himself that even though it was highly unlikely she was the guilty party; she might well have information that could help him confirm or reject Lemar's innocence. On his way across the room to her table, it occurred to him that she was the only model he had not truly interviewed.

There seemed to be a lull in the number of readers moving around the room when Noble reached her table. Ginger was sorting through a pile of stickers when he spoke, "Miz Ring."

Ginger flinched. "Goodness, Mr. Harris, you startled me," she gasped and placed a hand to her chest.

"So, sorry," Noble apologized, "that was not my intention at all. I need to interview you, and I was wonderin' if now would be a good time."

Ginger dropped her hand from her chest and scanned the room. "I think most of our visitors have gone to lunch. We don't seem to be all that busy, so I guess it won't hurt for me to be gone a few minutes."

"Wonderful," Noble said. "I'll meet you in the studio room then."

Ginger rose from her seat, "I'll be right there. Let me holler at Linda Rae so she knows where I'm at and can keep an eye on my table."

Noble nodded. He thought about waiting for her but then decided there was no need and made his way across the room. As he passed Jade Lee's table, he noticed that she was visiting with the author at the table next to hers. At the side door to the conference room, he stopped long enough to turn around and scan the room. Both the volume and the activity had declined drastically since the beginning of the book signing.

Noble turned once again and headed for the studio room. As he crossed the corridor, he pulled out his phone and checked the time. Three hours until the end of the signing. He shook his head. The odds of his solving the case before the end of the signing, when most of the authors and models would skedaddle, were not in his favor.

As he approached the studio, he noticed the edge of something white poking out from under the closed door. Shaking his head, he tried to remember if he had ever conducted interviews in a more unlikely place. He decided that if he had, he would definitely remember it, and since he could not, he chalked the studio room up as the most unlikely.

He opened the door to the studio and pushed it back, revealing the source of the white strip that he had seen peeking out from beneath the door. It was a standard legal-size envelope. Centered on the front of it in block letters was his name: NOBLE HARRIS. In the upper left corner in the same block letters where two words: THE GUARDIAN.

Looking down at it, his first thought was that he needed gloves and did not have any. He shook his head as the next thought entered his mind. Three hours or less to solve this case if possible, so even if the damn envelope was covered with bright red fingerprints and kissy lips, there would not be enough time to run prints, analyze the hand-writing, or even match the color of the lipstick. With a sigh of frustration, he reached down, picked up the envelope, and opened it.

Inside, he saw a single motel keycard and nothing else. He removed it from the envelope and made a thorough examination of both the key and the inside and outside of the envelope. No note with an explanation and no name, just the solitary plastic rectangle with a magnetic strip on one side and the word "Welcome" on the other side.

So, that's how we're gonna play this game, Noble thought, dropped the key back into the envelope, and made his way into the room.

Noble found it interesting that the killer had chosen to give them-self a name. He mulled it over and wondered at its significance. A guardian was someone who was responsible for others. Who here might shoulder that kind of responsibility?

As he laid the envelope on top of the case file, Ginger came through the door. "Sorry it took this long. I had to find Linda Rae; she wasn't at her table."

"Really?" Noble raised an eyebrow. "Where did you find her?"

Ginger blushed, and her gaze dropped to the floor, "She had stepped over to the ladies' room."

Noble felt a tinge of guilt for the embarrassment he had caused, but it faded quickly as he found himself mentally working on his next line of questioning. "How often do the authors and models step out during the signing?"

That Ginger looked like she was ready to flee did not escape Noble's notice. Her gaze moved upward from the floor, and for a brief moment, he thought she was going to look him in the eyes, but when her eyes reached his chest, it stopped and returned to the floor.

"Maybe you would be more comfortable if we sat down," Noble put his hand on the back of a chair as he spoke.

"I think so," Ginger agreed and slid into the offered seat.

Noble sat down in his usual spot and took out his notepad. Ginger looked up, and Noble realized she was staring at the pad. Not just staring, it was as if by concentrating solely on it, she hoped to build a wall between the two of them.

"I apologize if this makes you uneasy," Noble said.

"It's okay," she replied, keeping her line of sight on the pad, "and thank you."

"So, how often do the authors and models step out during the signing?" He repeated his question.

Ginger pushed a strand of red hair away from her face and tucked it behind her ear, then answered, "Not often. I guess it depends on the person."

"I see," Noble flipped to the next blank page in his notepad, then asked, "When was the last time you left the book signing room?"

Ginger blinked twice in quick succession and for a split second looked him in the eye before answering, "I haven't since the signing started, at least not until now."

Noble made an entry on the blank page, then without looking up asked, "So, you haven't been out of the main room all morning?"

"No," Ginger answered.

Noble took a deep breath and then let it out. He was fairly certain he knew the answer to his next question but asked anyway, "Is there any way to know who enters and leaves the room and at what time they do so?"

Ginger shook her head and answered, "No."

Noble had expected the answer but not the look that accompanied it. The look Ginger gave him left little doubt in his mind that she thought it was a stupid question.

Noble reddened and quickly asked another question. "How many keys does the hotel issue at check-in?"

Ginger shrugged, "I don't know about everyone else, but they asked me if I wanted one or two. I opted for one."

Another dead end. Noble tapped his pencil against the edge of the notepad twice in an attempt to redirect his brain. It did not work. After several seconds of silence, he gave up and said, "I may have some additional questions, Miz Ginger, but for now, I think that's all."

Ginger nodded, "Then I'm free to return to the signing?"

"Yes, ma'am," Noble answered as he rose and stepped to the door.

Ginger slid from her seat and crossed the room. "I hope you find out who did this awful thing," she said as Noble opened the door for her and she walked past him into the corridor.

Not sure how to respond, he replied in a half-whisper, "Me, too."

Feeling nearly hopeless once again and knowing there was not enough time to question everyone at the book signing about if and when they had left the room, he crossed to his seat and eased himself into it. He opened his notepad and flipped through it, looking for any sign of a string to pull. Finding none, he laid it aside and picked up the file folder and studied the report again. He found nothing there or in the Polaroids.

The envelope with his name on it and the key inside it lay on the table beside his notepad. His gut told him the key was the loose string that would unravel the whole case. But how? In frustration, he picked up his notepad, and under the two entries he had made, he wrote:

Ginger Ring: Almost certainly not a suspect.
Although if the shyness is an act, she well may be.

10

"No, sir, there is no way for us to tell, how many keys were made for a certain room," the woman behind the front desk informed Noble.

"I was afraid of that," Noble shook his head as he spoke.

"Is there anything else I can help you with?" she asked.

Noble looked around to make sure he was not holding up another customer. There was no one else in the lobby. Turning back, he gave her his most charming smile, "Actually, I do have a couple more questions."

The woman nodded as if to say "go ahead," but did not verbalize it. Noble wondered if he had indeed lost a step or if perhaps he simply was not this woman's type.

Damn, he thought, *I need to get out of my own head.*

"Perhaps, I should start again," Noble said, "I'm Noble Harris. I'm workin' with Kent Davenport, tryin' to help solve the murder that happened this mornin', and you are?"

"Oh, I see," the woman smiled for the first time since Noble had stepped up to the counter, "I'm Megan."

"Megan, I apologize for not explainin' the situation before I began askin' questions," Noble hoped that with introductions behind them, Megan would be a bit more forthcoming.

"That's okay," Megan leaned forward as she spoke, "you kind of caught me off guard, and I wasn't sure if I had made a mistake with someone's keys. You wouldn't believe how little it takes to get a butt-chewing around here. Now what was the other question you wanted to ask?"

"If I give you a key, can you tell me the number of the room it was keyed for?" he asked and held out the key that had been left for him in the envelope.

Megan leaned further forward as if she were going to take the key. Noble caught the floral scent of the perfume she was wearing before she stepped back and, with a shake of her head, answered, "No, sir. The only way to know if that key opens a particular door would be to try it. If the key hasn't expired and nothing has voided the magnetic strip, it should open the door it was keyed to open."

"What would void the magnetic strip?" Noble asked.

"I guess anything magnetic," Megan shrugged. "We get a lot of folks who come up to the desk with keys they have laid on their cell-phones while in the workout room or at the pool. For some reason, that seems to demagnetize the keys. I don't know the science behind it. I just know it happens."

Noble listened to her explanation and then asked, "Speaking of the workout room, do you have a camera in there?"

"We do," Megan answered.

"Does it record somewhere on the premises?" Noble asked.

"No, no recording," Megan replied. "They just have them so we can keep an eye out for anyone acting foolish."

Noble shook his head and muttered under his breath. Once again, one of the strings he had been pulling at refused to unravel any further. He had sure hoped there had been video with a timestamp of Robert arriving and leaving for his workout the previous night.

The lack of useful information from the hotel's front desk had begun to frustrate Noble. He knew it wasn't Megan's fault. Hoping his irritation had not been too visible, he thanked her and turned to walk away.

"You're welcome," Megan said. "Sorry, I couldn't be of more help. If you think of any other questions, I'll be here until four o'clock, but there is someone available twenty-four hours a day."

The phone rang as she finished speaking and she answered it, "The Lodge at Deadwood, how may I assist you?"

Noble was nearly out of earshot, when he heard her say, "I sure can. What room are they in?"

Mid-stride, Noble turned on his heels and headed back to the front desk. As he approached, Megan spoke into the phone, "I'll connect you now."

Noble waited for her to finish punching in the room number then asked, "Do you keep a record on the premise of incoming and outgoing calls?"

"Yes, we do," Megan answered, "Well, kind of."

"Kind of?" Noble could feel the excitement building up in his chest.

"Yes," Megan looked down at the phone as she spoke. "I don't have it all figured out myself, but I think the computer records it when I connect an outside line to a room and when someone calls from one room to another. I'm not sure if it logs all calls, but those ones I'm pretty certain about. You could talk to the I.T. guys about it?"

Noble thought for a minute, "I don't think that will be necessary, especially if you can do it yourself."

"Depends on what you need," Megan raised an eyebrow.

Noble gave her Lysa's room number. "Can you tell me what calls were made to and from that room yesterday between six and midnight?"

Megan's eyes lit up and she nodded her head. Noble watched as she moved a mouse around and made a couple of clicks. "Only one call during that time," Megan looked up, a bit wide-eyed, and Noble realized that to her it must be like playing detective. "It came from room 219."

As soon as he heard the room number, Noble asked, "Can you tell me who is in that room?"

After another couple of mouse clicks, Megan answered, "Robert Kelly."

Trying not to show too much emotion, Noble thanked her and stepped back.

"We did good, didn't we?" Megan smiled.

Noble could nearly see the excitement oozing out of her. "Yes, we did," he smiled back, "but if you don't mind, let's keep this between the two of us."

"Absolutely," Megan agreed.

Noble thanked her again and started for the elevator.

As he made his way down the short hallway past a sitting room near the main elevator, he mulled over what he knew. The suspect list had not changed all that much. Evidence still put Lemar at the top of the list, but all of it was circumstantial, and Noble's gut still had doubts about his involvement. Robert, on the other hand, had put himself directly in Noble's crosshairs when he failed to disclose the fact that he had called Lysa not long before she was murdered.

Noble had no motives for any of the subjects, and that bothered him. It bothered him almost as much as not knowing if the key he carried was indeed the key to Lysa's door or someone's idea of a bad joke. He watched the numbers above the elevator as they counted down. The hard clunk of it reaching the first floor sounded seconds before the door opened, and Noble stepped in. He pressed the button for the fourth floor and stepped back.

Just before the door closed, a hand appeared and pushed them back open. A woman with more salt than pepper in her hair, held the door open for two young children, both of whom wore swimsuits and carried towels.

"Mind if we catch a ride with you?" the woman asked as the three piled in without waiting for Noble to answer.

Even if I did, it's a bit late to say so, Noble thought as he said aloud, "Not at all."

The door closed, and while pool water dripped from the wet suits of the kids onto the floor, the elevator began its ascent. The woman quickly pressed the button for the third floor. Noble ran his finger along the edge of the key in his hand and waited.

A computerized ding sounded as the elevator passed the second floor and again when it thumped to a halt on the third. The door slid open. The two children stepped out, followed by what Noble figured was their grandmother, and the door closed once more.

Noble stared down at the puddles left by the children and wondered how many times someone nearly busted their asses when they stepped onto the elevator and hit the slick spot. Another ding announced his arrival on the fourth floor. Noble waited for the door to open, then carefully maneuvered around the water on the floor as he stepped into the hallway. A placard on the wall across from the elevator indicated Lysa's room was to the left. Almost immediately, another placard had him make another left.

As he strolled down the corridor, he subconsciously scanned the room numbers. It was not at all necessary. He knew where he was going. Her room was the one right next to the motel's secondary elevator, the one housekeeping used.

The elevator opened as Noble reached Lysa's room. A young woman pushed a cart out into the hallway and then blushed when her eyes met Noble's. Noble stepped back to allow her to pass.

Once she was several doors away, he tried the key. A green light flashed, and the door opened. One mystery solved. How many more to go?

~

Noble sat across from Lemar once again. Whether he should confront Robert about his lapse in memory before or after Lemar had been a toss-up. In the end, Noble decided Robert would have to wait.

"I need you to help me track the key to Lysa's room," Noble took the key out of his shirt pocket and laid it on the table as he spoke.

"So, you found it?" The relief on Lemar's face was evident. "Was it in Lysa's room?"

"No, it was not in Lysa's room," Noble tapped the key.

The relief on Lemar's face faded and confusion replaced it. "Where was it?" Lemar asked.

"That's what we're gonna try to figure out," Noble informed him.

11

The Guardian's phone indicated that Noble was nearly out of time. Soon it would be over and the great investigator who had never left a case unsolved would fall. A giant mental scoreboard flashed in the Guardian's mind; Guardian 1 – Noble 0.

Being new to book signings, Noble was learning a lot. He had seen the tables arranged with what looked like various gifts or door prizes near the back of the conference room but since they did not seem to have anything to do with the case, he had mostly ignored them. When he had asked Ginger where he might find Robert, she had pointed in the direction of the tables.

Robert was arranging the items on the table in a tighter formation as Noble stepped up and asked, "What's all this?"

"Well, Mr. Harris," Robert answered, "these are donations that will be raffled off for a good cause."

"What cause?" Noble asked.

"The Shiloh Horse Rescue here in Deadwood," Robert reached into a bag at the edge of the table and pulled out a keychain, "Here take one."

Noble accepted the keychain. It was a miniature horseshoe. As he turned it in over in his hand, he asked, "How does the raffle work?"

"People donate the prizes," Robert made a sweeping gesture over the tables as he spoke, "Most of the authors bring a basket with their books and swag in them but others also donate. Everyone who is interested in winning a prize purchases raffle tickets, or some get them from the authors who buy them then hand them out when you purchase a book from them. Each prize has one of these little bags in front of it." Robert held up a paper bag and tilted it so Noble could see the tickets inside and then placed it back where it belonged, "At the end of the day, Tony or I will pull one from the bag and whoever's name is on it wins that prize."

"I see," Noble said.

Whether it was because this was not an official interview or because, as Tony had suggested that Noble was not keeping him from his job, Robert seemed much more cordial and willing to cooperate.

Guess we'll test that theory, Noble thought, "I've got one more question for you, Robert."

"Shoot," Robert continued to move the prizes closer together as he spoke.

"Earlier when I asked you if the last contact you had with Lysa was when you left her in the elevator with Lemar and Tony, you told me it was," Noble stated.

Robert looked up from what he was doing and nodded.

"Phone records show that a call was made from your room to hers between the time you left the workout room and the time she was shot," Noble continued.

When he finished, Robert said, "I did not hear a question."

Noble smiled, not what one would call a friendly grin, more of a so-this-is-the-game smirk. "Why did you fail to mention the call?" Noble asked.

Robert shrugged, "You asked me if it was the last time I'd had contact with Lysa. It was. Yes, I called but she didn't answer. I figured the alcohol had finally gotten to her and she was passed out. I actually thought about telling you at the interview, but it didn't seem important, and I needed to get back to the book signing."

Noble was not entirely convinced but Robert's body language indicated he was telling the truth. It looked like Tony had nailed it.

"Okay, thank you," Noble said, turned and started across the room.

One more interview, he told himself. Noble hated to put all his eggs in one basket, especially when he had been unable to untangle so little of the ball of twine, but time was running short.

"Momma Carol," Noble said as he stopped in front of her table, "I need to ask you a few questions."

~

Noble watched and waited as Momma Carol leaned her walking cane against the wall and eased into the chair Noble had indicated. Her short stature and silver-gray hair did not fool him. Noble's grandmother had been running the farm long after she had passed Momma Carol's seventy-six years.

"Mrs. Brown," Noble began.

"No need to hold to formality, young man," she interrupted him, "Carol or Momma Carol will work fine. Mrs. Brown makes me feel old."

Noble chuckled, "Yes, ma'am."

"So, you have questions," Momma Carol leaned forward slightly. "Ask away."

Noble saw no sense in beating around the bush. A quick nod and he began again, "Mrs. Brown, I have questioned your son, Lemar, three times today. The second time we spoke, he was unsure whether or not he had taken the key to Lysa's room after he helped her inside last night. The key was found and so I was compelled to have a third visit with him. During that visit, I had him walk through his movements from the time he left Lysa's until this mornin'."

"I see," Momma Carol interjected. "You know I do that sometimes, like if I forget where I put the car keys or something."

Noble eased into the chair across from her before asking, "Did Lemar visit you after he left Lysa's room?"

"He did," Momma Carol answered immediately. "He's a good son. Always makes sure I'm okay before he calls it a night."

Noble inhaled deeply then exhaled slowly. Sometimes a case turned on the answer to a single question and he felt certain that the question he was about to ask could well dictate the outcome of his day-long investigation.

"Do you recall whether or not Lemar had a key with him when he arrived at your room?" he asked.

Momma Carol's eyes narrowed as if she were concentrating and then she closed her eyes. After several seconds, she opened them again, "I was visualizing him comin' into my room, but I honestly can't remember if he had a key in his hand or not. He was flustered. I remember that but I'm sorry, I don't remember a key."

"How do you know he was flustered?" Noble asked.

Momma Carol eyes lit up, "Oh, a mother knows, a mother always knows."

"Did you know what he was flustered about?" Noble asked.

Momma Carol grinned, "I'm a mother, Mr. Harris, not a psychic."

Noble shrugged, "Never hurts to ask."

"That's what I tell my kids." Momma Carol's eyes twinkled.

Not sure what to do or ask next, Noble pulled his notepad from his pocket and aimlessly turned its pages. The fact that Momma Carol and his Granny seemed to be kindred spirits made it hard for him to question her, and he had hoped that she would be able to give him a definitive answer on Lemar's arrival at her room with or without the key. As it stood, Noble felt like solving the case was going to be more like a guessing game than an actual slam dunk.

A confession was what he needed, but time constraints and lack of motive, were not in his favor. Frustrated, he flipped another page and found himself looking at his summary of Lemar's first interview.

Lemar Brown: Most likely not the killer.

Body language is wrong. Either he is innocent or one hell of an actor.

"You told me you knew Lemar was frustrated," Noble looked up from his notepad. "Did you ever figure out what is was that had him frustrated?"

Momma Carol nodded as she answered, "Yes, sir. It was Lysa Lynn. She got drunk and made a pass at him."

"I see." Noble took a deep breath, then asked, "How long was Lemar in your room before he left for his own."

"Fifteen or twenty minutes, I reckon," Momma Carol answered.

"And did he seem frustrated when he left?" Noble asked.

"Not really," Momma Carol replied. "After our visit, he seemed much calmer."

Noble began to flip through the pages of his notepad once again. What he needed was motive. Had Lemar returned to Lysa's room only to be turned down? What reason would Robert or Tony have to shoot the model? Was there jealousy between her and Ginger for some reason? Where was the motive? Noble shut the notepad and laid it aside.

"You look frustrated," Momma Carol stated.

Noble gave her a half-hearted grin. "Maybe just a bit."

"I'm sorry I couldn't be of more help," she apologized.

"I appreciate that but it's not your fault," Noble assured her. "It's too bad you can't attest to Lemar's whereabouts after he left your room."

Momma Carol shrugged, "I'm sure he went to his room and went to bed."

"That's what he says, but since he had a room to himself, there is no one to verify he was there all night," Noble said more to himself than to her.

"Well, I'm sure that's where he was," Momma Carol shook her head as she spoke, "and I'm sure it was not my son who shot Lysa in the head."

Noble nodded his agreement. "If only 'a mother knows' was admissible in a court of law," he shrugged and then added, "Ma'am, I'm out of questions."

Momma Carol reached for her cane as she spoke, "Well, I hope you are able to figure out who killed her."

"Me, too," Noble stood and ushered Momma Carol to the door.

12

Noble watched as Tony held up a big crate filled with books, large mugs, and an assortment of coffees and teas. Robert reached into the paper bag that accompanied the prize Tony held and pulled out a ticket stub.

"And the winner is," Robert paused for dramatic effect, before saying, "Lindsey Miller."

A woman three tables away from Noble squealed with delight as she jumped to her feet and began to point at the lady seated next to her. The winner stood up with a sheepish grin and made her way toward Tony.

As if by some preconceived agreement, Davenport stood up from the chair he was seated in and followed her to the front. While Jean snapped a photograph of her receiving her prize, Davenport gave Robert a thumbs up.

"Congratulations once again, Lindsey," Robert spoke into the microphone as the blushing young lady made her way back to her seat. "And now, folks it is time for us to take a short break from giving away the prizes. I promise for those of you with tickets in these last couple of bags, we will get back to the raffle as soon as possible, but as many of you know there has been a murder investigation going on while the book signing was in progress, so at this time I will be turning the microphone over to the Sheriff of Lawrence County, Kent Davenport."

All eyes, except Noble's, turned to Davenport as he accepted the microphone Robert offered. Noble had been scanning the room for Ginger. He found her just as Davenport began, "First let me thank all of you for allowing me to interrupt your book signing and a special thank you to Linda Rae Sande, Ginger Ring, and all those who helped put this event together. Do me a favor and give them a big round of applause." He waited while the room filled with the sound of hands clapping and more than a few whistles, when the room quieted once again, he continued, "Before I introduce you to the finest investigator, I've ever had the pleasure of working with, let me give you a bit of background."

Noble slowly worked his way to where Ginger stood as Davenport continued. "Last year a problem in the casino brought me to the Lodge at the same time your annual book event was going. When I finished taking care of the situation at the casino and started to leave, I noticed several people with name tags and books. My wife, Mary, is an avid reader, so I decided to see what it was all about. Long story short, I stumbled in, knew Mary would love it, and called her to meet me here. We met so many wonderful authors that when I got a call six months ago from a friend in Oklahoma, I reached out to a couple of them."

Davenport paused and looked around the crowd. Noble took the opportunity to lean forward and in a half-whisper say, "Ginger, I need to ask you one more question."

Startled, Ginger turned and nodded, as Davenport began again. "You see this friend of mine was worried about the investigator I spoke of earlier. She told me that since his retirement, he had slipped into a funk, and she wasn't sure how to help him. After several conversations with her, and many discussions with Linda Rae Sande and Ginger Ring, we put together a solution, a case if you will."

Noble leaned forward and whispered his question to Ginger. She shook her head and then turned back toward Davenport.

"I should also credit my wife for her help. She not only assisted Linda Rae with the mystery murder but also enlightened me to the best way to keep our investigator here once he arrived and discovered the case he was brought here to solve was not a real murder but more of a dinner theater put together just for him."

Several in the crowd laughed and Davenport grinned. "I know right. Who needs enemies when you have a friend like me?" he shrugged as his eyes caught Noble's across the room.

"Without further ado," Davenport motioned Noble forward as he spoke. "Allow me to introduce my good friend and retired Oklahoma Bureau of Investigation agent, Noble Harris. Noble get on up here."

Noble made his way to the front. While he was not nearly as comfortable or entertaining to a group as Davenport, he had spent his fair share of time in front of an audience. As Noble turned and gave the crowd a nod, Davenport clapped a hand on his shoulder, "Before, I turn this show over to Noble here, let me explain how this investigation was set up to ensure no one was given an undue advantage."

Noble gave him a side-eyed glance and shook his head.

"Noble and I have a little side bet going as to whether or not he can solve this case," Davenport chuckled as he pulled a white envelope from the breast pocket of his shirt. "And normally, I would do whatever necessary to win, including cheating." he wiggled his eyebrows and shrugged, then continued, "However, my wife decided to level the playing field. So, here in this envelope is the name of the person who shot Lysa Lynn. I do not know who it was, as a matter of fact, only Linda Rae, my wife, Mary, and...well, you get the idea."

Noble reached for the envelope, but Davenport pulled it away. "I think we should let Robert hold onto this until after you tell us who you think the killer is," Davenport grinned as he handed the envelope to Robert and the microphone to Noble. Finishing with a not-to-deep bow, he added, "the floor is yours, oh great investigator."

Noble looked out over the crowd as he gathered his thoughts. In a normal case, he would simply read the suspected killer their rights and haul them off to jail, but this was not a normal case or a normal crowd. Authors who entertained with their words, models who struck dramatic poses for the covers of novels, and the readers who begged to be wooed by the stories their favorite writers offered them, all stared back at him.

"To say this is a far cry from my usual investigations would be an understatement," Noble scanned the room from left to right as he spoke. "Sheriff Davenport was right about this was more of a dinner theater than a real murder case. I've not been to a lot of theaters, but the few I have attended always introduce the actors and actresses at some point. I think now would be the perfect time to do just that."

Noble paused long enough to take the notepad from his pocket, then continued, "I know there were more people involved than I have noted, but due to time constraints, I think I'll just call up the suspects and our murder victim. Robert Kelly and Tony Brettman are already up here."

He turned and nodded to each of them, then as he flipped through the notepad, he said, "Dan Frisbee, Lemar Brown, Ginger Ring, and Lysa Lynn, come forward, please."

Noble watched as the four made their way to the front. Dan Frisbee seemed shocked that he was being called up as a suspect. Noble noticed Lemar's body language. Lemar appeared almost resigned to the fact that his name was in the envelope. It was obvious to Noble that Ginger was not entirely comfortable with the attention. Lysa Lynn on the other hand seemed overjoyed at all of the eyes on her.

When Lysa Lynn and all five suspects were lined up behind him, Noble turned back to the audience. "If you all would please give a big hand for Lysa Lynn. She did a splendid job of playin' the corpse."

Lysa stepped forward and bowed as the room erupted in applause. Once everything quieted, Noble had the five suspects step forward and take a bow again. Another round of clapping along with a few hoots and hollers filled the room. Noble waited until the noise died down, "In any investigation, I look for opportunity and motive. In this particular case, every one of the suspects standing before you had the opportunity. Lemar, of course, had the greatest, or so it would seem at first glance. I found it hard to rule him out."

Noble glanced at Lemar and couldn't help but notice the droop of his shoulders. "Lemar if you would step to my right, please," Noble pointed to the spot he wished Lemar to move to as he spoke.

Lemar did as he was asked. "Robert," Noble nodded at the model, then turned back to the crowd and continued, "Well, I guess I'll put it this way. Robert had less of an opportunity but more of an attitude than Lemar. Add to that a bit of a discrepancy I discovered during my investigation, and I had to leave him on the suspect list as well. Robert would you be so kind as to step to my right and stand beside Lemar?"

Robert did as he was asked, and Noble continued, "Dan also had ample opportunity, so I'll ask him to join the other two on my right."

Dan shook his head in disbelief as he made his way to Robert's side.

"After interviewin' Tony and Ginger, I was thoroughly convinced that neither of them had committed the crime," Noble motioned for the two to move to his left and continued, "Durin' their interviews it was obvious to me that neither of them has the ability to lie convincingly. That is not to say they are not capable of murder, but if either of them ever commits a crime, they better hope they are never questioned about it, because their body language will most definitely give them away."

Noble paused and looked at the three suspects to his right, then scanned the room for Davenport. He found him leaning against Ginger's table listening intently.

"Now to motive," Noble held up his right index finger as he spoke. "As hard as I tried, I could not find motive for any of the three men standing to my right and so until just a short time ago, I feared I wasn't gonna be able to solve this case. What was more of a gut punch, though was the idea that I was goin' to lose a bet to Davenport."

Several people chuckled and Noble continued, "Motive. That's what I was missin'. Then I remembered an old Rhode Island Red hen my Granny had when I was growin' up on the farm. Granny called her Momma Red. Every year, Granny would let this old hen sit on a bunch of eggs until they hatched. Some of the eggs were her own eggs, but some of them were eggs Granny had harvested from other chickens and slipped into her nesting box. Once the baby chicks arrived, it did not matter to Momma Red that all those chicks didn't look the same. As far as she was concerned, every one of those little babies was hers and she was willing to fight to the death to protect them."

Once again Davenport paused. The room had grown almost silent. Someone off to his left clicked a pen twice. The sound of a vacuum in the front lobby floated into the conference room. Noble took a step forward before continuing, "Motive. Thinkin' about old Momma Red made me remember this time when I was sittin' on the back porch with Granny watching that old hen scratchin' in the yard with all her little chicks 'round her. I don't know where it came from, but suddenly a plastic grocery bag blew across the yard. I guess Momma Red figured it was after her babies because she squawked and went to floggin' that bag like those chicks' lives depended on it."

From his spot in the crowd, Davenport half-shouted, "I think you're stalling. If you don't know who did it just say so." Then he let out a hearty chuckle that caused nearly everyone in the room to laugh.

Noble held up a hand as he spoke, "Patience, dear Watson, patience. I have a point and I'm gettin' to it."

Davenport pushed himself away from the table he was leaning on and again spoke up. "Well, Sherlock, some of us have to get home to dinner, so..."

"So, I'll wrap it up," Noble finished his sentence, then continued, "Now where was I? Motive. That's right. I couldn't find motive for any of the men standing to my right. As a matter of fact, I couldn't find motive for anyone, but then a short while ago, during an interview a slip was made by the killer."

"So, who is the killer?" Davenport questioned from across the room.

"I'm almost there," Noble beamed. "You see, Lysa was shot in the back of the head while passed out on the bed in her hotel room. When she didn't come down for breakfast, Ginger had one of the hotel staff members open the door for her and found Lysa. The police were called and the good Sheriff Davenport showed up. For those of you who may not be aware, a crime scene is not generally open to the public. By deduction then, the only people who would know where the gunshot wound was on Lysa's body, would be those who manufactured this little murder theater, Linda Rae and Mary Davenport, as well as, Ginger, who found Lysa, along with the killer themself. Moments ago, I asked Ginger if she had spoken with anyone about what she had seen in Lysa's room and she assured me she had not. At the end of my last interview, Carolyn Brown a.k.a. Momma Carol assured me that her son, Lemar, was not the person who shot Lysa in the head. The only way she could have known that Lysa had been shot in the head was if she had fired the shot herself. So, Davenport if you would be so kind as to check the large black bag under Momma Carol's chair, I believe you will find a..." Noble paused long enough to pull his phone out and quickly tap the screen, "a .38 caliber pistol with pink grips and built in laser-sights."

Momma Carol pushed herself up from the chair she was in and

speaking loudly enough for all to hear said, "No need to check the bag. The gun is there, but how in the world did you know it had pink grips and laser-sights?"

Noble laughed, "I've still got connections back in Oklahoma where you purchased and registered it. The laser-sights were part of the gun description. The pink grips were just a guess."

"The motive still doesn't make sense," Davenport declared as he made his way toward Noble.

"The motive only has to make sense to the killer," Noble explained. "Lysa was just the old plastic grocery sack that threatened Momma Carol's little clan." Noble quickly turned to Lysa, "No offense, Miz Lysa."

Lysa feigned a pout then grinned, "None taken."

"I'm still not convinced," Davenport stated as he stepped up. "Robert let's have it. Open up the envelope and read the name out loud for us please."

Robert was all smiles as he tore the end from the envelope. Noble watched him as well as Lemar and Dan as he slid a single piece of paper out. The body language of all three indicated that a massive weight had been lifted. For their sakes, Noble hoped he was right about Momma Carol being the killer.

Robert slowly unfolded the paper, and as his smile widened, he said, "Drumroll, please."

To Noble's surprise, the whole room filled with the sound of people simulating a drumroll. Some used their fingers on the edges of their tables while others trilled their tongues. Robert stepped over to Noble and motioned that he needed the microphone. Noble handed it over and with a flourish Robert indicated the drumroll should end. As soon as it did, he raised the paper high above his head and spoke into the mic, "And the winner...oops, I mean the killer is...(pause for dramatic effect)...Carolyn Brown a.k.a. Momma Carol."

All eyes turned to Momma Carol. With a grin, she shrugged, and in a calm, confident voice stated, "It's best not to mess with a Momma's brood."

13

Noble leaned against the bar in the hotel's restaurant and watched as Sam served a fruity-looking drink to a lady several seats away. Davenport had been shaking hands and saying goodbyes to several of the authors and attendees when Noble slipped away. He knew Davenport would find him when he was done politicking.

With time to kill, Noble began to scan the bottles of liquor on the shelf behind the bar. He already knew his favorite, Jim Beam Devil Cut, was not there. He had been a whiskey or bourbon drinker all of his life, but as he looked from one bottle to the next, he considered the possibility that he should try something new.

"Get you something?" Sam's voice broke through his thoughts, and he turned to look at her.

"Absolutely," he smiled.

Sam stood silently waiting, one hip propped against the bar. Noble scanned the selections of liquor once more and was about to make a choice when Davenport stepped up beside him and said, "There you are."

"Here I am," Noble replied with a grin, "Time for you to square up on that bet."

Davenport looked from Noble to Sam and back again before putting his hand on his chest and saying, "Are you implying that I would welch on a bet?"

Before Noble could answer, Sam moved closer, "A bet, huh? Tell me about it."

Davenport opened his mouth to explain, but Noble cut him off, "Your sheriff here bet me that I couldn't solve a hypothetical case and lost."

"I see," Sam grinned, "so you're the one everyone has been talking about."

Noble felt himself redden and shrugged, "I guess so." Instinctively, he looked around the restaurant and was glad to see it nearly empty.

"Well congratulations," Sam said, then asked, "So what did the two of you bet?"

"If he couldn't solve the case," Davenport answered quickly, "he owed me a beer."

"And if he solved the case," Sam asked, her question directed at Noble.

Noble wiggled his eyebrows and grinned then answered, "He owed me a shot of my choosing."

"Just one shot?" Sam gave him a doubtful look as she asked.

"Just one shot," Noble confirmed.

A middle-aged man with a receding hairline pulled himself onto one of the barstools halfway down the bar. Sam nodded his way and held up a finger indicating she would be with him in one minute.

"So, what's it going to be?" Davenport asked.

Noble ran the first knuckle of his left index finger along the scar on his face and asked, "What's the most expensive spirit you have?"

Sam started to speak, but Davenport cut her off, "Hey man. I'm on a budget."

"Should have thought about that before you made the bet," Noble laughed, then turned to Sam, "Give me a shot of Jim Beam, please, ma'am."

Davenport feigned wiping sweat from his brow and pulled a money clip from the front pocket of his pants. Sam chuckled, "You got off easy, Sheriff."

"Don't I know it?" Davenport agreed.

"You want anything?" Sam asked him as she stepped over to the shelf and retrieved a half full bottle of Jim Beam.

"Can't," Davenport answered as he laid a twenty on the bar, then explained, "I'm still in uniform."

Sam poured Noble's shot, picked up the twenty, and made her way down the bar to the newly arrived customer. Noble took a long look at the amber filled shot glass in front of him. He had to admit to himself that he had enjoyed today. Would he admit it to Davenport? Most definitely not but interviewing the suspects and tracking clues had made him feel almost human again, and it felt good.

"What are you waiting for?" Davenport asked, breaking Noble's train of thought.

Instead of answering, Noble picked up the glass and tossed it back. A touch of sweetness followed quickly by heat and then he swallowed and enjoyed the feeling as his whole body flushed with the warmth of the magic elixir.

"You ready to go?" Davenport asked as Sam returned with his change.

"I reckon," Noble responded and nodded goodbye to Sam.

Davenport handed her a five from the change she had given him and thanked her. He and Noble made their way through the restaurant and casino without speaking. Once in the lobby, Noble asked, "What time is my flight back?"

Davenport continued through the lobby and out the sliding doors into the parking lot before answering, "About that. I wasn't completely honest when I told you I'd fly you up here and send you back today."

"What?" Noble felt his chest tighten slightly.

"Hold up!" Davenport put his arms up defensively as he turned to face Noble, "Just hold up a minute, partner."

"You've got about ten seconds," Noble's eyes narrowed as he spoke.

Davenport nodded that he understood and quickly began to explain, "Your return flight is Tuesday morning, but this part of the plan was not my doing. Mary and Carla put their heads together and decided a weekend up here away from your normal routine would be good for you and Carla and... well, your relationship."

Davenport retreated as Noble stepped forward and asked, "And just how is me being in South Dakota supposed to help our relationship?"

Davenport's face broke into a grin as he answered, "Because Mary is picking Carla up at the airport right about now and the two of you have a room booked for the weekend here at the Lodge."

Noble stood staring at Davenport as if he had lost his mind. Carla here? Booked a room for the weekend? Help their relationship? Had she actually said that or was Davenport making that part up?

"Partner, are you okay?" Davenport stepped forward tentatively as he asked.

Noble shrugged then a grin spread across his face as he answered, "I'm not sure. Ask me again Tuesday mornin' and I'll let you know then."

ABOUT THE AUTHOR

One Pen – Endless Possibilities. I cannot think of a better way to describe my writing. Born and raised in Southern Oklahoma by a high school English teacher and a newspaper columnist, there was little doubt that at some point I would turn to words for comfort. Surrounded on all sides of my family by spinners of yarns and tellers of tales, there was little hope that I myself would not become a storyteller.

DEADWOOD DYNASTY

LARAMIE CUMMINGS

and I nod my head in affirmation, "In ..." he sucked air in and I copied him, "out Oakley ... In ...." we push our air out, "Out ... good. Keep doing that." He rubs his hands up and down my arms.

"You're doing so well," he praised.

I kept doing the breathing exercises as he moved his hands and rubbed my back in circles with his left hand.

"Keep goin', Oak. You've got this," He said.

My breath normalized, and I felt the tightness in my chest dissipate.

"Good. That's it. Good girl. You're doing good." He kept rubbing my back in circles.

I finally felt calm enough after several minutes, and I turned around.

"Beau." I croaked out, trying not to show I was about to cry. I just had my first ever panic attack, and my biggest enemy, besides my dad, was comforting me.

"Hey, Oakley." His eyes shone with care instead of the usual hatred.

"Beau, please don't be nice to me just because Dan died." I hated having anyone see me be weak, let alone Beau.

He winced, and I looked away, back out at the darkened landscape. The tears streaming down my face were like I was caught in a downpour.

"Oakley, I'm not being nice to you just because Dan died. I mean, I am comforting you because you just lost the man who was your father figure. But I also don't hate you. Contrary to your prior assumptions."

I looked back at him, seeing this slight twinkle of hope cross his face.

"Beau, you were so mean to me growing up. You hated me. Hell, the one time I thought you liked me and wanted to hang out, you never showed up. You left me at the ice cream shop by myself, and I waited for over an hour. Then Carissa and her posse told me you were with your friends, and I was a loser for waiting for you."

"That is not what happened." He let out a deep, angry sigh. "Oakley, I—I never wanted to tell you this way. Especially not on the day you find out your uncle has passed. But I never hated you, okay? Never. I was in love with you, and I got scared. I stood across the street, hiding, trying to get the nerve. Then I left. It wasn't until I

DEATH & REVENGE

As a highly respected and formidable manager for many country music artists, I earned my money today. I love my job and its perks, but sometimes dealing with a whiney thirty-something-year-old man-child pushes me to my limits. Today I was dealing with my most famous client and the biggest pain in my ass, Maverick Austen. A person would hope and think that he would have realized by now that he couldn't continue being a belligerent idiot after his concerts and getting arrested. But what do I know? I was just a successful, ball-busting, powerful, yet normal adult. Not some celebrity who was never told the word 'no'.

My mission today was to free Maverick from one of those head-line-making arrest moments by springing him from jail. I was texting away to the publicist so that they could lock down any bad PR when my phone buzzed mid-text. On the screen, James Foster, my very estranged father, appeared.

I halted in my tracks. I hadn't spoken to my dad since graduating from high school, and I didn't even think he still had my number. For James Foster to call me out of the blue was shocking, and it told me one of two things: either something was seriously wrong, or that trouble was brewing.

"Hello. This is Oakley Foster." I said in the executive tone I used around males in the industry. Though I would have probably been better off asking what the hell he wanted instead of citing such nice pleasantries.

"Oakley. It's your father."

"Oh. Well, say what you need to say. You've got sixty seconds of my time and that's all you deserve after being radio silent for years." I paused, "Clock starts now."

After what felt like a full-length feature film, my father spoke again. "Oakley. It's your uncle Dan. He's dead."

"What? You're joking. What do you mean, he's dead? I just Face-timed with him on Sunday."

"He's dead. Died. Deader than a doornail. Good Riddance." He scoffed. I could sense my dad's smile through the phone. My father's happiness projected through the speaker.

"Dad? What the hell? You think you get to be the one to tell me this? That's rich coming from you. You don't talk to them. Hell, *we* don't even talk. So how the fuck would *you* find out before me? You disappear for years, then show up acting like you're still part of the family bulletin? No, that's not how this works. Start over, or hang up. I don't have time for your lies." I was seething, thinking this was some cruel joke from my mother's sperm donor. I was furious at my dad's callousness.

"He had a heart attack in his chair while he was watching the Broncos game. Anyway, he is dead. Your grandmother is planning the funeral for this weekend in Deadwood. See you then, daughter."

Silence.

He hung up, and James Foster hadn't even answered my question. Why was he the one calling? And how did he know before her? I hadn't spoken to my father in over fifteen years, and these were the first words we spoke. I stood in front of the jail with my phone still held to my ear, and a burning rage rushing through me. Here I was, the best damn music manager in all of Nashville and the Country Music industry, and I was dealing with an asshole of a dad and a man-baby country star. Why are men so disappointing? And why did the only man who ever meant something in my life have to die? Was Uncle Danny even really dead?

Still shell-shocked, I immediately called my grandmother, hearing the first ring, then the second. My nerves and anger grew to palpitating anxiety, waiting for my grandma to pick up the damn phone. After the fourth ring, my grandmother said, "Oakley Jane. It's true."

That's all my grandmother said. *It's true.*

Uncle Danny was gone.

When the words registered in my mind, the rage transitioned to overwhelming grief. My father figure, gone. Uncle Danny, who helped raise me, was dead.

Moving my phone away from my face, I could hear my grand-mother saying muffled words, but none of them made sense. Ending the call just like my father had done to me moments ago, I took three deep breaths, trying to calm myself. I couldn't fall apart in front of the Davidson County Jail. I had to get my shit together because the paparazzi filtering outside the station would absolutely photograph me breaking down in my saddest moment if I lost it. How was I supposed to be handling Maverick Austen's delinquent ass when my world was falling apart? After a few more deep breaths, I looked down at my cell phone and texted my assistant. I turned around and headed back to my car because I must get to Deadwood immediately. Maverick Austen can remain in jail until one of my other staff could bail him out.

I texted Joey Daniels, my best friend, COO, and executive assistant. I told him to book a flight to Rapid City, South Dakota, and to notify everyone that I had a family emergency. I'd never experienced an emergency before, let alone taken time off during my supposed vacations. But this needed to be my sole focus. Uncle Danny was the most important person in my life besides my mother, and his death was about to crush me and alter my life forever. I could feel it. All of my strength and armor were about to dissipate or harden. But his loss was going to change me in ways I had yet to fathom.

The drive from Rapid to Deadwood was always beautiful, but this time, immense grief and fury clouded the vision of beauty. Joey called our other best friend, Bethany Carthright, to loan out her private jet. Bethany joined this trip as moral support, and I was grate-ful. Joey also tagged along, having been to Deadwood several times with me. Joey was more like a brother than my assistant, and Uncle Danny's death was hitting him, too.

Bethany, Joey, and I had all attended school at the University of Tennessee and became best friends. Bethany married a famous football player, becoming a big-time socialite and influencer, while Joey and I got into the music industry. I moved fast and ended up starting my management firm and bringing Joey with me. Though he was my executive assistant, he was also a part-owner of the firm. He just didn't like dealing with celebrities, only me. He did a lot of the operational stuff for which no one ever gave him credit. His title was Chief Operations Officer, but he didn't want anyone to know. Joey's husband was the CFO for the firm, and the work dynamic worked out well.

But today, my friends came through for me as friends would do. They were my shoulders to cry on during this darkening time. As I drove the large SUV through the hills, I felt my eyes well with tears. Despite the beautiful fall foliage and crisp air, I remained grief-stricken. I hadn't physically shown my sorrow, but I could feel the sadness wanting to rear its ugly head. The tears were about to burst through my dam. I hated showing any emotion that I considered weak. It was one trait I learned from my evil father. But the loss of Danny had my steel walls crumbling. I pulled over, feeling the sting in my eyes, flinging open the door, I quickly exited to get some fresh air. Seeing the fall colored trees along the road, I couldn't prevent the tears from falling.

The dam of emotions broke.

"Awww, babe. I am so sorry." Bethany had gotten out and rubbed my back, a tissue in her hand.

"Let it out. Shhhh. Just let it out." Joey wrapped his arms around my stomach and leaned his head on my shoulder.

And I did. I let it out. I wailed and screamed, letting all emotions release from my body into the endless Black Hills. The hills echoed my wails and cries, but I kept going. I just needed to release it all into the universe.

My uncle was gone.

He left me behind.

My heart was left in the tiniest of pieces.

After several minutes on the side of the road, I finally pulled myself together. "Joey, can you drive the rest of the way? We are only about twenty minutes from the ranch, but I just can't do it."

"Sure, Oak. We got you." I turned and walked to the driver's side of the car. I hopped in the backseat, needing the space. As Joey was about to drive off, blue and red lights showed in the rearview mirror.

"Fuck. What did I do? I haven't even moved yet. I only turned on the blinker." Joey was panicking.

"Calm down, you ninny. They probably are just wondering if we need any assistance." Bethany said in her southern Tennessee drawl.

A knock sounded on Joey's window. He pressed the button, and it rolled down.

"I drove past a few minutes ago and saw you all huddled on the side. I was checking to see if everything is okay or if you need help." The deputy said.

I knew that voice.

"Carter?"

The sheriff's deputy looked back at me in the backseat. "Oakley Foster! Whatcha doin'? Oh! I am so sorry to hear about your uncle. The whole town's shocked by the news."

"Thanks, Carter. I'm shocked too." I said, not knowing how to reply.

"Gosh, I feel so bad. I'm sorry, Oak. Is there anything I can do for you?" Carter said.

"Nope. I um, just need to get home." I said, my voice cracking a bit.

"I get that. Everyone's talkin' about how your pops is coming into town. I think you beat him here. If you need anything, you have my cell number, right?"

"I do. Thanks, Carter."

"Seriously, if your dad even says one thing wrong, call me or the Sheriff's department. We'll handle him." Carter said sternly and confidently. More tears fell down my face.

I choked out between my new sobs, "Thanks, Carter. I am going to need all the help I can get dealing with that man. It means a lot."

"You bet, Oakley. We've all got your back. Anyway, I'll let cha' go. Seriously, call me if you need anything at all." He tipped his hat and walked away, back towards his cruiser.

"See, I told you, Joey. We are in South Dakota. People here are way too friendly." Bethany said.

"Oakley, do you know everyone here?" Joey asked, ignoring Bethany. I didn't respond, ignoring them as Joey drove and headed to my uncle's ranch.

. . .

As we pulled up the gravel drive and saw the huge log cabin with rock columns holding up the front porch, a rush of warmth and the feeling of home enveloped me. Then it hit me: the man who made this place a home for me was no longer here, and my heart broke even more.

When the car stopped, I looked out the window at the grand ranch house. This was my uncle and aunt's dream home. They had built it when I was in third grade. Before that, there was a modest ranch house that my uncle and father had grown up in. But this new house was the one I was raised in. This was the house my aunt and uncle had built for my mom and me so that we could be with family.

I finally got the courage to open the door, but the front screen door pushed open first. My grandmother stepped out with a handkerchief in her hand. She held it up to wipe away tears. I broke down at the sight and ran up like I was a child, to my grandmother, and threw myself at her into a hug. Uncle Dan's death hit me the hardest then.

"He really is gone, isn't he?"

Sobs came from my grandmother.

"Grandma, I'm so sorry you lost Uncle Dan. I'm so, so, sorry. No parent should have to bury their child, no matter how old they are."

We rocked each other, crying, and standing there on that front porch.

My grandmother, after a long, grief-filled embrace, let go. "My Oakley Jane. You're here." She beamed up at me and pushed a stray hair from my face with her arthritic hand.

"Yes, grandma. I'm here."

"Darling girl. I am so sorry you lost Danny."

"Grandma ... why didn't you call and tell me? Why did Dad?"

"I was going to, honey. I swear. Your dad and I were on the phone when Dan's heart attack began. After being at the hospital all morning and told he was gone, your dad called to check in, and I just spilled what happened. I told him I needed to get hold of you and that I needed to let him go. You deserved to hear this first."

"But he got to me first. Bastard." I said in a growl.

"He wants the Foster Love Ranch, the saloon, the gift shop, everything. He doesn't even care that his brother died. How did I raise such a man? He had called me before your uncle passed to threaten us."

Threaten them? I was so confused. I was wondering if she was just not in her right mind.

"Shhh...don't worry about that right now. Okay? What matters most is we are together." I say and hug her tighter.

"Okay. I love you, Oakley Jane."

"I love you, too, Grandma."

She broke away and grabbed my hand to pull me inside. "Let's get some whiskey and pour one out."

"Let's pour it out." I echoed.

My grandmother poured five shots of whiskey. I wasn't sure who the fifth one was for, but I was going to find out soon as she yelled, "Shots! Now! Kitchen!"

I waited for Bethany and Joey to come in. Joey had been here enough times to know the whiskey drill. They came in acting shy. I knew they were just trying to tread lightly since the air was so heavy with loss. Then I heard the back door slam and the loud stomps of boots. When the person finally walked through the kitchen, my heart stopped.

Approaching the kitchen island was the man I despised most in the world. The one person who bullied me like no other when growing up. I hadn't seen him in years because I avoided him like the plague when I was in town. But now here he was, in my dead uncle's house, and he looked good. Not that I should care how he looked. I was deeply mourning, but seeing him—over six feet of solid rancher muscle, a full dark beard and mustache, and wavy brown hair tucked beneath an SDSU ball cap—brought an unexpected spark to my otherwise bleak day.

"Beau, this one's for you." My grandma handed him the shot glass. He never took his muddy brown eyes off me as he took the shot from her.

"Thanks, Mrs. Foster." He said, still eyeing me.

"Well, my dears, we are goin' to pour one out for my son." My grandmother held her shot glass up, and cleared her throat, "Thank you all for being here for Oakley and me. Our family tradition, besides drinking, is to 'pour one out' and raise a toast. So, here it goes,

'Here's to those who wish us well. As for the rest, they can go to Hell'." And with that, my grandmother knocked the shot on the counter, brought it back to her lips, and downed it.

"Mrs. Foster!" Joey was trying not to laugh. "I expected heartfelt words from you."

"Oh! That was the best I could do, considering how my other son is showing up at some point tonight. He's destined for hell."

"Grandma!" I shouted. Though I had a smile on my lips. "Of course my dad belongs in hell, but damn. Sorry guys, we're a feisty bunch."

"We knew that already, hun," Bethany said in her Tennessee drawl.

A grunt sounded, and I remembered that my handsome arch-nemesis was in the room.

"What're you doin' here, Beau?" I asked.

"I live here."

"No, you don't. I would have known if you were living here." I said confidently.

"He lives here, Oakley Jane. He is renting out the old house while his house gets finished being built." My grandmother deadpanned.

"What do you mean?" I asked. I was confused as all hell.

"I am building a new log home on my property. Ya know, the one that butts up right next to yours? My home burned down in a fire last year." He was so serious and still staring at me. Was he even blinking?

"Oh. Well, sorry to hear about your home, but why are you at my home?" I couldn't hide my dislike any longer. My emotions were all over since my uncle had died, and I couldn't mask any of them anymore.

"Because Dan said I could rent out the old house." Plain and simple. He was always direct with me. But he always had a smile and smooth-talking words for everyone else.

The whiskey bottle slammed on the counter, and I looked back at my grandmother, who was slamming back a second shot.

"Oakley Jane, give Beau a break. He's been extremely helpful here on our ranch, still running his ranch, running his brewery, and helping with our businesses." My grandmother gave me the look that always let me know I was about to be in trouble if I didn't cool it.

I gritted out, "Can do ... for now." I said the last two words under my breath, aiming them at Beau.

Beau kept staring me down, and I probably shouldn't feel it, but I felt butterflies whisking around in my belly.

"Another shot, kids!" My grandmother was already going around and pouring more whiskey into the glasses.

"I always love coming here," Joey said.

"My turn to pour one out," Beau said, and I looked at him. "Here's to steak when you're hungry, whiskey when you're dry, a lover when you need one, and heaven when you die."

I blushed; the toast fitting this very moment. Beau took his shot, his gaze unwavering, compassion replacing his initial dislike. I did the same.

"Another!" my grandma said again.

"Grandma, I think we need to unpack. Then we can drown our sorrows some more." I walked over and hugged her, and she broke down in full-body, wrenching sobs.

I cried again, too.

"My baby," she cried out, "my baby. He wasn't supposed to go before me."

I broke.

A few hours later, I was sitting on the front porch. The evening was upon us, and I relished the Black Hills' quietness. I just finished a phone call with my mother, who told me she would be back for the funeral. She met a nice tourist a few years ago and is now married and living in Santa Fe. I also got an update from Carter that my dad had arrived at the Sheraton in Deadwood. Knowing he was here and so close had my nerves on edge.

I rocked back and forth, back and forth, lost to memories of my uncle and avoiding the creeping negative thoughts about my father. I didn't hear the footsteps approach.

"Oakley Jane Foster. It's been a while."

I didn't turn to look at the deep voice talking. "Yup. Wasn't long enough, though."

He scoffed, "Or it was too long."

Then I looked at him. What an odd thing to say to someone you bullied your whole life.

"What do you want, Beau Mason McGill?"

"I just wanted to–" he trailed off.

"To?"

"I, uh, I wanted to say I'm sorry for your loss. Dan was a great man." Beau cleared his throat, "I, I know we have never been close, but I am here for you. Dan always talked about you, and I just–I, well, I want you to know I am sorry."

I had never seen Beau frazzled, and I felt he was holding back on me.

"Beau, spit it out or leave me be. I just lost Uncle Dan, and I don't have the energy for bullshit."

He stares me down. Those butterflies I felt earlier awakened again. I tried to tamp them down since I was grieving, but the fluttering bastards wouldn't stop moving in my belly. What's wrong with me?

"Also, why do you keep staring at me?"

He didn't answer. He took his hat off, and with the hand holding his hat, he scratched his head, moving his fingers through that brown hair. His other hand moved to his hip. He was standing there like he was at a loss for words. I stood up and growled out my frustration.

"Seriously, Beau! Speak up! Between seeing you, my bully, the one person who loved to ruin my life today, and then seeing my fucking douche of a father tomorrow, I am not in the mood for mind games. I just lost the only man in my life who never treated me like shit. The only man who loved me. Please don't fuck with me right now. I can't take it."

I got up and paced, getting lost in my thoughts. My breath was racing, and I felt lightheaded. All the sadness, rage, hatred, love - everything was boiling to the surface. I grabbed my Alpaca-blend sweater, moving it in and out to get cool air and eliminate the panic. Then, I felt like I couldn't breathe. My heart was rapidly thumping, and I became dizzy. I knew I was not okay.

Then I felt warm hands on my shoulders, and Beau's face came down to mine, our lips mere inches apart. His nose was centimeters from mine, and I could feel his whiskey breath caress my lips. His eyes were deep brown and showed something like care with a mixture of despair.

"Oakley. Hey, hey, it's going to be okay. I am so sorry. You're having a panic attack. I'm here. Let's breathe, okay?" He nods at me,

heard Carissa and Mallory say that they lied to you I knew I had fucked up."

I looked at him in disbelief, wondering what alternate universe I had entered this morning. All in one day, I get a call from my estranged asshole of a dad after fifteen years. My uncle died, my grandma is drinking more than normal, and Beau tells me he was in love with me. This doesn't happen. I shake my head, throw up my arms, and head into the house. I stomped to my bedroom, slammed my door, and flopped onto my bed.

And then, because I am sad, confused, and angry, I cry myself to sleep, knowing that even more shit will come my way.

~

The funeral...

The last few days were a blur. I remembered little about getting everything ready for the funeral, dealing with community members and family coming in and out, and helping on the ranch. I cried a lot and tried not to sink too far into my grief, but I still tried to stay productive.

My mother had shown up the day before, and her arrival brought a sense of comfort I desperately needed. Sometimes, a girl just needs her momma. Her endless number of hugs, her crying with me, and her fond memories of Uncle Danny all helped me get through this difficult time. And she reminded me that even though I didn't get to say "goodbye" before he died, I still ended our last conversation with an "I love you." That was all that mattered. I knew how much Uncle Danny loved me, and he knew how much I loved him.

The morning before the funeral, I woke in my old bedroom, stretched, and basked in those few moments of waking up where I didn't realize I was there for Uncle Danny's funeral. Those few moments waking up and seeing the sun peek through my window reminded me how much I always loved being home. Though I loved living in Nashville, South Dakota would always be home for me. I vowed I would end up back here one day, especially knowing everything would be bequeathed to me. I just had anticipated it to be later on in my life. Not when I was thirty-three and still trying to make a name for myself. But life is a wild ride, as my uncle used to say.

I finally flung the covers off and got out of bed, throwing a crew-neck and some sweats over my pajamas to head downstairs to get coffee. Living in Nashville, people were shocked that I loved a good cup of black coffee. But that was how I grew up drinking it. Black Folgers coffee. My Uncle always said it would put "hair on my chest". Later, I knew the phrase was to help strengthen me. Black coffee was now my daily ritual to pep-talk me into being an assertive go-getter. Black coffee reminded me how tough, intelligent, and capable I could be.

I bustled down the stairs and walked down the hallway to the kitchen. I could smell the coffee and bacon lingering in the air. When I walked in, I still did not register that today would be the worst day of my life. I almost bounded in like it was any other time I visited home. I thought I would see my grandma cooking, but my mother's husband, Randy, was cooking breakfast. My mother sat at the table, staring at the coffee cupped in her hands. Joey and Bethany were missing—probably still sleeping. Then it registered: Beau was there. He was reading what looked like legal papers and sipping his coffee.

Instead of thinking, I blurted out, "Where's Gram?"

Beau, my mom, and her husband looked at me. I searched their faces for an answer.

Beau looked at my mother, expecting her to tell me, but she didn't. A giant tear trickled down her face.

Beau cleared his throat and set down the paper he held in his hand. "Oakley, your grandmother had a visit early this morning from your father. It didn't go so well. She's out walking the north pasture."

"My dad was here? What? Why didn't someone wake me up? It's only eight thirty! When did he get here?"

"Oakley, honey. Your dad surprised us. Randy opened the door for him at five this mornin', thinking it was an emergency. He just walked in and returned to the kitchen to talk to Lou. Their conversation got heated, so they went out to the barn. Then Lou came in and said she was going to walk her anger out. Your dad was already gone."

I became overwhelmingly angry. My dad was not the nicest man. He loved money and himself more than anything or anyone else in this world. I went to the back door, grabbed a random coat off the hanger, and threw on my grandma's wellies.

"Oakley, wait! Just let your grandma be. Today is going to be rough on her. She is putting her son in the ground." My mom said to me.

"Mom. Something isn't right. I need to go find her and talk to her." I could sense that my dad coming here for the funeral and coming this morning to see my grandmother had something to do with whatever my uncle was leaving behind, and the threats my father had spewed. My grandmother said my dad wanted Foster Love Ranch, the saloon, and all the other businesses. I wasn't sure what it all entailed. But I remember back in high school, on a visit to my dad's in New York City, he told me he couldn't wait to own Foster Love Ranch. I wondered if my dad thought he would get it all or had some plan to take it.

It took me about ten minutes, but I found my grandma at the creek that bordered our ranch and Elk Basin Ranch. As she always said, it was her go-to spot for thinking, naps, and reading. I walked up behind her, not hiding my heavy footsteps.

"I knew you would come looking for me, girl. You always knew when something was amiss, " my grandmother said, sitting on a log and staring at the creek. The morning sun was glistening and setting the water in a twinkle. Sunlight was bursting through the trees. The trickling sound of the water added an extra layer of peace.

"Well, you did what I would do, Grandma. I learned from the best. Anyway, I will not beat around the bush. What did my dad want? Why was he here at the ass-crack of dawn?"

"Oh, just to remind me, he gets it all. The lawyers told him everything Danny owned would soon be his and that he would sell this ranch off to developers or something else. I didn't fully pay attention to his lies. Unfortunately, your father thinks he knows everything when he knows nothing. He thinks he can lie his way back into owning everything. But really, he knows nothing at all."

I was confused. Why would my dad burst into the ranch thinking he was getting it all? If anything, I remember my uncle saying, "Everything the light touched was mine, and I would inherit all our family businesses and property someday. He even had me sign papers a few years back when I visited for a week. I wasn't sure what I had signed. I just knew that it was for when his time came.

"Grandma. Stop being vague and spill. What's going on? I haven't spoken to my dad since I was eighteen. Then he is the first one to call me and tell me Danny is dead. Then you spout off some vague sentences like you're a psychic. Tell me truthfully, what is goin' on? I can't help if I don't know."

"That's just it, Oakley Jane. You don't need to help. Your father's unaware his inheritance isn't guaranteed; he's powerless to change that. We have a meeting with the lawyers right after the funeral. I can tell you that shit will hit the fan. I just need you to be ready to handle it all." My grandmother stood from the log and looked at me, placing a hand on her hip.

That's when I noticed how much older she looked. She was newly seventy but still looked spry and in her fifties. She was lovely with blondish grey hair, tanned skin from working daily out on the ranch, and strong posture. Seeing her with a weakened look on her face, like all of her years had finally crept up on her, shook me.

"Grandma, of course, I'm ready. You, Momma, Danny, and Aunt Shell raised me to be strong. Working with rich celebrities and wealthy people in Nashville taught me other life skills that you would probably frown upon. But if anyone is preparing to fight my father. It's me. He won't even know what hit him. I lived with him and saw how he worked when I had to stay with him in the city."

"Good. That's what I was hoping for. I wish I weren't so vague, but I promise you will know everything right after the funeral."

"Alright, Grandma. If you say so." I went to hug her tightly. She embraced me fiercely, and I could hear her sniffling.

"Baby girl, I just—I can't believe it."

"I know, Grandma. I know." We hugged for a long time. The trees, water, sun, and soft breeze were the only ones to witness our sadness.

Before Uncle Danny passed, he had planned everything out. With Aunt Shelly's loss, my uncle ensured he would never leave us with a mess to clean up. He wanted everything done and done to his liking. My Aunt Shelly passed unexpectedly in a horse accident when I was twenty-five. When she died, her family tried hard to claim that the ranch was hers and that they were the inheritors. They also tried to get the businesses, money, and whatever they could get their hands on. Unfortunately, my uncle lost a small payout because my aunt had left her estranged sister as a beneficiary on one of her accounts. A significant sum sat in the account. The bank transferred it to the sister because of the lack of a will or trust.

That's why Uncle Danny's funeral and last wishes had been all planned out. Yes, we met with the funeral parlour, the florist, the band, and many others. But all the funeral vendors had all been paid previously by Danny, had a plan given to them by Uncle Danny, and were ready to tackle all the things needed to make today easy on those of us left behind on earth.

Walking down the church aisle to the front pew, I knew it would only be minutes before I broke down and cried. My grandmother held my hand, and I felt her squeeze it as we walked together towards the impending gloom and heartache. The whisper of mourning floated in the air in the church. Many attendees knew Danny well. My heart swelled with the love and support from so many, but it also made me exceedingly sorrowful because they had lost him, too.

As we approached the front, a man darted from the side, walked to the front pew, and sat down. I almost asked him to move, but realized it was my father. I hadn't seen him this whole week. Seeing him for the first time since I was eighteen had me pausing. He had greyish hair on the side of his head and a full grey beard. His blue eyes were still striking. He was wearing a Tom Ford suit, and it made me scoff. Here he was, showing off his opulence, but really, he was just reminding all of us how much of a prick he was.

My dad stared back at me and smiled a devilish smile. "Ahhh, there's my daughter. Look at you all grown up. What has it been, three or so years?" He stood back up from the pew and hugged me. I didn't release my grandmother's hand or move my other arm to wrap around him.

"What the–" I almost cussed, remembering I was in a church. I knew he was trying to gain sympathy and show he wasn't the horrible human he was.

"Why don't you sit next to me, Annie Oakley? I could use your support in this difficult time." He put on a face like he was distraught for the public. "I just can't believe my younger brother is gone." He said it almost too loudly.

I seethed. How could this man come in here and pretend to mourn his brother? How could he pretend to know me when we were estranged?

My grandmother still held my hand, holding it extremely

tightly. I whispered so as not to cause a distraction. "First off, it's Oakley. Second, you don't belong here." My dad lived for riling people up, and I wouldn't give him the drama he craved. I sat on the other side of my father, knowing he was expecting me to sit somewhere else, but I would give him the satisfaction. My grandmother sat on the other side of me, followed by my mom and Randy.

"Um, I'm sorry, you don't belong in this pew, Cynthia. You need to sit behind us." My father had leaned forward to tell my mother.

My mom looked back at my dad in disbelief. "No, Dad, she is family. She belongs in this pew. Don't make a scene."

"I am just saying she and her husband, who aren't family, should sit elsewhere. She is my ex-wife, for crying out loud. She shouldn't even really be here."

"She is more our family than you are, son. You're a disgrace to me and your father." My grandmother had chimed in, loud and clear for all to hear. "You're the one who shouldn't even be here, James."

My dad looked at his mother in disbelief, turned his head to the front of the church, and didn't move an inch or speak another word.

The sermon was lovely and reminded me so much of what Uncle Danny would have wanted. I had been previously tasked with giving a eulogy and realized the moment was approaching to stand up and deliver it. The pastor called me up, and I went to stand. My father, instead, tried to pull me back down.

"Oakley, your uncle wanted me to deliver the eulogy. I'm sorry, but your grandmother must have asked you, and she didn't know that Danny had asked this of me." I stood there in shock. Then it hit me that my dad was up to something.

I shook my head at him, "No. Uncle Danny asked me to do the eulogy. We'd talked about it a year ago. I'm doing it. He wouldn't have requested you to speak. I don't know what you're up to, but I will find out. And I will ruin your plans."

My father looked back at me with war waging in his eyes, telling me I needed to sit down. Because we were in public, he knew he couldn't fight me on this. Plus, the pastor had called my name, not his. I'd won this round, but I knew more rounds would come.

Reaching the podium, I surveyed the vast room. I knew I would cry, speaking about the most amazing man and striving to capture his essence.

My hands felt sweaty, and I felt the sense of panic I had earlier in the week come back to rear its ugly head.

"Um ... uh, thank you, everyone, for being here today. It means a lot to our family..." I trailed off, not knowing how to start. My heart was racing. I scanned the crowd more and found a familiar face standing at the back by the doors. Beau was there, and seeing him made my nerves settle. He smiled at me and nodded, almost like he was urging me to continue, silently saying I could do this.

"Um. Well. If you don't know, my name is Oakley Jane Foster, Danny's niece. Oh, where to begin? I planned an entire speech, but looking down, I don't think it would do him the justice he deserves..."

I thought for a moment. Taking some breaths.

"You see, Danny wasn't just my uncle; he was the man who helped my momma raise me. Aunt Shell, Grandma Lou, my momma, Cynthia, and Uncle Danny raised me on Foster Love Ranch. It was extraordinary to be raised by those four. Let me tell you. It was a gift full of adventure, love, and laughter, and what made my childhood perfect was the fatherly love that my uncle had given me.

You see, he and Aunt Shell couldn't have any kids. So when I came along, they spoiled the crap outta me. Then, when my mom and I moved on to the ranch with them in third grade, my uncle made me his number one priority.

Uncle Danny was my best friend—my dad. He taught me how to fish, hunt, mutton bust, and even French braid my hair." The crowd laughed. "He taught me to ride a bike and make my grandma's secret sugar cookies." More laughs. "Uncle Danny taught me to be strong, kind, and fight for what I believed in. And he also taught me how to love and make sure I accept only the best for myself. He was my biggest fan and biggest supporter. Without him, I don't think I would be even half the woman I am today."

Taking a deep breath, I looked back at Beau. He nodded again. "Most recently, Uncle Danny came out to Nashville. He came every quarter like clockwork. But this last time, instead of doing normal things like fishing and drinking beer. He decided he wanted to hit Broadway and see what it was like to be young again. I tried to convince him he wouldn't like it. But he would not take 'no' for an answer. So my two best friends, Joey and Bethany, came over. We got ready, and we went to hit Broadway and go to all the famous bars. We hit Tootsies, Honky Tonk and even Maverick Austen's new bar, Whiskey Bent.

We were having a blast, and I had not seen my uncle so happy. And then the booze started to hit. Uncle Danny decided he needed to ride this mechanical bull so badly and that he couldn't leave Nashville without riding it. He cut everyone in line and went right up and hopped on this bull. My friends and I went up and stood at the side, worried Uncle Dan would get thrown and break something. Then, my uncle yells, "Watch the bull riding master!" and we three just all started laughing our butts off. Before the bull started moving, a crowd formed to see him on the bull. He was yelling how he used to be a pro, which, as a side note, he wasn't, and people were just gawking. Phones were out ready to take photos and video, and my uncle is just sitting up there on this bull like he was the King of England."

I look down at the church carpet, a smile creeping up on my face at the memory. "Then the bull started to move. And my uncle looked so happy. Then it moved faster, and I could tell he was struggling to stay on. Then this mechanical bull got a demon in it or something because it was acting like an actual bull, and here I am worried about my uncle's safety. I overhear the guy running the machine say that he couldn't get it to slow down or stop. So I started to panic. Then everything moves in slow motion. Or at least that is how I remember it. But my uncle yells, 'Cowboy up!!!!!!' like he was reenacting a scene from *8 Seconds,* and he flies over several heads and lands on a table full of bachelorette party girls in pink cowboy hats. One girl screams, 'Oh my gosh, is he dead?'" I pause, forgetting I was at my uncle's funeral. And I laugh. Because I was telling this story at his funeral, and he is now, in fact, dead.

People in the audience laugh and also try to hide their laughter. I look at Beau, who is stifling his. I look at my mom, who is smiling. And I finally look at my grandmother, who has tears but is in a full belly laugh. Her laughter is echoing throughout the church.

"Well, I guess I didn't think that story through. The mechanical bull might not have killed Uncle Danny. But he sure is dead now..." I laugh. "And I think he would be proud that we are all laughing. Um. I will finish this story at a later date. But I wanted to end this with something my family likes to do. It's called 'Pour it out'. Some of you might have already been wondering why there is a shooter of Jack under your seat. If y'all would please join us in 'pouring in out', I would like to make a toast to the best man that ever lived."

People rustled, grabbing their shooters. I gave it a few moments, and finally, when it seemed like everyone was ready, I held up my shooter. "To Danny. The best friend, son, uncle, and father. We toast you with your favorite toast, 'Here's to those who wish us well, and all the rest can go to hell.'"

Cheers echo through the church. I toss back my shooter and feel the burn of the amber whiskey go down. Looking out at the crowd as people toss their shooters back, I say thank you one last time and head back to my seat. When I sit down, my father looks at me with evil in his eyes. My grandmother grabs my hand in support. And I knew that calling Danny, my father, in front of my dad just let him know I was ready for battle.

After the funeral, my mother, Randy, and grandmother all went in my grandmother's truck to the law offices. My grandmother had said she did not want my father to be at the house when the will and everything was read. So we headed to the law offices of Drakes and Marlow. My father beat us there and stood outside the office looking smug.

When we exited the car, he immediately strode up to me and grabbed my upper arm, tugging me away from my family.

"Oakley, a word." He tugged me to the side of the building, and I wrenched my arm out of his grasp.

"You touch me again, and I will have you arrested." I spewed, yanking my arm out of his grasp.

"Come now, daughter. Don't play that game." He looked down his nose at me like I was a piece of garbage. "Your speech at the funeral was atrocious. You embarrassed me. However, you have been pretty good at doing that your whole life. But this," he took a deep sigh, "this pushed me a little too far. You don't know what you're doing and who you are messing with. Calling my brother your father was embarrassing for me. You need to apologize."

"Are you threatening me?"

"Oh, honey. Yes, Yes I am."

I eyed him. I had known that my dad was a powerful man, but I still felt like I was missing something. "Dad, or I guess I shouldn't call you that since you didn't help raise me. How about I call you James, since you aren't anything to me?"

The anger welled up in him so fast that I didn't even register it. He lifted his hand to slap me across the face, but it never hit my cheek. I winced, expecting the slap to land, but he had gained his composure. My father paced away a few steps and returned, running his hands down his suit jacket to smooth out unseen wrinkles.

"Again, Oakley. Watch it. You don't know what you are doing."

My grandmother came around the corner just then. "James, if you try to lay a hand on Oakley, I will have the cops here so fast, but not faster than me pulling my pistol on you." She stared him down.

"Mother, I am just telling Annie Oakley here what is in her best interest."

"I can tell when you're lying, son. I know what you're here for and who you are. You might have it all sorted, but life will knock you down. I will make sure of it. Come Oakley. Let's go inside and get this over with."

I look at my dad before following my grandma. "It's Oakley. You don't have the right to call me Annie Oakley."

When we get inside, Mr. Drake from the law firm welcomes us into a large conference room. There is a female paralegal, Mr. Marlow, another clerk, and two other men in fancy suits. We all sit around the conference room, and I notice James sits between the two nameless men in suits. We wait for Mr. Drakes to come in, and when he does, he is followed by Beau. My mouth drops, wondering what the hell Beau could be doing here. He wasn't family.

"First off," Mr. Marlow says, "We are so sorry about Danny. He was a good friend to so many of us. Second, we will start reading the will, but we would like to introduce all the interested parties in the room."

"We have Mr. Marlow and I representing Mr. Daniel Redmond Foster's last will, which is dated March 17th of 2024. And representing Mr. James Randall Foster is his legal counsel, Mr. Bart Huckabee, and Mr. Larry Huckabee."

Feeling immense anxiety, I knew my dad was going to pull something nasty. I should have let my lawyer in Nashville know to get a team ready to battle, and what I had going on. Everyone emanated tension around the table, waiting for the shoe to drop. Mr. Marlow and Mr. Drakes took turns reading all the legalities.

"Now, we will get to the last wishes of Mr. Daniel Redmond Fosters, who said them in his own words through this video.

Hello All! Damn. If you're seeing this, then it means I keeled over. It's a shame, but I lived a terrific life. Besides bequeathing everything to all of you in this room, I have also written letters to each person. Please, all, remember to just be kind, love each other, and be better. And Oakley, I have one thing I need to say in this video that I didn't in your letter. Remember Lead and Ned.

Well, anywho, here it goes.

To my mother, Louise May Foster, I leave ownership of Deadwood Shoppe and Gifts. I also leave you $250,000 for when you get too old and need to go into a home. It is not the responsibility of Oakley or Cynthia to wipe your ass if you can no longer do so. Go into a home. I promise they will visit. Also, you're bequeathed 7.5% ownership in Foster Love Holdings. Love you, Momma. You were the best mom there ever was.

To Cynthia Renee Clearing, I leave $250,000 and the deed to the house in New Mexico. I bought it for you anyway. You did well. You were the best sister I could have asked for. You are also bequeathed 7.5% ownership in Foster Love Holdings. I love you, and thanks for sharing Oak with us. It was the best gift you could have ever given anyone, and Shell and I will never know how to repay you for that.

To Beau Mason McGill. I have high hopes for you, son. Your parents did such a good job raising you, and I just wish I could see even more of where you're heading. But looks like since I am dead, I will just need to bequeath you some things. First, Beau, you are bequeathed fifty percent ownership in the company of Bear Country Brewing. You are bequeathed $250,000 to do whatever you see fit. You are also bequeathed fifty percent ownership of the Foster Love Cabin in Story, Wyoming. You are also bequeathed twenty-five percent ownership in Foster Love Holdings. I know this is unexpected to everyone, but you will see why soon.

To James Randall Foster. First off, you can go fuck yourself. You were raised better, man. What happened to you? You went off to Harvard and came back a different person—someone I dislike. For my last will, I bequeath what Daddy left you, or at least should have left you. I kept it in a trust with your name. You will be glad to be bequeathed since all you care about is money and materialistic *things. In the trust, it is $300,000, and the stock is in Foot Locker. Is that store even around anymore? Oh, and you get some other stocks and bonds. The lawyers will get you everything. But for my last words to you, thank you for letting me be the father I should have been to your daughter. She is a great girl, and it is no thanks to you. And that's all I have to say to you, you bastard.*

Lastly, to my dear girl, Oakley Jane Foster, I leave everything else. You are now the brand new owner of Foster Love Ranch, 60% owner in Foster Love Holdings, 50% owner of Foster Love Cabin in Story, Wyoming, 50% owner of Bear Country Brewing, sole owner to all other property, cash, assets, stocks, bonds, items, you name it. It is yours. If it isn't listed in the will, it's yours. If it was listed in the will for someone else, well - it's theirs. I love you, Oakley Jane. You are the best part of all of us. Be strong, baby girl. I love you.

The video ended, and my uncle's smiling face filled the screen. I'm overwhelmed. I knew this would happen, but I didn't know all the in-depth details. Looking around the table, Beau looks like he is in shock, and my dad seems *too* calm. Then, that shoe we were all waiting for to drop, well, it drops.

"I am so sorry for your loss, everyone. But unfortunately, we are here to dispute the will read to you today by Daniel Foster, Mr. Drakes, and Mr. Marlow." Suit number one said. "We have an updated last will signed by Mr. Daniel Redmond Foster, stating otherwise. It is the most current will, unless he signed another with your firm. But this was signed and dated August 5th, 2024."

My mind went black, and I saw red. I knew my dad was up to something, but to stoop this low was infuriating.

"Can we please review this document?" Mr. Drakes said. He looked amused, like he knew they were trying to pull a fast one on him. Suit number two handed it over to our lawyers.

"We will need to have this reviewed. Unfortunately, when we spoke to Mr. Foster two weeks ago, he said nothing about this. We even have the conversation recorded. We asked him if he would like to update anything in his will dated March 17th, 2024. Mr. Foster stated he did not and that it was still accurate as his last will."

"You recorded your client, Mr. Drakes?"

"We did. Mr. Daniel Foster suspected that Mr. James Foster would try to pull something. So he came in regularly, and we recorded his statements with timestamps and witnesses. Your grandmother, Beau, our law clerk, Mr. Marlow, and I were all present at the last one."

I looked at my grandmother, who smirked at her son from across the table. I looked at my dad next and saw the red covering his face. He looked like he was going to murder us.

"It also seems that this document is a fake." Mr. Marlow piped up. "The signature is nowhere close to Mr. Daniel Foster's, and besides, I saw Mr. Foster for a beer and golf on Monday, August 5th. You see, we have a standing tee time every Monday and Friday at Elkhorn at 3:30 PM in the summer. So, please tell me how my client and friend could have signed this document in person in New York City on August 5th, 2024. I am not sure what you gentlemen are getting at, but I can assure you that this is the type of suspicious behavior our client discussed with us. We took the proper precautions to keep his interests safe."

The two suits looked shocked. It was almost like they couldn't believe that two small Western town lawyers had handled them. My dad shot up, slamming the table with his palms.

"This isn't the last you hear from me or my lawyers. Foster Love Holdings is mine." He got up and hurried out of the conference room.

Suit number one said, "We are sorry for the inconvenience. Our condolences."

Suit number two nodded his head and then followed my father.

I sat back in my chair, wondering what I was missing and what I was supposed to do now. I needed to pry the answers out of my grandmother, but we had to get to the celebration of life my uncle had planned for himself. We wrapped things up, got our to-do list from the lawyers, and headed out the door.

I felt a large hand grasp my arm before I followed my family to get in the vehicle. I turned around, ready to clock my father for grabbing me again, but stopped to realize it was Beau.

"What, Beau?" Looking at him, I could sense that I was losing all of my fight. I didn't know how long I could keep talking to people without breaking down.

"Can we go and have a drink? I think we need to discuss what just happened."

I stood, crossing my arms, thinking. There was something I was missing with my father, and I couldn't pinpoint it. Maybe talking to Beau could shed some light on the situation. Plus, I needed to know why he got so much from my uncle.

"Alright. We can talk. Let me tell my family to head home, and we can get that beer. I'm telling you now, though, I need answers, and you better have them."

"I think you'll enjoy knowing my answers, Oak. It will definitely give you more context." Beau replied.

I went to the truck and told my family to go on without me and that Beau would bring me home for the celebration. My grandmother gave me a curious look that I couldn't quite read.

We said our goodbyes, and I walked back to Beau. "So, Beau, where should we go?"

"How about we head to the brewery taproom? Grab a beer? It's closed today for your uncle, so we'll have some privacy."

"Sounds good." I didn't even know my uncle had owned a brewery with Beau until the will was read. I knew Beau had his brewery, I just didn't think it was "co-owned".

We walked the block down to the taproom in silence. I was trying not to let my grief and concern in. The silence was comfortable as we walked together, and I appreciated the moment to finally just be. We ended up at a red door, and Beau went to unlock it.

"I guess I knew nothing about the brewery," I said.

"There is a lot you don't know, Oak. And someone needs to catch you up." He pushed open the door and motioned for me to go in. I walked past him and into the taproom of Bear Country Brewing. It looked like an old saloon set in an old John Wayne movie. The wood, the bar top, all screamed "western". But there were also modern fixtures, sprinkled throughout. The barstools were cushioned. The lighting is more industrial, making it feel cozy and inviting.

"So what'll it be?"

"Hmm?" I asked

"What would you like to drink?" Beau asked again.

"Oh!" I scanned the beer menu chalked on the wall above the beer taps. "How about the Bear Necessities IPA?"

"Comin' right up." He poured my beer, and I kept scanning the menu. As I got further down, I saw my name on the wall. My heart stopped for a beat. There was a beer named after me, the Calamity Oak Pale Ale. I knew it was a play on my name. I was named after Annie Oakley and Calamity Jane—two notable women in Western history.

"There is a beer named after me. Was it my uncle who named the pale?" I asked. Trying not to tear up. Thinking about how my uncle included me in the little ways in his life made me sad and nostalgic.

"Um. Kind of–" Beau trailed off.

"What do you mean by 'kind of'?"

"Well, he said he would go into business with me as long as there was a beer named after you, his mom, your mom, and Shell. I agreed. And the first beer I ever made was the Calamity Oak Pale. I didn't even run the name by him. I just called it that, and it has been our number one beer along with our Shell Shocked Blonde."

"You named the beer?" I asked, dumbfoundedly.

"Yup."

"Why would you name your first beer after me? My uncle wanted a beer with my name on it, but your first one?"

"It tasted like you; honestly, when I was making it, you were the only thing on my mind at the time." He set the IPA down in front of me.

I looked at him curiously. This was not the Beau I remembered from my youth. He was almost nice to me. He told me he never hated me and liked me, but I still couldn't believe it.

"Beau, why don't you tell me what's going on? I feel like I have been missing something huge since I returned to Deadwood."

"You have. Shit's been stirrin' for some time. Your uncle was getting into some deep things, and your dad was also rearing his snake head. I finally got the full story a few weeks ago."

"Okay, well, start talking." I gulped my beer.

"Oakley, do you know who your dad is?" He asked.

"What do ya mean? He is James Foster. Money-hungry New York City millionaire who only cares for himself."

"I mean, besides that. Do you know how your dad gets money or what he does?"

"Not really. I haven't talked to him since graduation day. I haven't even looked him up online. I disowned him." I said in a matter-of-fact voice.

He snorts out an annoyed laugh. "You don't know anything, do you?" He looks at me deadpan. "Oakley, your dad is one of the most manipulative, narcissistic, conman *billionaires* in the world. Not a millionaire. *Billionaire.* He has dealings with Russia and the Middle East. He owns businesses worldwide, exploiting people to make another million. Do you not know this?"

"Nope. Maybe I should have put out a Google alert?" I tried to hide my disbelief that my dad was one of the wealthiest people in the world.

"Oakley, he can kill people just by asking one of his hitmen on payroll. His connections are so deep that how he hasn't already taken everything is beyond me. And honestly, today wasn't a mistake on his or his lawyers' parts. I almost don't believe he hired dumb lawyers. But I can't figure out his move."

"I will need you to tell me things faster here, Beau. What do you mean today wasn't a mistake? He brought a fraudulent will."

"Oakley, this was him trying to scare you and your grandma. It was to scare me. Your uncle had information to take your dad down once and for all. Your father could give two shits about inheriting all of this. But really, he just wants to scare us all. He wants us all to remain under his thumb in Deadwood while he keeps all his secrets buried here."

"I'm still confused," I say, getting scared.

"Your dad killed your grandfather, stole all the businesses, money, everything, and turned it into a global empire. When you were born, your dad let your mom and you, Danny, Shell, and Lou live in peace on the ranch as long as nothing came out. Your dad signed over the ranch, gift shop, and saloon to Danny, thinking it would be enough for y'all to live on. He didn't realize how smart and cunning Danny was, and that Danny could someday take James down. Danny discovered additional information regarding the ranch and James. He was just about to take James down, and then he had a mysterious heart attack? Your uncle's recent checkup in Rapid City revealed no problems. James knew Danny was coming for him, and I think he might've killed him. And now James is here trying to scare you and your grandma to keep you in line. He has more secrets and doesn't want them coming out, Oakley."

It was a lot to take in, and I was stunned.

"Oakley, I ain't lyin'. This shit is real. If we aren't careful, we will be dead next."

"Um..." I look away. Still trying to understand what Beau was telling me, all the actions of my family, the unspoken words.

"Oakley." He called my name to get my attention.

"I... I just knew something was going on. But I guess I am still trying to grasp everything and how big this is. I need to talk to my grams."

"I bet. It's a lot to take in. Danny only told me what was goin' on a few months ago because James threatened him. Now I'm not sure what your uncle's full plan was, but I know he had been working on it for some time. And everything was ironed out perfectly. He said he knew your father better than anyone, and that he was the only one who could take him down."

"I wonder what spurred this," I said.

"Your father came to Deadwood a few years ago and threatened Danny. I'm not sure of the full details, but Danny had been keeping tabs on your dad all these years. So I guess it made it so Danny was finally ready to take him down. I know your uncle had been building his network in secret. One that rivaled your dad's, and your dad still has no idea. I think if anyone learns everything, it is going to be you. And hopefully it will be soon."

"You are making it sound like my family is a mix between the shows *Succession* and *Yellowstone*."

"That's exactly what your family is." He says in all seriousness.

"Well, that's not good," I say seriously. And then it is like Beau reads my mind.

"Oakley, your uncle was so proud of who you have become. Starting your mini-empire. But now it's time to move home and take on the family business. Danny built Foster Love Holdings into something huge, all for you and to take your dad down. Your dad is desperate for it. I don't even think your dad knows exactly all Foster Love Holdings has. It's time to take down your father and all the other greedy men like him. And I'm here to help. Because I have a stake in this, too. We need to keep Deadwood, our family, and our lives safe. We need to take down your dad."

"You expect me to upend my life and move back to Deadwood? I am so numb right now, I am not sure I even believe any of this. It sounds like a soap opera."

"Yup. It sure does." He takes a big gulp of beer, "But you'll get your answers, and in time, your dad will rue the day he ever thought you were a nobody. You will defeat him. I'm going to help, and your uncle will look down on us with lots of pride."

"I think I will need a lot more discussion, planning, and beer to fully comprehend the gravity of this situation."

"Oakley, you deal with celebrities daily. You know the corruption inside and out. Now you get to take down the most corrupt person of all—James." He was so serious and so sure that I would be the one to take down my father.

I sat there in silence, thinking and drinking my beer. Although I knew we needed to leave soon for the celebration of life, I felt content staying put. I needed this break from everyone, even if it was an unbelievable information dump session. But I was here with Beau, learning about my history and trying to save my family's legacy. At some point, he had pulled up a seat beside me, sipping his beer. It was a comfortable silence.

"Beau, why you? Why did my uncle trust you?" I asked. I couldn't help but wonder why he had confided in the man who had caused me so much embarrassment and pain.

"You know why, Oakley. I told you the other night."

"You weren't being truthful. You were so mean to me growing up. Hell, you hated me and I never knew why." I said.

I was trying not to cry. This week had been so emotional for me that now I felt raw. Losing my uncle, seeing my horrible father, and now dealing with this bomb that just got dropped and Beau. I still hadn't even grasped the fact that he and I were co-owners of several things, including this brewery. The pain was turning to a numbness I didn't know if I could shake.

"And now I co-own a brewery with you!" I added.

"Oakley." He put his hand on my knee. "We can talk business later, but I will tell you again. I never hated you. Do you know the old saying that boys pick on the girls they like?"

I nodded.

"Well, I have loved you, no liked—loved, since we were three, maybe four years old. You are in my first memory." He chuckles. "I was wearing a cowboy hat. We were in the barn, I think. And I pulled it off, put it to the side of our faces, and kissed you. I was using the hat to hide our kiss. I remember my mom saying how cute we were. It wasn't until my parents died a few years ago that I saw an old VHS of that moment. But it is the first memory that I can remember pretty clearly."

I was stunned. I vaguely remember that, too, but I thought we were older.

"I remember," I said. Choosing to be honest instead of acting like I didn't know what Beau was talking about.

"I have loved you, Oakley, since we were toddlers. And your uncle, your aunt, your mom, and your grandma have known that. My parents knew it. The only one who didn't was you. It wasn't until a few years ago that I realized that you probably would have liked me back, but I was picking on you our whole lives instead of showing you how much I cared about you. I am sorry about that. Looking back, I shouldn't have treated you the way I did."

I couldn't look at him as he spoke. This week and today, with all of these revelations, have been a lot.

"I am not asking you to be my girl, or marry me today. But I have always loved you. I told your uncle when he came to me that I would do anything and everything to protect you. What we are involved in is big Oakley. Bigger than you can grasp right now. But if anyone can take down your dad, it's you. And I promise to help you and protect you the whole way. We have to save it all, Oakley."

I looked at him. The look in his eyes told me how truthful and serious he was. If I were honest with myself, his taunting hurt so much because I had loved him my whole life, too. Even to this day, he has this imprint on me. The confession didn't pierce me like it should have. My soul was shattered, and all my emotions were drained. I was a husk.

"I think we should get going to the celebration. I don't want people to question where I have been." I said.

"Yeah. You're probably right. We should get going. But I just. Fuck!" He growled, "I need you to grasp things because we don't have time to waste. Life has changed, Oakley. And we don't have time to dally." He said.

"I know. It's just been a lot. There is a lot on the line. There are a lot of emotions I am feeling. I was lost without Danny. And now everything you told me. It's so much. One minute, I am trying to bust Maverick Austen outta jail, and the next, the one man in my life who cared for me is dead. Then you confess your love for me. And my dad, I knew he was bad, but this. This is a lot. It's hard to believe." I'm spiraling now.

Beau stands up from his chair. And pulls me into a hug. "I know Oak. I know." He holds me in his arms, and I sob. I cried forever, and he just held me. It had been a long time since I had felt such comfort from a man, especially a man who wasn't related to me. All my other interactions with men were quick one-night stands or short-term situationships. Dating wasn't feasible, given my demanding lifestyle. My last situationship was when I was twenty-eight, and I don't even really remember his name. If I were being honest, I had always had love and a pull for Beau.

After crying my eyes out, I pulled away and looked up at Beau. He looked down at me and brushed the hair away from my face.

"You've always been so beautiful. I hate seeing you cry. I'm sorry for the past, for the present, and for the future. But I'm here for you and'll help you through it all." Beau said.

It was like a declaration. The proposal marked the pivotal moment when I knew my life would change significantly. Yes, Uncle Danny died. Yes, I inherited a bunch of stuff. But this was the moment that made it clear. My life was no longer the same, but at least I would have Beau.

"Beau ..." I said and couldn't get out the rest of my words.

"Oakley Jane." He said, cupping my cheek with one of his large, calloused hands.

And then I leaned up on the seat and pressed my lips to his. He kissed me back. The kiss sent lightning throughout my body, and I knew this was what I needed to dissipate the numbness. All the hairs on my arms and neck stood up. My heart fluttered. I'd never felt this chemistry with anyone else. Still being on my stool, I used my legs to pull him closer. He deepened our kiss, and the numbness I was succumbing to lifted completely.

Then my phone rang.

I pulled away from Beau, trying to catch my breath. The interruption gave me that moment to think about the gravity of what had just happened with this man.

I pull my phone off the counter and stagger out, "Hey, hello?"

"Oak. You need to get here. Your father is yelling at your grand-mother, and some musician just showed up."

"My dad is at the celebration?"

"Yup." My mother said, "He doesn't have the suits with him, though. It's just him. Your grandmother has a gun in her hand. And this Mav kid is singing some songs for the crowd."

"Maverick Austen is there?" I said in disbelief.

"Yes, honey. This boy said he needed to be here to support you. Seems so sweet. But get here now. Your daddy is going to have his head blown off if he doesn't leave."

I looked up at Beau, and the weight of everything fell like bricks stacking on my chest. My uncle is dead. I am connected to Beau. Maverick is here, and I need to outsmart my corrupt father.

"Come on, Oak. Let's get this goin'." Beau takes me by the hand, leading me out of the brewery, locking it up, and taking me to his truck.

We climb in, strap our seatbelts, and head to Foster Love Ranch, where a showdown is about to begin.

Beau slows down as he drives down the way. I see my grandmother and father spitting words back and forth. She's holding the rifle, and I hope she won't use it on her son.

"We should call the police," Beau says.

"Not yet. I need to handle this. I signal you to call if shit really blows."

"I climb out of the truck and walk up, head held high like Beth Dutton.

"Can I help you, James?" I ask, strolling up, masking my anger, and putting on my executive face that I use with men in board rooms. I can't let him smell my fear. If anything, the music industry has taught me that I need to play the game and have bigger balls than the men who think they own the world. I need to manipulate him or scare him.

"You can help me by signing over everything. If you're not here to do that, then butt out of this conversation. I have nothing else I want from you," James spat at me.

"Oh, but you see, James. I am going to be involved in this conversation. I'm also going to remind you that you're trespassing, and one signal from me, I have Beau over there calling the Sheriff."

James gives me a death glare.

"You see, Father, I know. I know it all, and I won't bend over willingly and have you steal everything back. You messed up."

"Listen here, you little ..."

"James, I will not have you speaking like that to my granddaughter. Get your ass outta here or I'll blast you." My grandmother holds up the rifle.

I saunter closer to my father, "Trust me—"

"No, trust me, Oakley, when I say you shouldn't get involved. But if you are, know that I will take all of you down. Your inheritance will go," he motioned with his hand, "poof. Just like that. Don't fuck with me. Don't start a war you can't win. You're just a little girl trying to learn chess, and I am the Grandmaster."

"No, James, don't fuck with me. You don't know me, and what I can do." I murmured low into his face, "But if I find out you had anything at all to do with Dan's murder, or you try anything, you're going to learn how much better I am at the game than you are. I will demolish you. All that money, all that power, everything you give a damn about will be gone. Or 'poof' as you like to say." I smile my deep snake-like smile, "You might play chess and think you're the Grandmaster, but I am flipping the godsdamn board over and lighting everything on fire."

"Don't do this, Oakley. You don't know how powerful I am. I'm your father. You should join me. You can have so much more. Just hand it all over."

"The man who was my father is now dead. You think I don't know you, I learned from you dad when I had to be with you in New York. I watched, and I learned. Instead of making me in your image, you made me your consequence. I also learned from Uncle Dan, Grams, Deadwood, and I will be that final bullet that will take you down if you so much as try to fight me." I stared him down with so much hatred filling my eyes. "You did something to Dan, and I will figure it out. When I do, I will end you."

He glared back at me. I fix my gaze on him, letting him see the fight in my eyes. I hope he can tell how serious I am.

"What's a dumb girl in heels going to do to a man like me? This is your last warning. You don't know shit Oakley Jane." My father says.

"Oh, Daddy, don't you know I wear heels to make me taller than the bodies I bury? I wear lipstick as my war paint. This dress—I will bury you wearing it. You may think I am some little girl just talking and playing dress up, but I am your biggest enemy, giving you a warning. You want a war, James? Well, you should have buried me first, not Dan. Now get the fuck off this property and don't set foot back in Deadwood. If I hear that you do, well, you're done for. I will take my gun and aim it with intent. And I sure as hell won't miss." With that, I turned on my heels and walked away, confidently harnessing all my anger.

Then I turn around and add, "Oh, and James, watch your back. I'll be comin' for ya." I aim a finger gun at him, shoot, and then blow my invisible smoke. I turn back around and strut into the house.

The celebration of life ended, and I sipped my scotch in my uncle's office. I sat in his big leather chair, staring out the window at the back property. Being here by myself is what I needed to end this horrific and devastating day. All the exhaustion is catching up to me. I needed some solitude. I hadn't been by myself long enough to just breathe and mourn. I take another sip, turning the chair around to face forward.

I searched the drawers, hoping to find something my uncle left behind—something that would give me a clue to what he had on my dad and how to take him down. I kept looking and looking, staring down at the planner on my uncle's desk, and sipped another taste of my scotch.

I get lost in how my father thinks he can win this "war", but he doesn't know me. He's unaware that I understand him completely, and I intend to keep what belongs to the family rightfully. If he wants to show me how truly awful he is, well, I can be worse.

Getting lost in my thoughts, I'm interrupted by three quick raps on the door. A head pokes in, and I see Maverick. His brown hair is hidden under his typical ball cap, and his brown eyes shine with that youthful glint.

"Maverick," I take one more sip and forcefully put my glass down. I can't take off even a week for personal matters, can I? What the hell are you doing here?"

"Ahhh, Oak, you're like family. I wanted to come and be here for ya. You're always there for me." Maverick said.

He was right. I was always there for him and exceeded what a manager would do. But this kid was almost like a little brother to me. Yes, he did dumb shit, but he had worn me down over the years, making me care.

"Well, I appreciate you caring about me. But you didn't need to come." I sighed.

"I needed to. I know how much your uncle meant. And the few times I met him, he was always so nice to me. Just a genuine guy."

"He was. Thank you, Maverick." I was hoping he would leave so I could get back to my thoughts.

"Ya know, since the tour is over, I'm considering taking a break. I need to find myself again. This last arrest really did a number on me, and I—uh, well, I need to just reset." There it was. Why was Maverick here?

"So you want to take a break? How long?" I ask, thinking of the endless list of to-dos I would need to get done just for him to go on a sabbatical.

He takes his hat off and runs a hand through his hair. "I'm not sure, Oak. I don't feel right. I was wondering, well, your Grandma said I could stay here, and I think I might—"

"Stay here? What do you mean, Mav?"

"I mean, I want to take her up on her offer and stay here in Deadwood at the Ranch. Or I could rent a cabin somewhere here in the Hills. But I just need to find myself again, and honestly, I think you could take a break too. Seems like you and your fam need to get some shit figured out." He said, and he wasn't wrong.

I didn't know what to say, so I went into my scary thinking mode. I stood up and paced the room, my face stoic, and my hands clasped behind my back. This mode frightened onlookers. After several paces back and forth, I turned to look at Maverick Austen.

"Fine. You can stay here, but there will be hard labor involved. Your hands will get dirty."

"Not a problem, Oakley. Works for me." He came over and grasped me in a firm hug. "Ya know, Oaks, I love you. You're the sister I never had. I'm sorry about Dan."

I hugged him back tightly. "Thank you, Mav. Now go. Get out of here. If you're staying, you need to get your rest every night since you'll be up at the ass-crack of dawn each morning."

He laughs and walks out.

I go to shut the door behind him when a hand pushes it back open. My anger starts to flare when I realize it's my grandma.

She comes in and shuts the door, leaning back against it.

"Oakley Jane, we need to discuss a lot. And there is still much you don't know. But I don't want you to get hurt. You weren't supposed to get involved." She was shaking as she finally came forward to grab my hands. "Oakley, go back to your life. I can't let your father hurt you, too."

My stomach dropped—those words.

I can't let your father hurt you, too.

Was she confirming my father had killed my grandfather, or uncle, or both?

I tamped down the worry, hurt, and fear. I let the anger and rage boil to the surface.

"Grams, you're going to tell me everything, and you will not leave out even one tiny detail. If anything, I will give my dad the rope he uses to tie his noose."

"Oakley, your father, he isn't the boy I raised. He is evil incarnate. He knows the right people. Your uncle thought he could beat James. But he couldn't. No one can."

"Well, I am James' daughter. And if anyone knows manipulation and corruption, it's me. You're going to tell me everything, and then I am going to burn my father's empire to the ground. I'll leave him amongst the ashes. I may not know everything that he has done and why you're showing the first signs of fear. Rest assured, nobody, not even James, can fuck with me or my family and avoid the repercussions. He may have built this empire in fear, but I'm gonna burn it down and rebuild a dynasty on his bones."

"Oakley, don't let this turn your heart hard." My grandmother says.

"It's too late. My heart was already hardened, but now it's as hard as a diamond. We lost Danny, and knowing my dad and what I suspect is true, this is going to be a war. And I am tired of him winning. I'm going to ruin him."

"Maybe revenge isn't the best way. Maybe Danny was wrong, and we should just try to live in peace with your father."

I stared my fearless grandmother down. How could this formidable human being start to crumble now? I knew losing Danny broke her, but I didn't realize just how much.

I walked behind the desk and went to sit in the leather chair. I poured another scotch and poured one for my grandma, too.

"Grandma, of all the people, you taught me to fight. You may have taught Danny, James, and me how to shoot guns, but I got the best aim out of all of us. And hell, I am pissed now. Plus, I learned all my father's tricks when I was younger. It's about time someone puts my dad in his place and who better than me? So I'm going to invite my friend revenge in for a whiskey and see what happens."

"All I'm sayin' is be careful, Oak. Once this war between you and your father truly starts, I don't think there is any end to it unless one of you comes out dead."

I snort, realizing my heart is hardening. I am going to do what I need to do to protect what is mine. I need to protect the family, and I need to come out the victor. But to do that, I need to know everything.

"Start talking, Grams. Tell me everything and give me the information I need. Because James' castle is crumbling and I am the storm about to knock it the rest of the way down." I say in a calm but calculating tone.

My grandma sits in a chair on the other side of the desk after pouring her scotch. She takes a big gulp and stares at the unlit fireplace.

"Alright, Oaks. If you're goin' down this road, I may as well make sure you've got all the ammo and supplies. Here it goes."

ABOUT THE AUTHOR

Laramie Cummings is a rising author who refuses to stay boxed into just one genre—her imagination knows no limits! By day, she navigates the fast-paced world of fintech, but off the clock, her life is a delightful juggling act. She's a proud mom to two rambunctious kids, a spirited partner to her husband, and the ringmaster to a quirky pet duo: a dog and a cat who's convinced it's one too. When she's not spinning stories or chasing the next big idea, you might catch her reading, skiing, or being outside with her kids. Laramie lives in Wyoming—and no she is *not* named after the town.

You can find out more about her books on her website: llcummingsbooks.com.

ECHOES OF LOVE AT MT. MORIAH

LYNN DONOVAN

BLURB

Brian Rourke only planned to spend two days in Deadwood, paying respects at his grandfather's favorite historical site. But when ethereal violin music leads him to a haunted grave at dawn, those two days stretch into a destiny he never imagined.

Echo Maugham has been playing her supernatural concerts in Mt. Moriah Cemetery since 1882, waiting for the right moment— and the right man. Now she's found him, and she has just one chance to guide him to her great-great-granddaughter Mary, a local historian whose emerald eyes mirror her own.

As Brian finds himself caught between two worlds, he discovers that Echo's music isn't just a tourist attraction— it's a bridge between past and present, between loss and love, between what was meant to be and what still could be.

In this enchanting supernatural romance, the Black Hills hold more than gold and gunfighters' graves. They harbor a love story that took over a century to complete, and a ghost who won't rest until the final note of her matchmaking waltz is played.

1

Brian Rourke stepped out of his white Toyota Corolla Cross LE but didn't move. Not one step. He stood paralyzed by the mesmerizing specters of steam dancing across Mt. Moriah Cemetery's parking lot. Intellectually, he knew the spectacle was created when the cool morning air passed over the warmth retained in the black asphalt. Still, a shiver rattled his teeth as it skipped down his spine.

This spooky sensation seemed befitting for what he was about to do. The eerie silence starkly contrasted the city of Deadwood's hustle and bustle day or night. "Come on, Brian. You promised Grandpa," he whispered, squaring his shoulders.

Inhaling the cool, crisp air blended with the aroma of fresh dirt, pine, and dewy aspen leaves, he pressed his key fob to lock the vehicle— out of habit, not need. A water jug was his only cargo, but city instincts died hard. He rolled his eyes at the ridiculousness of himself.

An unexpected sound drifted through the morning stillness, catching his attention. He paused, leaning against his car, straining to determine if what he heard was real or imagined. The vibrations of a solitary violin floated on the otherwise empty air, faint and ethereal, like a whispered memory. At times the melody seemed to fade completely, only to return with the shifting wind, haunting and sweet. The notes quivered and danced, sometimes clear as crystal, other times barely distinguishable from the rustling aspen leaves that sounded remarkably like rain.

It was an old tune, perhaps a love song, its longing enhanced by the distance, making it impossible to tell if it came from the cemetery, the old church beyond, or somewhere deeper in the shadows of Mt. Moriah. The sound wove between the tombstones, rising and falling like a woman's soft laughter turned to music.

Brian glanced up the steep terrain toward the iron gate that had been bent and shaped into the name of the cemetery— he listened. His assumption that coming early would allow him to be completely alone on this self-guided tour of Mt. Moriah was wrong. Whoever had gotten here before him had brought a violin and played it beauti-fully. Perhaps to soothe restless spirits that might wander aimlessly beyond their graves.

"Okay, let's see..." Brian fumbled with the self-guided tour map and the creaky, rusted latch that kept the iron gate closed. The gate's hinges protested with a long squeal that seemed to echo off the weathered headstones, blend with the ethereal violin notes, and fade like a dust-devil running out of wind. Dew still clung to the grass, and the morning shadows stretched long across the uneven ground.

Whoever played that instrument, wherever they were playing it, would surely not be surprised by his presence in the cemetery after making all this noise just to get inside the fenced, sacred grounds.

He shook out the creased two-dollar map, turning it this way and that, painfully aware of how tourist-like he must appear. None-theless, something in his gut cautioned him to be quiet, like when one entered a library, so as not to disturb anybody who might be concen-trating. Brian's lips twisted as he traced his finger along the cemetery map, remembering his grandfather's last words, "Promise me you'll visit Wild Bill before you settle down."

Grandpa had moved in with Brian's parents— something about his ticker not keeping time right— but his presence seemed to cause a rift between the folks that ten-year-old Brian couldn't understand. What Grandpa's watch had to do with it was a mystery.

But with Brian's track record of failed relationships— none lasting past the six-month mark— that promise to visit before settling down could have stayed unfulfilled forever if fate hadn't intervened. Last week's layoff notice still branded in his mind. Edward Jones's prestigious letterhead couldn't soften the blow, but the severance check and unused vacation pay had opened an unexpected door.

After five years of college and one soul-crushing year at a desk in Colorado Springs, getting downsized should have felt worse. Instead, standing here at Mt. Moriah's gates, it felt like his grandfather had pulled a few strings from above.

Surreal. Being here at last could only be described as surreal— he was about to enter a place he had only dreamed of since he was ten years old. Finally, he would meet Wild Bill Hickok and Calamity Jane, well, sort of. He had opted for the self-paced walking tour rather than the crowded, squawky tour-guide, quick-and-dirty one-hour bus tour that included the city of Deadwood. This way, he could come when he liked, take his time, look at each headstone, take pictures, walk at his own pace, and simply enjoy his time in the quiet ambiance of a cemetery.

Especially this cemetery. Wild Bill Hickok, Calamity Jane, Potato Creek Johnny, and Seth Bullock were all buried here.

Each step up the incline sent Brian's pulse drumming against his collar. His palm grew damp against the folded map. He'd read their stories a hundred times in those thin dime-store novels that belonged to Grandpa. Each dog-eared page a refuge when his parents' shouts echoed down the hallway. Now, after all these years, he was finally going to meet these childhood heroes. Even if it was just their headstones. They had saved him, one story at a time.

The swelling sound of the violin drew Brian's attention from the map. He looked across the grassy knolls but couldn't see who played the lovely instrument. Returning his eyes to the map, he followed the suggested route and paused before Wild Bill's brass bust and tombstone. Sadness filled his heart. If only Grandpa could be here with him. Physically, for real, not just in his memory.

They gave Grandpa the last room at the end of the hall, next to Brian's. He and Grandpa shared a wall insulated by closets. Momma had cried when she repainted the room a pale robin egg blue, instead of the strawberry pink it had been ever since Brian could remember. A white wicker dresser and a white bent wood rocker had been removed to make way for Grandpa's favorite dark-stained pieces of furniture. Something they said would make him more comfortable.

"Good day, sir." Brian nodded to the brass replica of Bill's face. "I am a big fan. I've read every story written about you."

Among Grandpa's comfortable furniture pieces, there was a desk hutch that held every book imaginable, but the bottom shelf— right at Brian's height— stored those precious dime-store novels. Brian had permission to come in and get one of the small books anytime he felt like it. And he felt like it often when he was ten and eleven. Gone these fifteen years, those two years with Grandpa next door were precious to Brian. The impression Grandpa made on him shaped who he had become.

Imagining Wild Bill humbly waving his comment off, Brian could almost hear Bill say, "Well, thank you, son."

Brian smiled to himself. Bill would have called him son. Understanding this pilgrimage, even if he couldn't fathom the seven-hour drive that had replaced weeks of dusty horseback travel.

Coming here to Deadwood and standing before Wild Bill Hickok's grave made Grandpa seem close. Grandpa had been his refuge. He told fantastic stories, made Brian laugh, and occasionally tossed the baseball while Brian broke in his new mitt. It was good to feel Grandpa's nearness once again. Like he was just a room over, quietly living at the end of the hall.

The muted silence of the cemetery suddenly transformed as the violin's tune grew louder, jerking Brian's attention away from Hickok. Through the trees, something moved atop a massive boulder. As his eyes adjusted, he made out a dark slender silhouette, one arm swaying like a branch in the wind as the bow drew forth notes that floated like mist between the stone markers.

Brian stepped away from the object he had primarily come to see, drawn toward the sound that now intrigued him. The music pulled at him like a siren's song. Would this alluring melody lead him to dash against hidden rocks or simply drown him in its ethereal strains?

Ignoring his map and the planned route to see each historical burial site, he moved toward the figure, his feet carrying him forward as if by their own will.

"Excuse me." Brian spoke softly.

"Oh." The woman whirled around, flinging the bow as if knocked off balance and nearly tossing it in the air. "Oh my! Good day to you, sir. Have I disturbed your solitude?" She stumbled back from the boulder.

"No, not at all." Brian shook his head. "You... you play beautifully."

"You are most kind..." She dipped her eyes coyly. "This dear instrument has been my constant companion since I was but a slip of a girl. Father insisted all proper young ladies should master at least one musical accomplishment." She gestured wildly with the violin and bow. "One does try to maintain one's practice, though finding appreciative listeners can be rather scarce these days." Her eyes remained on him as if to determine his sincerity. "Indeed, you are most welcome to tarry while I practice."

"I-I had to come see who you were. I couldn't imagine who would be out here... at such an early hour... playing a violin."

"Well," she quipped. "I find the morning air most agreeable for practice. The spirits are gentler at this hour, wouldn't you say?"

He too had considered her tune to be for the purpose of soothing restless spirits that might wander aimlessly beyond their graves, but to hear her state her intentions so exactly with his thoughts made his stomach tighten uncomfortably. He bobbed his understanding as if he had not been so viscerally affected. "But... why here?"

She lifted curious emerald eyes and stared at him. Dark brown hair framed her creamy smooth face, bright green eyes that seemed to have a light of their own, and soft, kissable, full lips gave her an impish mischief that made him want to laugh.

Did she not understand his question? "I mean," he chuckled in spite of himself, "Why do you play in the cemetery?"

She shrugged, placed the violin under her chin and dragged the bow across the strings, drawing out two harmonious notes that floated like the focus-music he'd played during late-night study sessions back in college. "Is there a more fitting place for music than among those who can no longer make their own?" she said at last.

Brian jerked his chin in an affirmative nod, accepting her answer. "I'm Brian, by the way."

She grinned. "I am called Echo." She played a quick, lively set of notes... "Echo Hannah Maugham, if you please." She dipped into a small curtsy, violin and bow held gracefully to her sides.

"Brian Everett Rourke, if you please." He mirrored her deep bow.

She laughed. "Nice to make your acquaintance, Brian Rourke... Uh, I assume you do not utilize your middle name?" Her brow lifted high on her forehead. "As I do not."

"You would be correct in your assumption," he answered, delighted with her whimsical personality. "So, do you come here often?" he wagged his eyebrows.

"Everyday." She tilted her head, turned, placed the violin under her chin, and continued to play a slow and melodic tune that Brian recognized from old Victorian movies his mother had watched. It was a waltz. Brian racked his brain to think of the title.

"Roses from the South!" He snapped his fingers.

Echo looked up at him, delighted. "Indeed. How delightful that you know the waltz! So few gentleman callers appreciate such refinements these days."

She tucked the violin under her chin again and continued with the song. She swayed and twirled as if she were dancing the waltz with a partner, rather than the violin. Brian found himself swaying with the tune too. The enthusiasm with which she played the waltz, twirling and swaying as she played, filled his heart with joy. She reached the end and plopped down on the giant boulder, sitting gracefully, but panting and swallowing hard.

Brian clapped his hands. "Bravo!" he shouted. "Bravo!"

Echo glanced toward him, grinning as she fought to regain her breath. "Thank you, kind sir. Thank you. I dare say, you have quite an ear for music." Her breath evened.

The front-gate hinges protested loudly, carrying the teeth-gnashing sound across the cemetery. Echo's smile vanished. "The hour grows late" Her eyes darted to the gate. "I, uh, and I must take my leave." she said quickly.

Brian's heart sank. "If I come tomorrow morning, will you be here... playing?"

She grinned nervously, her eyes darting toward the entrance. "It's a good possibility."

When Brian turned to see who was entering Mt. Moriah and looked back, Echo was already retreating through the headstones. Her dark figure fading into the morning mist like watercolor bleeding into paper.

"Until tomorrow," he called out, but his words fell into empty air.

He watched the spot where she'd disappeared, wondering what lay beyond that hill. More houses? Another part of town? The landscape was still foreign to him. Sighing, he lifted his self-guided tour map. He'd come to meet his childhood heroes but now found himself eager for tomorrow's sunrise for an entirely different reason.

2

Brian rose in the pre-dawn darkness and rushed to breakfast at the restaurant inside the Historic Bullock Hotel. He could not wait to enter Mt. Moriah again and see if Echo Maugham was there playing her violin. Wolfing down the "hearty home crafted breakfast" that should have been savored, he hurried to the parking garage and took off in his Corolla.

By the time he reached Mt. Moriah, the first rays of sunlight were filtering through the trees, and faintly, as if carried by the breeze, he could hear a lively tune that danced and played in the current.

"Echo," he uttered and walked quickly through the creaky old gate. Giving a gentleman's nod to Wild Bill as he walked past the sepulcher, he moved deeper into the cemetery to the large boulder on which the dark figure sat enthusiastically playing the lively tune.

It sounded Gaelic, like the river dance tunes he had heard in the online advertisements for the Denver Performing Arts Center. He could almost hear the accompanying tapping of leather shoes.

"Good morning." Brian said softly.

Echo swirled around, leaping off the boulder as she had done the day before. Her smile seemed radiant, and her emerald eyes twinkled with delight. "Brian Rourke! You've returned to call upon me once more."

"I said I would come back," he replied, slight hurt mingled in his voice.

"Indeed, you did." She seemed to marvel in the truth of his return. "Well, and so, here you are."

"Yep, here I am. And you are here too, playing your violin. Was that an Irish folk dance?"

"You are correct. Do you know about Irish dance songs?"

"Only from what I've seen on the internet," he replied.

Confusion drew her face tight. "The what?"

He paused. Was she appalled he had never attended one single performance of the traveling Celtic dancers? Or any cultural performance at the Performing Arts Center? Ashamed he had let his work dominate his life, he wished to move quickly away from this faux pas.

"Never mind," he said quickly. "Please, continue playing."

Her frown quickly flipped into a smile.

"Did you know," she began as she put the violin under her chin. "That the exact roots of the early Irish dancing are lost in the annals of time?" She touched her bow to the strings and produced the happiest set of notes Brian had ever heard. He felt himself bouncing in place to the rhythm.

Echo moved with preternatural grace, each step a whisper across the grass as she swayed and touched with pointed toes, one foot in front of the other, alternating against the ground as if dancing while playing. And yet she never actually touched her toes to the wet grass. Her movements were so fluid, so ethereal, she seemed to float above the dewy earth rather than walk upon it. Her dark maxi-dress hem swayed against the grass, and yet it never seemed to absorb the moisture from the dew.

What was more interesting was her dress itself. Not that he knew anything about women's clothing. The women he had worked with only wore skirts and pants under suit jackets and elaborate blouses with large billowy bow ties, or turtlenecks, or silk shirts with laced collars and long decorative necklaces that hung down past their bosom.

Echo's dress could even be a costume. It wasn't uncommon for people to dress period appropriate to the eighteen hundreds and walk around Deadwood doing ordinary things... like playing a violin at the cemetery.

His eyes shifted to the ground on which she danced. Unpolished toenails on pink toes peeked out from under the hem as she hopped from one foot to the other. Pink toes... her feet were bare!

Brian halted. "You're barefoot!" he gasped.

"I am." Her eyes dropped to the ground. Sadness seemed to fill the space between them. "My momma insisted they take my shoes."

"Leave your shoes? Where?" Brian furrowed his brow as he waited for Echo to explain.

She hesitated, then lifted her eyes and with a mischievous smile she said, "Did you know... the Celts were sun worshippers. They practiced pagan dance within a circular formation. It was said that a clockwise circle celebrated a happy occasion and a counter-clockwise dance meant mourning." Lifting her violin and bow, she continued to play the peppy tune and hopped to her left and right, touching her toes to the ground in front of her with each movement.

"I did not know that," he replied, almost forgetting the question that lingered between them. How she played and danced at the same time was beyond Brian's comprehension. But he loved the sound and sight of it. He couldn't help but smile and clap his hands to the rhythm.

Watching her tiny bare feet, he tried to imitate her dance moves. Clumsily, he danced, mirroring her movements.

Seeing him try made her face light up with joy and she continued to play and dance.

Breathless, they both plopped down when she played the final note. Laughing and panting, Brian closed his eyes. "This is the most fun I've had in a long time."

"Do tell the truth." She tilted her head. "You don't normally dance Irish jigs where you come from?"

"No." He chuckled. "I do not dance at all. I'm an accountant... er, I was. I'm officially unemployed right now. But I've spent the past six years either in school or at work, and I didn't take the time to go out or dance, or anything fun. My friends always invited me, but for some reason I just never said yes."

"Never said yes?" she looked truly sorrowful. "For heaven's sake, pray tell what would keep you so serious?"

"I honestly don't know." He smiled pitifully. "I plan to change that. I'll get another job, as an accountant, I'm sure, but I will go out with my friends and dance up a storm. Maybe you can come go with me?" he said cautiously.

Would she accept his offer? He hadn't asked anyone out on a date since his senior year of high school. He wasn't even sure if this was how it was done. But he had said it and now it was out there.

Her smile melted into a frown. "Oh, it wouldn't be proper."

Tossing his head back, he laughed nervously. "Why not?" Letting his eyes focus on hers, his heart quickened. "I never expected to meet anybody out here at Mt. Moriah, but here you are."

"Indeed, here I am," she said, but there was a lingering sadness in her voice.

"Well," he continued. "I can't tell you how much I am enjoying hearing you play and talking to you. Would you want to come into town and have lunch with me?"

"Quite so, that would bring me great pleasure..."

His spirits soared.

"But I must decline."

Those same spirits dove and crashed to the ground like a badly constructed kite.

"I see." His eyes darted to her hands as she adjusted her violin, searching for any glint of gold or diamond that might explain her reluctance. Her fingers were bare.

"No, I really don't see," he blurted. "Do you not feel what I feel? An attraction between us?"

"Oh, yes, I feel the attraction." She stood. Placing her violin to her chin, she began to play again, hopping and skipping within an imaginary three-foot wide boxed area, she smiled at him, and he felt his heart lift with gladness again. Perhaps it didn't matter that she would not join him for lunch. Perhaps this serendipitous encounter was just that. A vacation fling that amounted to nothing more than talking and dancing and making a memory he would measure all other encounters against for the rest of his life.

"Well, then," —he leaned closer to her— "Could I leave you with a kiss?"

Her smile quivered on her lips. "That would be delightful..." She coyly dipped her head. "But we had better not." Her eyes flitted to the entry where the sound of the gate creaked open, exactly as it had the day before, indicating others would soon be walking through the cemetery. The private moment gone.

Brian turned to see who had ruined this special moment. When he turned back, she stood, precariously balanced on top of the boulder. Her arms stretched out wide, with the violin in one hand and the bow in the other. She seemed to be reaching to absorb as much of the sunlight that filtered through the trees as she could. He smiled up at her.

"Be careful." He reached to steady her, but she gracefully twirled just out of his reach and landed on the grass behind the boulder. She laughed and he found himself laughing too.

Yet something niggled at the back of his mind as he watched her, making his heart sink. He took one step back, pursing his lips. He'd wanted to pull her into his arms for a farewell embrace, perhaps even a kiss, but the moment had slipped away like she had. They both knew he had to leave.

If only she would reveal what kept her from spending more time with him. Was it some big secret? Was she married, engaged, going steady? If she needed to leave, why couldn't he take her to lunch?

"Will you be here tomorrow?" he asked.

"It's a good possibility," she said playfully, exactly as she had done the day before.

He smiled. "Okay, then. I'll see you tomorrow."

Her brow scrunched into three lines above her petite nose. "Time will tell," she said teasingly.

What did she mean by that? Hadn't he already proved that if he said he would return, he would definitely return? He laughed, just to gauge if she was kidding.

A giggle escaped her lips, and she turned, tucking her violin under her chin and dragging the bow across the strings as she walked and played a tune quite the opposite of the happy Irish jig from before. Was it a reflection of her sadness for having to leave?

Sadness replaced the giddy feeling Brian had felt coming here today as he watched her walk into the mist that seemed to reach for her like eager fingers. The further she went, the thicker it grew, until he couldn't tell where the mist ended and Echo began. Her music lingered in the air long after the mist had swallowed any trace of her presence.

She was gone.

He turned and slowly left the cemetery. Thoughts of Echo skipping across his heart much like the Irish jig they had danced to.

3

"I'd like to change my reservation." Brian stood at the front desk of his hotel, hoping he could extend his stay. He simply was not ready to leave. While he had fulfilled the obligation to his ten-year-old self and his grandpa by visiting Wild Bill and the others in Mt. Moriah, he wanted more time with the mysterious violinist he had met out there.

"We have already booked your room, sir." The young lady tapped furiously on the keyboard. Did it truly require the cacophony of keystrokes to verify his room was already obligated.

"Could I move to another room?" he asked, hopeful.

"Let... me... see..." She squinted at the computer screen as if that would help her to find an available room. "Looks... like... all... we... have..." —she lifted her eyes to meet his, but sadness filled them— "is a basic room. It's one double bed, no refrigerator, and a standing shower."

Brian bit back a comment that there was no such thing as a sitting shower. He didn't take baths, so a "standing" shower was fine.

"I'll take it," he said quickly, before she determined it was reserved for someone else.

"But parking isn't included like the room you were in. You'll have to pay for parking."

"I don't care, I'll take it." He shoved his credit card toward her.

"Okay..." Her eyebrows stretched high on her forehead. He

wondered if the little silver-colored ring piercing her brow gave her any pain when she did that. "But please do me a favor," her eyes pleaded. "Don't complain to management if the paranormal activity keeps you up all night."

"The what?" Brian flipped his card back toward his palm.

The gal shrugged. "That room has been particularly 'active' lately." She made air quotes.

Brian considered his options. Did he believe in ghosts? Really?

"I-I don't care." He shoved the credit card back toward her.

"Okay..." She said in a sing-song, mocking sort of tone. Tapping her keyboard in an endless succession of keystrokes, she finally lifted her eyes. "You're all set. You'll need to move out of your current room and into this one no later than eleven o'clock."

"Is the room ready now?" he asked.

She looked back at the screen, as if she needed to verify. "Oh, yes, it's available now."

What did that mean? Did they normally not put a guest in that particular room unless they were full and had no other choice? A tense sensation hummed in his gut. Would paranormal activity keep him from sleeping tonight? Or was it a matter of self-fulfilled prophesy that people witnessed this so-called paranormal activity. As an accountant, he had a tendency to view events as black and white, facts over fiction. Surely, with the right attitude, he would have a restful sleep, just like he did in the room he would soon vacate.

He'd worry about any paranormal activity if it happened. Right now, his mind was too preoccupied with a far more enchanting mystery— one that played waltzes and Irish jigs in a cemetery.

Rushing back to his room, he tossed his razor and comb back into the leather shaving kit, closed his suitcase, and tossed a five dollar bill on the loosely made bed for the cleaning people, and moved to the basic room one floor up. It was a lot smaller, but he really didn't care. A bed, a bathroom, a shower. That was all he needed.

Plopping the suitcase on the scissor-legged stand next to the three-drawer dresser he would never use, he turned to leave. A growl in his mid-section reminded him he needed to eat first.

The hotel's restaurant stopped him in his tracks this morning. Yesterday he'd rushed through, focused only on getting to Wild Bill's grave. Now, he actually saw the place. A massive fireplace dominated one wall, its 1895 potter's tiles gleaming in the morning light. Carved woodwork framed emerald green walls adorned with period artwork. History breathed in every corner.

But even surrounded by such carefully preserved beauty, his thoughts kept drifting to Echo. He followed the hostess to a seat, barely glancing at the menu she handed him. The sooner he ate, the sooner he could return to the cemetery. Would Echo be there a third time?

She had said she played of a morning while the earth was still and quiet. But did that mean she played her violin at the cemetery exclusively, every single day? She had been so secretive about where she went when she left, why wouldn't she be open about whether she would be there every single morning?

Not looking at the menu, figuring on telling his server he'd take whatever the restaurant was known for, he lifted his cell phone and slid his thumb across the screen. Opening Google, his thumb hovered over the search bar.

"Echo Hannah Maugham," he typed, each letter another promise of answers. The results loaded. He leaned closer to the screen, scanning entry after entry. Sponsored ads. Wikipedia unreliability. Historical records. Museum archives. Tourist information about old Deadwood. But nothing—not one single hit—showed an Echo Maugham in the present day.

That couldn't be right. He tried again, adding "Deadwood" to the search. Same results. A third try with "violin" added yielded nothing new. It was as if she didn't exist in the modern world at all.

A server stepped up next to him. "Would you like some coffee?"

"Yes, please." Brian lifted his gaze to the young redhead who looked to be of college age, or she just simply worked here for a living. Her name tag read, "Amanda." Why was he so curious about her schooling? "And just bring me whatever is the special." His eyes shifted back to his phone screen.

She paused. "I, uh, we don't have a special, actually."

"Oh." He lifted his eyes again to meet her worried expression. "What do you recommend, then?"

Now she really looked worried. "I, uh, I don't know. People order all kinds of stuff, it's all really good."

Brian smiled. "How about bacon, two eggs, over easy, hash browns, and sourdough toast."

She looked relieved.

"Of course," she blurted and entered his order on a device that looked a lot like the calculator he had used back in high school.

Brian returned his attention to his phone. Scrolling past the results— endlessly scrolling past the sponsored ads, Wikipedia entries, historical archives, again. There was nothing recent. No social media profiles, no current mentions. He shook his head. Nothing but historical links. That was odd. Her name, so unique, how could there be nothing about her online?

His food arrived. Shocked at how quickly his breakfast had been cooked, he stammered, "Uh, thank you."

"Of course," she responded. "Can I get you anything else?"

Suppressing the irritation her response caused in his chest, he replied. "No, thank you."

His fork scraped against the plate in rapid succession, each bite hardly chewed before the next. The other diners' leisurely conversations faded to background noise as he focused on getting back to Mt. Moriah as quickly as possible.

In the parking garage he remembered he no longer had the better room that allowed him free parking. Exiting through the automatic arm that sensed his vehicle and lifted to let him out, he turned right to head straight to Mt. Moriah Cemetery. When he came back, he'd have to enter a credit card to get back in.

His stomach clenched and churned, the heavy breakfast sitting like a stone. He pressed a hand against his abdomen, wishing he'd chosen something lighter than eggs and bacon. Maybe he should stop at a convenience store to buy some bottled water.

Back on the road, he soon pulled into the parking lot next to the cemetery. Carrying two bottles, since he anticipated seeing Echo, he couldn't show up without enough for both of them. He entered the creaky gate. A waltz floated on the breeze, quickening his heart and broadening his smile.

She was here.

4

As he entered the cemetery, the early morning silence was broken only by Echo's waltz and the distant rumble of a bus engine warming up somewhere in town. He checked his watch— still too early for tourists. The cemetery would be theirs alone, at least for a while.

Walking directly to the boulder where he always found Echo, he saw her sway in a three-step pattern— one, two, three; one, two, three. Twirling as she drew her bow with a long note as if she had been turned under the guidance of a partner— she stumbled back, startled, realizing he was there. "Oh! Brian Rourke! You have returned once again."

"Yes," he said, curious when she would understand that if he said he'd be back, he would indeed be back. "I extended my stay at the hotel. I wanted more time... to get to know you."

"You hadn't planned on being here this long?" she asked.

"No. I figured two days were enough to do what I came here to do... but then I met you."

As if considering what he had said, she nodded slowly, but her face had confusion written all over it.

Then she smiled. "Did you know..."

She put the violin to her chin and positioned the bow to begin playing, yet she did not start. Lowering the instrument, she said, "A lot of people came here in 1874 because of the great gold rush?

Everybody dreamed of striking it rich in the gold mines. Deadwood was hidden, you see, because it was in such a deep gulch, and terribly treacherous to get into. They literally had to lower wagons and horses by rope to get down here. It was terrifying!" she lowered the violin to her side and stared at him as if she measured his response.

"My family came with hopes of entertaining those miners, even though the very nature of this hidden gem of a town attracted outlaws, gamblers, and gunslingers too. My family figured even outlaws had money to spend, and money was money no matter where or who it came from. So long as they spent it on a troop of performers, we were alright with it. See, we sought our riches in other ways."

Brian's brow wrinkled. What brought that to her mind? For lack of knowing what else to say, he blurted, "Yeah, it's a smooth highway to get here nowadays."

She tilted her head, her smile wavering. Then she continued the waltz she had stopped playing when she spotted him. It was lovely, three notes, a slight pause, three more, a pause, then a long note in which she swayed, setting her feet into motion to twirl in a full three-sixty circle. It reminded him of the cotillions his mother spoke of back in Florida when she was a young debutante.

He stood still on the higher ground behind the boulder, listening and watching her, framed by the trees. When she finished the waltz, she bowed deeply as if she were on a stage, and he were her only audience. He clapped enthusiastically. "That was beautiful."

"Thank you," she said softly. Echo cocked her head toward the town below. "More visitors will be coming soon." She smiled wistfully. "The living are so curious about the dead, aren't they?"

Brian stared at her. What an odd comment.

"Did you know," Echo continued. "As famous as Wild Bill Hickok is, he wasn't actually here very long... before he was shot? Folks called the hand he had, those aces and eights, the Dead Man's Hand afterward. Just makes me shiver to think about how gruesome it was to be killed over a card game." She physically quivered, wrapping her arms around herself with the violin and bow in opposite hands. "What if we had been performing in that saloon when he—" She shivered.

"Things were different then," she continued, her eyes darting occasionally toward the road below. "Much quieter, except for the occasional shout when someone did strike gold. Not like now, with the regular parade of tour buses and cameras."

Sadness filled her eyes. "Things smelled different, too, back then." She closed her eyes as if she were reminiscing. "You could smell coal burning in the chimneys, fresh baked bread along main street where the German bakery stood." Her eyes flew open. "It burned down, you know, in '79." Shaking her head, mournfully. "Such a sad thing to happen to such good people."

She lifted her bow again, but her movements seemed more hurried. "We should make the most of our time. They'll be here soon."

"Hey." Brian blurted, hoping to lighten her mood. "I'm not much for selfies, but..." He lifted his phone. "Come stand by me. I want to take a picture of us."

Her eyes dropped to his phone, her brow slammed together hard. She didn't move from her spot.

"The City Commissioner had a violin competition about that time." She spoke with a tone of distraction. "He wanted to encourage a more sophisticated migration into Deadwood. It was held at the old opera house. I wore a lovely emerald green performance gown." Her eyes grew distant as she described the gown.

Brian staggered back a step. The maxi-dress she wore, he had remembered it being black, but now he realized with the morning sunlight burning off the opaque mist, it was a dark emerald green. Just as she had described. This was no costume. This was her performance gown.

His jaw went slack, parting his lips. "Echo?" he stammered.

She lifted her eyes to meet his gaze. Sadness filled them, making the shining emerald orbs fade to a dull washed-out green. She sighed. "Yes?"

He couldn't utter the question burning in his heart. Instead, he walked around the boulder, easing down the incline to the grassy area where she stood. Turning back toward the boulder where she often sat and played her violin, he realized there was a marble headstone at the base of the boulder.

Here Lies
Echo Hannah Maugham

Accomplished Violinist,
Beloved Daughter,
Adoring Wife and Mother
Died 1882

Brian swallowed the sudden rush of bile at the back of his throat. Really regretting the greasy breakfast he'd eaten too fast. "Is... this you?"

He turned to look at her.

She nodded sadly. "You knew, didn't you?" she asked before he could speak.

He only stared at her. Unable to shake his head or nod to give her any kind of response. He hadn't known. Not until a second or two ago.

"I thought perhaps..." she continued. "Well, it's been wonderful having someone to play for again," she said.

The gate creaked. Her eyes darted toward the sound. "The tour bus is coming. It must be Thursday."

Movement caught his eye— a flash of red and yellow through the trees as the converted school bus wound its way up the hill. Echo began playing again, this time more urgent, as if racing against time.

He had avoided the tour bus in town. Now it encroached on their time together. People stepped down the three rubber-matted steps and meandered about on the blacktop as the group reassembled, waiting for their tour guide.

"You should go," Echo offered.

Brian turned back toward her. "Why?"

"The tour guide." Echo smiled. "She's my great-great granddaughter."

"Your what?" Brian turned back to the people strolling through the gate, chattering and laughing.

"She plays too, you know," Echo breathed. "Not violin, but piano. She's lonely, like you. Like I was." Her voice faded.

Turning quickly to look at Echo again, Brian gasped.

She was gone.

Far away, somewhere beyond the trees, he could hear the violin's voice swelling with longing and yet fading into the mist. The waltz began softly, almost hesitantly, before gaining confidence with each measure. One, two, three; one, two, three— the rhythm carried like a whispered promise. The higher notes shimmering like a crystal chandelier above deeper tones that anchored the dance. The melody twirled and dipped, now rising in joyful turns, now falling into bittersweet passages that tugged at the heart. His heart.

"Go to her. She is who you came here to meet." Echo's voice whispered in his ear, carrying the same musical lilt as her violin.

The tour group filtered through the gates, their voices breaking the cemetery's spell. At their head walked a young woman in a park service uniform, her honey-brown hair caught in the same kind of loose braid Echo had worn. Brian's breath caught. Even from this distance, something in her stance, the way she gestured as she spoke, echoed the woman who'd just vanished.

The violin's final notes still seemed to hover in the air, and for a moment, Brian could have sworn they harmonized with the tour guide's voice. She had Echo's cadence, that same way of letting certain words dance off her tongue as she described the cemetery's history.

He found himself drifting closer, drawn by a familiarity he couldn't explain. What would he even say to her? "Your great-great grandmother's ghost just played me a waltz and suggested we meet," hardly seemed like a winning opening line.

But as he watched her interact with her group, saw the same sparkle in those emerald eyes when she spoke of Deadwood's past, he understood what Echo had meant. This wasn't just about history anymore. This was about futures, too.

His mind was still reeling from the realization that he had been visiting all this time with a ghost and not a live person, he stepped in with the people following their tour guide, walking with them through the cemetery. When the tour guide stopped to speak directly to her group, Brian smiled.

Her mannerisms and gestures, so identical to the woman he had felt... he had thought... he was falling in love with.

When the tour ended and she gathered her people back to the bus, Brian approached her. "Excuse me," he said casually. "I realize you're working right now, but could I meet you somewhere in town after you're done? I have something interesting to tell you about this headstone right here."

He pointed at Echo's headstone.

Her eyes widened. "That's my great-great grandmother," she stammered.

"Yeah." He nodded. "Can we meet later?"

"Uh, sure." She seemed extremely hesitant. And he couldn't blame her. What sensible girl would agree to meet a stranger after work?

"Nowhere isolated, I assure you. We can meet somewhere very public. I just want to tell you about something I learned today."

"Right... okay." She glanced at her people milling toward the bus. "Yeah, I get off at three, but I'm gonna ask a friend to come too, alright?"

"Of course." Brian bobbed his head. "I completely understand. Where do you want to meet?"

"Uh, how about Mustang Sally's? We gather there after our shifts to eat."

"Perfect. I'll be there at three." Brian pursed his lips into what he hoped looked like a non-stalker smile. "My name's Brian Rourke, by the way."

"Mary." She said but hesitated as if she were uncertain she should reveal her name. "Mary Echo Stephens." She giggled and rolled her eyes. "I have no idea why I told you my entire name. But I was named after her." Mary pointed at the headstone.

Brian put out his hand to shake hers. She stared at his proffered hand, then slowly put her palm against his. It felt warm and real. "That's okay. I think I know. We'll talk about it at Mustang Sally's, my treat, by the way."

"What?"

"I just mean, I'm buying. Whatever you want at Mustang Sally's, I'm buying. It's the least I can do for you letting me tell you my story."

She nodded slowly, her eyes very cautious. "You a writer?" Regret seeping into her gaze.

He shook his head.

She sighed. "Okay. See you later, then."

"See you later." Brian stepped back and watched her join her tourists. He turned back to the boulder. The space around it was empty. With a two-finger salute, he turned and walked to his Corolla.

Three o'clock couldn't get here soon enough.

5

Mary and another girl, the one that had waited on him just this morning at Bully's dining room, approached the table where Brian sat. He had intentionally asked the Mustang Sally's hostess to let him sit at one of the outdoor tables where he figured Mary would be the least uncomfortable meeting him even though the sun bore down on them at a balmy ninety-eight degrees.

He grinned when he saw them. Mary, so familiar with her dark brown hair contrasting her creamy smooth face, so pretty. Her bright green eyes, identical to her ancestor's and soft full lips that gave off an impish mischief. She and Echo looked the same, and yet, he knew they were not. And Amanda, his breakfast server.

He stood as they approached.

Their giggles faded quickly. Mary cleared her throat. "Hi."

Brian swallowed. "Hi." His eyes shifted to Amanda. "Hi, again. Please, have a seat." He gestured to the empty chairs.

Mary sat across from him and her friend, by default, sat in the chair adjacent to his. Neither one of them looked comfortable being here.

"I know this is weird." Brian began, "and it may not get any better after I tell you what I have to say, but—"

A server approached them. "Hey, Mary" the server said. Turning to the other girl, he continued, "Amanda."

"Hi, Angelo."

"Y'all want your usual?" Angelo asked.

"Um," Mary's eyes flitted to Brian's. "Sure." She leaned into him and whispered, as if Angelo couldn't hear what she said. "We always get the chili cheese fries and split it." She shrugged. "It fills our bellies and doesn't cost too much."

"So," Angelo said. "That what you want?"

"Yes." Mary smiled at the server whom she obviously knew well.

"I'll have the same." Brian said. "And three sodas."

Mary's eyes widened. "We usually just get water, but sure, I'll take a Dr. Pepper." Had she remembered that he said he was paying?

"Same for me." Amanda said.

"Three Dr. Peppers." Brian confirmed.

Angelo smiled. "Of course." He returned to the interior of the restaurant.

Brian settled his eyes on Mary. "Forgive me," he said. "You look so remarkably like—" realizing he couldn't just blurt it out that he knew her great-great grandmother, he pursed his lips. "I mean..."

The wariness in Mary's expression melted away, replaced by a familiar sparkle— the same one he'd seen in Echo's eyes when she played.

She glanced at her friend, a silent conversation passing between them. Then, her gaze shifted to his.

"The cemetery's different in the mornings, isn't it?" Mary finally said, her voice careful, measured. "Especially near the old boulder."

Brian's pulse quickened. "How did you—"

"Some say they hear music up there." She leaned forward, dropping her voice. "Sweet and clear, like crystal. Always the same songs. Always at dawn."

"Mary..." Amanda touched her friend's arm in warning.

"No, it's okay." Mary's eyes never left Brian's face. "He knows, doesn't he? You've heard it too, haven't you? The violin?"

Brian's mouth went dry. The way she watched him now reminded him so much of Echo it made his chest ache. "I... might have."

"Just heard it?" Her gaze intensified. "Or did you see something more?"

The air between them seemed to crackle with possibility. Brian wrestled with how to respond, knowing his next words could either open a door or slam it shut forever.

Mary drew a shaky breath. "Did you... see her?"

There it was. The real question hanging between them like mist in the morning air. Brian's heart stopped for two beats.

"Who?" he managed, though they both knew.

Mary's fingers trembled slightly as she traced the edge of the menu she no longer needed. "Echo," she whispered. "My great-great grandmother."

He couldn't utter a word. She knew about Echo and her violin? Slowly, he nodded.

"Wow." Amanda breathed.

Now that the cat was out of the bag, Brian breathed a sigh of relief. "I came here on Monday," he began. "To see my childhood heroes at Mt. Moriah. But..."

"You heard her playing the violin," Mary said.

"Yes, I did."

"We've all heard it." Amanda said quickly. "You can't live here in Deadwood and not know about Echo and her violin music."

"I'm so glad to hear you know about her. I had no idea how to convince you that I saw her... talked to her, she's amazing, really."

"Wait!" Mary said abruptly. "You... talked to Echo?"

Brian hesitated. "Yeah."

"And..." Mary continued. "She talked back?"

"Yeah. I honestly didn't realize she was... wasn't... I had no idea... I thought she was just somebody playing a violin in the cemetery—"

"Wow." Amanda stated, her vocabulary reduced to the one word in her stupor. The girls exchanged a look. "I mean, wow. Nobody's actually talked to her. A few have seen her. We've all heard the violin."

"Yeah, there was a group of seniors who went up there after prom." Mary added. "They claimed they saw her, and she was barefoot."

Brian nodded. "She is barefoot. She said her momma made her leave her shoes. I don't know what that meant."

Mary's smile pressed into a frown. "As I understand it, my great-great grandmother's family was so poor that when someone died they removed the person's shoes before they buried them so someone else could have them. Waste-not-want-not, sort of a thing, I suppose."

Letting this information sink in, Brian murmured, "Well, she certainly knows you," he started slowly. "She was excited that it was Thursday and your tour bus would be arriving. She told me then who you are to her and that I should meet you... before I go back home."

"Where are you from?" Mary asked.

Amanda gently poked an index finger into Brian's arm. He jerked, turning to look at her. She shrugged as if to apologize and giggled. "Just checking to see if you were real."

Mary giggled. "Amanda!"

"Well?"

"It's alright," Brian chuckled. "I don't blame you really. I'm from Colorado Springs, Colorado. I had intended on making this a two-day vacation, but then I saw and heard Echo Hannah Maugham playing her violin. I decided I needed to stay longer... to get to know her."

The girls tucked their fists under their chins and stared at him, enthralled with his tale.

"That's amazing," Mary cooed.

"Here we go." Angelo said, breaking the spell everyone had fallen under.

Over his shoulder he balanced a large round tray with two massive plates of cheese-smothered chili fries and Dr. Peppers, the restaurant's logo faded on the blue plastic cups. He set a large plate of cheese-smothered, chili-covered french fries between the girls and another in front of Brian.

He could see why they shared the dish, it was huge. Angelo pulled three paper covered straws from his pocketed apron and laid them in the very middle of everything. "Will there be anything else?"

"Angelo!" Mary squealed. "This is Brian Rourke, he's seen my great-great grandmother out at Mt. Moriah!"

"For reals?" Angelo's mouth hung open.

Amanda took a chili fry and gingerly plopped it in her mouth. "For reals!" she said around the scorchingly hot food.

Angelo glared at Brian with a new admiration before he zipped off to answer a call across the patio.

Mary's worried eyes shone with joy now. She folded her arms in front of her, leaning her elbows on the table, and pulled a french fry out from under the sloppy chili and cheese. Blowing on the hot mess, she gingerly placed it between her teeth. "What did she say?"

Brian gulped. Should he tell her that Echo had said Mary

was the one he had come here to Deadwood to meet? Just because she believed him about seeing and speaking to Echo, didn't mean she would understand such a prophetic statement from her ancient ancestor. "We talked about a lot of things, actually."

Mary's eyes widened. "You really liked her, didn't you?"

Brian paused. "Well, yeah. She's a really awesome person."

"Was she?" Mary's enthusiasm faded into a sad, regretful tone. "Gosh, I wish I could talk to her."

"They appear to those that are meant to see them." Amanda stated wisely.

Mary nodded. "I know, but she's *my* great-great grandmother. Why wouldn't she want to show herself to me?"

Her eyes shifted to Brian's in a pleading way that made him feel obligated to give her some sort of explanation. "Maybe, since you are related, she doesn't need to appear to you. Perhaps, you feel her in your heart."

"Awww." Amanda mused.

Brian gazed at Amanda, had he taken it too far? Revealed too much of his own feelings? "Mary, may I tell you that you look just like her?" he said, testing the waters.

"Really?" Mary softened.

Brian nodded. "Sound just like her, too."

Mary gaped at him. "For reals?"

"Yep." Brian answered, finally taking a bite of his cheesy chili fries. Oh, they were still very hot. He swigged some Dr. Pepper to cool the burning spot on the roof of his mouth.

The girls giggled. He chuckled with them. "This is good, but dang, it's really hot."

They nodded in agreement and set to eat more of their food.

"What was she wearing?" Mary asked after a while.

"A lovely emerald green dress, apparently it was what she wore—"

"At the violin competition." Mary finished his statement.

"Yes." Brian marveled that she knew.

"She won that competition, you know?"

"No, I didn't know that," he said. "She didn't mention it."

"She's modest." Mary turned to Amanda, expressing the realization about her ancestor's personality.

"What else did she say... about me?" Mary asked, absently stirring her Dr. Pepper with her straw.

Brian watched the ice cubes dance in her glass, buying time. Echo's words reverberated in his mind— 'She is who you came here to meet.' But how could he explain that without sounding crazy? "She said..." He paused, choosing his words carefully. "She seemed to think our paths crossing wasn't an accident."

Mary's eyes widened slightly. "What do you mean?"

"Well..." Brian shifted in his seat, suddenly aware of both girls watching him intently. "You know how some people say everything happens for a reason? I was only supposed to be here for three days, visiting the cemetery. But then I heard the violin, met Echo, and..." He met Mary's gaze. "Now I'm wondering if maybe there was more bringing me to Deadwood than just visiting Wild Bill's grave."

Amanda glanced between them, a small smile playing at her lips. "You know, Mary's always giving tours about Deadwood's history, but she rarely gets to hear stories about her own family."

"Really?" Brian turned to Mary. "There must be so much more you'd like to know about Echo."

Mary nodded eagerly. "Oh, absolutely! The family stories only go so far, and the historical records..." She trailed off, shrugging.

"I'd love to tell you everything she shared with me," Brian said. "Maybe... over dinner?"

The words hung in the air for a moment. Mary's cheeks flushed slightly, but her eyes sparkled— just like Echo's had when she played the Irish jig.

Amanda cleared her throat. "You should take him to Diamond Lil's, Mary. They do those historical tours between courses."

"That's if... if you'd like to," Brian added quickly. "No pressure. I just thought—"

"I'd love to," Mary interrupted, then caught herself, blushing deeper. "I mean... yes, that would be nice. Diamond Lil's is perfect, actually. It's where they used to hold the town's social gatherings back in Echo's time."

"Really?" Brian smiled, feeling his nervousness fade. "Sounds like exactly the right place, then."

"For reals?" Mary squealed. "Wow." Her gaze swiveled to Amanda. They smiled at each other.

"Well," Mary turned back to Brian and extended her hand. He

took her hand into his and they shook as if meeting for the first time. "Hello. I'm Mary Echo Stevens."

"I'm Brian Rourke. May I take you out for dinner this evening?"

"That would be lovely." Mary smiled sweetly.

"May I ask you one more thing?" Brian asked.

"Of course."

"How old are you?"

Mary laughed. "I'm older than I look."

"Which means what?" Brian pressed.

"I'm twenty years old. The same age Echo was when she died of scarlet fever." Mary pursed her lips.

"So, are you in college? Doing this tour guide gig in the summers?" Bryan ventured.

"Yes." Mary said. "I'm majoring in Accounting, and I take the summers off to work so I can earn my tuition for the next year. That's why it's taking me longer than some." She turned glaring eyes toward Amanda. "I don't take summer classes."

Amanda just shrugged. "Well, not everybody had parents to foot their entire college bill. I only work so I've got something to do while you're working your butt off."

Brian listened to the two bicker back and forth. Realizing he still wore a silly smile. "Amanda, would you like to join us for dinner? Is there someone you'd like to invite?"

"There is." Amanda looked surprised Brian had asked. Swiveling to Mary, "Would you mind if Brendon and I join you two? Make it a double date?"

"Not at all." Mary said quickly. Turning to verify that Brian didn't mind either, she turned back to her friend. "The more the merrier."

Brian smiled too. He had not given his hotel an exact date when he would be leaving, and since there was no job he needed to hurry back to, he was free to stay here in Deadwood as long as he wanted, within reason, of course. "Great. It's a double date. One more question." He grinned, remembering his promise to Echo.

The girls glanced at each other.

"What?" they both said.

Brian laughed. "Do they have a dance floor? Uh, at Diamond Lil's?" he added. "And may I pick you up?"

"They do and sure." Mary grabbed a napkin and wrote on it,

sliding it over to Brian. "Here's my parents' address." Turning to Amanda, "You and Brendon will meet us there?" she told her friend, more than asked although her tone was in the form of a question.

Amanda nodded. "Yes. I'll text Brendon now." She lifted her phone and began thumbing the keys.

Angelo returned at their side. "Any dessert?"

"No." Mary said, as if out of habit more than what she might actually want.

"If you want a dessert—" Brian started.

"No, no. I need to save my girlish figure," she laughed.

Brian laughed with her. "Don't we all."

"Say," Mary looked at him through veiled eyelashes. "How old are *you*, anyway?"

Brian chuckled. "I'm twenty-six."

"Oh good. We're not that far apart." She grinned mischievously like Echo, then hesitated. "Though Daddy's pretty protective. He might have concerns about the six years."

Brian's stomach knotted. He hadn't considered needing her father's approval. How could something that felt so destined be derailed by parental caution? But then he remembered his grandfather's lessons about treating every woman like a precious gem, about what it meant to be a true gentleman.

He straightened his shoulders. "I'm happy to meet with your father before dinner," he said. "If he'd like."

Mary's eyes lit up. "Really? Most guys wouldn't offer such a thing."

"My grandpa taught me better than that."

"You are amazing, Brian Rourke."

"No, not really. I'm just a boy falling for a girl he never knew could exist until a ghost pointed her out."

Mary's grin faltered. "Yeah, can't get much stranger than that." She swallowed. "Let's leave that part out when you meet my dad."

Brian agreed.

Later, as twilight settled over Deadwood, a familiar Irish jig floated down from Mt. Moriah. Brian paused, catching his reflection in a storefront window. The melody shifted into Echo's waltz, and for a moment, those emerald eyes seemed to twinkle at him from the glass.

"Thank you," he whispered.

The music faded, but its echo remained, leading him forward. He'd come seeking childhood heroes and found something far more precious— a future wrapped in the threads of the past. In a few hours, he'd see those same enchanting green eyes again, this time looking toward tomorrow instead of yesterday.

Somehow, he suspected his grandpa had known all along he would find echoes of love at Mt. Moriah.

The End

PERSONAL NOTE FROM THE AUTHOR

Readers,

If you would like to be part of the development of my stories and are not a member of my reader's group on Facebook, Books by Author Lynn Donovan, join today. Click here.

Stay in the know, by joining my Facebook group or join my newsletter subscription https://lynndonovanauthor.com/newsletter for updates and news.

AFTERWORD

Newsletter and a Free Gift for You

Hey! Thank you for purchasing and reading this book. I'd like to give you a parting gift to show my appreciation. Sign up for my newsletter here. I will send you an e-copy of a collection of

short stories I wrote purely for your entertainment. I will happily send you this e-copy for FREE, if you ask. I will also add you to my NEWSLETTER list and you will receive up-to-date information on new release before anyone else.

This book will **not** be sold anywhere, at any time, I am keeping it exclusively for you, my readers, and only if you ask for it.

Thank you again, and God Bless.

~Lynn Donovan

ABOUT THE AUTHOR

Lynn Donovan is an author, playwright, and director who spends her days chasing after her muses trying to get them to behave long enough to write their stories. The results are numerous novels, multi-author series, anthologies, dramatizations, and short stories.

Lynn enjoys reading and writing all kinds of fiction, paranormal, speculative, contemporary romance, and time travel. But you never know what her muses will come up with for a story, so you could see a novel under any given genre. All that can be said is keep your eyes open, because these muses are not sitting still for long!

Oops, there they go again...

Want More?

You can learn more about Lynn on her blog and her website LynnDonovanAuthor.com.

DEADWOOD'S DEADLY PUZZLE

LOUISE FOSTER

BLURB

Who complains about having too much money?

Answer? My latest client.

I'm Tracy Belden, being a PI is one of my three jobs. My new client recently acquired a company which is showing an unexpected spike in profits. Worried about illegal activity, she's demanding answers.

So, me, my precocious, crime solving twelve-year-old son, and my family are headed to Deadwood, South Dakota. However, the possibility of fraud turns to tragedy when I find one of the former partners poisoned.

Was his death suicide or murder? Either way, to complete my puzzle, I have to find the secret his death was meant to hide.

1

14 Across; 8 Letters;
Clue: Antagonistic manner.
Answer: Attitude.

"I don't like you." Pam Isley, co-owner of a major corporation in Nevada, didn't bother to disguise her disdain.

If I were kind, I might put her rude comment down to the fact that she was fighting a takeover bid by her disinherited deadbeat sister. However, that wasn't the cause of her imperious attitude. She'd been born that way.

What amazed me was that Pam or anyone else believed that I, Tracy Rae Belden, P.I., cared what they thought of me. Outside of my family or friends, the world could go whistle in the wind and I wouldn't lose a minute of sleep.

"Yeah, that's great. I'm crushed." I managed to swallow the long-suffering sigh that rose up. No way could I keep the boredom out of my voice.

What did she expect me to say? "I don't like you either", came to mind. However, as of this morning, she was a paying client of Crawford Investigations, owned by my boss Crawford.

Thankfully, Pam's company was headquartered in Lake Tahoe. I lived in Langsdale, Nevada, a three-hour drive north of Vegas.

"What you did to the Prushark family was unforgiveable." The woman continued in a strident tone. "Your investigation crushed them. I grew up with their children."

"Hey! Don't kill the messenger." The words broke through what little restraint I had. "I didn't kill old man Prushark. All I did was prove who murdered him."

I was losing patience with her attitude. I'd been in a good mood before this phone call. Glancing at the crossword puzzle I'd been working on creating, I pushed away the laptop. That would also prevent me from being distracted by looking at the spreadsheet of B&T, Inc.

My ten-year bestie, Kevin Tanner and I had joined forces in the handyman company a few months ago. Only weeks ago, we'd joined in marriage.

Determined to focus on my P.I. job, I told myself to act like an adult. In an effort to recoup the situation, I stifled another sigh and decided to focus on the case. "Let's move past the pleasantries. What's the case? Crawford didn't provide me with any details."

Actually, the froggy voiced rat had told me next to nothing.

"Pam Isley has a job." He'd growled when he called. "She paid up front and insisted on you. She'll call you. Keep quiet and get results."

What was I supposed to do with that lead in? Play nice with a woman who disliked me?

"I asked for you because you come up with results." Pam spoke in a tight, autocratic tone. "How you manage to succeed, I'll never know. However, I have little to lose by throwing you at the problem."

"Isn't that sweet?" My impatient hindbrain took control when I wasn't looking. Was it good or bad that the words dripped with a syrupy, patently fake tone? "What is the high stakes issue I'm going to spend my time on?"

Stony silence met my comeback. Her long, drawn-out exhale signaled her rising temper. "You are *so* annoying."

"It's what I do." I shot back. "Go with my strength."

"One of the companies I recently acquired is having issues." Pam's voice reverted to a professional tone.

My brain clicked over to business as well. We'd both be better off sticking to the facts. "What kind of issues? Personal? Financial?"

"Both." Came the terse reply.

That was going to be my third guess. "How long have you owned the company?"

"Almost three months." She answered immediately. "The ninety-day probationary period is coming up next week. Our people audited the books before and after the sale. Everything balances, but the numbers aren't what they should be based on the market and the supplies. The area doesn't... shouldn't have the base to justify the recent sales."

Her words brought me up short. "Wait a minute. Your new business is bringing in too *much* money?"

My brain grabbed hold of the dichotomy with both hands. I had to give the other woman points for originality. Very few clients complain of an excess of profits. However, while touchy, feely emotions aren't my strength, numbers are, and in any equation both sides have to balance.

"I realize this isn't a common problem." Pam clipped off her words with a knife's edge. A hard anger colored her tone.

Her ire flowed over me without effect as the puzzle caught my attention. "How many audits have been done?"

A small huff sounded over the line.

"A full audit before the purchase, of course." When she spoke this time, her voice was much calmer. "No problems were flagged. Three weeks after the sale the first reports came in. We'd put money into renovations. However, I never expected this rapid of a turnaround. The VP in charge and I agreed a second audit was needed."

I focused on her update. "The second audit balanced also?"

I knew the answer. If the numbers hadn't balanced, Pam would have dug into the discrepancy on her own. She wouldn't have hired Crawford, and she wouldn't be on the phone with me.

"The sales and profits matched to the last dollar." Her strident tone betrayed her worry. For the first time in the conversation, I felt a kinship with the woman. "I *know* something is off, but I have no proof."

It was the gut, as Marcus, my precocious twelve-year-old son often said about me. If an answer didn't silence my internal worries, I kept looking until I was satisfied.

A deepfelt exhale echoed over the line. "I bought the business on the advice of a longtime employee. Warren Kitt was born in South Dakota. He's worked for me for twenty years. The business was under performing. It's a minor company in my portfolio, but I don't appreciate being made a fool of."

"Did you have someone local investigate?" I asked. "Or do you think they'll be too close to the issue?"

"I don't want anyone who might be compromised." Her stern tone brooked no argument. "For all your rumored faults-"

Gee, thanks. I rolled my eyes at her jab.

"All my reports agree that you can't be bought." Pam sounded disappointed. "Honestly, it sounds like you don't listen to anyone. I don't understand why Crawford tolerates you."

"Because I solve puzzles," I retorted. "And I get results."

"Fine. I want answers." Her tone turned professional. "I'll forward you the information I have. You leave tomorrow."

"Tomorrow?" No one mentioned such a quick deadline. "You might not think so, but I have a life. A husband. A child. A business of my own."

Pam scoffed. "I'm certain they can live without you for a few days. This is important."

I gritted my teeth as our fellowship evaporated. "I'll make arrangements with Crawford regarding when I can leave."

In a remarkable show of restraint, I hung up before I said something Crawford would regret. I stuck my tongue out at the phone. My brain calculated the cost of insisting on a first-class plane ticket against turning it in for five cheap seats.

There was no way I'd be able to leave town on a case for Crawford without taking my twelve-year-old Sherlock Holmes wannabe along. Then, there was the rest of the Belden-Tanner Detective Agency as my son Marcus had dubbed our adopted family.

And where would Holmes be without his seventy-plus Dr. Watson? Mrs. C, my landlady and friend, was even British.

I tapped the phone against my chin. A surplus of money was a difficult oddity to explain. At least, this case had no dead bodies.

2

11 Down; 5 Letters;
Clue: A ploy or scheme.
Answer: Trick.

Marcus, my twelve-year-old adopted son, grimaced at me from the other side of the gray sectional in our loft apartment. His dusky skin and straight black hair were clear evidence of his Korean heritage. "Couldn't you find a crime in San Diego? Or Orlando?"

"I'm sure I *could* find a crime there," I said, staring right back at him. I'd taken the boy child off the streets four years ago after he stole my wallet, and ran away with my heart. "But no one's paying me to fly to a coast and solve those fictitious crimes. Pam Isley *is* paying me to investigate what's happening at her newly acquired business in Deadwood, South Dakota."

Mrs. Alice Colchester, otherwise known as Mrs. C, set a second large bowl of buttery popcorn on the coffee table. "I've never been to Deadwood. This could be a bit of a lark."

Kevin Tanner, my hubby of only a few weeks, filled a smaller bowl with popcorn and passed the large one to Jack Rabi. "South

Dakota's new territory for me, too. We can check out old western towns, Mount Rushmore, the Badlands."

I nudged his shoulder. "That's the spirit!"

Marcus's expression morphed into one of excitement. "The Badlands! That sounds right up our alley. They must have gunfights set up in some of those towns, too."

Rabi, a black man with ashen skin and shoulder length black hair that fell in waves to his shoulders, put the large bowl of popcorn between him and Marcus. "Got the week off."

That was a display of wild enthusiasm for him. A former member of Special Ops for twenty-two years, he'd been adopted as family within a week of Marcus moving in with me. The lean man was slightly over six-feet tall but his frame had slightly more meat on it than a cadaver.

"Good!" I cuddled up next to Kevin. "Let's start the movie. What are we watching by the way?"

""The Sting" with Newman and Redford." Marcus aimed the remote at the television. "Rabi and I chose it for Kevin."

Which meant Marcus picked the movie. I frowned at the boy's supposed motive. "Do you think this movie can teach Kevin anything about grifting?"

My hubby had been born and raised in the internationally famous Feilen family of con artists. At six-foot-one with black hair and eyes the color of sapphires, his charm and brains had landed the family millions of dollars in scams. Unfortunately for them, he'd been born with a conscience. Ten years ago, he walked away from it all for the glamorous life of a construction worker and living paycheck to paycheck.

Kevin chuckled at my question. There was nothing he didn't know about running scams.

Marcus waved away my comment. "This movie is a kinder, gentler view of grifting. Besides, I like it."

Kevin put a hand on my leg. "What business did Pam Isley invest in, and why did she choose South Dakota?"

Having spent the last couple of hours reading over the material Pam sent me and doing my own research, I had an answer at hand. "Pam has some interests in that area. She also took advantage of several tax incentives for investments in agribusiness research and tourism. Her new business researches the use of solar panels on farms and ranches to benefit crops and livestock. The company also sells rare and specialty wines, and they have a micro-brewery."

"That's an odd range of interests." Kevin eyed me as he munched popcorn. "Tax dodge?"

"I think so." My head hurt from trying to decipher the various holdings of the company they'd bought out. "One of Pam's trusted managers, Warren Kitt works remotely from South Dakota. He proposed the takeover after doing the initial prospectus."

Mrs. C looked up from her knitting project. Under her perfectly coiffed white curls, her green eyes narrowed. "Green energy is the latest golden child, innit? Solar panels should be bang on for a company."

"You'd think, wouldn't you?" I was still getting a handle on the case. "The solar panel division was on top of the latest research. Development was getting off the ground. They had some sales, but their grants ran out. Loans were coming due and they'd failed to show a profit after four years."

"Ripe for a buyout." My hubby looked absorbed in Paul Newman's struggle to get a carousel running in the movie.

Grifters knew how businesses worked. Kevin had faked being an executive or an investor numerous times in his short life as a con artist.

"You nailed it." I confirmed his supposition, not surprised he'd guessed correctly. "A young couple and three friends got together in college. None of them could make a go of it by themselves. They pooled their business acumen and their money."

Marcus, munching popcorn, split his wide-eyed interest evenly between Newman and my report. "This is where it gets good. Money. Envy. Hurt feelings. Anger. I like it."

I wanted to tell him to concentrate on the movie. However, having survived the streets on his own for a few years, he'd seen the seamier side of life. Besides, the decision to sell was the most likely spot to plant seeds of discourse.

I tipped my head to the boy child. "Two of the guys signed non-competitive forms regarding the solar panel division and took a buyout. One is working in Deadwood."

Kevin seemingly watched the movie with undivided interest. Until his eyes narrowed. "He oversaw the winery and the brews?"

At my nod, Marcus slapped the sofa. "How did you know?"

The boy had taken the words right out of my mouth.

Kevin didn't take his gaze from the television screen. "If he was interested in the solar panel development, he'd have stayed rather than walk away. A high-end restaurant or shop that deals in fine wines would give him leave to dabble without competing."

"Score one for Tanner." I thought back to my notes. "The other buyout returned home to North Carolina. He's working at his family's boating business on the coast."

"That leaves three." Marcus held up three fingers. "Are the married couple the brains? What about the third person?"

This was the crux of the issue as I saw it. "The married couple, Natalie and Matt Crocker, along with Yvonne Dunston stayed with the company. They were given titles as VP's of Research and Development. The other staff were left intact. A handful of Isley employees were shifted to oversee the whole. Development was set to continue uninterrupted."

Mrs. C, who'd added jalapeno salt to her popcorn, followed my report with interest. "When did the problem first develop?"

I met the older woman's gaze without glancing at my notes. "A month after the sale, the wineries and micro-brews showed a marked rise in sales. It's seen steady growth ever since."

"Wait a minute!" Marcus yelled and threw up his hands. "What was all that about the solar panels and research, lady?"

Seeing equally puzzled expressions on the others, I held up my hands to forestall the protests. "The original five partners figured diversity would give them a greater chance of success. Atherton, the guy in town, inherited a huge wine cellar and wanted to build on that. The other buyout, Hayden had a micro-brewery business. They bought a small company dealing with solar panels, which was supposed to bring in the big bucks."

The explanation mollified some of the outrage.

I continued painting the picture. "They share the profits from any part of the venture."

Kevin watched me closely. "Deadwood is built on tourism. The wine sale and microbrewery should have been a shoe in. What went wrong?"

"That's the question." I'd been studying the issue and the people all day. "Natalie Crocker is skilled in getting grants and loans, but the solar panel division ate money from the beginning. They poured cash into research and production. The wine and beer sales kept them afloat, but not enough. Once the sale went though, the wine and beer sales shot up."

Marcus abandoned Newman and Redford. He leaned his elbows on his knees and faced me with a scrunched-up expression. "You were hired because the company's making money? Who does that?"

I threw my notes on the coffee table that sat in the middle of the sectional. "That is the one thing Pam and I see eye-to-eye on. Having those sections of the company turn a profit *now* doesn't make sense."

"If the original partners were so close to making good, why sell?" Kevin's face wore a thoughtful expression. "They had to know how the numbers were running."

A low, ruminating hum sounded from Mrs. C. "The men in charge of the two divisions turning a profit took the money and walked away? That's rather odd."

"Exactly!" My mind had been stacking the information all day, probing for holes or threads to pull. "I don't have any answers in my puzzle."

"This trip should be great." My son grabbed a handful of popcorn. "We're going to Deadwood, except nobody's dead."

With his laughter echoing around the room at his feeble joke, I shook my head and turned to the movie.

Pam hadn't warned anyone except her manager, Warren Kitt, that I was coming. If there was fraud, the answer had to lie in the partnership. I doubted the remaining trio would welcome my arrival.

3

24 Across; 6 Letters;
Clue: Opening move.
Answer: Gambit.

I'll skip over the packing and travel. With Marcus fresh out of school and Rabi able to get the week off, we landed in Rapid City, South Dakota two days after I'd spoken with Pam Isley.

Given the exorbitant price of my first-class ticket with only two days warning, turning it in to cover five last minute economy tickets didn't leave too much of a gap. I also flipped what I considered a pricey hotel for a three-bedroom Air B-N-B with a foldout sofa.

I was feeling pretty pleased with myself as we drove down the main street of Deadwood, South Dakota. Small shops and restaurants lined both sides. Colorful awnings mixed with historical names and buildings.

After an early lunch that included chicken fried steak bites at the Nugget Saloon, we settled into our rented house.

Marcus exited the small den after depositing his suitcase on the floor. "Does she really expect you to solve this in, like, five days? Why don't her people look into the problem? Why the hurry?"

"Her people searched for an answer with no luck." I took his rapid-fire questions in stride while glancing at the spacious living area. I was looking forward to mixing my investigation with trips to the Crazy Horse Memorial and Mount Rushmore, along with all the other sights. "The remaining partners are due to receive a final payout this week. She wants answers before that happens, and she's willing to pay extra to get them."

Marcus stopped halfway into the living room. His wide eyes stared out the French Doors at the back of the house. "We have a pool and a hot tub! Hallelujah!"

He threw his arms over his head and stomped in place. "We are rich!"

"We're traveling on someone else's dime." Which was my favorite way to travel. I smiled at my son's antics. "The water does look nice. No reason we can't reconnoiter poolside."

While the rest of us swam, Mrs. C sat under the overhang in a muumuu splashed with bright blooms of every color.

After I'd abandoned the pool for a spot in the sun, Rabi, Marcus and Kevin swam for a while. Finally, they got out and flopped into the remaining chairs, dripping wet.

"Okay," Marcus breathed out the word as he filled a corn chip with an abundance of dip. "Stop stalling. If the Belden-Tanner Agency is going to solve this case, we need all the facts."

I stared at my boy child over the rim of my lemonade. There were several things wrong with his statement. "*I* haven't been playing in the pool for the last half-hour. Besides, I gave you all the facts I have."

We also weren't a detective agency. Only I was an actual PI. The Belden-Tanner Agency was a figment of Marcus's imagination. Although my adopted family had done their part to help me solve several murders, it was strictly voluntary. As in, I didn't share my paycheck. However, they did benefit in other ways. Ala, we were sitting by a pool in Deadwood.

Mrs. C, my seventy-plus landlady, shuffled over in her ever-present slippers. In honor of Deadwood, she'd brought the pair with sheriff badges on them. "What roll are you expected to play? You'll need access to the businesses."

Her British accent was decidedly at odds with the western setting.

Marcus pointed a second chip over-burdened with dip at me.

"Are we undercover? We could sneak into places and find their stash."

His dramatic whisper had a sinister tone that was completely at odds with the sunny day and the slight breeze.

"We don't need to sneak in anywhere." I told him in a firm tone. "Only Warren Kitt, Pam's on-site rep knows I've been hired to look into the situation."

Kevin twirled a fork in his fingers. His blue eyes held a discerning gaze. "Does she want you to find answers or does she want to make sure no one else can find the problem? That would explain why she hired someone she considers too stubborn for their own good."

Grabbing a chip for myself, I rewarded my hubby with a smile. "You get the door prize. This investment is a tax dodge. She doesn't want anything illegal, but more than that, she doesn't want trouble."

Marcus snorted back a laugh. "And she hired *you*? Didn't she learn anything from your case with the Prusharks?"

I joined in the round of laughter. "I have a meeting with Warren Kitt in an hour. He's been on-site for several months. He chose the company to purchase. He's followed their profits for a few years. Why he chose them over other contenders, I don't know. An easy sale evidently. He also negotiated and oversaw the sale. As the man in charge, he relocated here."

"He's responsible." Rabi's low drawl cut across the conversation for the first time in several minutes.

"This is his baby." I wondered where Kitt stood on my involvement. "If I find major trouble, he'll have to explain how he missed whatever is going on. I'm not sure he'll welcome me sticking my nose into the game."

Mrs. C unfurled a large fan with orange and yellow flowers on it. She fanned herself with a languid air while eyeing me. "What's your next step?"

Her tone held a skeptical note, knowing my penchant for jumping into cases with no plan at all.

I took a deep breath. I'd considered my options over the last few days. "Pam wants to keep the investigation on the down low. I'll get Warren Kitt's input. See how far he's willing to help or if he has any ideas."

Kevin tapped a rhythm on the table's edge. Water dripped off his black hair. "How did he explain the abnormal jump in profits?"

"He's the one who pointed out the trend to Pam." I was as baffled as everyone else. "He says he's been watching the books, tracing down the new orders, and the businesses they originate from. Everything looks legit."

Mrs. C's pale green eyes narrowed. The older woman had done her share of dancing on the wild side of the law during fifty years of running from a murder charge. A murder, we discovered a few months ago, that she wasn't guilty of. However, she had an excellent understanding of the shady elements of society.

That, coupled with Kevin's grifting background, gave me a wealth of knowledge to draw on. I watched the woman in anticipation.

She leaned back in the chair. "Very odd affair."

My hopes plummeted. I know this is my case, but I'd been hoping for words of wisdom. When I blinked, her Hawaiian themed muumuu, coupled with the puffy sheriff's badge slippers, and the tangerine fan, hit me in the face. What was I thinking?

To be honest, I couldn't blame Mrs. C. I needed more input than Pam saying something was off with this acquisition.

"Here's the plan." I shoved the chips away and dusted off my fingers. My audience eyed me with no visible reactions. "I'm going to meet with Wallace Kitt. You..."

I pointed at them in a slow arc. "Are going to hit the sights of downtown Deadwood."

Marcus perked up. "Like bakeries and ice-cream parlors?"

I eyed the boy child. He, even more than the rest of us, traveled on his stomach "Sure. Check out everything. But you have had three meals already."

He shook his head with a mournful sigh. "Desserts go to a different stomach, T.R. You know that."

Kevin nodded in agreement. "It's true."

"Whatever." I couldn't win when the two of them were in cahoots. "Visit local wine stores and breweries. Does Prairie Sun and Spirits have a good reputation? What's local opinion on Wallace Kitt and the buyout?"

Kevin studied me with a flicker of suspicion in his eyes. "Does something have your goat about this case, Belden?"

I never could hide anything from him. After ten years of being besties, he knew me too well. "I'm wondering if Pam expects me to fail. This set up doesn't make sense, but she knew I couldn't resist a puzzle."

"And you fell into her evil trap." Marcus summed up the affair in a deep, falsely menacing tone.

"I was helpless." I admitted, admitting my inability to turn away from a challenging puzzle.

Kevin's expression softened. His low chuckle morphed into a smile. "We'll scour the town for innuendo and rumor."

Marcus stiffened like a dog on point. "Do these places have like, finger food? Munchies?"

"Seriously?" I eyed our son. "Is that all you think of?"

"I'm a growing boy." His straight, black hair, drying in the hot sun, flew around his face as he threw back his head. "You can write it off on the expense report, and we'll get the information you need. People love us."

He pasted on a charming expression.

I sighed. It was true. Heaven help the denizens of Deadwood. "I'm glad I have a meeting to go to. Please don't call me with any catastrophes."

4

42 Down; 6 Letters;
Clue: Critical situation; _____ play.
Answer: Clutch.

Warren Kitt's office was as non-descript as the man himself. He was two inches shorter than my five-nine height. He made no pretense of hiding either his thinning hair or his growing belly. At forty-four, he was almost a decade older than me. Though he had a laidback manner, the hazel eyes behind his eye-glasses held a sharp intelligence.

Housed in an unassuming building several blocks away from the small, but thriving downtown area, the front man for the Isley Corporation led me into a twelve-by-fifteen-foot room. Ignoring the oak desk opposite the door, he led me to a polished oval table containing several folders and a laptop.

"Please, have a seat, Ms. Belden." He waved me to a chair facing the door before sitting next to me. "The files regarding the Prairie Sun and Spirits Company are at your disposal. Pam asked me to give you any help I can. I only hope you're able to get to the bottom of this manner. Where would you like to start?"

I couldn't stop the groan that escaped at the sight of the reports or the offer to go through the figures again. Raising my gaze from the death traps, my eyes locked in on the espresso machine on a counter behind the door.

My entire body froze. Putting a hand over my heart, I let myself get lost in the moment. Next to my family, coffee is my first love. I pointed at the gleaming silver. "Does that make coffee? And call me Tracy."

A smile wreathed his face reminiscent of a proud papa. "Call me Warren, and that makes the best coffee in the entire state. I recently received a bag of orange Amaretto coffee beans. Would you like a cup?"

I couldn't even speak. All I could do was nod and hope Warren wasn't guilty of any wrong doing, because he was my new best friend. Kevin would understand.

Moments later, I inhaled the delicious aroma of the freshly brewed cup. The scent alone was enough to breathe new life into my veins. Taking a sip, I let the hot brew settle on my tongue. "Ooohh! This is ambrosia."

"Wait!" Warren's satisfied expression grew even more excited. "I have fresh baked Ginger Snap cookies from the local bakery. You have to try them with this coffee. They're to die for."

"Oh, my!" With a bite of the cookie still on my tongue, I took another sip of coffee and let the flavors mingle. "This is delicious. I may never leave."

Warren chuckled. Then, his mouth flattened. "Not if you're looking for answers."

"And reality rears its ugly head." I set down my cup and turned my attention to the case. "I know numbers, but I'm no expert. If you can't find fault with the figures, I doubt I will. For the moment, let's say you're not behind the issue I've been hired to investigate."

Crawford's people were actually going over the books right now. I'd learned not to show all my cards in an investigation.

"Thank you for your trust." He spoke in a heartfelt tone.

"It's not that." I couldn't afford to trust anyone on a case, not even people who served me heavenly tasting coffee and cookies. "You pointed out the... let's call making too much money a problem for the moment."

Warren gave me a rueful smile and toasted me with his I Love Deadwood coffee cup.

I continued. "Also, if your goal was to commit fraud, there are more options in company headquarters in Tahoe."

"Along with greater scrutiny." Warren pointed out in a show of honesty.

"Why did you ask to oversee a company in Deadwood at this point in your career?" I asked. A quick check had showed he hadn't been born or gone to school in South Dakota. "Your social media shows pictures of a Mason family reunion in Mitchell, South Dakota."

"You *are* thorough." Surprise and admiration showed in his eyes. "My family settled here four generations ago. My sister and brother moved to the state in the last five years. One for a job. The other to help with the family store in Mitchell, South Dakota. When I read about the diverse interests of Prairie Sun and Spirits and their failing cash flow, the company seemed like the investment opportunity-"

"Tax dodge." I inserted with a smile.

Warren chuckled. "The Isley Corporation has been looking for smaller companies to invest in. If it goes well, I'll transfer here full-time. I have nothing keeping me in Nevada."

His unblinking gaze and manner lent him an air of honesty, but I don't get paid to take people at their word. "Would you mind giving me your siblings names and addresses?"

With an expectant look on his face, he took a piece of paper out of a folder and slid it toward me.

"Due diligence." I explained, glancing at the names before sliding the paper into my purse. "Currently, I'm stuck on the motive. I can't figure out an end-game. The profit ends up in the Isley account. Nobody launders money without wanting the cash back somehow. I assume the profits are safe?"

"Absolutely. The money is in our accounts." Warren adjusted his accountant-like glasses. A slight tightening of his eyes increased his wrinkles. His glance strayed to the files and reports on the table.

I noted his reaction while cringing at the thought of more reading. I also believed the answer lay in the ties that had bound the original partners together. "Tell me about Natalie and Matt Crocker. The married couple that put their dreams into spreading solar panels across the open fields of South Dakota."

Warren's eyes relaxed along with his shoulders as we shifted topics. Most of what he told me, I already knew. Natalie could have made a living as a grant writer. Matt was the front man and a whiz at sales. Yvonne Dunston was a computer expert. She'd created the computer programs they still used after the buyout. He hadn't had much contact with Bruce Atherton, the wine guy in town, and had never met Tom Hayden, living on a boat off the east coast.

Warren couldn't point to any red flags, but my brain was busily arranging clues and a grid for my mental crossword puzzle. After conning him out of a cup of coffee for the road, Warren stopped me at the door.

"Tracy, this venture was my idea." He met my gaze with a desperate air. "I want to stay here permanently. I've grown to love this area and being close to my family. If there's anything I can do, let me know. I'll throw in a bag of the orange Amaretto and Ginger Snap cookies if you find the answer."

"You know how to hit me where I live." If I needed additional incentive to solve this puzzle, I had it. Perhaps I should get the promise in writing in case he was guilty. "I'll keep in touch."

"Great. You can copy me on the reports you send Pam."

I shook his hand, throwing in a smile at his assumption. I didn't mention that my boss would be lucky to get a report. I had no intention of communicating with Pam Isley.

Several moments later I connected with the rest of the Belden-Tanner Agency at a small park by the Halloway Rodeo Cowboy statue. They were eating ice cream from the Big Dipper. I ditched my empty cup of amaretto coffee. Planting a kiss on Kevin's cheek, I settled myself into a wooden picnic table. Situated under a row of trees, the place provided a perfect spot for people watching.

Marcus's eagle eyes nailed me with a stern stare. "What have you learned? Do you know who did it?"

In the act of stealing a drink from Kevin's smoothie, I made the boy wait before gifting him with a frown. "I've been in town for a few hours. I'm gathering information. What about-"

"Good." The boy breathed a sigh. "There are cowboy reenactments and we need to go on the stagecoach ride. We have to stay long enough to do everything."

"I'm glad you have your priorities in order." I gave the boy a flat stare. "As long we're making lists, no one can go on the tour of Victorian houses without me."

Mrs. C, looking comfortable with her muumuu, waved her fan at me. "I can't wait to see the Victorians. I'm with you."

Marcus's initial grimace deepened. He looked wildly back and forth from Kevin to Rabi as he made a slashing motion across his throat.

Kevin chuckled. "I'll be happy to escort you both. Rabi and Marcus can find something else to do. Maybe find the barns where they keep the horses."

"That would be cool!" Marcus jumped at the alternative. Then, like a camera shutter, his manner shifted. He looked around our mostly deserted corner of the park before leaning forward. "What have you learned? You go first. Then, we'll tell you what we heard."

With his tantalizing promise hanging in the air, I gave an abbreviated version of Warren's updates. "Hayden has made brief visits, but Kitt's never met the guy in person. Atherton jumped at the buyout because he was unhappy with the partnership, possibly from the beginning. The venture was built on his business acumen and a wine cellar of rare vintages he inherited that partially funded the early years."

"An outlier." Narrowed eyes accompanied Rabi's judgement.

I was struck with the accuracy of his guess. "The five of them came together during college. The three remaining partners have always been a united front."

Mrs. C's sly smile and knowing green eyes met me when I looked up. "More than you know, luv."

Her British accent and intriguing comment put me in mind of an Agatha Christie scene at a country house.

The boy child, having scanned the table, leaned forward. "Bruce introduced Yvonne to Matt in college. That's when Matt joined the scheme with those two. Tell her, Kevin."

My hubby, having waited his turn, nodded solemnly at being given the stage. "Matt and Yvonne dated for several weeks. Natalie and Hayden had been soulmates for two years. She was the driving force behind the business, but she needed money."

Mrs. C snapped her multi-colored fan together. Her eyes twinkled at the whiff of intrigue. "Matt inherited a trust fund a few months later when he turned twenty-one. That's what Natalie wanted, and she got it, didn't she?"

"She dumped Hayden for Matt Crocker, who left Yvonne? And the partnership survived?" I couldn't imagine why Yvonne or Hayden had stayed. I said as much. "Perhaps they were banking on the profits coming in after the lean times."

"Too much lean time." Rabi's mouth barely moved as he delivered the summation. His gaze continued to scan the area.

I sipped the dregs of Kevin's smoothie, flashing him a smile. "The team invested heavily in the solar panels anticipating sales and a grant that didn't materialize. The loss of capital sapped the bottom line."

Mrs. C clicked her tongue. "And the dominos fell into the Isley's lap, didn't they?"

Marcus cupped his chin in his hands. "Can't the increased sales just be, like, a cycle or something?"

I nodded at the insight behind his observation. It wasn't a bad question. "On the surface, that's a possibility. But when Warren considered what's selling, the numbers don't make sense."

"Why not?" Marcus held out a hand as he spoke. "And, you still can't solve the case before the end of the week."

"I don't think that's going to be a problem." Since I had no clue what was going on. "The increased profits aren't tied only to the sale of the wine and beers. The sale of merchandise like t-shirts, hats, and cups is topping out. The rate is out-performing more established wineries and breweries. The purchases are legitimate as near as the accountants can tell."

Interest sparked in Kevin's eyes. His fingers beat a rhythm on his glass. I waited but he said nothing.

"You have an idea?" I prompted. I was out of my depth. I'd never had any excess money to worry about.

He met my gaze before shifting to Mrs. C. "Have you ever laundered money?"

The older woman pursed her lips. "I've had the odd occasion to shift money, shall we say, luv."

Marcus's eyebrows rose. "Your family probably moved money lots of times, huh Kevin?"

"On occasion," Kevin parroted with a smile accompanied by a

thoughtful look. Finally, he shook his head. "This doesn't follow any pattern I've seen. This company isn't on the stock market."

"Nope." I shook my head. "Privately owned from the beginning, still is under Isley. The money is rolling in for Isley and no one knows why. How would you like to discuss rare wines with Bruce Atherton? I made an appointment with him in your name. We could eat at the Legends Steakhouse."

Kevin narrowed his gaze at the teasing note in my voice. "A walk in the park and a fancy eatery, all in one day? I could be convinced."

A loud slap on the table made me jump.

"No!" Marcus wailed. "There's a shootout tonight. We have to go. Rabi, you'd rather go see cowboys, right?"

"Every time." The man sounded insulted at even being asked.

"Mrs. C?" the boy pointed at the older woman. "You're in, too?"

"Wouldn't miss it for the world." The woman's face was wreathed in a smile of anticipation. "I do love a good shootout!"

If it were any other soul over seventy, I'd take the comment for a joke. With Mrs. C, it was probably the truth.

"Oh, no!" Kevin slumped in his seat. His face was a mask of anguish.

Concern coursed through me. "What's wrong?"

My hubby groaned. He leaned toward Marcus. "I have to go to dinner alone with Belden?"

I glared at Kevin while trying to keep a straight face.

Marcus roared with laughter and pointed at Kevin. "You like her, Kev. That's why you married her. You have to take her."

I playfully pushed my hubby away as he reached for me. "For that, you're buying me dessert, and you aren't getting an invitation to the pizza party when we solve the case."

Kevin laughed in the face of my threat, kissing my cheek.

Marcus waved his hand. "You can be my plus one, Kev."

"You're lucky you have him." I grinned at my husband and best friend. "Now, take me home so I can get dolled up for this dinner. I intend to ambush Bruce Atherton, and you're going to help."

"Let's go!" Kevin leapt to his feet. "I better be looking good for this, too."

As if the man could look bad.

~

Fast forward to late afternoon, Rabi, Mrs. C, and Marcus were last seen headed for the shootout. Kevin and I had strolled hand-in-hand down Main Street. We meandered through two art galleries and strolled through multiple tourist shops with their colorful awnings. I'd noted the sign for Big Dipper offering ice cream, then spent several minutes admiring the stunning jewels in the Ponderosa Trading Company. Finally, we ate a delicious meal at Legends with matchless service.

Kevin squeezed my hand. "The Buffalo Wine Barrel's up ahead. I reviewed their wines in stock. It's good stuff."

I hugged his arm and kissed his cheek. "That's why I keep you."

"Had to be something," he said with a teasing smile. "How do you want to handle this? Subtle? Or your way?"

"I'm not in the mood for subtle."

"Are you *ever?*"

"My gut thinks the problem lies with the odd combination of people." I admitted. "That back story doesn't add up for me, and Miss Marple told me not to believe what people say."

"Miss Marple should know." Despite his serious tone, mischief sparkled in Kevin's eyes as he reached for the door handle of the store. "Let's find out what Atherton has to hide."

5

56 Down; 5 Letters;
Clue: Move. Change gears.
Answer: Shift.

The wine store was better dressed than any of my apartments had ever been. A seating with leather chairs. Rows of gleaming bottles with multicolored labels. Stacks of wooden cases displayed various vintages.

Kevin eyed the shelves with a discerning gaze. He lingered over a bottle of red wine with a local label. "They have a good collection. A wide variety. Good décor."

"It's nice." My murmur of agreement brought a sideways glance. I fought to hide my laughter. "What do I know of fine wine? Or any wine?"

Kevin nodded in response to a clerk currently checking out another couple's purchase. "You can smell intrigue in the air, but not the aroma of a good wine."

My gaze scanned the aisles and corners. One woman was emptying a small crate of bottles. A slim man stopped her for a whispered consultation.

I tugged on Kevin's hand. "Bruce said his office is in the rear of the store."

Kevin and I strolled toward the corner where the man and woman stood.

As we approached the man looked up with a slight smile on his face. His gaze narrowed. Touching his co-worker's arm, he walked toward us. "You're Tracy Belden."

I started in surprise. Kevin, unlike me, kept his composure. No one other than Warren Kitt was supposed to know I was coming. "I am, but how do you know my name?"

"Bruce is expecting you." The words came with a sigh and an easing of the tension in the man's face. George, according to his nametag, gave a slight smile.

George included Kevin as he turned and waved a hand toward a corridor in the back corner. "His office is this way."

With my suspicions on full alert, I followed him. "Did Bruce discuss my arrival with his former partners?"

"I don't know. Bruce didn't tell me anything. I saw a Vegas news outlet on his computer with your picture." George slowed and glanced at us with a look of anticipation. "Are you buyers from one of the Vegas casinos? That would be amazing."

I answered with a smile and a wink. Best to play it cool, since I was completely confused. Either someone had blabbed or Pam had a major leak in her organization. Or perhaps the multiple audits had lit a fire under a guilty conscience.

The short hallway to the office left little time to ponder. The man rapped his knuckles on a closed door at the end of the hall. "Bruce? Tracy Belden's here."

No answer came.

George smiled apologetically. "I know he's here. I spoke with him an hour ago when someone called for him."

"We'll go in." The clerk spoke with a lilt in his tone. "I know he's waiting for you."

Part of me wanted to hold back, which was silly since I'd specifi-cally arranged this confrontation. Perhaps the tension tap dancing up my spine accounted for my hesitation.

"Bruce?" George opened the door to a small office. "Tracy Belden's here."

Images flashed on my brain: A small desk by the window, paperwork piled on a spare chair, three crates of wine from different companies stacked by the front corner. A man sitting behind the desk faced the lone window in the room. A wine bottle and a glass with the dregs of a red liquid reflected in the sunlight.

And the stillness.

The closed-in silence smacked me in the face. I tensed instantly. I heard nothing from Kevin. Not even the sharp intake of breath that gave evidence of my own shock. However, I felt his hand touch mine.

"Bruce?" George's voice sharpened. "Hey, bud. Wake up! You have visitors!"

When the clerk started forward, I grabbed his arm, forcibly holding him back. I returned his puzzled look with a stern one of my own. "I'll check on him."

Pushing him toward Kevin, I walked forward.

"What's going on?" George's confused tone gave no indication of alarm. "I can't believe he dosed off."

Two strides was all it took to put me behind the desk. Bruce Atherton's blank eyes stared at the blue sky outside above a slack jaw. His loose hands lay in his lap. He'd been thirty-two. A few years younger than me.

No pulse. No breath.

I looked at Kevin and shook my head. He already had his phone in his hand. He gave a nod and gently grabbed George's arm.

The clerk's wide eyes shifted from me to Kevin, fighting against my hubby's grip. "No! What are you doing? He's fine. He's napping. Does she think he's dead? Bruce can't be dead."

Actually, he can be, my brain answered irreverently. And he is dead.

As they turned to leave, I leaned over and smelled the dead man's mouth. The only aroma I could discern was sour wine. Using the back of my finger, I tipped the remaining liquid in the glass. No obvious residue, but it was a red wine. The laptop was closed. No notes on his desk. Nothing in the inside pockets of his jacket.

Kevin and George stood in the hall. Kevin was still on the phone. George glared at me with growing confusion.

I put out my hands out and pasted on a puzzled expression.

"Next time, leave a clue," I muttered to the dead man before walking away.

When I joined them in the hall and shut the door behind me, Kevin raised his phone. "The police are on the way."

George stared around as if lost. "He's not really dead, is he? How is he dead?"

"I don't know." I'd come to investigate fraud and ended up with a dead body. Was it suicide? Why? He'd just taken a buyout. But who would murder him?

Someone with something to hide.

Kevin put a hand on the man's shoulder. "Wait here with Tracy. I'll meet the police."

I exchanged a nod with Kevin as he turned to the front of the store. His move put him face-to-face with two women barreling toward us.

A chubby blonde with short curly hair wore a frown. She was whispering to her companion. "... am I here? You said you'd talk to him."

Seeing us, she shot the clerk a flirtatious smile. "Hey, Georgie. Bruce is expecting us."

The taller brunette with a model thin figure scanned Kevin and I with a quick once over. "Consulting on setting up your wine cellar? Bruce is the best."

"Hey, Natalie." George put out a hand to block the brunette from sidling past us. He'd finally found his voice, though it was breathless. Then, he turned and nodded to the blonde. "Yvonne. They're buyers from a casino in Vegas."

I didn't bother to correct the man. I was too busy studying two of the other partners. Neither woman blinked at Kevin and my supposed roles. Nor did they show any flicker of recognizing me as George had.

The clerk remained in the middle of the hall. "You can't see Bruce."

Yvonne, the blonde, tightened her jaw in defiance.

Behind them, a police cruiser pulled up to the curb. No lights or sirens. Like Langsdale, Nevada, the resort town where I lived, police don't like to alarm the tourists. They wouldn't believe Atherton was dead until they saw the body for themselves.

"George." Natalie added a touch of steel to the man's name. "This is important. Obviously, his previous meeting is over."

She raised a brow in my direction.

Kevin, standing beside George, looked pleasant enough, but no way would either woman get past my husband, or me.

Stepping around Kevin, I took a breath and considered how to play my hand. "You need to speak with the police. There's been... an accident."

Both women stiffened at my words. Their quick, silent exchange of startled looks was interrupted as the chime sounded from the door. Turning around, Natalie and Yvonne gasped as a uniformed police officer walked into the wine store.

The white guy was fifty-something. Curly, light brown hair had escaped from his cap. His wide build showed the beginning of a belly, but his quick gaze was intent and sharp. After a quick scan of the shop, he zeroed in on the five of us clogging the corridor. He nodded to his right before striding toward us.

After a cursory look at the three locals, the man locked in on me and Kevin, ending with my husband. "Did you call 9-1-1?"

"I did, officer. I'm Kevin Tanner." Kevin moved to one side of the narrow hall and pointed to the door at the back of the hall. "He's in there."

"Wait a minute." Natalie's strident tone betrayed the uncertainty in her eyes. She evidently disliked not having all the facts. "I demand to know what's going on. Why have the police been called? What happened to Bruce?"

Yvonne's face was pinched with worry. "Is Bruce going to be okay?"

Fear bordering on panic threaded through her voice, as she registered the arrival of the police rather than an ambulance.

I held out a hand to Officer Clark, per his nametag. "Perhaps we should all wait in an empty office if one is available?"

George pointed wordlessly to a closed door slightly behind us.

Kevin stepped back and opened the door. A small table with four chairs was offset with a set of shelves and various brochures.

Officer Clark quickly seized control. "Everyone wait in here. No talking until I get back. Don't call anyone. George, come with me."

The wine clerk tensed instantly. Too bad Clark hadn't asked me. I wouldn't have minded another look at the scene.

Being in the room with the two woman was like being caged with a pair of wild-eyed tigers. No one sat except Kevin, who took the chair farthest from the door. I was too busy studying the other women.

Yvonne stood with a hand over her mouth, leaving only her scared, worried gaze flickering back and forth.

"He can't keep us here." Natalie got in Yvonne's face so quickly, her long, straight hair swung out behind her. She swiveled to face Kevin and me. "Who are you two? How do you know Bruce?"

"I'm Tracy Belden." Pause for recognition. Again, not a flicker at hearing my name. "This is my husband, Kevin Tanner. As George said, we flew in from Vegas. We came to speak with Bruce."

"Did you?" Yvonne demanded. With her fists clenched by her chest, she looked like an angry pixie. "What have you done?"

The door opened before I could answer. Officer Clark's solemn expression confirmed what Kevin and I already knew. His demeanor put the other two women on alert. Both tensed like tightly strung wires.

He met their eyes with a sympathetic look. "Bruce is dead."

Their exclamations of sorrow and shock appeared genuine. Both gasped. I didn't have to look at Kevin to know his intense gaze was studying them as well.

Yvonne collapsed in a chair. Burying her head in her hands, her shoulders shook.

Natalie put a hand to her chest as if she'd been struck with a lance. After the denials that it must be a mistake, the woman turned toward the outsiders. Her gaze slid by Kevin's sympathetic expression to land on me. "Bruce was fine when I spoke with him this morning. What did you say to him? What have you done?"

They'd talked this morning? Yet she didn't know my name and Bruce had. Interesting. I met her gaze and shook my head. "We never met him. George led us back to the office. When we found him, Bruce was already dead. It was right before you came in. You said you had an appointment with him also?"

"No." Yvonne raised her head, wiping at her eyes. Her lip quivered as she spoke. She took a trembling breath. "We just dropped in."

Natalie opened her mouth. Her body tensed. Her narrowed eyes pierced her friend with a hard look.

Cautioning her to silence?

Officer Clark studied all four of us equally. "The lieutenant's on his way. The coroner's been called."

Deadwood's population of fourteen hundred people coupled with its low crime rate, including zero murders for the last year, meant there was no homicide detective. There was simply no need. The police force of less than twenty officers would handle the investigation.

I kept my gaze on the other two women. "Bruce called and asked you to come here."

Yvonne nodded. Her gaze slid sideways to me. Then, she tensed.

Natalie's expression tightened. "You have no right to ask questions of us."

I shrugged at her rising ire. "The telephone records will prove who called who, as well as the timeline."

Clark eyed Kevin and I with an intense gaze. "Let me see your I.D.s. George said you were wine buyers from a casino in Las Vegas. Who do you work for?"

Exchanging a look with Kevin, I reached in my bag. Should I speak with the police officer privately? Or come clean now? In a town this size, the truth would ripple through the streets within moments. Best to see the women's reactions in person.

I held out my wallet to Clark. "George made an assumption regarding my business with Mr. Atherton. I'm a private investigator from Langsdale, Nevada. I'm here on a case."

Clark stiffened but didn't stop. He studied my Nevada P.I. license and made a few notations in his small notebook before handing it back. His eyes narrowed at seeing Kevin's driver's license. "You're her partner?"

Kevin shrugged. "In a manner of speaking. I'm her husband. I'm just along for the ride and to see Deadwood. It's a lovely town."

My brain came up with a comment about eye candy. The smart aleck quip was on my lips, but I managed to clamp my jaw shut. I'd alienated a few police officers in Nevada. With no Crawford on-site to bail me out, I figured I should play nice for now.

I hadn't even bothered to check whether my P.I. license was reciprocal in South Dakota. My report on possible fraud would have gone straight to Crawford, then Pam Isley. I'd never expected to be involved in a death, whether it was suicide or possible murder.

Clark handed back our I.D.s. He loomed over us, not giving an inch. "What exactly are you investigating that involves... involved Bruce Atherton?"

I raised my chin and looked him in the eye. "I'd rather not go into detail without contacting my client."

Yvonne groaned. "It's the buyout. Of course."

"Yvonne!" Natalie turned on her friend. Her raised fists were clenched. "Keep quiet!"

"Oh, please, Natalie!" The other woman struck the table with her open hand in the first show of defiance since they'd arrived. "Everyone is town already know. Why else would a P.I. be here? Pam Isley is doing another on-site review. Did you think they'd hand over this much money without due diligence?"

Clark had watched the women during the outburst. He turned to me with a raised brow.

Still digesting the scene, I nodded. "That's pretty much it."

"Good to know." A new player filled the open doorway, closing it behind him. A white guy with a solid build, high cheek bones and light brown hair, he looked to be in his mid-forties. Brown eyes flashed above a nose that had been broken more than once. He nodded a greeting to Clark, then surveyed the rest of us. "I'm Lieutenant Lawrence Hawken. I'll be looking into Bruce Atherton's death."

Clark jerked his head toward the end of the hall. "Phillips and Lloyd are taking pictures. They're bagging everything, including the bottle of wine and the glass. I closed off the office. George is in the next office. The coroner is waiting for you before she moves the body."

"Good." Hawkens nodded approval. His gaze touched briefly on the rest of us as his hand moved toward the doorknob. "I'll be back in a few minutes."

The closing of the door seemed to mark a new chapter. The police investigation had officially begun. My own case had taken a darker turn. With no signs of violence on the body, Bruce Atherton had almost certainly been poisoned.

Was it by his own hand? Or had someone wanted to silence him before he spoke with me?

6

26 Across; 5 Letters;
Clue: Friends. Partners.
Answer: Mates.

I wanted more than anything to confer with Kevin. However, under the eagle eyes of Officer Clark, that was impossible. I settled for sitting next to him at the small table and holding his hand.

My hubby was on one side of the table, within arm's length of Yvonne. Despite the woman's stunned expression and downcast gaze, her eyes were alert.

Natalie stalked the narrow end of the room. She spun suddenly and pointed at me. "You did this! You're responsible for his death!"

Being an outsider, I took her accusation in stride. However, I noted she didn't accuse Kevin.

"Natalie." Clark voice was calm yet stern. He walked toward her. "Everyone's in shock. You're distraught. Sit down and try to relax. Hawk will talk to each of you in turn. Until then, I'll have some water or coffee brought in."

Knowing how long questioning by the police could take when a dead body was involved, I squeezed Kevin's hand. "At least we ate at Legends before coming here."

Diverted by Natalie's outburst, Clark hadn't noticed my comment. The woman finally sat. Unfortunately, she was directly opposite me and continued to stare daggers at me.

Clark diverted her attention by asking about Atherton's next of kin.

I continued to study Natalie. Her hostility seemed out of proportion considering Yvonne's reaction. Misplaced guilt, perhaps?

The door opened on my musings. Hawkens stepped inside. Clark held up his notebook and explained about the contact information for the family.

"Good." Hawkens nodded. "I've arranged for water and coffee to be brought. I'll need to speak with each of you. There's another room down the hall. Officer Clark will remain here. I'll start with Ms. Belden and Mr. Tanner together."

Kevin and I followed him down the narrow hall. I caught a glimpse of George in the main part of the store. Another police officer and the female clerk we'd seen initially stood with him. He met my gaze with an angry frown. Probably annoyed I hadn't corrected his assumption.

The exchange lasted only seconds before Hawkens opened the door to an even smaller office. A narrow desk filled one corner. File cabinets and shelves of binders covered the walls. One wheeled office chair faced two straight backed chairs. Kevin and I sat side-by-side facing Hawkins.

"The Isley Corporation hired you." After a glance at Kevin, Hawkens addressed me. "Warren Kitt has been working with the Prairie Sun and Spirits for months."

The accuracy of the rumor mill in Deadwood didn't surprise me. I'd grown up in a small town. "The buyout is a done deal. Everyone in town must know about it. Do you know why Natalie and Yvonne argued about keeping a lid on it?"

He shook his head, silently studying me.

I returned his gaze. "Is there any indication if it's suicide or murder? I see no motive for either."

His tense expression relaxed slightly. He leaned back in the chair. "Nothing obvious. Bruce and three of the other partners were well known. They've been in the area for almost five years. One, Tom

Hayden worked remotely. Tell me, exactly what are you here to investigate?"

Pam Isley already didn't like me. I wasn't going to blab. "I can't tell you that without speaking with my client."

Hawken's mouth tipped up ever so slightly. "The accountants found a problem with the records. They're trying to close the barn doors after the horse is out by sending you here. Bruce and Tom Hayden both received the buyout."

Despite his on-point guess, I kept my mask in place.

"Don't bother denying it." He waved a hand as I opened my mouth to repeat my disclaimer. "Who knew you'd been hired? How did Bruce find out? Natalie and Yvonne didn't know."

I threw my hands up. "I've been wondering about Bruce's source of information since George greeted me by name. Only Pam Isley and Warren Kitt were supposed to know. There have been e-mails back and forth, but-"

A bell rang in my brain. "Records. Computer programs."

Kevin met my gaze. An answering light sparked in his eyes. He faced Hawkens. "Yvonne was the computer wizard. Who did most of the actual work on the computer?"

The police lieutenant hesitated only briefly. "Bruce."

I ran through the scenario. "Yvonne created the program the company used, but Bruce worked it. When Warren was made CEO after the buyout, he was given a sign-on to the Prairie Sun and Spirits program."

Hawkens smiled at my logic chain. "Bruce traced the e-mails regarding your hire. Why not tell the others?"

"That could be why Natalie and Yvonne were here." As I spoke several questions appeared on my list of clues. "I was contacted two days ago. Travel plans were finalized yesterday. Bruce couldn't have known for long. What did he tell George?"

A buzzing sounded from both Kevin's and my phone.

Kevin glanced at the readout before smiling at me. "I'm surprised it took this long."

I chuckled until I saw Hawken's expression stiffen. "Our son came with us. He's at the shootout with some family friends. He's a twelve-year-old Sherlock Holmes."

Hawken grunted. "Deadwood's grapevine is alive and well."

Kevin shook his phone. "Can I assure him we're not dead?"

"I think that's safe." Hawken expression turned serious. "As for George, he saw your picture on Bruce's laptop. Bruce shut it immediately and said you'd be stopping in and to watch for you."

I leaned forward. The timing of Bruce's death was too close to my arrival not to be suspicious. "Did Bruce see anyone else today? Did he receive any calls?"

After an assessing look, the police lieutenant rubbed a hand over his face. "After speaking with George, I checked Bruce's computer history."

A jolt shot through me. "His computer wasn't locked?"

Hawken shook his head. "An officer found the laptop in a partially open desk drawer. His search history brought up a few articles regarding your cases over the last few months."

When I groaned, Kevin nudged my arm. His over-wide grin matched his teasing expression. "You're a star."

Hawken chuckled. "You have an impressive record, Ms. Belden."

"Call me Tracy. The truth is: I like to solve puzzles, and I'm good at it. That's my main qualification."

Hawken nodded. "I don't remember the last time we had a murder in Deadwood. I'm happy for any help you can give me. I don't have the records for the office phone. Bruce's cell showed multiple calls to and from Tom Hayden today."

"The other buyout." Kevin noted as his fingers tapped his thigh. "Now on the North Carolina coast."

"At last report," I muttered. When Hawken stiffened, I waved a hand at the enigmatic look in his eyes. "I've learned to verify everything."

Kevin snorted. "Miss Marple warned Belden that people lie."

Hawken snorted at the name of the fictional sleuth. "Excellent advice. Why would Tom be the person Bruce called rather than his friends in town? I'll contact the local police. If they confirm Hayden is there, they can talk with him."

"Let me know what you find out." I grimaced at another buzzing from my phone and Kevin's. "The wine cork was on the table. A third of the wine was gone. The date on the bottle was early twentieth century. Does the store carry that vintage?"

"No." Kevin's no-nonsense reply came before the lieutenant opened his mouth. My hubby's self-deprecating expression was by way of an apology. "That's a rare vintage. Sixty known bottles in the world. High five figures."

"He's a man of many talents." I explained to Hawken's stunned expression. "Raised in Europe."

"I see." The police officer recovered his composure. "You two make an interesting pair. I'll ask Natalie and Yvonne about the bottle. It and the glass will be tested. There's no sign of a visitor. The other three employees say he was alone for the last hour."

"Back door?" I asked. There had to be one for deliveries.

Hawken nodded. "He could have let someone in. Which would explain the amount of wine that's missing."

Kevin flipped a gold dollar over his knuckles. "Or he was working up his courage by enjoying the rare vintage, before..."

The lieutenant looked thoughtful. "Possible. I'll have to wait for the autopsy to confirm cause of death. It might have been a heart attack or a stroke."

We three exchanged skeptical looks.

Hawken sighed. "We'll know more once the lab completes the tests. George watched Bruce open the bottle. How would someone add poison to a closed bottle?"

"Another question to add to the list." They were piling up. "I wonder what secret is out there that's worth killing for."

7

33 Across; 8 Letters;
Clue: Where things join.
Answer: Juncture.

Marcus's exuberant energy from Monday evening hadn't abated by Tuesday morning. Our discussion of the case last evening had been interspersed with a retelling of the gunslinger shootout. At the moment, after starting the dishwasher, I was nursing a second cup of coffee.

Mrs. C had resurrected her knitting needles and yarn. Her latest project was a set of shawls for the ladies in her reading group. Since they were currently watching our two newly acquired felines, Kevin and I had popped for the yarn. The older woman eyed me with a placid expression that left me wary. "What's your next step, eh, ducks? Having a dead body in the mix complicates the matter, I'd say."

I took a sip of the dark roasted coffee, savoring the heat before nodding. "Pam and Crawford agreed with you. Neither was happy about the news. Although I don't think it's fair for them to blame me for the man's death."

Kevin sat down at the table with a carrot cake muffin in one hand and a fresh cup of coffee in the other. "Hawken should have a preliminary autopsy report today, along with the results on the wine."

"That should answer a few questions." I stared across my coffee cup while inhaling the tantalizing aroma. "My next goal is to talk with Matt Crocker. Other than Hayden, Crocker is the last main player I haven't-"

A high-pitched scream cut me off.

I gasped and jostled my cup. Fortunately, I escaped scalded fingers. "I'm assuming that's not Rabi."

"Look what I found!" Marcus's scream drug out the last word as he ran through the house. He skidded to a stop in the wide arch connecting the dining and living rooms. He held a whiteboard out for all to see. "Ta-da!"

Rabi followed him in at a far more sedate pace. He brandished a handful of markers and a small smile.

I put a hand over my heart. This boy and his melodrama might be the death of me. "Good grief."

Marcus was already clearing off the top of the bureau with Kevin's help. I cringed at the boy's hurried handling of the decorative items. Fortunately, Kevin rescued them before any damage was done.

"People! People!" Marcus threw his hands up in the air. He looked like a preacher addressing his congregation. I almost threw in a Hallelujah, but I didn't want to get in trouble. The boy child waved several colored pages in the air. "I printed off photos of the people involved."

Wanting to do my part, I headed for the kitchen. "I'll get tape for the pictures."

Moments later, Marcus faced his audience. "This is an official meeting of the Belden-Tanner Detective Agency. We are here to discuss the Case of the Purloined Profits."

"Purloined?" Kevin questioned. "That means stolen. The problem is too *much* money."

"Allegedly." Marcus pounced on Kevin's comment. "If they have extra money, it had to come from somewhere. Every one of us mentioned having too much cash makes no sense."

I frowned. "Rabi never actually said that."

My son stabbed a marker at me. "He thought it! Didn't you? And no rabble rousing in the meeting!"

Rabi nodded, a twinkle in his eye softened his stern looks.

Kevin pointedly moved his cup farther away from me. "If you can't behave, I'm moving seats."

I gently kicked his leg at his snarky comment. "Where did you get a photo of Hayden and Matt Crocker? Bruce and the two women are on social media, but the company web-site only has avatars for the five partners."

"I had to dig." Marcus busily wrote the names and titles of the principles, adding Warren Kitt to the lineup. "I found a group picture from college."

The last photo he put up showed the five partners smiling for the camera. Two dark haired men of medium build, Crocker and Hayden, bookended the group with Atherton in the middle.

"It's hard to tell them apart from here." A red lettered 'dead' was written above Bruce's photo. Under motive was written a single word: money. When I read it out loud, Marcus faced me, tossing the green marker up and down.

"Too much money led us here." The boy child narrowed his eyes. "Did you ever start a scam with extra cash on the books?"

He aimed the question at Kevin. My hubby was the only one in the room who had any real experience with high finance.

Kevin's expression turned serious. "In scams you have to flaunt money to get money. We created our own accounts. We could have any amount of cash we needed to grab the mark's attention."

"Get their attention." Discussing the facts out loud helped me see things clearer. "The Isley Corporation wouldn't have bought out the Prairie Sun and Spirits without confirming the bottom line."

The tapping of Mrs. C's knitting needles sounded in the silence. "The excess didn't present itself until after the purchase. Days, weeks afterward. The timing of the fraud and the man's death are highly suspicious."

Her words echoed in my mind. "Both events seem to be orchestrated. Who could do that?"

A spark lit up several of my synapses. I grabbed Kevin's arm, who, despite his threat, still sat beside me. "You padded your own accounts."

His eyes narrowed. His expression was watchful. "It's the easiest way to make yourself look rich."

Marcus laughed. "Have to have an inside man cook the books."

I froze as my mind's eye turned to my mental crossword puzzle which had stubbornly refused to come together. Suddenly, a portion of it rearranged and made some kind of sense.

I had one answer and an untold number of questions, but at least I was moving forward. "There's only one person who could have messed up the Prairie Sun and Spirits' books and gotten away with it. One person who forced this investigation: Warren Kitt."

Reactions varied from Kevin's agreement to Mrs. C's surprise.

"Why?" Marcus asked.

"I don't know." I'd dug heavily into the history of the five partners. I'd done some research on Kitt, but not as much. A mistake I planned to correct. "Kitt discovered the Prairie Sun and Spirits and brought it to Pam's attention. He orchestrated the background checks into the company and sat in on the negotiations for the purchase."

Mrs. C was knitting like her needles were on steroids. "Why would he throw a monkey wrench into the works after the fact?"

Kevin rapped the table. "He couldn't have known Pam would send you."

"I wasn't the target." I waved my hand at his false assumption. "His false records drew attention to the company and to the partners. That was the only foreseeable outcome of his machinations."

Marcus finished circling Kitt's photo with several red circles. "Why?"

I went back to the basics. "The five partners met while attending the University of South Dakota. Neither Hayden nor Crocker graduated. They left school to concentrate on the company."

"The University of South Dakota?" Mrs. C stiffened. "I met a lovely lady yesterday who retired from there after thirty years. I'll be happy to check for any news related to your case."

"Anything would help." I could only find so much from the official channels. "The Prairie Sun and Spirits had a steady flow of money coming in before the sale. Yet they didn't show a major profit until after the business left their hands."

"Missing money?" Rabi's eyes hardened with a cynical look.

The others perked up, but I had to shake my head.

"All the grants and loans are accounted for." I hedged my defense with a knowing look. "At least on paper. The wines and beers got good reviews. Sales were slow, but steady. Atherton and Matt were the face of the company. They made the contacts and pushed the sales of the liquor."

Kevin leaned forward, setting his elbows on the table. "They were successful enough to get Isley's attention. Yet bad enough to sell the company. In a perfect scam, you need to get the money and get out before anyone knows they've been had. If you get greedy and stay too long, it's bad news."

"People get all kind of mad about being tricked." Marcus who'd been updating the board, turned. Though his tone was serious, his eyes were puzzled. "But how does blowing grant money tie into Kitt setting up the investigation? What did he think would happen?"

Mrs. C's knitting needles had stilled. "I'm not seeing the threads tie together either, luv."

I tapped the table as I poked at my crossword puzzle I'd built for this case. "I don't have all the answers, but I'm on to something. The puzzle says so, and the puzzle never lies, well not often, maybe sometimes. But not this time."

"Very reassuring." Mrs. C raised her brows. Her concern for my mental state was apparent. Her needles slowed as she cast me a sideways glance. "What would you have of us?"

"Arrghh!" I raked my hands through my hair. "We don't have our usual contacts here."

"Just remember one thing." Marcus left the security of the whiteboard and put his hand on my shoulder. His left hand gripped the blue marker. His expression was somber. "No matter what happens, we're not leaving until Friday."

I smacked the table and glared at the boy. "Why did I expect a serious response from you?"

He spread out his hands. "I *am* serious! There's cool stuff going on all week. More gunfights, a train from the eighteen-eighties, the Crazy Horse monument, and tons more."

I sucked in a breath. I could hardly blame the boy. We'd never been in this area. Gunfights, giant carved mountains. What more could a boy want? I put on my mom hat.

"Fear not." A chuckle accompanied my words. "We'll get to all of your planned activities. We don't fly out of Rapid City until Friday. What did you have planned-"

Marcus's loud gasp over-rode my words. "This is perfect!"

"-for today?" I finished my sentence despite the boy's outburst.

Mrs. C's nimble fingers paused as the boy turned to her, his eyes full of expectation. Their gazes met. Marcus's jabbing finger almost met the older woman's eye before her wrinkled brow cleared. "Oh course! That will work out like a treat, luv. Our trip must have been meant to be."

Thankfully, Kevin and Rabi looked as confused as I felt. "What trip?"

"Tour of the Prairie Sun and Spirits Brewery," Rabi inserted.

I put a hand to my forehead. "I forgot all about that. The Crockers and Yvonne live on-site. Matt should be there. Between the five of us, we can find a way for me to question him."

My hopes rose. A little more digging into the backgrounds of everyone involved should serve me well.

Marcus clapped his hands. "Even better... they have food."

Kevin gave the boy a thumb's up before winking at me. "You may also get another shot at Natalie and Yvonne. A trifecta!"

8

37 Down; 4 Letters;
Clue: Center of operations.
Answer: Base.

After several aborted discussions on the all important topic of where and when to eat, Marcus stated that for politeness's sake we should have an early lunch at the brewery's café.

His pretense of manners fooled no one. He wanted to pursue the case.

"I have to get something." He started to put down the markers. Then, he spun on his heel and pointed them at us like weapons. His narrowed eyes glared at each of us in turn. "Nobody touch the white board."

Mrs. C saluted him with her loose knitting needle. "I'll keep them in line, ducks."

I sipped my coffee and hoped Pam Isley never learned about our methods for solving cases.

After a few minutes of rustling from the other room, my errant son returned. With a triumphant smile on his face, he held up both hands. Cords and pieces of electric equipment peeked out from his clenched fists.

"Are those earbuds?" I asked.

He walked to the table. "And a mic and a receiver. You're wearing a wire."

I took a long drink of my coffee. "Why did you bring that stuff?"

The boy heaved a long-suffering sigh. "We're on a case, T.R. As detectives, we have to be prepared. How did you solve any cases on your own?"

Kevin, resting his chin in his hand, smirked. "I've often wondered that myself."

Aiming a mock glare at my smart aleck hubby, I focused on our son. "This tape may not be admissible in court if I don't tell them they're being recorded."

"Of course, don't tell them!" Marcus looked at me as if I were crazed. "This isn't for court. This is so the rest of us can be in on the kill. Although, South Dakota is a one-party state. So, the tape will be admissible in court. You have to make them confess."

"I'll do my best, but I doubt I'll get anything crucial." I added my own long sigh. "And I get the last of Mrs. C's homemade scones. I'm also going to need more coffee."

Several minutes later, the small mic was in place, and the receiver had been tested. The range was over one hundred yards. Marcus told me with a serious expression that he had invested in quality. Of course, he'd used my money to do it.

Kevin, herding us toward the car like cats, raised a brow. "Are we eating before or after Belden accuses one of them of murder?"

"Before." Mrs. C surprised tone left no room for argument. She clutched her smaller knitting bag. "Eating afterward would appear heartless, wouldn't it? We don't want that."

"Of course not." As if accusing someone of murder wouldn't seem heartless? My sarcasm was apparently lost on the older woman and Marcus. "Besides, we don't know it was murder. It might have been suicide or natural causes."

"It wasn't natural causes." Marcus snorted. He waved his hand without turning around. "And suicide still implies guilt."

A call on my cell phone saved me from agreeing. "It's Hawken. I wonder what's he got?"

"You were right." The lieutenant's serious tone returned my greeting. "Poison. Hemlock, which can be found in any meadow or ditch in South Dakota."

"Hemlock." I repeated the poison for the benefit of my audience. "Was it in the bottle, the glass, or both?"

"Both." His voice grew heavier. "If the poison was added to the bottle first, it was premeditated. How could the killer know only Bruce would drink it? It would have been injected through the cork. That's so damaged, there's no proof of anything."

"Unless Bruce or the murderer added it to the open bottle." I stroked my lip in thought. "Any word on what Hayden and Bruce discussed on the calls?"

A thud sounded over the line. Whether from Hawken smacking the desk or his boots hitting the floor was hard to tell. "I haven't found Hayden yet."

It took me only seconds to decipher the meaning behind his harsh tone. Surprised, I looked at Marcus, who was planted right in front of me. "Are you saying Hayden's in town?"

My son's eyes grew wide.

"Yes." Disgust mixed with anger in Hawken's tone. "I got a download from his cell phone. The location shows he was in the area of the main house by the brewery during all three calls. Natalie and Yvonne didn't mention they had a visitor."

I narrowed my gaze. "How long has he been in Deadwood?"

"Off and on for several days by the look of it." Hawken's increasing ire showed in his tone.

That didn't add up in a town the size of Deadwood. "It's odd no one mentioned seeing him: in town, at the brewery. Word should have gotten should."

No immediate answer came. "I hadn't thought of that. I doubt anyone in town would recognize him by sight. His family has tour boats on the coast of North Carolina."

And the questions kept multiplying in my puzzle. "He worked remotely the entire time. He received a full buyout at the sale. *Then,* he returns to town?"

Mrs. C cocked her head to one side. "Perhaps it was a visit for old time's sake?"

The gleam in Marcus's narrowed gaze spoke differently. "Or he wanted more money to keep secrets buried."

"This story doesn't add up." Hawken's determined voice rang in my ear. "I'm headed out to talk to Hayden myself. I'll see what he had to say about his calls to Bruce."

"You might see me there." Best to warn him of my intentions. "My family and I are headed to the brewery now. We're going on a tour and having a bite to eat."

From his chuckle, Hawk evidently didn't believe in my rampant curiosity about the process of making beer. "I'll look for you. Good luck to us both."

Marcus stomped his feet in excitement. "No one mentioned Hayden was in town! That's super suspicious. Let's go!"

Mrs. C tapped my arm. She had a smug look on her face. "I'll wait until we're in the car for my news."

My interest meter shot sky high. "You spoke with your friend at the college? Did she know this group?"

"Yes, to both." The woman's British accent rang out across the warm summer air, sounding distinctly out of place on the plains of South Dakota. "Rather intriguing."

I could barely wait for the car to pull out of the driveway before I turned around and demanded the full story.

Marcus sat in the middle of the backseat with Rabi on the passenger side behind me. The man's dark eyes didn't share the sparkle of interest that covered my son's expression.

"There are several key points." Mrs. C settled her traveling knitting bag on her lap. "Mrs. Stone worked in the Young Entrepreneurs Department, which assisted students endeavoring to begin their own companies. That's where the five students coalesced as it were during their junior year."

Kevin gave a nod. "I wondered how they came together."

"Atherton had already started his business selling rare wines," the older woman went on. "Natalie and Tom Hayden were developing plans for an international computer company with Yvonne."

That tidbit caught my attention. "Natalie and Hayden."

Mrs. C sat back. Pleased with the effect of her bombshell. "The two had been an item all through college. Yvonne was dabbling her toes with no solid plans."

Marcus had followed the narrative closely. "Yvonne was dating Crocker first, right?"

"Mrs. Stone confirmed their romance." The older woman

warmed to her tale. "Bruce introduced the pair. He and Matt had spoken of a partnership. Matt had no drive to start a company. What he had, *unlike the other four*, was capitol from an upcoming Mason Family Trust fund."

She paused expectantly.

The name rang a bell, but my brain was busy organizing clues. "Are you saying Matt Crocker funded the whole thing with his inheritance?"

"Exactly." Mrs. C's grin looked like the Cheshire Cat's. Her red tipped nail stabbed the air, underlining her words. "Without Crocker's money, there would have been no Prairie Sun and Spirits."

"And no eventual buyout," I muttered.

Marcus poked Mrs. C's arm. "When did Natalie and Matt get together?"

"Shortly before his twenty-first birthday, which was when he received access to the trust." Mrs. C's cynical tone belied any romantic notion.

"Love at the first sight of his money." After delivering his judgement, Marcus laughed along with the rest of us. "Yvonne was left out in the cold."

Kevin glanced at me, a grin on his lips. "Neither of us had to worry the other was marrying for money."

"Not hardly." I chuckled. Our marriage of a few weeks ago had brought us a sliver of breathing room after Kevin moved into my and Marcus's loft apartment. That, my P.I. paychecks, and our fledgling handyman business was all that was keeping us off the streets.

I faced the front of the car. While my gaze absently watched the scenery of South Dakota stretch away to the horizon, my brain took note of the tangled relationships the group had built their company on.

"It lasted most of five years." Longer than I would have thought considering the usually volatile nature of broken romances.

I had a few more pieces for my puzzle and far more questions. However, my black-and-white grid was mostly empty. I was so preoccupied, I didn't realize we'd arrived until Kevin drove through the wooden gates of the Prairie Sun and Spirits' brewery on the city limits.

The scenic landscaping coupled with the stone patio of umbrella covered tables could have been in the English countryside. The situation would have been more enjoyable if I hadn't been hunting a killer.

As Kevin turned off the car, he faced me. "They have a bar and grill in the city. Your quarry might be there."

Why question the decision now? Was he testing me? "Hayden's hiding out. He's not in town, and neither are the others. Bruce's death is a perfect excuse for them to lay low."

Cozy looking stone worked buildings made an idyllic scene. Several tables were filled with couples or groups of friends. A soft breeze stirred the leaves. A rustic sign with an overflowing mug and an open wine bottle swung over the wide door leading to an open tavern.

My gaze lingered on the sign.

Kevin followed my line of vision. "What are you thinking?"

I shifted closer to him, though only the five of us were on the path toward the tables. "I'm thinking there's more than one way to get poison into a bottle of wine."

Marcus, who'd followed our conversation from behind us, pushed between us. "Why would the killer put the poison in the bottle after it was open?"

"To create confusion." Which I had aplenty in this case. "If the poison was only in the glass, the killer had to be present the day Bruce died. If it's in the bottle..."

Marcus jumped on my open-ended comment. "The police have to trace who had access to the bottle. All the killer had to do was wash their glass and put it back. You're good at being sneaky, T.R."

"Thanks, I think." Impatience boiled inside of me at the chance to waylay Matt Crocker and Tom Hayden. I dragged my feet. For once my stomach was over-ridden. "I'm going to the main house. I can't sit here."

Kevin kissed my cheek and stepped away. "Okay."

"That's it?" I eyed him suspiciously. "No protests about facing a possible killer alone? Just, see you later?"

He gave me his best innocent look. "You can pretend you're going off alone, and we'll pretend Rabi's not going to show up at the first sign of trouble."

I chuckled. "Deal. At least Hawken should be there as back-up."

I walked back and took the fork in the path. The others walked toward the patio. Other than a couple of signs warning me not to go this way, nothing stood in my way. High hedges and a row of trees gave way to a low built ranch house to one side and a two-story cottage on the other side. Each structure had a two-car garage.

Despite space for several cars to park, there was no sign of a police cruiser. Hawken would surely have used an official vehicle. Perhaps he'd been delayed. After a moment, I opted to try the ranch house. Rather than the front door, I slipped around the side.

The murmur of voices carried easily on the still air. Most people fail to appreciate how far a conversation can be heard, especially out in the country with no traffic sounds to mask the words. I slowed my steps.

"I didn't see him that morning!" The man's voice sounded desperate and trapped. No telling if it was Hayden or Crocker. "*You* drove in to talk to him."

"I was delayed!" Natalie's composed tone seemed a little patronizing. "How could you not warn me about the private detective? What does Pam Isley know? What does the Belden woman know?"

Not as much as I'd like.

"Stop it! Both of you!" Yvonne's guttural tone joined the fray. Her stern voice teetered on hysteria, but her command brought silence. "We have to pull ourselves together. Lieutenant Hawken will be here soon. He must have the cause of death by now. Obviously, Bruce committed suicide. None of us would have killed him."

That sounded rather naïve and certainly more hopeful than realistic. Who else knew him well enough to murder him?

"She's right." The man was obviously speaking to Natalie. "We have to stick to the same story. Bruce was depressed. He kept his feelings hidden from everyone."

"Bruce?" Yvonne's astonished tone put a lie to the story. "He's been complaining about the set up non-stop from day one."

I did a quick look around the area at my back, but saw no one. If I got caught, I could come up with an excuse. No way would this group be this forthcoming under direct questioning. Obviously, they had plenty to hide.

"We're so close to making this work." Natalie's voice broke on the last word. Unlike her competent pose yesterday, the woman had turned into a doomsayer. Her nerve was breaking. "After all this time."

Neither Kevin nor Rabi would have anything but disdain for her lack of composure in the face of a crisis. Even Marcus and Mrs. C would have faced a catastrophe with more resolve.

"Natalie!" Yvonne's voice was filled with anger. A high-pitched yelp of fear mixed with her exclamation.

A quick glance through the window showed the blonde gripping her friend's arms. I slipped out of sight rather than risk being seen.

"Listen to me." Blonde Yvonne sounded like she was about to blow a fuse. "I didn't come this far to fail now because you lost your nerve! This was your idea from the beginning. This whole thing is your fault! Both of you!"

Another quick glimpse showed the man-Matt Crocker? I couldn't tell from this angle. Crocker and Hayden's coloring was almost identical, and I only had Hayden's college photo to go on. Either way the man forced his bulk between the two women. He had to pry Yvonne away from the model-like brunette.

"We can make this work!" The man fought to maintain a calm tone.

Yvonne raked her hands through her short blond curls. "Talk to your wife. This sandcastle is built on a lie. You two talked me into this scheme. I'm not going to watch it crumble because you chicken out at the eleventh hour."

Keeping my body close to the wall, I risked another look. This was like watching a live action soap opera. What stunning revelation would come next? Fortunately, their actions had turned their faces away from where I stood.

Where was Hayden? Evidently not in the main house, but would he remain in the cabin at this crucial juncture? I looked at the other building, but saw no signs of life. Could Hayden have killed Bruce? Had Bruce, like Natalie lost his nerve within sight of the finish line?

They obviously wanted the final, ninety-day payout. However, I still wasn't sure what their secret was. If Lieutenant Hawken delayed long enough, I might learn the full story without any more detecting. I turned my attention to the unfolding drama.

Yvonne had retreated a few steps after her confrontation with Natalie.

Matt put a hand around his wife's shoulders. Cupping her face, he looked into her eyes. "We just have to get through the next few days. If we present a united front, there's nothing the police or that nosy P.I. can prove."

Natalie's tense shoulders relaxed. She wiped her hands across her face before straightening.

He shifted to get Yvonne's buy in to the new strategy.

The screech of tires on gravel had me spinning around as I tried to be one with the side of the house. No one driving up to the front could see me from here, but tell that to my rapidly beating heart.

"That must be Hawken." Natalie took the words right out of my mouth. With the windows open, the sound carried easily into the house. Fortunately for them, the police officer had arrived during a lull in the screaming match.

"Listen!" Matt's voice was low and stern. "Bruce always had issues with depression. We thought he'd put it behind him, but he talked recently of not deserving our good fortune."

Yvonne had her arms crossed over her chest. "That's true enough."

Her enigmatic words stuck in my brain. What could she mean? They'd developed their business from the ground up. They'd sold it after a full audit. Yet, Warren Kitt had stumbled on a sticking point during his work with their company. Why hadn't he exposed them? Would Pam Isley have been liable after the purchase?

I couldn't make sense of their dilemma, but I had yet another question at the top of my list.

A car door slammed out front. Footsteps crunched on the gravel.

"Fine!" Yvonne threw up her hands at Matt's dark look. "I'll go along with the party line."

"So will I." Natalie's stiff voice sounded more like her tone from yesterday. "I lost control for a minute. We can get through as we have before. It's just us now."

A spike of alarm rang in my brain. Had Hayden skipped town? Or had he had to be silenced as well? Either would explain his absence.

Hawken's sharp rap on the door echoed through the house.

"I'll get the door." Matt's voice sounded through the window.

I inched my way toward the front of the house. I'd have to time my retreat carefully. The two men exchanged greetings. Waiting until the front door closed, I made sure no one was in sight. Fortunately, the women had remained in the seating area off the kitchen. So, the man headed toward the middle of the house.

Once I hurried to the gravel drive, it was a simple matter to turn and walk up the main path. I retraced Hawken's actions and climbed the few stairs to knock on the front door.

Yvonne opened the door just wide enough to block the entry path with her body. She greeted me with a stiff, harried gaze. "Ms. Belden, Lieutenant Hawken said you might be arriving. This is obviously not a good time. We'll speak with you-"

She raised her hand in front of her body, palm out and started to back up, closing the door in my face.

I almost laughed. If she thought telling me to leave was all it took to get rid of me, she quickly learned how wrong she was. I stiff armed the door open and thrust my body forward. Stepping into the house, I followed her as she retreated into the open living room.

Fury exploded in her eyes as a red flush colored her face. All her anger at her partners found a release. "How dare you! You have no right to push your way in here. You rude, intrusive bit-!"

"Call the police!" I thrust myself into her face. Satisfaction spread through me as the words stopped her cold. I stepped back before pointing behind her. "Hawken is in your sitting room. It'll be a short trip. Better yet, let's go talk to him together."

The dark flush on her neck only increased. She was practically seething with fury, but there was nowhere for her to go. She raised a clawed hand toward my face, ready and willing to strike out at someone.

I took a deep breath and relaxed my confrontational stance. "This situation isn't of my making, Yvonne. You and your friends started this."

She stiffened. Her anger melted away as she retreated half a step. Blinking rapidly, she pressed her lips together.

"The scheme was going to unravel at some point." I paused to let the words sink in. "Reality just caught up with you. Now, shall we join the others?"

I gestured to where the others waited. She made no move, but turned willingly when I put a hand on her elbow.

Hawken nodded to me at our entrance. "I thought that would be you. I'm surprised you didn't beat me here."

I decided now wasn't the time to mention I'd been listening at the open window for ten minutes. "My family's touring the brewery. I walked up."

Matt Crocker frowned. "This is private property. There are signs posted."

"And since the Isley Corporation hired me, I walked right past them." I watched his expression darken as the words sunk in. "You work for Pam Isley now. She sent me here to find answers. She won't stop until she's satisfied. Neither will I. It's the one thing we have in common."

The three remaining members of Prairie Sun and Spirits exchanged shuttered looks. Whatever their plan had been, the scheme seemed to be turning into quicksand beneath their feet.

I took advantage of the moment to study Matt Crocker. The forty pounds he'd gained since college rounded out his face, but something jarred with my memory. My brain refused to reconcile his college picture with the man before me. However, his profile showed the same broken nose from his photos.

Hawken stood by the window I had recently vacated. "I informed Bruce's friends of the cause of death. I've started tracing the sale of the wine to see who had access to it. The rest of the staff didn't record any other visitors."

Natalie put a hand on her husband's arm. Sorrow filled her eyes. "Bruce was prone to depression in college. Achieving his dream with the brewery put him on an even keel. But when sales didn't materialize and we had to sell, his depression returned worse than ever."

I fought to keep my expression neutral. Kevin can call up any emotion at a moment's notice. For some reason, knowing the tale was spun out of thin air, I was having a harder time than usual.

"Bruce fought against selling the brewery." Yvonne's soft notes held more truth than Natalie's. "He loved the business. It was all he wanted."

She opened her mouth as if to say more, but her voice seemed to drift away into memories.

Matt rubbed a hand over his face. "I can't believe he's gone. I never thought he would end his own life."

"There are several problems with a determination of suicide." Hawken watched each of them closely. His words drew everyone's attention. "If he killed himself, why was the poison in the bottle? He drank a third of the wine. He would have had symptoms long before drinking that much."

Natalie's eye narrowed. She put a hand over her heart. "You can't think someone murdered Bruce. Everyone loved him. There's no motive for anyone to kill him."

Her anguish and confusion sounded amazingly heartfelt. I had to admit, motive was the sticking point.

"Perhaps Tom Hayden could shed light on Bruce's state of mind." Hawken spoke quietly as he lobbed his grenade into the mix. "He's the one I came to speak with."

9

14 Across; 8 Letters;
Clue: Antagonistic manner.
Answer: Attitude.

From the stunned expressions of the three partners, the lieutenant's bombshell was more than satisfying. Stunned expressions. Guilty looks. Pale faces.

Natalie, recovering first, scoffed. "Tom's not here. He's in South Carolina with his family. You must know that."

The disbelief in her final words added just the right touch.

"Tom and Bruce took cash from the buyout." Hawken confirmed. "Hayden worked remotely the entire time. However, Bruce spoke with Hayden three times yesterday, and the location on Hayden's phone puts him in town. If anyone can shed light on Bruce's state of mind, Tom Hayden can."

You could have heard a pin drop. It's a cliché for a reason. The whole house seemed to hold its breath.

"That was me. I talked to Bruce yesterday." Matt seemed to jump at his own words. Shock gleamed in his eyes. "I can't believe I used Tom's phone."

Hawken simply stared at Matt.

The other man held out his hands. An apologetic smile touched his mouth. "I can explain. Tom and I got together when I traveled to South Carolina on a business trip. I just returned two days ago. When I left, I accidentally grabbed Tom's phone. He thought he lost it. I didn't realize I had it until last night. I'm the one who called Bruce. Tom was never in town."

Parts of the convoluted explanation struck me as true, but most of it had all the substance of cotton candy. The bottom line was: they couldn't produce Tom Hayden. The man seemed to be an integral part of the on-going mystery. At least they had Matt and his inheritance. As Mrs. C had said, where would they be without *that*?

Hawken's patent disbelief mirrored my feelings. The police officer pointed at Matt. "You called Bruce three times using the wrong phone."

"I used the one in my pocket." Matt shrugged as he returned Hawken's look. "I didn't realize it was Tom's. I called and told him this morning."

On the surface, the explanation sounded almost plausible, but these three had had years to... I frowned as my thought faded away in mid-sentence. Years to... what? Lie? Perfect their story?

I stepped back, literally and figuratively. When I lose my way in creating one of my crossword puzzles, getting an overall view of the whole usually puts me back on track. A crossword puzzle has to be symmetrical from top to bottom. All the clues and answers have to fit.

This puzzle, er case had too many clues that didn't flow together. Why did Warren Kitt cook the books to draw attention to the Prairie Sun and Spirits company after the sale was complete? Then, there was the Mason name cropping up with Matt and Warren. How did that tie in? The seemingly small detail was too coincidental not to be crucial. What was this nebulous scheme these three had touched on?

"What did you and Bruce discuss?" Hawken's carefully neutral tone brought me back to present.

The doorbell's chime interrupted any possible answer.

"Who could that be?" Natalie's strident tone matched the full-blown seething anger in her eyes.

"It's probably Warren Kitt." I raised my hand, then faced Hawken. "I may have forgotten to mention it, but I asked him to come. I think he can fill in the background. I'll get the door."

I didn't want Yvonne or the others to turn him away. A minute later, I escorted the Isley manager into the room. "I think you all know each other. You've been working together for months."

Then, like a perfect hostess, I introduced Warren to Hawken. Since I had the stage, I decided to throw a match into the volatile situation. I faced the police officer while pointing to Warren. "You see, Warren cooked the books on the Prairie Sun and Spirits account just enough to draw Pam Isley's attention. He wanted to force an investigation into the partnership."

The collective gasps and outrage of the three partners was surpassed only by Warren's shock. His open mouth and wide eyes were picture perfect.

"What are you saying? I..." When he stared at me, I met his gaze with a knowing look. The tightness left his face, replaced with resignation. "How did you know? Not even the accountants caught it."

"Your expertise was your downfall." I admitted. "You're too good not to have caught financial trouble in advance of or after the sale. Abnormally high sales could only have been manufactured from the inside, *after* you had access to their books. You should have been able to find the problem or dismiss it as nothing. If Pam trusted you less, she probably would have realized that fact."

Natalie stared at Warren with a hurt expression. "We've worked together for months. If you had a problem, why did you push the sale to begin with?"

Her dismay appeared to be genuine, and probably was.

Warren simply stared at her for a moment. "There was no problem with the initial sale. My siblings live in South Dakota. They're the only family I have left, and I wanted to relocate here. To justify the move, I needed to broaden the Isley interests in the area, and your company caught my interest."

Siblings. Family. All he had left. As my brain grabbed hold of his answers, an entire square of my crossword puzzle filled with answers. I sighed in relief. It's so nice when the answers fall in place.

Yvonne stared at him in growing confusion. "She said you messed up our accounts *after* the sale. Why?"

This time Warren couldn't come up with an answer.

I answered for him. "Once he was on the inside, he couldn't ignore the fact that something was off with your bottom line. Even I had to wonder how you could have so much money coming in from grants and loans yet *not* make a profit. You were selling green energy combined with wine and beer in a tourist mecca like Deadwood. During the first audit, he may have overlooked the dichotomy because he wanted to save your company."

Surprise and confusion showed on all of their faces.

I eyed Warren before continuing. This part of the picture was in focus now. "He's been tracking Matt's career for years. Haven't you, Warren?"

While the accountant looked surprised, Matt was totally freaked out.

Hawken was as taken aback as the others. "Why would he do that?"

"A common ancestor." I kept my gaze on Warren, who looked at me as if I had a rabbit in one hand and a top hat in the other. His lack of extended family had been the final clue I needed.

Yvonne appeared equally stunned. "How can you know that?"

Now I knew how Crawford, my boss man and a former police detective of twenty-five years, felt when I said dumb things. "You realize I'm an investigator, right? It's literally in my job title."

Hawken, more subdued, folded his arms over his chest. He zeroed in on me with a laser stare. "What's the connection?"

I pointed at Matt, who'd been strangely silent during my revelation. "Matt's money came from the Mason Family Trust. It was funded from a patent on a Mason gear that was commonly used in farm engines decades ago. Money poured in. The patent was sold. The name was changed. A trust fund was set up."

"We *know* that!" Natalie stomped her foot. She looked ready to launch herself at me.

I gave her a flat stare. "Did you know Warren's sister works at the Mason Family Grocery in Mitchell, South Dakota?"

Warren gasped. "You checked my family?"

I threw my hands in the air. "I verify what people tell me during my cases. This might surprise everyone except Hawken, but people sometimes lie during criminal investigations, especially ones involving *murder*."

My heavy dose of sarcasm drew a chuckle from Hawken. None of the others had a comeback. "When I investigate six people and find the name Mason connected to two of them, it makes me suspicious."

"Enough!" Matt closed the distance between us. "You're done. I'm not listening to your TV like summation for one more second!"

"Yes, you are." Hawken moved up to confront Matt. "She's working with the police in a possible murder investigation. You can listen to her here. Or we can all go the station, and you can listen to her there."

Matt glowered, but after a momentary stare down, he retreated.

Natalie put a hand on his shoulder, and the two stepped away together.

I still wasn't sure what plan these people had hatched, but the random details I'd learned over the last few days were finally coming together. And somewhere in my brain a picture was forming. If I could just put the clues in the right place.

Hawken nodded at me. "Go on."

"The other side of the equation begins with the partnership in college." I faced the trio with a sunny smile. "Natalie, Yvonne, and the missing Tom knew each other for years. Bruce had a fledgling business. He'd recently met Matt. They planned to go into business together, using the trust fund that was coming to him on his twenty-first birthday."

"Wait." Hawken's stiff tone cut across my scenario. "The grapevine said Yvonne introduced Matt to the others."

"Not according to the administrator of the program." I didn't add my theory that the rumor had been deliberately planted to mislead. "She remembered the players. Bruce and Matt had their business papers drawn up when the other three caught wind of their plans. Isn't that right, Matt?"

The man looked shell shocked. He swallowed hard and nodded. "Yeah, I knew Bruce first. The others brought their skills to the mix. Bruce and I couldn't have done it without them."

"Sure, you could have." I scoffed at his disclaimer, ready to incite the masses. "Bruce was in business already. You had money coming to you. People have made a success with much less. The others only had technical skills, which could be found anywhere."

"That's not true!" Yvonne leapt to her feet. "We were a team! Matt was all for the idea. He wanted to be part of something. He agreed. He was ready-"

She broke off abruptly. Her body seemed to lock in place.

Matt, who'd been dumbstruck at her diatribe, shook off his stupor. "Of course, I was. It all worked out for the best."

"Did it?" I turned to Warren who'd been following the scene with rabid interest. "You know how much money they started with and the grants they received. If you add in the contracts they have and their sales, how are their profits so low?"

"Excuse me?" Natalie stepped into the ring, ready to land a few blows. "A bad economy. Supply line disruption. We made mistakes. We invested too much into infrastructure and development. We kept trying."

"No, you kept getting money." I stabbed my finger in her direction. "That was your skill. That was your dream. Not hard work."

Hawken put out his arms to separate the combatants. As Natalie took a step back, the lieutenant looked at me. "What exactly are you implying, Tracy?"

"I arrived at the house before you did. I listened outside the window while these three discussed how close they were to pulling off some... scheme." I waited for the eruption.

All three attacked me with such ferocity that I couldn't help but laugh at their communal outcry.

"Let's wrap this up, okay?" I out yelled them with a voice that would have carried to the paddocks on my parent's Kentucky horse ranch. "Because, while I might be wrong on a few details, this little meeting put the big picture in focus."

Wallace eyed me with a guarded, but hopeful look.

Hawken snapped his fingers and motioned them to silence.

I caught Wallace's attention. "Next week's final payoff is rather large I'm assuming."

He started at my words. "Pam told you that?"

"She didn't have to." My careless tone was at odds with his surprise. "If the amount wasn't sizeable, they'd be gone by now."

"Where would they go?" Wallace asked in a puzzled voice.

"Probably out of the country." I faced the three partners. "Their dream was about striking it rich. Bruce's business and Matt's money were all they needed as a cover. The only question is: How did the real Matt Crocker die?"

I locked eyes with Yvonne. She flinched instantly. As the other two drew breath to refute my claim, I held up my hand. "Don't bother. It's like Wallace cooking the books. Once you know the answer, it's obvious. I saw the resemblance between Matt and Tom in a college photo. Same height and weight. Similar coloring."

Eyeing me with matching stares, Natalie and Matt locked hands and stepped close to each other. Stiff with fear, they swallowed their ire.

I met Matt's gaze. "You had a nose job, a little work on Tom's drooping eyes. The weight gain masks your other features. Fortunately, Matt was an orphan with no close family. Your move to the other side of the state left any acquaintances behind."

"It can't be." Hawken's face went slack. He studied Matt, er, Tom with wide eyes. "All this time? Why?"

The police lieutenant rounded the sofa. Picking a pale Yvonne as the weak link, he loomed over her. "Tell me!"

His overbearing tone pointed to his fury at being played for a fool. I jumped as his tone reverberated off the walls. Yvonne looked ready to faint.

Hearing his loss of control, Hawken took a deep breath and stepped back. "Yvonne, what happened? Why did the rest of you kill the real Matt Crocker?"

"We didn't kill Matt!" Yvonne raised her tearstained face. She took a shaky gulp and swiped at her wet cheeks. "Everything was in place. Bruce and Matt were on board. Natalie and I would do the tech side. T-Tom was... is a born salesman."

Hawken looked at the other two partners. "What happened?"

Tom's jaw tightened. He met my gaze with a stare that melted in seconds. His shoulders slumped. "It was an accident. A stupid, careless curve in the road after we'd been drinking. Matt was the only one hurt. He died instantly."

"I'm confused." Warren pushed forward. "How did you get the money from the trust? The bankers would have known the real Matt Crocker."

"Matt died *before* his twenty-first birthday." My gaze swept over the trio. "The money was never his, but they were so close to their prize. They weren't going to let a little thing like a man's death stop them. Tom took his place when they met the lawyers. Tom and Matt both conveniently dropped out of college. No one saw the real Matt Crocker after that."

Tom gave a rueful chuckle before his expression drooped. "Eight days. Matt wanted us to have it. So, I changed my hair, wore glasses, grew a beard. They didn't even blink when I signed Matt's name. How did you know?"

"Little things." No need to confess how totally confused I'd been until I overheard them talking. The final answer hadn't fallen in place until I realized the elusive Tom Hayden hadn't been seen by *anyone*. Then, I saw Tom up close and my brain refused to slot him as Matt Crocker. "All the grants and loans Natalie got, yet your profits were minimal. Why would Bruce, who wanted the business more than anything, exit?"

Natalie thrust her shoulders forward. "He was so determined to leave! He could have stayed with the company."

Her absolute confusion for Bruce's choices rang in her irate tone.

I felt an odd sympathy for her blindness. "It wasn't his company. You corrupted his and Matt's dream."

Part of me wondered if Matt had tried to withdraw from the devil's bargain he'd made. Should I mention it? Could my hunch be proved five years later?

The police lieutenant straightened his shoulders. "You'll all have to come to the station for questioning."

"For what?" Tom erupted. "This is water under the bridge. Matt was an orphan. He had no family."

I stared at him, dumbfounded at the man's entitlement. "The money in the trust would have gone to the next person in the Mason family line."

"How do you know there's anyone left?" Natalie's looked down her nose at me. "Matt didn't have any relatives."

"Matt didn't have any *close* relatives." I pointed to Warren Kitt, standing in silent shock to my left. "Why do you think he followed Matt's career? Why else would he check on an obscure business in Deadwood? Why would he get involved in bailing out a seemingly failing company?"

All eyes turned toward Warren.

Yvonne's jaw dropped open. "The trust would have come to you?"

Warren blinked away his surprise. "Me and my siblings."

"It still will." I crossed my arms over my chest. "Once the courts recover the money from your accounts. Warren and his family will have what they should have been theirs all along."

Natalie licked her lips. Her shocked expression gave way to a closed, thoughtful mask. "Fine. We didn't think through the implications. We thought we were doing what Matt wanted. We can make it right."

Hawken scoffed at her words. "Bruce is still dead."

Tom put out both hands. "That wasn't us."

Yvonne rose, shaking her head also. "He was our friend. We would never hurt him."

"Are you sure?" I asked the blonde. "Yvonne, do you remember what you said to Natalie in the hall yesterday as you walked toward Bruce's office?"

Her brow furrowed, then she shook her blonde curls.

I shifted my gaze to Natalie. "You said, "Why am I here? You were going to talk to him.""

Yvonne's face tightened. Suspicion filled her eyes.

"How do you know Natalie didn't see Bruce earlier? Entering through the back door. Asking him for a glass of wine." I eyed the tight-lipped brunette. "He told you I was coming. He was going to confess everything. You three were within days of leaving with the final payment. Add in all the grant money you stashed in hidden accounts and you'd be on easy street. But not if Bruce talked."

Natalie was already shaking her head. "The whole town knows there was hemlock in the bottle and the glass. It's also well-known George saw Bruce open the wine bottle in his office that afternoon. I couldn't have poisoned him. I was just running late. I didn't get a chance to speak with Bruce."

I laughed in her face. "Then you have less imagination than I do, because I'd have poured the hemlock in the open bottle after I dosed Bruce's glass."

"How dare you?" Tom stormed toward me with his fists clenched. When Hawken stepped between us, the other man stopped. "You mouthy, good for nothing busybody. You have no right to accuse my wife of murder."

"I do." Hawken spoke in a deadly voice. "I've called for back-up to transport all of you to the station."

"Since you're getting personal." I moved forward to stand next to Hawken, still staring at Tom. "How about getting justice for Matt, too? Because I have to wonder if he didn't change his mind about including you three in the partnership with him and his friend, Bruce."

Tom's expression froze ever so slightly. "What are you talking about?"

"Who was in the car at the time of the accident?" I stabbed my finger in his face. "It wouldn't happen to have been you and Natalie alone with Matt? Or perhaps just you? Did he happen to mention that he'd changed his mind about handing over the trust money?"

Tom retreated a step. "I didn't hurt Matt. I would never do that."

"Oh, my God! How could you?" Yvonne sobbed as she stared at her partners with a dawning horror. "It was the two of them. I never understood how Matt could have been that drunk. He told me he was going home, and he *had* changed his mind. He was going to keep control of the money."

Tom moved toward her. "Yvonne, nothing happened."

The woman sent him a scathing look. "I loved Matt! We were going to be married!"

Natalie gripped her husband's arm. "You can't prove anything. I don't even remember where we buried the body."

"I do." Yvonne spoke in a chilling voice. "You two would have done anything to get your hands on that trust fund."

A wail of sirens punctuated her words.

And a quick check showed my crossword puzzle was complete. No empty squares.

~

When I rejoined my family, Marcus was jumping up and down clapping his hands. "That was so cool! We heard everything! Well, Mrs. C and I did. We were sharing the earphones."

The Belden-Tanner Detective Agency was currently driving down the road toward our home for the week.

"I have to go to the station and give a statement." I rested my hand on Kevin's shoulder as I spoke to our son. "Before I forget, Hawken wants a copy of the tape."

"Whoo-hoo!" Marcus danced in the middle of the backseat. "We get to visit the Deadwood police station! I have to get pictures, so I can e-mail them to all of our contacts."

Kevin, sitting at the wheel, looked over. "We were asked to leave the restaurant very early in your confrontation. Then, we were asked to leave the grounds."

I hid a smile behind my hand. Despite Rabi's straight face, I could only imagine Marcus's reaction to the revelations.

"All for the best really." Mrs. C sat placidly next to the twelve-year-old bundle of energy. "We listened in the comfort of the car. You put on a masterful show, ducks. Well done."

Marcus shook my shoulder. "Warren's going to get the trust fund money back, right? What about the Prairie Sun and Spirits accounts?"

The tangled web of money made my head spin. "I'm certain Warren and his brother and sister will be able to claim the money from the trust fund. If the partners stashed most of the grant and loan money they received, Warren said it could add up to millions of dollars. That was their plan all along."

Mrs. C clicked her tongue. "When Matt and Bruce objected, they were each killed in turn. Natalie and Tom are heartless tossers."

I relaxed into the seat as the tension from the faceoff eased. "Yvonne didn't know about either murder. She started talking to Hawken on the way to the police car."

Marcus chuckled in glee. "Smart woman. The one who talks first gets the best deal. Remember that, everyone."

Rabi slid the boy a sideways gaze. "We won't get caught."

I laughed along with the others.

Kevin smiled into the rearview mirror at our son. "Yvonne will do time for fraud, but if they can find Matt's body, Natalie and Tom will go away for murder."

My son clapped me on the shoulder with more force than necessary. "Good job solving the case so soon! This clears up the rest of the week for sightseeing. I have a list of like twenty places. We'll start with Mount Rushmore, the Black Hills, and every ghost town within a hundred miles."

"Oh, my word." I closed my eyes. "If that doesn't scare the ghosts out of the saloons, nothing will."

"South Dakota, here we come!" Marcus howled in the backseat.

ABOUT THE AUTHOR

Louise Foster is the author of the Crossword Puzzle Cozy Mysteries. A lifelong love of reading and solving puzzles proved to be good training when the writing bug bit. While she enjoys many genres, mysteries have always intrigued her.

Working on jigsaw puzzles and crossword puzzles with her family has also been a constant part of her life. A habit that carries through to today. In the Crossword Puzzle Mystery Series, her love of writing and solving puzzles came together.

WHEN ENEMIES COLLIDE

SAVANA JADE

PROLOGUE

Deadwood, a town where the mountains whisper secrets and every street corner has a secret. Iconic figures like Wild Bill Hickok and Calamity Jane carved their names into history. But was the quaint, historic town truly prepared for the delightful chaos that Genevieve Martel and Colton Monroe-self-proclaimed mischief makers and the reigning king and queen of pranksterdom were about to unleash?

Genevieve unpacks her suitcase, filled not just with clothes, but with an eager heart thirsting for adventure. A ten-day retreat is precisely what the doctor ordered. Work has been suffocating; and above all, what she desperately needs is a detox from Colton Monroe.

"I promise you won't regret it." Pamela barges into Genevieve's sanctuary and flops down on her bed, exuding enthusiasm.

"Oh, I know," Genevieve replies, mirroring her excitement. "This is exactly what we all need. No kids, no responsibilities—and most importantly, no men. Especially after Colton had my last date literally running out of the bar." She playfully yanks Pamela off the bed, and together they head out back where the rest of their girl gang has gathered around the fire. Nikki is pouring strawberry margaritas from a pitcher into the two glasses, that were waiting for them while the aroma of the fire fills the air.

Yep, just what I need, Genevieve thinks to herself.

1

As dawn breaks over the peaks of Deadwood, the town awakens, casting long shadows along its storied streets. Soon, those antiqued pathways will buzz with the footsteps of residents and curious tourists alike. The girls have decided to kick off their adventure with an early breakfast and a splash of window shopping.

"I can't believe you brought your daily planner," Nikki teases, giving Genevieve's notebook a playful slap.

"And you didn't?" Genevieve counters, a smirk on her lips. All four women—Genevieve, Nikki, and Pamela, who are high school teachers, with Amber as the resident nurse—have been the best of friends since the first grade. Inseparable is an understatement. "It's not like I plan on bringing it out and about."

"Well, yeah. But it's just for the drive," Nikki defends her planner like it's a treasured artifact.

Genevieve rolls her eyes. "I swear, if I see that planner make an appearance at any point during this trip, you owe me big time." After years of friendship, Nikki wisely chooses silence, knowing the queen of mischief sticks to her word.

"Alright, kids. Enough of that," Amber scolds gently, taking control of the situation. "What about this place?" she asks, expertly maneuvering the car into a parking stall.

"Sure," the ladies chime in unison, exchanging glances that clearly indicated they have no choice in the matter.

~

"Oh my God, this French toast is divine!" Genevieve rolls her eyes and moans, savoring the delightful bite.

"One might think you just had an orgasm," a voice interrupts, halting her in mid-revelation.

"Please tell me I'm imagining things," she mutters, swallowing hard and dropping her fork in shock. Pamela's eyes widen in terror, Nikki's jaw drops as she looks over Genevieve's shoulder, and Amber also freezes mid-bite. "From the looks of it..."

"What the hell are you doing here?" Colton interjects, cutting Genevieve off before she can catch her breath. Summoning all her composure, she turns slightly, squaring her shoulders defiantly.

"The real question is—what are you doing here?" she mirrors his question, trying to regain control of the conversation. "Did you follow us?"

"Follow you?" Colton chuckles, squeezing into the booth next to her, further heightening her annoyance. "Sweetheart, we were here first."

"Oh my God, are you two?" She tries to shove him off the edge of the booth, but he's as solid as a rock. "Get away!" she grunts. "Go back to where you are from and leave me alone. You're ruining my vacation!"

"Your presence is ruining mine," he replies nonchalantly, snatching her fork and jabbing at her French toast. "Not bad," he mutters, chewing a piece of her breakfast. "I'm here with Tommy, Brad, and Kellen—bachelor party vibes."

"For how long?" Pam inquires, her curiosity piqued. "And how did we not know about this?" When Colton shrugs, she presses further. "Does Tommy know we're here?" As if summoned, Nikki suddenly spots her fiancé across the room, excusing herself to join him.

"He does now." Amber shrugs with a hint of mischief.

"Does anyone realize that this jackwad is about to ruin my entire vacation?" Genevieve gestures dramatically in his direction.

"How long are you here for?" Amber continues, clearly unfazed by the brewing tension.

"Ten days, same as you," he responds, stabbing another piece of French toast. "This is pretty damn good," he adds, and Genevieve feels her blood begin to boil.

"Am I the only one who thinks this was a planned vacation? I mean really, he knows how long we're here for and everything."

"Wanna bite?" he grins, and with all her might, she shoves him as hard as she can. He lands hard on the floor, looking more surprised than hurt, impressed she had the strength to move him. "Well," he observes, "that was rude."

"Oh, I haven't even started," she retorts, a fierce glint in her eye.

This was merely the beginning.

The tour bus rattled along the bumpy road from Deadwood to Black Hills, its leather seats filled with laughter and playful banter. Genevieve sat in the front, her mischievous mind bubbling over with ideas as the bus swayed gently from side to side. To her left, Pamela, Amber, and Nikki engaged in a spirited discussion about the best places to grab lunch in the Black Hills, but Genevieve's attention was elsewhere.

In the back, Colton lounged with his friends Tommy, Brad, and Kellen, a smug grin plastered on his face. Colton had been particularly obnoxious after winning their last prank battle—a classic 'whoopee cushion' under the 'cushion' of her seat that had made Genevieve squeal like a startled goose. She was determined to reclaim her title as the reigning champion of pranks, and today would be no different.

"Okay, ladies," Genevieve leaned closer to her friends, lowering her voice dramatically as if sharing state secrets. "Here's the plan. We're going to prank Colton so spectacularly that he won't know what hit him."

"Can we please just enjoy this trip without getting kicked off the bus?" Tommy interjected from the back, his eyes pleading. The engaged couple were always trying to channel the chaos of their friends into something resembling sanity. "You two could seriously ruin everything."

"Ohhh, don't be such a spoilsport!" Genevieve shot back, her eyes twinkling with mischief. "This is precisely why we are here. To break the monotony of life and have a little fun!"

Nikki chimed in, "Last time you pranked him, he retaliated by dyeing your hair pink in the middle of the night!"

"It was magenta," Genevieve corrected, frowning in mock annoyance. "And it was fabulous."

"Yeah, until you had to explain to your boss why you looked like a cotton candy machine exploded on your head," Pamela chuckled, flipping her hair over her shoulder.

Colton's laughter erupted from the back, ringing out louder than the chatter in the front. He caught Genevieve's eye and raised an eyebrow, his expression a mix of challenge and amusement. "What are you plotting, Genny? Maybe just a quiet ride to enjoy the beauty of the Black Hills?" he taunted, leaning back in his seat like a king on a throne.

Genevieve's heart raced with competitive spirit. "I'll show you beauty," she countered, her eyes narrowing playfully. "Just wait until we stop for a photo op."

"See! This is what I'm talking about," Tommy groaned, slumping back in his seat. "Just try to keep it civil!"

But before anyone could react, Genevieve had already concocted her brilliant plan. When they reached the iconic Crazy Horse Memorial, the perfect spot for a photo op, she very carefully, snuck a rubber chicken under her shirt. It was juvenile, it was silly, and it would be spectacular. To prevent premature squaking, she had to make sure no one would bump into her on that side.

As they arrived, the landscape opened before them. The majestic stone face loomed in the distance, and excitement filled the air. Genevieve seized her moment, nudging her friends as they disembarked. "Alright, ladies, it's time to put the plan in action."

"Just to be clear, we are not involved in this, right?" Nikki asked, eyeing Genevieve warily. "I don't want to end up on the receiving end of Colton's wrath."

"Relax! You'll just be the innocent bystanders," Genevieve assured her, her voice dripping with confidence. "I'll do the dirty work. I always do. Besides, this is completely innocent."

She made her way toward Colton, who was already setting up his camera with the ease of someone who had spent far too many weekends indulging in photography. His back is turned, and the rubber chicken is tucked safely under her arm, a prize ready to be unleashed.

"Hey, Colton!" she called, feigning her sweetest tone, the kind that could convince a toddler to eat broccoli. "Do you want a picture with me?"

"Not if you're going to make me wear that hideous hat again!" he shot back playfully, turning his head just enough to see her smiling face. "You've already haunted my dreams with that thing."

Genevieve pouted dramatically. "But think of the Instagram likes!"

"Ah, fine! Just this once," he relented, shaking his head but unable to hide his amusement.

As he stepped away from his camera, Genevieve dove into action, by placing a sticker on the lens as quick as she could. She secured the chicken under her arm, giggling to herself as she rejoined her friends, her heart racing.

"Do you think he'll notice?" Amber asked, a giggle escaping her lips.

"Not until he tries to take a picture," Genevieve said, already anticipating the moment of realization that would send them all into hysterics.

Moments later, Colton positioned himself, lens ready, and aimed at the girls. "Say cheese!" he called, a wide grin on his face.

Genevieve held her breath, waiting. As Colton clicked the shutter, the unmistakable noise of the rubber chicken's squawk filled the air, causing him to freeze mid-laugh.

"Where'd you get that?" he exclaimed, his eyes narrowing with mock indignation as he recognized the telltale squeak.

Confusion washed over his face, and Genevieve erupted with laughter, all her friends joining in as Colton stood there, utterly baffled.

"Oh, come on! You must admit, it's brilliant!" she replied, ignoring his question, tears of laughter glistening in her eyes. "I mean, who doesn't want the sound of a rubber chicken when they press the button in front of Crazy Horse?" When he returns to his camera to view the picture on the screen, he notices a sticker silhouette of a middle finger on the lens. Nodding, because he got duped, twice, his wicked smile grows on his face.

"Okay." His smirk couldn't hide the admiration behind his playful annoyance. "This means war." She wouldn't expect anything less. Especially since his presence ruined her vacation already.

As the laughter echoed across the hills, Tommy sighed in resignation. "And here we go again," he said, rolling his eyes, while Nikki grinned, caught up in the chaos. "I hope you're ready for the fallout, Genevieve!"

With pranks on the horizon and the landscape sprawling ahead, the day promised to be anything but dull. As the sun began to dip low in the sky, Genevieve and Colton's playful rivalry already set the tone for another round of hilarity, laughter, and love in the heart of the Black Hills.

2

Genevieve poked her head out of her bedroom door, her heart racing with anticipation. Nikki invited the guys to the cabin which she advised would be a horrible idea. Colton was plotting his next move. On her turf no less.

"You're looking a bit nervous there, Gen. Planning your next move? Or just trying to avoid Colton?" Tommy teased, rocking on the porch, his arm around Nikki.

"Shut up, Tommy. It's called strategy," she snapped. "Besides, I have every right to be cautious. We all know Colton's a revenge artist."

Nikki, who was scrolling social media stops to chime in. "I can't wait to see what he comes up with. I mean... He could be plotting something with a goat or glitter bombs."

"No more glitter bombs," Genevieve replied with an exaggerated eye roll, the threat of a glitter bomb sent shivers down her spine. "Can you imagine explaining glitter everywhere in this cabin? I mean, it's one thing doing it at home, but here. Besides, we both agreed to not use glitter anymore."

Meanwhile, Kellen and Colton were sitting at the table with Pam and Amber. Colton, pacing back and forth plotting his next move.

"I can't believe she just pranked me like that. She won't get away with it." He turns to pace back to his starting point. "I have to hit her where it hurts."

Kellen, the most neutral of the bunch, sits back in his chair and suggests. "What about her obsession with that overpriced face cream she has?" With all their group trips to the mall, everyone knows how passionate she is about her skin care.

"I could replace it with something."

"Like mayo or something," Pam chimes in without even realizing she gave them ammunition.

"Pamela." Amber sounds shocked. "What are you doing? Whose side are you on?" Pam shrugs.

"I mean, when in Rome. If they're going to prank each other while we're all on vacation, might as well make it entertaining."

"Perfect!" Colton exclaims. "This is going to be epic." He turns to the table. "Now, all I need is a distraction."

"Don't look at me." Brad waves his hands. "Nope. I want nothing to do with this."

"You're no fun."

"Do you remember the last time you two sucked me in it? I ended up face-planting in freshly laid concrete."

Genevieve enters the kitchen. "That was not my fault." She glances at her nemesis. "It was his. You're still here?" she asks, knowing full well that he won't leave until the rest of the guys do.

"Where else would I be?"

"I don't know," she replies, filling a glass of water. "I'd thought you'd be chasing a chicken or something."

"Real funny, Genny." Colton steps up to her and becomes unbelievably close, clearly putting her in an uncomfortable position as he pins her to the counter. "Careful, maybe I'll get my cock out," he teases causing Genevieve's face to flush while Kellen and Pam begin laughing.

"Is that supposed to scare me?" She does her best to hold her ground.

"Fuck around and find out." He winks and heads out of the room.

~

Colton leans against the bar anticipating Genevieve's arrival. He sent her a text a while ago. Of course, at first, she didn't believe him, which knowing their history, is understandable. That's what Pam told Kellen anyway. The neon light flickers just over the swinging door.

"Dude, she's coming, are you ready?" Kellen nods at the side entrance of the bar. Colton's eyes dart towards the entrance.

He straightened, smirking at the thought of his plan, thankfully getting the idea from his friends this time. "Absolutely. Just remember, you're the distraction. You forgot your phone and you have to go get it. And Pam is going to take you."

Kellen rolls his eyes. "Right. Because I'm the sidekick in this romantic comedy we call your life. Let's just hope she doesn't take it out on me."

"What do you mean romantic?" Kellen shakes his head, brushing his question off.

As Genevieve walks in, her hair glistens under the bar's low lights. Colton felt a flutter in his stomach, filled with dread and excitement combined. Throughout the years, she hadn't changed all that much. She used to be the little girl whose pigtails he would pull and torment. She has always been a challenge. Both ending up in the principal's office or grounded because they both would get caught at the same time. Things shifted during high school for Colton. When he died her hair pink and she sported it like it was meant to be, he couldn't stop the slight attraction he felt for her. And as the years have gone by, the attraction has grown.

Genevieve, with her girlfriends in tow, looks for her rival. When she sees him, he's looking straight at her, smiling. She flushes at the sight of him with the memory of his promise from earlier. His smile, when it's genuine, has always done things to her in ways she wouldn't ever admit. Nikki steps past the mischievous duo right into Tommy's arms.

"What took you so long?" Colton asks.

"We were in the hot tub when you texted. I didn't believe you at first. Still don't if you want the truth," she admits when the bartender places a captain and coke in front of her. "Mine?" she asks.

"Yours," Colton confirms. "I told him you guys were coming. He assumed you were the one."

"Did you do something to it?"

"Genny. You saw him bring it to you." He huffs when she still doesn't touch it. "Here." He takes the glass and takes a drink of it to prove that it isn't tainted. "Better?"

"Yes." She takes the glass and takes a sip. "Thank you."

Kellen walks up and pats Colton on the shoulder. "Sorry, I left my phone at the hotel. Pam is going to take me to get it." Colton nods. "We'll be back soon." He discreetly gives Colton a wink as he and Pamela walk out of the bar.

Colton orders another beer and excuses himself to use the restroom, and this is a perfect chance for Genevieve to plan her next attack. She takes her darkest shade of lipstick and runs it along the rim of the bottle the bartended just delivered.

~

"I hate him." She tosses her brand-new jar of face cream in the garbage. "I absolutely hate him." Yesterday, she noticed that the cream felt a little greasy and it didn't smell very well. It wasn't until her face started to get itchy when the cat was out of the bag. Pam admitted helping Kellen get into the room to put some strange oil in the cream. Evidently, there was some sort of chemical reaction with whatever the cream was made of and the oils he put in it. Kellen, feeling horrible, admitted that he couldn't find fish oil, and ended up with whatever he could find.

"I just don't know why you don't just jump his bones already." Nikki sighs. Her eyes double in size when she realizes she said that statement out loud. "What?"

"No." Genevieve cringes. "Just, no."

"Whatever." Nikki shrugs and finishes her coffee. "Will you be ready soon? Tommy wanted to take a tour of the brothel today."

"So now our entire vacation revolves around the guys?" Amber asks.

"They're paying for it." It's apparent Nikki wants to spend every second with Tommy.

"Do I have to go?" Genevieve asks.

"What? Why?"

"That's an easy answer," Genevieve says. "Revenge."

3

The sun was setting over Deadwood, casting shadows across the uneven streets, where the whispers of the past mingled with the laughter of friends looking for a thrill. The girls and guys are walking along the sidewalk headed to the historic brothel.

Genevieve, with her loose curls tumbling over her shoulders, even though she asked if she could skip the tour, was super excited to be going inside the brothel, not just for the history, but for the perfect stage to unleash her latest prank on Colton.

"Are you sure this is a good idea?" Tommy asked, adjusting his glasses as he eyed the creaky old building that loomed before them like a reluctant ghost. "I mean, it's a brothel..."

"Relax, it's just a tour." Genevieve said, feigning innocence. "Besides, it's educational. We'll learn about the history of... uh... companionship." Her eyes sparkled mischievously as she turned to Colton, who was walking behind her, his confidence radiating like a warm glow.

"Let's just see if you can handle it," Colton smirked, leaning closer as if to share a secret. "I mean, you're only here for the historical context, right?" He winked, and Genevieve felt her heart flutter, just as the plans for her prank began to crystallize.

Inside the brothel, the air was thick with the scent of old wood and something sweetly floral. Nikki and Tommy walked ahead, holding hands, while Kellen and Amber bickered playfully over who should lead the tour. Pam hung back, rolling her eyes at their antics, but even she could not suppress her smile.

"Welcome to Pam's Purple Door," the tour guide chimed, an exaggerated smile plastered on her face, clearly well-rehearsed. "This establishment has been at the heart of Deadwood since the gold rush. Behind these doors, secrets, laughter, and—ahem, a lot of history, unfold."

Genevieve nudged Colton, her heart racing. "I bet I can make you believe in ghosts tonight," she whispered, her voice low and teasing.

Colton raised an eyebrow, intrigued. "You think you can scare me, Genevieve? I'm not that easily spooked." He returned her playful tone with a cocky grin, leaning back slightly. "But if you want to try, I'll just have to up my game."

"Challenge accepted," she replied, her eyes sparkling with mischief.

As they made their way through the dimly lit rooms filled with vintage decor and the echoes of stories long past, Genevieve began to plot. She whispered her plan to Nikki, who quickly stifled a giggle. The fact that everyone was already on edge made it the perfect backdrop for a little ghostly trick.

They reached the parlor, where the tour guide shared tales of the ladies who entertained during the town's rowdy days. Genevieve took a deep breath and slipped away from the group, her heart racing with anticipation. She found a dusty corner and grabbed an old lace shawl, draping it over her shoulders.

Just as she was about to execute her plan, she caught sight of Colton, who was leaning against a wall, scrolling through his phone, utterly oblivious. A mischievous grin spread across her face. This would be fun.

She crept back toward the group, moving silently like a cat in the night. With her shawl swirling around her, she approached from behind, her voice low and ghostly. "Colton..."

He turned, eyes wide. "What the—"

"Beware!" she chimed, her voice barely above a whisper, as she floated the shawl just inches from his face. "I am the spirit of the

Purple Door, here to haunt the souls of those who dare to mock my home!"

The reactions were instantaneous. Kellen and Amber burst into laughter, Tommy clutched Nikki, who was giggling uncontrollably, and even Pam had to cover her mouth to stifle a laugh. Colton, however, had a momentary look of shock that quickly morphed into an amused grin.

"Nice try, Genevieve," he said, rolling his eyes but clearly entertained. "But you'll have to do better than that to scare me."

"Oh, I will!" Genevieve shot back; her confidence reinvigorated. "You just wait."

Outside, the group fell into a series of playful banter over who had the best ghost story, and Colton, still riding the high of Genevieve's prank, decided it was time for a little revenge. "Alright, everyone, gather around," he said, his voice dripping with mock seriousness. "Let me tell you about a legend. They say if you call the name of the ghost three times, they'll appear."

Genevieve eyed him suspiciously, her heart racing. "You wouldn't dare."

"Genevieve, Genevieve, Genevieve..." he called, his voice booming, and suddenly, everyone's laughter stopped. They turned to see what would happen next.

With perfect timing, the tour guide popped out from behind a door, holding a fake skull and screaming, "Boo!"

The shriek echoed through the hall, and Genevieve jumped, clutching her chest. Everyone erupted into laughter, and Colton doubled over, his laughter infectious.

"You jerk!" she exclaimed, but she couldn't help but laugh too. "You got me!"

"Game on, Genevieve," he said, winking at her. "Next time, I'll be ready."

As the night wore on, the pranking escalated, and what had begun as a simple tour turned into a delightful contest of one-upmanship. The air was charged with playful tension, teasing glances, and lingering touches that made Genevieve's heart race.

When the tour concluded, and they were back outside under the stars, Genevieve felt a pull towards Colton, an attraction blooming amidst the laughter and pranks. She leaned in closer, teasingly whispering, "Just wait until the next time we're in a haunted house—this is far from over."

Colton grinned, his eyes sparkling with challenge and mirth. "I wouldn't expect anything less."

And as they stood together, the night rich with promise, Genevieve knew that whatever came next, it would be filled with laughter, mischief, and possibly even a little bit of romance.

4

Genevieve stood at the edge of Whitewood Creek. The gentle breeze rustling her hair as she surveyed the scene with a mischievous glint in her eyes. Colton, the unsuspecting prankster in the game of their flirtatious rivalry, was balancing on a rock nearby, trying to look like a modern-day Tarzan. Today is supposed to be a day of fishing. Unfortunately, the only two left to catch a fish are Genevieve and Colton. They would catch one if they would put as much effort in it like they do trying to torture one another.

"Careful, Colton! You might actually hurt yourself trying to impress me!" Genevieve teased, arms crossed and a smirk dancing on her lips.

Colton turned and snorted, one eyebrow raised, and shot her a playful grin. "Impress you? Please! I'd never fall for someone who spends their weekends throwing rocks at my head."

"Those were just friendly warnings!" she shot back, suppressing a laugh. "I was trying to save you from falling off that rock."

"Just admit it, you're secretly hoping to see me plunge into the creek," he quipped, leaning back just a little too far in a show of bravado.

She raised an eyebrow, a spark of mischief igniting in her chest. "Maybe I was hoping a little splash might cool your overheated ego."

"Overheated? Please," he laughed, taking another bold step out onto the precarious stone formation. "I'm as cool as—"

Before he could finish his sentence, Genevieve made her move. With a swift flick of her wrist, she threw a small pebble straight at his foot. Colton yelped and lost his balance, arms flailing as he tried to regain control.

"Whoa! Genny!" he shouted, half-terrified and half-amused.

"Oops, my bad!" she called out, biting her lip to suppress her laughter as she watched him teeter on the brink of disaster.

With a dramatic wave, Colton tipped backward. "This is your fault!" he yelled as he plummeted into the creek with an impressive splash that sent water flying in all directions.

Genevieve doubled over, laughter bubbling out of her, the sound bright and carefree. "Oh my God, Colton!" she gasped between fits of giggles, her hands on her knees.

Emerging from the water, Colton wiped his face and shot her a mock scowl, his hair sticking to his forehead like a wet mop. "You'll pay for this, you know," he said, his voice half-strangled by the creek water.

"Oh really?" she replied, trying to sound playful but unable to contain her amusement. "What are you going to do? Throw a rock at my head?"

"Consider this a challenge," he exclaimed, splashing water in her direction.

Before she knew it, Genevieve leaped back, her laughter echoing through the air. "You think you can scare me with a little creek water? Please!"

"Little?" Colton scoffed, his heart racing not just from the chill of the water but from the thrill of the chase. "That was a tidal wave!"

"Then let's see how you handle a splashdown round two!" Genevieve declared, running toward the creek, her feet barely touching the ground as she lunged into the water.

With another shriek of delight, she dove in, sending a wave of cool water crashing over Colton, who had barely managed to recover from the first assault. He sputtered, laughing despite himself, and lunged toward her, attempting to pull her under.

"You are so going to regret this!" Colton declared, his eyes sparkling with mischief.

"Regret, what?" Genevieve retorted, her breath hitching in the thrill of the moment. "This is the best fun I've had in ages!"

With that, the two found themselves locked in a playful water fight, splashing and laughing, the creek becoming the stage for their romantic comedy. Colton lunged forward, capturing Genevieve's waist and pulling her closer. "Alright, you got me," he said, panting lightly, the distance between them shrinking. "But now we're even."

"Even? Not a chance," she replied, her voice softer now, their laughter fading as they locked eyes. The water swirled around them, reflecting the golden light of the setting sun, and for a moment, everything else faded away.

"Then I suppose I will have to find a way to get you back," he whispered playfully, inches from her face. The air crackled with tension; the laughter replaced with a charged silence as both of them realized how close they were in that moment.

"Well," Genevieve said, heart racing, "I look forward to seeing what you come up with. Just don't try to drown me!"

With a teasing smile, she waded back, splashing him one last time before she turned to head toward the bank. Colton watched her—a blend of admiration, attraction, and the thrill of mischief swirling in his chest.

"Just you wait, Genevieve," he called out, already plotting his next move. "This isn't over yet."

And as the sun dipped below the horizon, a sense of undeniable chemistry lingered in the air, echoing the promise of more pranks, laughs, and perhaps something deeper, waiting just beneath the surface.

5

After the group made their way back to the girls' cabin, laughter bounced off the trees as Genevieve recounted her latest escapade, the prank she'd pulled on Colton after their tour of the old brothel.

She'd swapped his drink with a particularly pungent herbal tea, leaving him gagging as he tried to impress a couple of female tourists. The memory made her giggle, and the sound blended perfectly with the rustling leaves of the breeze from the gentle wind.

"Just wait until Colton gets a taste of his own medicine," she said, her eyes glinting mischievously as they approached the cabin. "He thinks he can prank me and get away with it? Not on my watch!"

Inside the cabin, the ambiance was cozy, scented candles flickering on the dining table while the aroma of homemade pasta filled the air. Pam and Amber were setting out plates, while Kellen and Brad debated the best strategy for a game of charades later that evening. Meanwhile, Nikki and Tommy had retreated to the bedroom to 'change'—which everyone knew was code for a prolonged debate over what to wear.

"Don't take too long!" Genevieve called playfully. "We want you to join the fun, not take it hostage!"

Kellen laughed, then shot a sideways glance at Genevieve. "You've caused enough chaos for one day, G. Maybe you should just sit back and relax."

But Genevieve wasn't done yet. She edged over to the sliding glass door that led to the deck, peeking outside toward the hot tub where she had seen Colton last. "Where's Colton? He should be in there, soaking his troubles away," she mused aloud, her brow furrowing slightly.

Just then, Tommy and Nikki emerged from the bedroom, each adorned in matching shorts and shirts—an endearing sight that made everyone snicker. "We're ready for fun! What did we miss?" Nikki asked, her hair damp from their quick change.

"Not much, just plotting revenge on Colton," Genevieve replied, trying to keep her smirk hidden.

"Wait, is he still in the hot tub?" Tommy raised an eyebrow, exchanging a knowing glance with Nikki.

"I don't think so," Genevieve said, biting her lip to suppress her excitement. "We should check!"

Nikki, sensing the energy in the air, grabbed Tommy's arm. "Let's go! I want to see whatever mischief you're up to."

The group, with Genevieve leading the way, slipped out onto the deck. The warm evening air embraced them as they stepped toward the bubbling jacuzzi. To their surprise, it was empty.

"Where did he go?" Genevieve pouted, her eyes scanning the area. Just then, a chuckle echoed from behind the trees.

"Over here!" Colton's voice called out, sounding innocent yet mischievous.

Genevieve narrowed her eyes, instantly feeling a surge of adrenaline. "What are you up to, Colton?" she shouted back, a playful challenge lacing her tone.

"Just making sure the hot tub is safe for you," Colton replied, stepping into view, his perfectly tousled hair glistening from the twinkling patio lights. He wore a towel draped over his shoulders, and Genevieve's breath caught at the sight of his confident grin.

"Safe? Or should we be worried?" Genevieve teased, stepping closer.

"Depends on how good you are at swimming," he shot back with a wink, leaning casually against a tree as if he owned the place.

Genevieve felt her cheeks flush slightly, but her competitive spirit kicked in. "Oh, I can swim just fine," she shot back, crossing her arms playfully. "But can you handle a little prank?"

Before Colton could respond, Genevieve darted back to the hot tub and scooped up a handful of water, splashing it in his direction. He quickly dodged, laughing heartily as the water droplets caught the last rays of sun and shimmered like diamonds.

"Is that how you want to play?" Colton yelled, feigning shock. "You've just signed your own prank warrant, Genevieve!"

In an instant, Colton was charging toward her, his eyes alight with the thrill of the chase. Genevieve squealed and dashed away, her laughter ringing through the trees.

"Get her, Colton!" Kellen cheered, his enthusiasm fueling the friendly rivalry. Brad, Pam, Nikki, and Tommy joined in the chase, urging Colton on as he closed the distance.

Genevieve managed to outmaneuver him, weaving around the bushes and dodging the deck chairs, but she could feel Colton's presence looming behind her, calculating, ready to pounce.

Just when she thought she had lost him in the cover of the trees, she stopped short. Colton appeared right in front of her, his chest heaving gently as he grasped her shoulders, both of them panting from the exertion.

"Gotcha," he whispered, his eyes locking onto hers. The world around them melted away, leaving just the two of them standing in a bubble of laughter, anticipation, and undeniable chemistry.

"Okay, okay! You win!" Genevieve laughed, unable to resist the magnetic pull of his gaze.

"Not yet." Colton grinned, then swiftly leaned in, distracting her while one of reaching behind his back where a surprise water balloon was tucked in his waistband. With a sudden flick of his wrist, he sent it flying towards Genevieve.

She squealed instantly, ducking just in time, but the balloon splashed perfectly into the hot tub, the pop echoing like a cannon. Water sprayed everywhere, and amidst their shared laughter, Genevieve caught sight of their other friends breaking into fits of giggles on the sidelines.

"Prank war initiated," she declared, her heart racing at the thrill of it all. "Just remember, you started it!"

As the evening sky deepened into twilight, the group erupted into a playful battle of splashes and laughter, each moment bringing Genevieve and Colton closer together, the foundation of their budding romance solidifying amidst the light-hearted chaos.

Maybe, just maybe, this would be the summer that changed everything.

6

The following night, the air was thick with the aroma of mischief as the steam rose from the bubbling hot tub, swirling around Colton and Genevieve like a warm blanket. The moon hung low in the sky, casting a silver glow on the cabin they had rented for the weekend. Inside, their friends Nikki and Tommy had long succumbed to sleep, while Amber, Pam, Kellen, and Brad had also retreated to their respective rooms after yet another round of laughter and chaos.

Genevieve rested her head against the side of the tub, her dark hair fanning out like a halo around her. "You know, I thought that prank would be funny," she said, a mischievous grin dancing on her lips. "But I didn't think it would smell *that* bad."

Colton chuckled, leaning back against the opposite edge of the hot tub, the warm water lapping at his sides. "You stole Brad's room key and unleashed a fart bomb apocalypse. Of course, it was going to be a disaster. But hey, it's all in good fun." He gave her a sideways glance, his eyes glinting with attraction. "And now we're stuck here while they all complain about the smell."

Genevieve smirked, the corners of her mouth twitching. "I'd say it was worth it. Besides, now we have the hot tub all to ourselves. Just you and me, with no one to interrupt."

"True," Colton replied, a hint of challenge in his tone. "But what do we do about this truce we were supposed to discuss? You know, after our *epic* prank war this week?"

"Truce? What truce?" Genevieve teased, poking her foot against his leg, sending ripples through the water. "I thought we were just getting started."

"Okay, okay." Colton laughed, splashing her lightly in retaliation. "We can agree on one thing: you're a menace, and I'm the only one brave enough to face you alone."

"Brave or foolish?" she shot back, tilting her head, her gaze locking onto his. The tension between them simmered like the hot water around them.

He took a deep breath, letting the warmth envelop him. "Maybe a little bit of both."

As if on cue, Genevieve leaned forward, the water lapping at her shoulders, and grabbed at the nearby bottle of wine. "How about we celebrate our remaining hours of freedom with a drink?"

"Drink and discuss terms?" Colton raised an eyebrow, accepting the glass she offered him. "That could lead to even more trouble."

"Exactly." She clinked her glass against his with a playful smirk before taking a sip, the alcohol warming her from the inside out.

The light laughter faded into a comfortable silence, the kind that buzzed with unspoken words. Colton watched Genevieve, captivated by the way the moonlight illuminated her features, the way her lips curled into a smile as she took another sip of her drink. When they were in each other's presence, neither one had to worry about the other.

"Can I ask you something?" Colton said, his voice low, the alcohol loosening his resolve.

"Sure, shoot," she replied, tilting her head toward him, her eyes sparkling with curiosity.

"Why do we always end up at each other's throats, even when we're having fun?"

Genevieve hesitated, her gaze drifting away. "I think it's because we're both too stubborn to admit that maybe we like each other. It's more fun to fight than to acknowledge that there's actually something more."

"That's a strong possibility," Colton admitted, feeling the weight of her words. The unspoken chemistry crackled between them like the hot water swirling around. He floated across the water and leaned closer, their faces inches apart. "What if we stopped fighting? Just for tonight."

In one bold move, Genevieve bent forward, her lips brushing against his in a tentative kiss. It was soft, electric, and everything else melted away. Colton responded instinctively, deepening the kiss, their surroundings fading into the background.

The taste of wine lingered on their lips as the heat of the moment took over. "Oh wow," he breathed, pulling back slightly to catch his breath. "That escalated quickly."

"Maybe we should have done that sooner," Genevieve replied, her cheeks flushed, a giggle escaping her lips.

"Maybe," he echoed, the playfulness in the air shifting into something more serious, more intimate.

"You know," she started, her voice low and teasing, "I bet we could create a whole new kind of trouble in here."

Colton raised an eyebrow, the intrigue lighting a fire in his belly. "What did you have in mind?"

"Let's just say, I have a feeling this hot tub can handle more than just bubbles," she whispered, her eyes glinting with mischief.

With a grin, he pulled her against him, the warmth of the water swirling around them as they surrendered to the heady mix of attraction and laughter. The night stretched on, filled with playful banter, stolen kisses, and the undeniable chemistry that bound them, leaving behind the echoes of fart bombs and pranks and creating new memories in the steam of the hot tub.

As the stars twinkled above, Colton and Genevieve embraced the chaos of their evening, ready to plunge into the uncharted waters of romance and laughter, oblivious to the world around them.

7

The sun streamed through the tinted windows of the tour bus, illuminating the faces of Colton and Genevieve, who sat at opposite sides of the bus, pretending to be absorbed in their surroundings. The air was thick with the unspoken tension of last night's hot tub activities. The rest of their friends clustered happily together, completely oblivious to the simmering awkwardness.

"Nikki, did you bring the snacks?" Tommy leaned closer to his fiancée, grinning like a kid on a sugar high.

"Of course! But only if you promise not to eat them all before the first stop," she teased, swatting his arm playfully.

Amber, sitting directly across from Colton, raised an eyebrow. "What's up with you two? You're quieter than a mime convention."

Genevieve glanced at Colton, who was suddenly fascinated by the view of the passing countryside. "Maybe they're just—contemplative," she replied, trying to keep her voice light.

"Contemplative? More like avoiding each other like the plague!" Kellen chimed in. He leaned closer, a mischievous glint in his eye. "What happened last night? Were you guys plotting world domination in the hot tub?"

Colton shot Kellen a look that could only be described as a mix of daggers and desperation. "No world domination here, just—personal reflections."

"Personal reflections? You mean you're both dealing with the fact that you've crossed the forbidden line of friendship?" Pam interjected, her voice dripping with playful sarcasm. "Admit it, you two are in love now, aren't you?"

"Hardly! We're not even speaking," Genevieve retorted, her cheeks flaring a shade of pink that was hard to miss.

"Oh, right. Because silence is the ultimate sign of affection," Brad chimed in, his arms crossed, clearly enjoying the drama.

"Can we just enjoy the scenic views of Mount Rushmore?" Colton groaned, sinking lower in his seat. "I mean, that's what this trip is about, right?"

"Aw, come on! This is way more entertaining," Amber laughed. "We're all dying to know why the dynamic prank duo suddenly decided to take a vow of silence. Are you two just saving up for a big prank reveal later?"

Genevieve shot Colton a knowing glance, her eyes sparkling with mischief despite the tension. "Maybe. Or maybe we're plotting a prank on you all!"

"Doubt it," Tommy said, crossing his arms. "The two of you couldn't prank your way out of a paper bag right now. You're too busy wallowing in embarrassment."

"No wallowing here!" Colton exclaimed, shooting up from his seat. "Just planning our next move..."

Genevieve smirked, leaning forward to get a clear view of his face. "Oh? Care to share?"

"What happens in the hot tub stays in the hot tub," he replied dramatically, throwing his hands up as if warding off their prying eyes.

"Right, and what about the weed whacker incident last summer?" Kellen replied, grinning. "You can't just drop that line on us. We demand entertainment!"

"Okay, okay," Colton relented, running a hand through his hair as he leaned back into his seat. "Let's just say that last night was a little —unexpected. But we're over it. Not a big deal."

"Not a big deal?" Pam repeated, incredulous. "You guys are practically radiating enough tension to light the entire bus."

The bus bounced over a pothole, causing Genevieve to laugh. "Hey, if it gets us to Mount Rushmore without any more bumps in the road, I'm all for it!"

Tommy leaned forward, his eyes narrowing in mock suspicion. "So, what you're saying is you two *have* to prank each other before we reach the monument? Like a bus rule or something?"

Colton exchanged a glance with Genevieve, who shrugged and smirked. "Sounds like a plan!"

"Ha! Let the games begin!" Amber squeaked, her eyes sparkling with glee.

"Alright, alright," Colton said, his competitive spirit stirred. "But first, we have to establish the rules of engagement."

"Agreed. And just to be clear—no pranks involving water this time!" Genevieve declared, her tone half-serious, half-joking.

"Who says? Maybe that's the perfect way to break the ice!" Kellen shot back, winking.

"Please, let's not drown anyone," Tommy chimed in, shaking his head in mock exasperation. "Last thing we need is a wet t-shirt contest on the bus."

"Hey, we could start a whole new trend!" Genevieve teases. "But seriously, I'm up for some harmless pranking."

Colton grinned at her, warmth spreading through him. "Game on then. Just remember, what goes around comes around."

"Or, in our case, what stays in the hot tub!" Genevieve shot back, her laughter ringing through the air, finally breaking the tension.

As the bus pulled up to Mount Rushmore, the group erupted into excited chatter, the earlier awkwardness forgotten. Colton and Genevieve exchanged glances, a spark of a silent understanding passing between them. The pranks were bound to get messy, but maybe—just maybe—this time, they wouldn't be the only ones getting swept up in the chaos of laughter and romance.

8

The moon lit up the sky over the town. While Genevieve and Colton stood side by side, pretending to be absorbed in their ghost tour brochure. In reality, they were plotting the ultimate prank against one another, mischievous twinkles dancing in their eyes.

"Okay, so here's the plan," Genevieve whispered, her voice low but laced with excitement. "When we get to the old cemetery, I'm going to 'accidentally' drop my phone, and while I'm pretending to look for it, I'll sneak up behind you and scare you."

Colton chuckled, leaning closer to her taunting her with a fictitious thought "Nice try, but I've got something cooking too. When you drop your phone, I'll act all concerned and then shout 'Boo!' right when you turn around. That'll get you for sure."

"Game on, Colton," she replied, a playful glint in her eyes. "But remember, all's fair in love and pranks."

Their friends—Nikki and Tommy, who were practically inseparable since their engagement, Amber, the bubbly and adventurous one, Kellen, the innocent one, Pam the sceptic, and Brad, the troublemaker—were gathering nearby, oblivious to the undercurrents of mischief swirling between the two.

"Are we ready to meet some ghosts, or what?" Amber exclaimed, bouncing on her toes. "I've heard this place is haunted by a lovesick specter who can't find her soulmate!"

Tommy threw an arm around Nikki. "Good thing I'm not a ghost then. You're stuck with me."

"Or you could be a ghost," Kellen quipped, smirking. "You know, haunt her with your 'undying love' or something."

Nikki rolled her eyes playfully. "Please, if you die first, I'm just going to be stuck haunting the same old arguments."

Genevieve and Colton exchanged amused glances; their previous plans momentarily forgotten amid the banter of their friends.

"Alright, everyone, let's move!" Brad shouted, waving for them to follow. "The first stop is the old cemetery, where we'll learn all about the town's past... And maybe a little about our future, right?"

"Let's get a selfie with the ghost!" Amber said, leading the charge. "I want proof!"

As they approached the cemetery, Genevieve felt her heart race. This was it—the moment she would execute her prank. She positioned herself next to Colton, who was casually leaning against a gravestone, looking completely unfazed.

"Hey, Colton, can you help me with something?" she called, feigning innocence.

"Sure, what do you need?" he replied, turning his gaze toward her.

"Just hold my phone while I check my bag," she said, holding it out toward him. As he reached for it, she shifted suddenly, letting the phone 'slip' from her fingers and tumble to the ground.

"Oh no!" she exclaimed, dropping to her knees. "My phone!"

Colton's reflexes kicked in. "Whoa, are you okay?" he asked, stepping closer, a mock-concerned expression on his face. "What if it's haunted?"

That was her moment. As he leaned in, she spun around and shouted, "Boo!"

Instead of screaming, Colton erupted into laughter. "Nice try, Genny, but—"

Before he could finish, Genevieve snagged a handful of grass and tossed it at him like confetti, catching him completely off guard.

"Hey!" he shouted, wiping dirt from his shirt. "That's not fair!"

"Oh, come on! That was a classic!" she teased, reveling in her victory.

"Alright, two can play at this game," Colton said, his eyes

narrowing playfully. He picked up a tiny stone and discreetly rolled it in her direction when she wasn't looking.

"Colton!" she shrieked as it hit her foot. "What was that?"

The group turned with eyes wide. "Is this a part of the ghost tour?" Kellen snickered, already predicting the chaos.

"Maybe a ghost just threw it at you!" Tommy suggested, barely containing his laughter.

"Very funny," Genevieve said, sticking her tongue out at Colton. "But you better watch your back!"

As they continued their ghost tour, the pranking reached new heights. Genevieve and Colton exchanged exaggerated warnings about the 'lost souls' around them, often breaking into fits of laughter, while their friends tried to keep up with the antics.

"Hey, what if we end this tour with a ghost hunt of our own?" Amber suggested, bouncing with energy.

"Yeah, let's split into teams," Nikki chimed in. "Genevieve and Colton can be one team since they're practically a married couple."

"Only in pranks," Genevieve shot back, winking at Colton.

"Can we prove that love is in the air, or just haunted?" Colton smirked, leaning in closer.

"Maybe both," she replied softly, the teasing glimmer fading for a moment. "But watch it, I'm still coming for you!"

"Bring it on," he whispered back, their eyes locking for just a heartbeat longer than intended, the surrounding laughter fading into the background.

In the end, the tour was filled with ghost stories, laughter, and harmless pranks, but underneath it all was a growing tension that neither could ignore. As darkness enveloped the town and the night stretched on, Genevieve and Colton found themselves not just caught up in their competitive spirit, but in the undeniable spark that flickered between them like the glow of a distant lantern—inviting and a little spooky all at once.

After all, who knew what would emerge from the shadows?

9

Genevieve leaned against the cold metal bars; arms crossed tightly over her chest. She's doing her best to refrain herself from killing him. She glanced across at Colton, who was slouched against the opposite wall, a bemused expression on his face that only made her more irate.

"You seriously thought it was a good idea to pull a fake robbery in a town like Deadwood?" Genevieve huffed, keeping her voice low but fierce, as if that would suppress the echoing laughter of the ghosts of outlaws past that seemed to taunt her from the shadows.

Colton chuckled, the sound both infuriating and oddly charming. "I just thought it would be funny; you know? A little bit of mischief. They see a fake cowboy in a mask at the saloon, everyone laughs, we move on. No one was supposed to get arrested!" He tried, half-heartedly, to suppress another laugh, but failed.

"Funny for you, maybe! I didn't realize your idea of fun included spending the night in jail!" she snapped back, waving her hand around the small space. "How do I explain this to Principal Lewis?"

Colton raised an eyebrow, leaning closer to her, his voice dropping to a conspiratorial whisper, "What, are you upset you didn't get a chance to prank me back first? I thought you loved a good prank war, Genevieve."

"Yeah, well, I didn't sign up for having the sheriff scowling at me while I sit on a bench that smells like foot fungus!" She tried to glare at him, but the corners of her mouth were threatening to betray her resolve. It wasn't just the irritation of being in a cell; it was the lingering spark between them that made her heart race, and the cell was becoming an unexpected breeding ground for tension.

"Okay! Okay! I get it. I went too far," he admitted, his tone shifting from playful to genuine in an instant. "But can you blame me? You're the queen of pranks! I just wanted to keep up!"

Genevieve rolled her eyes, refusing to acknowledge the flutter in her stomach at his words. Did he just admit she's a queen? "You call this keeping up? You could have landed us both in real trouble!"

He smirked, and she wanted to punch him, but the way his eyes sparkled in the dim light had her heart beating faster. "But look at us now: locked up together, just us against the world. Isn't it kind of romantic?" He's been tossing the word around ever since Kellen mentioned it the other day, causing him to soul search his feelings for her.

"Romantic? Is that what you call this?" Genevieve laughed. "I call it a disaster! You can't just throw around the word 'romantic' because we're literally behind bars!"

"Maybe not literally romantic, but you know..." Colton leaned closer, a serious note darkening his playful demeanor. "Sometimes, you discover that you care about someone when you're in tight situations. I do care about you, Genevieve."

The words hung in the air like a poorly timed balloon—full of promise yet perilous to pop. Genevieve's heart raced, and she felt the heat rising in her cheeks. "What are you saying?" she managed, the surprise seeping into her tone like the fading light in the cell.

"I'm saying that I like you. I like you more than just as a prank partner, okay? But that prank? I thought it would be fun to do it together." His eyes softened as he searched hers for understanding, his brow furrowing slightly.

But instead of joy or embarrassment, Genevieve felt an overwhelming rush of annoyance. "Are you serious right now? You spring this on me while we're in jail? This is a terrible time for confessions!"

"I know! But it's kind of fitting, don't you think? We're here together—"

"What, you think being stuck in a cell brings people closer together?" She shot back, crossing her arms tighter.

"It worked for Bonnie and Clyde!"

"Colton, they ended up dead!"

"Yeah, but only after a lot of romantic escapades! Look, I might not have chosen a great way to confess, but this is better than getting shot at!" He leaned closer, a cocky grin sliding back into place, and a spark lit the air between them.

"Are you kidding me? You think this is better?" Genevieve laughed incredulously. "We're in a jail cell because of you!"

"But I still like you!" he reiterated, and for a second, the humor faded, leaving behind something more raw, more real.

"And I like you too," she finally admitted, the rush of the confession spilling out faster than she could contain. "But—"

"No 'buts.' We're locked up together, we can't run away from this," he challenged, his intensity making her heart beat faster than any prank war ever had.

She stared at him, mouth slightly ajar, letting the moment stretch. "Fine. But as soon as we're out of here, you owe me dinner. And I get to pick the place! Just no more jail cells, okay?"

Colton grinned wider than she'd ever seen, and the weight of the bars around them lifted just a little. "Deal. And I promise to be on my best behavior for the rest of the trip. No more masks or cowboy get-ups. Just us. Together."

"Right! Because that's what every girl wants—an apology from a would-be bandit!" Genevieve laughed, the tension between them shifting into something else entirely.

"Well, at least I know it won't be boring," he replied, leaning back against the wall again, his grin infectious.

"Let's just hope the sheriff lets us out soon, or I might have to come up with a way to prank our way out of this one," she quipped, playfully flicking her hair over her shoulder.

"Now that's the spirit!" Colton declared, his eyes twinkling with mischief—and something much warmer.

As they bickered and joked in their makeshift prison, the cold iron bars seemed to fade into the background, and Genevieve couldn't help but smile. Because sometimes, even in the most absurd situations, love has a way of finding a path through the chaos—and maybe, just maybe, this was the beginning of a whole new adventure.

EPILOGUE

The evening air was warm, carrying the sound of laughter and distant music from the patio. Colton leaned against the wooden railing, his gaze darting over the dimly lit backyard. He couldn't help but smile as he remembered last night—the chaos that had led to a wild ride in the back of a police car, the prank gone too far, and the surprising confession that followed.

"Fancy seeing you here." A playful voice broke through his thoughts.

Colton turned, his heart skipping a beat. Genevieve stood there, her dark hair cascading over her shoulders, a sly smile playing on her lips. She wore a floral sundress that twirled around her knees, and he couldn't decide what he found more intoxicating, the dress or the devil-may-care expression on her face.

"Funny how we both ended up on the same side of the river after the jailbreak," he replied, trying to keep his tone light.

Genevieve stepped closer, her eyes sparkling mischief. "Truce, right? No more pranks for the rest of the night?"

"Right," he confirmed, their eyes locked in an unspoken challenge. "No pranks. Just—us."

"Just us," she echoed, her gaze softening. "Tonight feels different, don't you think?"

Colton nodded slowly, his heart swelling with newfound courage. "Yeah, it really does."

Behind them, laughter erupted as their friends gathered around the fire pit, s'mores in one hand, drinks in the other. Pam, with her ebullient charm, was amusing Kellen with an exaggerated tale about how Genevieve once put an entire jar of mayonnaise in Colton's car as a prank. Colton shifted uncomfortably, eyeing Genevieve, then Pam, who was stuffing marshmallows into her mouth to suppress her laughter.

"Okay, okay! Truce!" he shouted, trying to bring the focus back to their romantic tension. Everyone turned to him, eyebrows raised. "We're just here to enjoy the night."

"Speaking of enjoying the night," Amber chimed in, wrapping her arm around Brad, "Colton, you're not going to let Genevieve get away with just one night without a little friendly competition, are you?"

"Competition?" Genevieve raised an eyebrow.

Colton smirked. "What did you have in mind?"

"Let's play a game!" Tommy shouted, glancing at Nikki who nodded enthusiastically. "How about a prank war with a twist? You two are on the same team for a change. If we hear about any pranks or trickery tonight, you owe us drinks for a week!"

Genevieve's eyes lit up with mischief. "And if we win?"

"You get to pick the next date activity," Pam added, her smile encouraging.

Colton felt the thrill of the challenge tingle through him. "You're on!" he said, glancing at Genevieve. "But remember, we're only playing for fun. No crossing the line this time."

"Of course," she replied, her voice warm with sincerity. "You know I'm not that cruel."

"Ha! That'll be the day," he teased, and they both laughed, the air buzzing with an exciting anticipation.

As the game unfolded, laughter filled the air, and the pranks flew thick and fast—mostly playful jabs at each other orchestrated by their friends. Genevieve managed to slip a tiny whoopee cushion onto Colton's seat, earning a round of applause from the group when he sat down.

"Alright, alright," Colton laughed, shaking his head in disbelief. "That was clever."

A mischievous glint sparked in Genevieve's eyes. "Just warming up!"

As the stars twinkled from above, the group gathered around the fire pit. Colton and Genevieve found themselves sitting side by side, their shoulders brushing against each other, sparks flying more than from the crackling flames.

"Do you think we'll end up like Pam and Kellen?" Colton asked, still caught in the moment.

Genevieve rolled her eyes playfully. "Only if you keep your pranks in check. I'm not going to be the one to end up in the police station again."

"Good point." He chuckled, nudging her shoulder. "But I think we can keep it fun. You and I, we make a pretty good team."

She turned to him, the laughter fading from her eyes, replaced with something deeper—something he could get lost in. "You really mean that?"

"Yeah, I do," he said, his voice sincere. "I think we're just getting started."

They shared a quiet moment, the world around them fading into a gentle hum of laughter and music. Colton reached for her hand, intertwining their fingers as if they'd been made to fit together.

"Are you ready for our first official date?" he asked, his voice barely above a whisper.

"Only if you promise no pranks," she replied, grinning teasingly.

He raised his hand in mock surrender. "Scout's honor."

"Good! Because I have an idea for revenge already."

"Oh really?" Colton raised an eyebrow skeptically, half-excited, half-nervous.

Genevieve leaned closer, her voice lilting in a conspiratorial whisper. "Let's just say, when you least expect it..."

And with that, the romantic comedy of their lives resumed, both of them knowing that the truce was only temporary, and the real adventure was just beginning.

ABOUT THE AUTHOR

Savana was born and raised in sunny Southern California. But, for the past few decades, she has embraced a new chapter of life in the picturesque surroundings of Wisconsin. Her passion for writing and reading fuels her creativity, while her hands find solace in knitting and crocheting during precious moments of downtime. A dedicated sports enthusiast, Savana holds a special place in my heart for baseball and soccer, which often brings her family together for spirited discussions and lively games. As a skilled surgical technologist, she thrives in the dynamic environment of the operating room, where precision and care are paramount. On weekends, Savana cherishes the joy of family life, spending quality time with her husband and their three adult children, weaving together the threads of love, laughter, and shared experiences that define who we are.

ALSO BY SAVANA JADE

Live Today Series
Focused Series
Broken & Brave

FORGETTING DAKOTA

V.J. LEE

BLURB

Dakota promised he would always find her. However, after suffering a traumatic brain injury, he can't seem to remember her.

Hadley promised always to love him, but he chose his ex, the one who made him feel comfortable—the one he remembered—the same woman who would do anything to get him back.

They both promised to create heaven for one another, but now she's living in hell.

Dakota may have forgotten her, but for her, there will be no forgetting Dakota.

HADLEY MOORE, SOON TO BE MAXWELL

2 years earlier

My sleeveless dress was crafted with delicate tulle and sheer lace. It effortlessly combined elegance and romance. The moment I slipped into this enchanting gown, I felt like a princess ready to walk down the aisle.

The dress's bodice was adorned with intricate black lace appliqués that ran to my waist. This created a stunning illusion neckline that beautifully framed my collarbones. The sheer lace continued onto the back, adding a touch of allure and sophistication. The fitted waistline accentuated my curves, while the full ball gown off-white skirt cascaded in layers of ethereal tulle and created a mesmerizing silhouette.

I felt beautiful as I walked down the aisle on the arm of my uncle, Bob, who came to Deadwood from Colorado, because he was the last of my family.

My brown and burgundy hair was curled, my nails were black to match my sparkly cowgirl boots and my makeup was perfect. I felt more beautiful than I ever had.

I wasn't nervous; I was excited to marry my best friend and the love of my life. Our love was so strong it was almost scary. The small church was packed with all our friends and his family. After the ceremony, we'd proceed to Farmhouse Barn for our reception.

At the end of the aisle, Dakota Maxwell stood in his black suit, with his black cowboy hat covering his black hair. Tears flowed from his green eyes. His best man and friend, Jake, patted him on the back with a huge smile.

Halfway to him, he took off down the aisle, grabbed me in his arms and carried me bridal style to the front of the church. Laughter rang out.

When he sat me down on my high-heeled, booted feet, he kissed me. "You are the most gorgeous woman in the universe, and I love you more than anything."

"That's not how we rehearsed this," Pastor Davis said. More laughter ensued.

I handed Tink my black-and-white rose bouquet. She took it with a smile and a wink.

As the pastor spoke, all I felt was Dakota's calloused hand in mine. I also smelled his intoxicating, spicy scent mixed with fresh hay. I was marrying my best friend—the love of my life.

It was time for Dakota to say his vows. "Hadley Rae Moore, or Hads, you are my everything. You brought a sense of peace to my heart I never thought possible. I love you more than Orion." That made everyone laugh, because we knew how much he loved his horse. "My love for you is all-consuming and will last for every life-time we have together. My life would be nothing without you. Your unconditional love for me is more than I ever hoped for. There is no one for me, but you. I promise to love you for the rest of my life and never forget how you make me feel. Know I will always find you."

If only he had kept those vows.

1

HADLEY

Present day

I was sitting in the stands, watching my husband of two years get ready to ride Demon. The big black horse was part draft horse and American Quarter Horse. No one had been able to stay on him longer than five seconds. I rubbed my sweaty palms on my jeans.

"He'll be fine; he's the best." Tink leaned over and yelled at me above the crowd. She wore a pair of cut-off denim shorts, a tank top and cowboy boots. Her pink and purple hair was cut in a pixie style, making her look like a fairy. The woman stood barely five feet tall. To say the name Tink fits her is an understatement.

"I know, but I'll always worry." Dakota's parents wanted him to take over running their ranch, but he wanted to try the rodeo circuit first. We had been traveling all over, and he proved he was one of the best; he had the belt buckles to prove it. I was proud of him, but it still sent dread racing through me every time I watched him.

"Go, Dakota! You got this!" Dakota's ex, who never got over him, shouted.

"Why the fuck is Shawanda screaming for him like she's his wife?" Tink asked. "They may have been an item for a while in high school, but once you started Lead-Deadwood High, there was no one else but you. I never believed in love at first sight, but damn, when he saw you, that was it. No other girl existed for him."

My cheeks heated. "The same goes for me. He was everything to me, but he had a girlfriend hanging off him like a leech."

"As soon as he broke things off with her, you two were joined at the hip."

As if she knew we were talking about her, Shawanda's blonde head turned toward us, glaring. Tink flipped her off and snapped her teeth at her. Shawanda hated me, ever since Dakota broke things off with her. Shawanda's posse all turned in unison, flipping us off.

I didn't do anything to her, and she wasn't worth my time.

The smell of horses and their shit was usually soothing for me, but today my stomach was twisting and turning. I put a hand on my stomach as I swallowed several times.

"You okay?" Tink asked.

"I have a bad feeling." I looked at my husband on that big black horse. He smiled and winked at me as he mouthed, *"I love you more than a horse loves hay."*

Shawanda put a hand to her heart as if he was talking to her.

I mouthed, *"I love you more than an angel loves the heavens."* We were love-sick fools, still hopelessly in love after two years of marriage and six years of being together.

Dakota nodded, indicating he was ready, and all sounds stopped. My breathing ceased, and my heart stopped as I watched the gate open. The horse, with my love on top, took off, bucking like crazy. I had never witnessed a horse buck and kick so violently. Dakota hung on for what felt like an eternity, then was thrown into the fence. However, the horse kicked him in the head as he fell.

Someone was screaming so loudly it hurt my ears. It took several minutes of that blood-curdling scream before I realized it was coming from me.

"I'm going to be sick." My hand went to my mouth, and I ran to my love without thinking. Before I could get to him, I was hauled into strong arms.

"You can't go in there. Let the EMTs do their job," Jake whispered in my ear. I squirmed, trying to get out of his hold. I needed to feel Dakota's heartbeat against my hand.

"Let me go, Jake, or I swear to God, I'll kick you in the nuts." I was crying so hard, I could hardly breathe.

"You know I can't do that, Hads. You can ride in the ambulance with him."

"How bad is it?" I asked, my voice shaking as tears ran down my cheeks.

When he shook his head, I buried my face in his chest and cried even harder. I barely noticed the smell of sweat on him, because my nose was stuffed up from crying so hard.

Once the EMTs got him loaded into the ambulance, I jumped in, vaguely remembering that I told them I was his wife.

They let me hold his hand on the way to Monument Health Hospital. It was only seven miles from the rodeo grounds, and in the ambulance, it would take no time. But it felt like I had been in the loud, cold and hard back of the ambulance for a lifetime—all because my husband was unconscious and blood was covering the bandages they put on his head.

Once the ambulance stopped, the paramedics sprang into action, getting him into the hospital.

I answered questions and filled out paperwork with shaking hands and in a daze. Then, I went to wait in a small room that had a few rows of chairs and a couple tables with old magazines.

Dakota's parents weren't even in the waiting room before his mom, Lilly, started screaming at me. "This is all your fault. If you supported our wishes for him to work the ranch, instead of all this rodeo nonsense, none of this would have happened." Her brown hair was sleek and straight, falling to her shoulders. Her brown eyes were red-rimmed from crying.

"It's not her fault, Lil." Dakota's dad, Matthew, spoke up for me. "He's an adult, and making his career choice is not Hadley's fault."

Lilly clutched onto Matthew's button-up western shirt and cried so hard it broke my heart again. Falling into a chair, I covered my face and cried harder than I ever had before.

I was in a daze as many people came and went while we waited to hear something. Finally, after what seemed like days, the doctor came in to give us the scary update. The love of my life had a severe skull fracture and needed a cranioplasty using titanium mesh. I cried so hard, I thought I was going to pass out. Thankfully, Jake and Tink were there to help me get to a chair.

At some point, Shawanda showed up and ran to Lilly as they both cried. I didn't care; I kept praying my husband would be okay.

Three and a half hours later, the doctor came in and sat down. "He did very well. There will be a lot of work to do for him to get back to normal, but he will recover. We'll let you see him once he is out of recovery and into a room." He squeezed my shoulder before walking away.

~

I sat in Dakota's room, holding his hand, unaware of time passing by as I watched the strongest man I knew struggle with something so severe. Time slipped away from me. I sat there so long, the smell of disinfectant no longer phased me.

Dakota woke up in recovery, but with all the pain meds, he fell back asleep. He looked so horrible with all the bandages. The constant beeping of the monitors became the background sound of my personal narrative. I refused to leave him. The nurse came in to check on him regularly and would smile at me with a look that showed she felt terrible for me.

Finally, I felt his hand twitch in mine. I sat up, watching him, while holding my breath. The nurse told me he would need water when he awoke and to give him small sips, so I did.

Holding the straw to his lips, I said, "Take slow sips, not too much yet."

Once he finished, I put the water back down, looked at him and smiled. Even with bandages wrapped around his head and bruises all over his handsome face, he still made my heart skip a beat.

"Do you need me to get the nurse?" I knew all his lush hair was gone, but I didn't care.

"What happened?" he asked in a deep, hoarse voice.

"You don't remember?"

"I wouldn't have asked if I had." I let him be upset. He had every right to be pissed.

"You were riding Demon, the bucking bronco, and he kicked you in the head when he threw you off. You have a skull fracture. The doctor had to dig out the bone fragments. They put a piece of mesh in your head." He reached up, to touch the bandages on his head.

"Why was I riding a bucking bronco?"

"You're one of the best bronc riders in the nation."

His eyes scrunched up in confusion, but he didn't say anything for a while. I figured he needed to process, because this was likely the end of his rodeo career. I texted the group thread, letting everyone know he was awake.

The nurse came to check his vitals. She asked about his pain level and asked if he wanted something to eat. Once she was satisfied he was okay, she raised the head of his bed.

Once she left, I told him, "I was so scared. I thought I lost you." I took his hand, but he let his lay limp in mine.

"Why are you here?"

I was shocked by his question. Why wouldn't I be with my husband? Before I could respond, the door opened and his parents rushed in the room to him.

"Oh baby, we were so worried," his mom said, pushing me out of the way.

"You took one hell of a kick to the head, son."

"Did Wanda come with you?" The hope in his voice had my heart racing.

"Why would she be here?" his dad asked.

"Because she's my girlfriend."

Four words and my world shattered.

2

DAKOTA

I felt like I was kicked in the head by a horse. Come to find out, I was. I thought it was strange that Hadley Moore from high school was in my room, because I barely knew her. But when I asked about Shawanda and saw the devastation on her face, I was baffled.

My dad cleared his throat and looked away.

My mom smirked at Hadley. I knew how much my mom loved Wanda.

Hadley looked as if her world was ending. Tears pooled in her pretty blue eyes and her hand covered her mouth.

"I'll get Shawanda to come," my mom said.

"Lilly," Dad warned.

"What? He wants her here. It will help him heal faster."

"Son, you know Shawanda is not your girlfriend, right?"

Those words confused me, until I looked down at my hands and saw the tan line on my left ring finger. "Did we get married?"

"Yes!" Mom yelled.

At the same time, Hadley said, "No," and Dad shook his head.

"Which is it, yes or no?"

Hadley stepped by my dad, and tapped my finger. "You and I are married. You don't remember ... us?" Tears streamed down her face like rivers, making my heart twinge with pain.

Then the door flung open and Shawanda ran in. My mom must have texted her. I knew how close those two were.

"Baby!" She grabbed my hand, squeezing it. It was good to see her and it made me relax back down into the bed.

Mom turned to Hadley and told her, "You should leave. I think you're upsetting him."

It looked as if Hadley was frozen in place. The sign she wasn't was the hiccupping and tears she shed from crying so hard.

There were parts of my memory I was having a difficult time accessing. Years seemed to be blank and were hurting Hadley.

Hadley stepped away as Shawanda held onto me with a death grip.

"It would probably do you some good if you and Shawanda spent some time reminiscing," Mom said.

"Lilly, she's not even supposed to be in here. It's family only right now," Dad admonished.

"She's family." That was the last word. My eyes flicked to Hadley. She was breaking in front of everyone, and though I didn't remember our relationship, something deep within me knew this wasn't like her. She would need time to let her hurt shine through alone.

"Actually, can all of you leave so I can sleep?" I asked. "I need some time to think and sleep."

Mom and Dad said their goodbyes and left. Shawanda bent down and kissed my cheek. "You remember how in love we are, right?" She touched my bandaged head, then said, "Don't worry, your hair will grow back." I put a hand up to my head, not even realizing all my black hair was gone.

My eyes flicked to Hadley before I answered. "I do remember how in love we are." Wanda squeezed my hand, before smirking at Hadley on her way out.

Hadley stepped up to me and kissed my lips. I didn't respond to the kiss. "You promised me you'd never forget. You promised me you'd love me in all lifetimes. Just know that, whether you remember how much you loved me or not, I will always love you in every life-time." With tears in her eyes and slightly slumped shoulders, she laid the bed down flat and stood. "Get some rest." She shuffled out.

As I lay there thinking, my head told me I was still in love and in a relationship with Shawanda, but my heart was breaking at seeing Hadley so upset and hurt. I tried everything to remember the sad, but gorgeous brunette with the burgundy highlights. It caused me to get worked up, and the pain in my head started up again. I pushed the nurse call button and she rushed in. I asked for pain meds and she came back in minutes to administer them. Soon, the drugs kicked in, and I let the darkness overtake me.

~

"He needs to come home with us," Mom said. "He has the most memories there."

I had been in the hospital for a week and a half and was finally getting discharged. Everyone was arguing over where I should stay. Dr. Woods told us I should be where I was most comfortable, but also where I had the most memories, hoping that would trigger something in my blocked head.

"He should come with me, because he remembers our love," Wanda said, looking at Hadley.

"He has all his things at our home, where his most recent memories are. He needs to be in our marital home with his wife." Hadley was not going to be swayed by the rest. "As his wife, it's my job to care for him and see to his every need."

Thankfully, Dr. Woods came back in the room right then. "I agree. Going to your home is the best plan. However, spending time with others will also help you regain your memories. Try home for a bit, and if that doesn't help, move to your parents' home."

"Just so I know I'm hearing you right, you want him to keep seeing me, right?" Shawanda asked with a smile, even though the doctor never said that.

Dr. Woods looked from her to Hadley, then over to me, before nodding as he answered, "It's possible your memories will be jogged by something that happened in your relationship with Shawanda." He looked at her with a hint of remorse. "There's a reason you broke up, which could be what unblocks things."

"I'll do my part to help," Shawanda exclaimed.

"You broke up, because it was love at first sight when he saw me," Hadley said. "Now, if you all would leave so Dakota can get dressed. I'd like to take him home."

"I think I should help him dress," Shawanda said, looking at Hadley with a twinge of malice. "I mean, he doesn't even know you."

Dr. Woods, seeing there was about to be an issue, intervened. "I'll have the nurses help him. The rest of you can wait out in the hall."

The nurses got me ready and put me in a wheelchair. Hadley went to bring the car around. As we headed to the doors, Shawanda took my hand, and I had to admit, it felt right. She was comforting, because there were no gray areas where she was concerned.

Once I was loaded into the car and Hadley was in the driver's seat, Shawanda leaned in, kissing the corner of my mouth. Hadley's knuckles turned white on the steering wheel, but she remained silent.

"My number is still in your phone. Call me if you need me for anything." Shawanda stepped away so my parents could say goodbye, and then we were off to a home I had no idea about—a place that would be strange to me.

Would Hadley expect me to sleep with her?

How could I do that when she was basically a stranger?

As we drove through town, I remembered all the casinos and businesses where I hung out as a teen. But I couldn't remember the woman beside me, who was too quiet.

"Thank you for being at the hospital with me and driving me home," I said as we drove through town.

She stopped at a stoplight and looked at me. "I would do anything and everything for you," she said, her voice sad, hurting my chest.

We reached upper Main Street when she pulled into a steep driveway of a white Victorian-style home with light blue accents—the blue that was my favorite color. We pulled into a detached garage. There was a big gunmetal gray Ford F-250 in one spot. Hadley parked her Rav4 next to what I assumed was my truck.

"Everything okay?" she asked.

"I was thinking that's my dream truck."

"It is. You worked so hard to get the truck. You worked for your parents between rodeos, until you could afford to buy it outright. You don't have any debt. Our only debt is the house, but we are making double payments, so we won't have that debt for too long." She took a deep breath. "That is, if you ever remember us." She looked at me, her blue eyes shining with unshed tears. "What if you never do?"

"Let's not think about it right now," I said and grimaced with pain. She gave me a tight smile and a sad nod.

"I'll help you out." Before I could tell her I could get myself out, she was there, opening my door and helping me out of the car and into the house.

"It's a gorgeous home."

She smiled. "It is. We spent so much time remodeling to make it everything we dreamed of. All our friends and family said starting a home renovation project so early in our marriage would lead to divorce, but we laughed, cussed and made love on every surface."

I had no desire to hear about our love-making. I took in the modern kitchen with granite countertops and modern appliances, but the rest of the place featured restored hardwood floors, a fireplace and double-hung windows. It was a house I would love to live in.

I walked into the living room, taking in the hominess of it all. There were pictures of Hadley and me, some with my parents and friends. There was one where I was carrying her bridal style. I was in a suit with my cowboy hat on, and she was in a gorgeous black-and-white gown. I was looking down at her as she looked up at me. We both had so much love shining in our eyes that it was apparent even coming through the photo.

"I was halfway down the aisle," she started, but chuckled and continued, "You couldn't wait any longer for me to get to you. So you rushed halfway down the aisle and picked me up, bringing me to the altar so we could start our lives as husband and wife sooner. It's my favorite."

Looking at the silver-framed picture, I said without turning toward her, "I'm sorry, I can't remember."

I felt a slight touch on my back, as if she feared I wouldn't want her to touch me. "It's not your fault." She walked away.

Walking through the house without remembering any part of it upset me and pissed me off.

I was standing in the master bedroom, with the door leading to a balcony, when Hadley came in. She pointed to two doors. "That's your closet, that's mine. The bathroom is through there. Your dresser and mine."

"I can't sleep in here with you," I said before even thinking how it would affect her.

The silence was deafening. It was so quiet, I could hear the pieces of her heartbreak breaking off and clattering to the floor. Then, there was a sob and footsteps leaving me. I knew I was hurting her, but she was also a stranger to me, and sleeping with her would be uncomfortable.

Why couldn't I remember?

I understood the injury was severe, but I also saw how much I loved her in those pictures. She looked at me like I was her entire world.

3
HADLEY

"I'll sleep in the guest room," I said when he finally walked back into the living room. He sat down in his big chair as I got up from the couch, my favorite spot. I needed to sleep with my head on his chest to hear his heart beating, so I knew he was alive and well. However, he wasn't comfortable around me and I wouldn't push him. I finished getting both our main bedroom and the guest room in order. I walked back into the living room and found him on the couch, in my spot, watching TV. He had the afternoon news on, like that would help him remember our life together.

"There's no reason for you to leave your room. I'll take the guest room."

"It's our room, but thanks." I was dying inside. Dakota was my person, my other half, and he didn't know me. He didn't want to sleep with me. I shook off the melancholy and told him, "I'm making your favorite for dinner."

He looked at me with a gleam in his eye. "Pizza?"

It would seem I couldn't do anything right. "Before you got hurt, it was my shepherd's pie. But if you want pizza, I'll order from Marco's."

"No, that's fine. I'd like to have the shepherd's pie. That sounds like it would be comforting. If there's time, I want to lie down here and rest." He got comfortable on the couch and I got a blanket out of the ottoman to give him. I wanted to tuck him in and snuggle with him like we always did in the evening, but instead I just placed the folded blanket on his lap and went into the kitchen.

I started cooking and heard snores. I stopped and went to cover him up with the blanket, since he fell asleep with it still folded on his lap. I couldn't stop myself from leaning down and lightly pressing my lips to his. "I love you so much."

"Shawanda," he mumbled in his sleep. Pulling away, I returned to cooking what I hoped would still be his favorite.

I took a family leave of absence from my job at the rodeo to care for Dakota. I tried showing him videos of us, our pictures and told him about our time together. I reminded him of our favorite restaurants and bars. During the three weeks he was home, I talked to him and showed him our lives, but he became increasingly interested in his phone.

Our friends came over for dinner so we could reminisce. Jake, Emmitt and Tom all talked to him about his rodeo days. Tink told him he broke his head, not his heart, so he should start thinking with the organ in his chest. Candice and Andrea explained to him that our love was pure and perfect—it had restored their faith in relationships.

Dakota would engage, then get up and take a call or text.

One night after dinner, he shocked me by saying he thought we should make love. Maybe that would help him remember. My heart beat like crazy. I was so excited and happy that he wanted me.

He led me up the stairs to our room. Slowly, I undressed him, even though I wanted to rip his clothes off his body. I ran my hands and lips over every exposed part of his skin, kissing his stubbled head even. When we were both naked and panting, he laid me down and made love to me, but I felt he was only going through the motions. I could tell his heart wasn't in it.

Once the love-making was over, he said he still didn't remember and got up, leaving me there to cry all night long. I could feel him slipping away from me. I couldn't sleep that night, so I got up to ensure the doors were all locked. That's when I heard him on the phone. He must have been on a video chat, saying, "Turn around, let me see that one from behind." There was a whistle. "Yeah, that's the one for sure. You look fucking hot."

I didn't have to ask who he was talking to. Shawanda told everyone on social media how she and Dakota were getting close again, like they had been in high school. He never once ignored any of her calls or texts. Her friends were all over the moon, while mine told her she needed to stay away from him.

The longer he stayed here, the more I saw him pulling away. He started working on the Maxwell Ranch, and on the second day, he came home and told me we needed to talk.

We were in the living room and I broke out in cold sweats. He held his Maxwell Ranch ball cap in his hands, squeezing the bill.

"What are you worried about?" I asked.

"What makes you think I'm worried?"

"Even though you don't remember, I know you better than anyone, and you do that with your hat when you're worried." I nodded toward his hands.

"Working at the ranch, I went into my old room and felt comfortable there."

I tried to smile ... I really did. "You want to move home."

"I still don't feel like this is my home. But it does feel like home at my parents' place. The doc says it's because my last memories are from high school and that's why."

Looking at my hands, I couldn't talk yet, because the tears would come if I did. Trying to stop the sobs from escaping wasn't working, and soon my shoulders were shaking with my grief. I didn't want to make him feel bad, but how do you stop your heart from breaking?

I felt the couch next to me dip and a big hand rub circles on my back. "I need to see if this helps me remember. Please don't be upset."

Wiping my face with my shirt, I told him, "You need to do what is right for you." Then I got up, but before leaving, I said, "Please keep in touch with me. I may not be your everything anymore, but you're still mine."

~

A week had gone by with very sporadic texts from Dakota here and there. I would send good morning texts, ask him how his lunch was, tell him good night, and send several "I love you" texts throughout the day. I would get one-word replies.

Shawanda's other posts showed them eating burgers at Mustang Sally's, walking down Main Street and sitting around the fire pit at her home. All I was worth were one-word text replies.

I threw myself into work at the rodeo, doing all the clerical and accounts payable tasks. Everyone who entered my office gave me pitying looks.

Nothing I did seemed to reach my husband and I missed him so much. Sleeping alone in our bed was killing parts of me little by little every day.

The thought of him touching her, kissing her and making love to her was killing me. You can't live without a heart and Dakota was my heart. But he was gone. I felt I had lost him.

The longer he was away, the more I worried he didn't want to remember the memories of us together. Instead, he was creating new ones with her.

During week three of his absence, he texted me to ask if I wanted to have lunch with him at Dale's restaurant. I was happy. I wore my best burgundy sundress with black wedge heels and even curled my hair the way he liked.

I was disappointed when he wanted to meet me there instead of coming to pick me up, but I got in my car and drove to him. As I entered, I couldn't help but smile. The smell of coffee and grease greeted me, causing my stomach to roil with nerves.

But as soon as I saw him, my smile faltered. Shawanda was seated next to him with her head on his shoulder. They were laughing. I made my way to them and sat down. Dakota moved so her head fell from his shoulder, but she still smirked at me.

"I thought we would be alone."

Shawanda looked over at him before meeting my gaze. "We thought doing this in public and together would be best." The waitress brought me water, but I asked her to return to take our order in a bit. I had a feeling I wasn't going to be hungry.

"What do you need to say to me, Dakota?"

He swallowed. "I tried staying with you and my parents, but my memories haven't returned." He took a drink. "Now I ... we've decided it might help if I stay with Shawanda for a while." It felt like the floor opened up and I was falling into a black vortex of despair.

"So now you two are a 'we' and make decisions together?"

"It is me he remembers."

Dakota said, "I remember my love for Wanda." He looked at her with so much love it hurt. "Someone or something would have had to do or say something false to get me to leave her."

I looked at her with so much contempt, I hoped she would feel it for days. "I'm sure you filled his head with lies for him to leave me, she said.

"Or maybe you were fucking the entire baseball team and he didn't want to get an STI."

Shawanda gasped. Dakota scolded, "Don't speak to her like that."

"Have you made your choice, then?" I asked.

"Like there was a choice," Shawanda snarked.

"It's not like that, Hadley. I'm doing everything in my power to try to remember, but Doc says it could take months, if not years. And I want to be in places I know and where I am comfortable." Shawanda nudged his shoulder. "I also think it would be best if you stopped calling and texting me constantly."

"We need time to concentrate on us ... I mean, he needs time for himself," Shawanda smirked.

My mantra was—I would not let them see me cry, even though I was in the most pain I had ever felt in my entire life, which included my parents' deaths. "Is this what will make you happy, Dakota?"

"Yes."

I nodded, trying like hell to accept my fate. "I once told you I'd never do anything to make your life harder and would always ensure you were happy. If this makes you happy, I'll leave your life." I got up and walked away from the man who held my bloody heart in his hands.

4

DAKOTA

I had been staying in Wanda's guest room for a few days, but the part of my brain that needed to remember things still wasn't working. I was getting frustrated, and it felt like a boulder was on my chest, crushing my physical body and soul. The look on Hadley's face when I told her I was moving away from her haunted my dreams.

Deadwood had always been my home. It was a safe, comfortable place for me, but now I was afraid of walking down the street and seeing Hadley. Even though it was a small town of under fifteen hundred people, it never felt small. But now it was a different story—it felt stifling. I didn't want to go out much, so I threw myself into work at the ranch. I thought my dream was to help run things there, but Hadley told me that changed when I started the rodeo. That explained why I didn't feel content working on the ranch now. Mom was ecstatic, but I could see the worry in my dad's eyes. Wanda was there for me no matter what. She was becoming my safe haven.

Dad pulled me aside today, asking if I was sure living with Shawanda was a good idea. I was married to Hadley, after all. Shawanda had been pressuring me to file for divorce. She said it wasn't fair to Hadley if I was living with another woman. She kept telling me Hadley poisoned my mind against her, which was why we broke up. Hadley didn't seem like the type to do that, but I couldn't remember much about her or our life together. I kept thinking about that wedding picture of me holding her in her beautiful dress. And the love in our eyes. That was soul-crushing not to remember.

True to her word, Hadley hadn't called or texted me. We made eye contact one day on the street, but she put her head down and crossed so we wouldn't run into each other. For some reason that hurt. My head was healing and the hair was actually starting to grow back. Soon, I wouldn't need to hide it with my ball cap. But that didn't mean I was remembering anything, which was upsetting.

A knock on my bedroom door brought me out of my musings. I opened the door to Shawanda in a see-through robe with nothing underneath. Her dark nipples were hard and her body was perfect. Her blonde hair was curled, hanging down around her perfect breasts.

She held up a carton of ice cream with two spoons. "This always makes me feel better." She walked past me, bringing her floral scent into my room. She wanted me to stay with her in her room, but I couldn't. I might not remember my wife, but I'm not about to cheat on her.

"I think you should leave."

She pouted. "Come on, do you think you won't be able to keep your hands off me?" She smiled while running her hands over her breasts and down between her legs. With no more thought in my head, I left. This was getting way too confusing and I began to get a headache. I walked out of the house without a word, leaving her in a negligée in her guest bedroom, complete with my favorite rocky road ice cream and two spoons.

I called my boys when I got in my truck to meet me at the Brass Rail Lounge. When they showed up, I was already there, sipping a beer.

After they got their drinks, we sat there, not saying anything for a bit. "Am I screwing up by staying with Wanda?"

"Yes!" It was a unanimous declaration.

"I feel comfortable around her; I don't know Hadley."

"You should let Hads go. Then I can be with her," Jake said.

I glared at him.

"What? You don't know her? You don't remember all the sacrifices she made to be with you by helping you make your rodeo dreams come true? I'd give my right nut to have a woman who loved me the way she loves you."

"Me, too," Emmitt added.

"When we were in school, Shawanda fucked around on you like crazy. Hadley doesn't even look at other men. Her eyes and heart are only for you. I know I've said it before, but yours had only been for her. It was like fucking lightning striking all over the place when you two were together, and I, for one, can't believe you can't feel that love."

I felt like a grade-A ass. "I told her to stop texting and calling me."

Jake snorted. "And yet, when you were staying at home with Hadley, trying to remember shit, you couldn't get your nose out of your phone, texting Shawanda all the time."

"Let me guess. You asked and Hadley obliged you," Tom said and took a swig of his beer.

A nod of my head was all I could manage.

"You might be comfortable with Shawanda, because she is what you remember, and it makes you feel as if you have some control over this shitstorm that is your life. But what happens if Hads has enough and leaves you for good, then you get your memories back? Because we've all told you, man, that woman is your everything. Your heart song. Your person. You two were so fucking in love, it made everyone around you want the same thing," Jake ranted.

"Or made us want to puke," Emmitt said.

"If Hadley and I loved each other so much, why can't I remember her? You'd think I'd feel something if we had a love as perfect and big as you say."

Tom brought the beer down from his lips, his hazel eyes bright in the bar light. "You don't feel anything at all?"

"We had sex and I couldn't even stay in the same bed after."

"Wow, that's fucking harsh, man." Tom wasn't telling me anything I didn't know.

"Tom, you don't have to tell me. I felt like a slimeball afterward."

"Then you moved in with your ex-wreck of a girlfriend?! You know none of us ever liked her, and she came on to all of us," Jake said. He got up, threw some bills on the table and left.

I looked at Tom and Emmitt. "Why didn't you guys tell me about her coming on to you?"

"We did. You didn't listen."

"You claimed you two had an all-consuming love, but before Hadley showed up, you started seeing Shawanda's tricks and decided to leave her. When you saw Hadley, it was over for you and Shawanda. You said Hadley was the best thing to ever happen to you, that you were happier than you'd ever been, and she supported your dreams."

"Wanda thinks I should divorce Hadley, because it's unfair to her." I swallowed the last of my beer and held it up for another.

Tom sighed. "I both agree and disagree with her. I agree, because if you're not going to stay with Hads and give yourself a chance to remember her, you must let her go. I disagree, because you need to give the two of you a chance, and I don't think you're doing that."

Emmitt added, "As long as you're around Wanda, you never will give Hads the time she deserves."

"Hads might be sweet and will put up with your shit for a long time, but once she's done, you won't get her back. I suggest you think long and hard about what you want to do," Tom told me. I could hear the disappointment in his deep voice.

Emmitt put his elbows on the table and leaned his colossal body in. "I suggest if you let Hads go, you let Shawanda go as well. Take time for yourself and work on getting your memories back. I'm telling you as your friend, if you don't work on remembering your wife and lose her when you regain those memories, which had her in them, you're going to hate not only yourself, but life in general."

"We aren't kidding when we say the love you two have is relationship goals, and losing that kind of love will wreck you."

"Looks like I have a lot of soul-searching to do."

~

I made up my mind to tell Wanda we were done. I could see the sneaky tricks she had been playing. I was walking down the hallway at school when the air was knocked out of my lungs.

Standing at a locker was the most gorgeous girl I had ever seen, including on TV and in movies. She had long brown hair, sky-blue eyes and a curvy body. And when she smiled, everything stopped. She wore blue jeans with pink sparkly high-top Converse, a tank top that matched the shoes and a jean jacket.

I don't know how long I stood there watching her struggle to open her locker, but Wanda pulled me out of my fog. "New trash alert, girls!" She linked her arm with mine.

I was done. I looked down at her, and said, "Don't touch me. We're done." Not the best way to break up with someone, but I knew I couldn't take her any longer. I walked over to the new girl with my hand out. "I'm Dakota Maxwell, a junior, star baseball player and your new best friend."

Instead of taking my hand, she threw her head back and laughed. I stood there, looking at her in confusion, but I loved how her laugh made me feel. It washed over me like silk. She straightened up when I wasn't laughing with her. "Oh, you're serious."

"About what?"

"Your parents named you Dakota while living in Deadwood, South Dakota."

"It's a good name. What's your name?"

"What do you think my name would be?"

My eyes went to the ceiling as I thought. "Bella, when I hear it, I think of all things beautiful."

"You're cheesy." She stuck out her hand and I took it. "Hate to disappoint you, but it's Hadley Moore. Nice to meet you." When I took her hand, it was as if I was struck by lightning.

"Maybe someday it'll be Hadley Maxwell." I wasn't kidding. She had me from the very start.

I awoke with a start, not knowing if that was a memory sneaking into my head or just a dream. My head was pounding after having one too many beers. One of the guys must have brought me home, or I should say to Wanda's house.

There was a warm body next to me—a very naked body. I looked over at Wanda, who was sleeping with a small smile, her lips turned up. Thankfully, I had my clothes on. I prayed we hadn't done anything. I was still married, and Hadley did seem like a wonderful woman, so I wouldn't want to hurt her more than I already had.

A delicate hand wrapped around my waist before I could sneak out of bed. "Don't leave me. Stay and cuddle."

"Why are you in my bed naked?" I asked, unable to hide the disdain in my voice.

"Actually, it's my bed in my home." She pulled me down and

pressed her naked breasts into my side. "I think you should pay me rent."

I removed her arm and got out of bed. "I'm married."

She rolled her eyes, getting out of bed as well. She stood on the other side in nothing but her naked glowing skin. I swallowed, trying to get the arousal under control. She was a gorgeous woman with a banging body.

"Please, it's only a matter of time before you two divorce. You picked me and you always will." She turned toward my bathroom. "Now, I'm going to shower and you are more than welcome to join me."

I ran a hand through the stubble on my head and grabbed a pair of sweatpants and a T-shirt to go downstairs for coffee. My phone had several messages from my boys and Hadley's friends. I may have asked her to stop texting, but I haven't told them to stop.

They started sending me photos of Hads and me, along with some videos and text messages I sent them over the years, telling them how much I loved their friend, promising never to hurt her and that I would always choose her.

There was a video from Tink of the reception at our wedding. In every clip, I looked at my wife like the sun rose and set with her and her alone. She smiled at me like I was her savior.

> Tink: You promised you wouldn't hurt her.
> You promised you'd always choose her. You
> lied!

Then she sent me a GIF of a guy getting kicked in the nuts by a horse.

5

HADLEY

How much could one person cry?

Once I thought my tears had dried up, I would see something or smell something that reminded me of him, and I would start all over again. It wasn't fair he was living with her. She was going to poison him against me. Not being able to reach out to him for every little thing happening in my life was hard.

He didn't want to hear from me.

He didn't want to stay with me.

He didn't want to remember me.

I decided he needed to come home. We couldn't make things work if he wasn't here with me, and if he didn't, I'd let him be happy with her. I want him and I'll always love him, but I won't force him. I also want him to be happy and if that's with Shawanda, then I'll wish them the best. And if that's the route our lives take, I love Deadwood, but I'll leave, because there is no way I can stay in town with them living their best lives.

If I was bringing my husband back home, I would need to ensure we had food. I plan on winning him over with all his favorite foods, so I needed to head to Lynn's in Lead.

I considered everything I would say to my husband during the entire four-mile drive. God, why did I love him so much? If we had a horrible marriage, this would be easy. Throughout our time together,

I never once feared he would leave me for anyone, even Shawanda. Now, I was so afraid this was it for us.

While shopping, I heard some women talking in the next aisle. "OMG! I can't believe you two are finally back together," one woman said.

"Since middle school, you two have been relationship goals!" another chimed in.

"I'm so happy he finally dumped his wife and figured out you were the most important person in his life. Please, tell me you're getting married!" another yelled before the rest shushed them.

"She has nothing on you. Your family has the most expensive, prestigious horse breeding program in all of the Dakotas, and his family is generation upon generation of successful ranchers. She's an orphan who had to come live with her grandma when her parents died. She's a nobody," the first woman explained. I knew it was Shawanda's posse of bitches.

"They probably died to get away from her." They all laughed. I guess once a mean girl, always a mean girl. It was the same nonsense they pulled in high school, until I punched a couple of them out.

"Ladies," a deep masculine voice I'd know anywhere acknowledged the group, rooting my feet to the spot.

"Dakota, we were just asking Wanda when you two will make things official and finally get married, as you should have done years ago."

"Girls, he's already married. Don't put him on the spot like that," Shawanda laughed.

"Didn't the two of you wake up naked in the same bed this morning?"

That's when I couldn't stay one minute longer, if I wanted to keep my morning coffee from being puked up all over the white tile floor. I left my cart of food and ran out the doors.

Before I got to my car, a large, calloused hand grabbed my arm. "Hadley."

The tears in my eyes made him blurry. Between running and crying, I couldn't catch my breath.

"You need to calm down so you don't hyperventilate." He bent me over so my hands were on my knees. "Slow, deep breaths. There you go."

I didn't want to cry, but figured, fuck it, let him see me dying inside. So I looked up at him with big, fat tears running down my face. "This would be so much easier if I didn't love you so much or know how much you loved me."

"How much did you hear in there?"

"Everything."

He rubbed at the back of his neck. "I didn't have sex with her."

"You expect me to believe you woke up naked in the same bed, and you didn't have sex?!" I knew I was bordering on hysteria, but I couldn't keep my emotions at bay, just like I couldn't stop the rest of my heart from shattering.

He took me by the shoulders and crushed me to his chest. "I got so drunk last night, I don't know how I got home. If I was that drunk, there's no way in hell I could get it up. She got in bed with me."

With my fists gripping his shirt, I let myself fall apart. "That's not your home. We have a home we bought together. We spent months side by side, fixing it up." I knew I looked like a hot mess, but I looked up at him, letting him see my ruination. "Please, I need you home with me. We can't make our marriage work if you're not there."

He was too quiet.

"I know you're not comfortable with me," I continued when he didn't answer. I couldn't help myself, I raised myself on my tiptoes and pressed my lips to his. The kiss was soft and sweet, until it wasn't. He grabbed the back of my head and angled his mouth over mine, until he pushed his way inside. We kissed like we never wanted to stop.

"What the fuck do you think you're doing?" Shawanda screamed. Dakota pushed me away, as if I had an infectious disease.

When I looked over Dakota's shoulder, Shawanda and her posse stood there with their arms crossed over their chests, glaring at me as if I was the other woman.

"If you're not home tonight by six, I'll take it to mean you don't want to remember us." I got in my car and drove home, unsure how I would deal with it if he didn't come home, wondering how my life would change.

How I managed to get home and into the house was beyond me. I curled up on the couch and let the pain out, while wrapped in the blanket I gave him when he came home from the hospital. It still held his scent and it broke my heart more.

At three, I found the groceries I had left at Lynn's on my

doorstep, I figured Dakota had dropped them off. By five, I was getting ready, praying with everything I had that my husband would be home in an hour.

I made a lasagna with garlic bread and a nice salad. I set the table with the beautiful dinnerware his parents gave us for our wedding and lit candles. Then, I waited.

Five minutes after six, my heart sank.

By six-thirty, I couldn't swallow.

At seven, I cleaned up the food.

When eight o'clock came around, I texted my friend, Jeff.

Nine, I sent my boss an email.

By midnight, I had loaded three suitcases into my car.

At one-forty-five in the morning I pulled up to the small, five-hundred-square-foot cabin in Deadwood Canyon, which stood before Whitewood Creek. My grandma had left it to me.

At three in the morning, the tears stopped. There was no reason to spill any more tears or waste time on a man who didn't want to put in the effort.

I spent the next few days getting my life in order. I unpacked, decorated the cabin and got a virtual assistant job so I could work from anywhere. I had enough savings to figure out where I would go when I was ready to take the next steps in my new life.

The hardest thing I did was press block on Dakota's number.

6

DAKOTA

She was the most beautiful bride in all of existence. All I knew was that I needed to ensure she would continue walking the rest of the way to me. I couldn't wait. I ran down the aisle, picked her up and brought her to the altar.

She looked at me as if no one else existed. I could feel her love for me to the depths of my soul. I knew I never wanted to be in any life without her by my side.

I understood what she gave up to help me make my dreams come true. No one else supported my career in the rodeo, but she told me she would stand by me, no matter what I chose.

"Hadley!" I jerked awake. I was on the couch in Shawanda's living room. I remember setting my alarm to get up so I had time to talk to Hadley before I passed out on the couch to rest. I must have fallen asleep, but it was dark outside. Grabbing my phone, I noticed it was off.

"Fuck! What time is it?" I turned on my phone, seeing it was midnight. "I missed meeting Hadley." I knew I set my alarm. I suspected Wanda turned my phone off since she was becoming more and more obvious in her nefarious ways.

Without another thought or caring about the time, I grabbed my keys and took off. The entire way to her house ... no, our house ... all I could see was the tears pouring from her eyes as we stood in the grocery store parking lot. I remembered and heard her voice asking me to come home like a song only my heart could hear.

At the house, I pounded on the door for ten minutes before I realized I lived there, too. I must have a key on me. It took a bit to find the right one, but once I did, I opened the door. The first thing that hit me was the smell of garlic and spices—she cooked for me and I didn't show up—and I ran upstairs to our bedroom. "Hadley! I'm sorry. I fell asleep." But when I opened the door, the bed was made. She wasn't here.

The thought of her being with another man caused the breath in my lungs to seize up. I may not remember her, but my heart and body sure as hell did. I've been dreaming about our sex life. And if any of it is true, it was fucking amazing. The dreams I've been having are more like memories. I've also been getting memories of us while awake. I stumbled to the dresser, which she told me was hers, and opened the top drawer, because that's where all women keep their bras and panties. That thought stopped me in my tracks, because I remember her telling me that while we were putting our clothes away when we moved into our home.

With a shake of my head, I pulled open the top drawer of her dresser and found it empty. Then, I went to the bathroom, and everything she used was missing from her side of the sink.

My legs wouldn't hold me. I stumbled to the bed and fell onto my ass. It felt like someone was prying my ribs apart and pulling my heart out. All she wanted to do was help me remember us. She tried to help me.

There, on my pillow, was a piece of paper. I unfolded it and, in elegant script, she left me a note.

Dakota, my love, my life, my heart, my everything.
The only thing I have ever wanted for myself was you.
I'm glad I had you for a few short years. Thank
you for showing me so much love while you remembered

me. I want nothing more than for you to remember, but you don't seem to want that. So, I'm releasing you to be happy. I love you enough to want your happiness more than my own. I pray you don't regret your decisions when your memories return, because I refuse to believe they're gone forever. I both wish for you to remember and do not want you to, because once you remember, you're going to hate yourself, and I only ever want you happy and content.

If I can't give you that, then it's time for you to move on. It kills me that you don't remember me or us. We were good ... no, we were great together. A love like ours is rare. Know I'll always be proud of you, whether you go back to the rodeo, work for the family ranch or help Shawanda raise horses. No matter what you do, you'll be great at it.

I'll never stop loving you, but a one-sided relationship will never work. I wish you and her a long, happy life."

With all my love, Your Hads.

I couldn't figure out why the page was getting wet, until the words became blurry. I wiped the tears from my eyes, feeling like the best thing that ever happened to me was slipping through my fingers.

I locked up the house without caring what time it was and went to find Tink. If anyone knew where Hadley was, it would be her.

Tink lived in a studio apartment off Kirk Road.

I started pounding on her door, not caring if I woke her neighbors up. Something in me told me I had to find Hadley. I couldn't lose her, because if I did, I would never be happy again.

Soon, the lights came on and I heard grumbling. The door swung open to reveal a pissed-off Tink. She was no more than five feet tall, with her pink and purple hair sticking up all over her head. She was wearing a huge black T-shirt that went past her knees. I had a feeling I had interrupted something.

"What in the fucking hell are you doing here at this hour of the morning?"

"Please, tell me you know where Hadley is."

Her brows scrunched in confusion. "I haven't heard from her. Is she not home? I thought you two were supposed to have dinner and talk. She was making lasagna and was going to make you stay home or leave for good. She wouldn't have missed that."

I rubbed at the back of my neck. "I fell asleep and missed her. When I woke up, my phone was off, but I took off to see her. She's not home and her stuff is gone."

Her little fists clenched at her sides. "You piece of fucking shit. You may have lost your memories, but nothing is wrong with your heart. And that woman is your heart, as you are hers, and if you can't feel that, you do not deserve her." She took a step toward me, but was pulled back.

I looked at Emmitt as he tucked her into his side. "Down, bull-dog." I wondered when they started hooking up.

Her intense glare shot up at him. Emmitt was almost six feet six inches tall, muscular, with blond hair and brown eyes, and I had no idea they were together like this. "Did you just call me a dog?"

He ignored her, turning to me. "What's going on? As you can tell, we've been busy all night long." He waggled his eyebrows at me and thrust his hips, smiling.

Tink, still giving him a death glare, snorted. "Three minutes does not all night make." Emmitt lost the smile real quick.

"I was excited." She rolled her eyes.

I didn't give a shit about all their bullshit. "Have you heard anything from Hadley?"

"No, and even if I did, I wouldn't tell you!"

"I'm worried something happened. I've been calling and texting, but they're bouncing back to me."

She stepped up to me, poking my chest with each word. "She probably blocked your ass. She was doing everything to make things work, and you went and moved in with your ex-slut. Go back to her and forget about the love of your life. Admit you failed your marriage and move the fuck on like Hadley has."

"I don't remember!" It's not like I was trying to hurt anyone, but if I couldn't remember, it wasn't something I planned. Why am I the bad guy?

She let out a sigh. "Okay, you don't remember, but tell me, in one word, how you feel about never seeing her again?"

"Terrified." I didn't have to think about it.

"That's a start. But I don't know where she is either. If you didn't show up for dinner, she would have been devastated. And if she left, she might have left the state." It felt like pieces of me were falling to ash and blowing away through the Black Hills, scattering the ashes of my perfect life with Hadley.

The thought of Hadley leaving Deadwood was not something I was willing to accept. "We need to find her."

"I doubt she wants to be found, but I'll keep trying to get in touch with her. If I hear anything, I promise I'll at least let you know she's okay."

The only thing I could do was nod.

As I was leaving, I heard Emmitt say, "I'm ready for another round."

"Oh, you've got another minute in you? Are you going to go for four minutes, instead of only three?"

I heard a growl and a giggle. I remembered the last time I was with Hadley. I wanted so badly to remember her that I dragged her to bed and lost myself in her. She felt as if she had been made for only me, but when I didn't remember, I had to leave. Now, the regret of those actions weighed heavily on me. What was I going to do now?

Wanda had been blowing up my phone, demanding to know where I was. If I was out with Hadley, then I had better choose between the two. Maybe I should go back to my parents' house. I couldn't imagine spending the rest of my life with Wanda and never seeing Hadley again.

7
DAKOTA

A month passed, and I was still looking for Hadley. No one heard from her. The town was small, so it made sense she wouldn't tell anyone where she was. The news would have spread like wildfire. I had been having more dreams and memories about our lives.

From my dreams, I knew she was a doting wife. There was nothing she wouldn't do for me or to me. I woke up more than once with my hand on my cock, because of the things she had done to me in my dreams.

I moved out of Wanda's and back to our home. I couldn't spend time in Wanda's or my parents' house with them all looking at me like I was an alien. Wanda was not happy and had not stopped sending me shit from when we dated in high school, telling me we were so happy, until *that bitch* corrupted my mind. My parents knew better than to bother me with the choices I was making. Mom was clear that she wanted me to pick Wanda, but Dad seemed to want me to pick Hadley. They both thought it was good to step back and stay in my home, so I could figure out my next move.

Shawanda sent me a picture of us at our sophomore prom, saying, "Don't we look happy?" Before Hadley left, I would have enjoyed the pictures from Wanda. Now, I wished she would stop.

I noticed a box in the closet. I picked it up and removed the lid. When I saw what was inside, I took it back to the bed I shared with my wife and sat down to go through it. It contained all the mementos of Hads and me.

There were ticket stubs from a movie, which she had written on it that it was our first date. There was a small scrapbook. There was a dried wild mountain rose where she had written: **The flower he put in my hair on our hike.** There were little stuffed animals. Each one had a tag with when, where and why she got it from me. I found two prom pictures, one for junior and one for senior prom, and the look on our faces said it all. In all the pictures Wanda sent me, I never looked at her the way I looked at Hads, and she looked at me the same.

When I saw our wedding photos, tears swelled in my eyes. Although I didn't remember her, my heart missed her. If she left town, I knew Deadwood wouldn't be the same without her.

I needed to fucking remember. I decided to go to the rodeo and look around where I got hurt. It might help knock something loose in my brain to help me remember.

On my way, I got several texts from Wanda.

*Wanda: **Why won't you come back home?***

*Wanda: **I miss you.***

*Wanda: **I won't pressure you anymore if you come back. We need to talk.***

*Wanda: **You promised you'd never leave me.***

∽

"I will always find you."

I knew I told Hads that in our wedding vows. I remembered that as clear as day.

I walked around the rodeo, trying to remember something.

Then, something pushed its way to the forefront of my mind.

∽

"His name is Demon for a reason, babe. I'm scared."

I pulled her into my arms, taking in her cherry blossom scent. "Then, after this ride, they'll call me the Demon Slayer." I kissed her. "Don't worry; nothing will happen to me."

"I trust you." She looked at the giant black monster of a horse. "I

313

don't trust him." She stuck her tongue out at him. "If you die, I'll follow after you."

I kissed her hard. "Same, babe, same."

My stomach was doing somersaults as I walked away from my wife. The fact that she was my wife made my lips kick up into a smile. Hadley was my wife, and nothing would ever come close to making me so freaking happy.

"That's quite the smile for someone about to die," Jake said, handing me my gloves and my good riding hat.

"If it's my time to go, I'll go a happy man, because I knew the love of that perfect fucking woman."

"You two are sickening."

"You're just jealous," I teased.

"Fuck yeah, I am."

I got ready to ride.

~

After getting on that horse, I remembered nothing else, but I recalled something about Hadley, which had to mean something.

Shawanda continued to blow up my phone. I needed time to think, but more importantly, I needed time to remember. My stomach was twisted in knots and I felt a sense of impending doom.

Wanda: You know Hadley never really loved you. She only wants your money.

Wanda: You need to get a divorce so we can be together.

Wanda: Come home. I miss you.

Wanda: You need to come so we can talk!

Wanda: Where are you?

I slid my phone back into my pocket, still looking out over the rodeo grounds, when I felt a slap on my back.

"Are you thinking of coming back?" Fred Carr, the operations manager, asked in his raspy baritone voice.

"I'm still trying to remember."

He pulled the ever-present pipe from his shirt pocket. He poured cherry pipe tobacco into the wooden pipe and lit it. His white mustache was stained yellow from where the smoke billowed around his lips. His light gray eyes held a wealth of wisdom. His cowboy hat was sweat-stained, covering a full head of snow-white hair. The lines on his face spoke of years spent in the sun and working hard.

We stood there in silence for a bit, the warm South Dakota breeze swirling the scents of the rodeo and his pipe smoke around us. The smell wasn't pleasant, but it felt comforting.

"I left her desk exactly as she left it," he broke the silence.

"It's been a month. Don't you need to hire someone for her position?"

He blew out smoke, shrugging. "We're good right now. If you could remember her, I bet she'd come home."

"That's why I'm here, hoping something breaks free in my head."

"It's the trauma of the fall. Remember that ride and you'll remember the girl." He tapped out the burnt tobacco from his pipe on the fence, then headed to the office. I knew he expected me to follow without him saying a word. When I fell into step with him, he said, "You two share a love that most people never understand. Even though you can't remember, you should still be able to feel her in here." He slapped a hand over my heart. "You should have never shacked up with that other woman."

I now understand what an enormous mistake I made by moving in with Wanda, but it's too late. "I have to find Hads, but I feel I need to remember first."

He pulled the door open. "Ask yourself how you'd feel if your memories came back in a year and, by then, some other man realized what an amazing gift she was and that she was now his. How would that make you feel?"

"We're still married."

"Not what I asked."

"I would fucking hate it," I admitted. He nodded his head and then headed straight to a desk.

"This is her space. It's like a fucking shrine to you and her. To your love."

There was a metal desk with a corkboard on the wall, filled with nothing but pictures of me and a few with Hadley and me. Little stuffed animals lined a shelf. There was a license plate that read "Dakota" and had red hearts drawn all over it. Right by her computer monitor was the picture from our wedding, where I held her in my arms, carrying her to the altar to marry me. The space still smelled like cherry blossoms.

"Every month, you would send her a bouquet of flowers. They were always on a different day of the month and a different type of bouquet, so she never knew when they would arrive. Even though she knew they were coming, she never knew when, and every single time she received those flowers, she would tear up. But they always had the same message." He opened a drawer in her desk filled with notecards and pulled several out.

I will always follow you. I love you more than Orion, more than anything, and I need you more than my next breath.

Your loving husband.

"She kept them all?"

He bobbed his head. "She did. You promised to follow her. Now get your ass out there and keep your promise."

"Yes, sir." I saluted him.

"If you want to come back to the rodeo, there will always be a place for you."

I nodded as I left. I was trying to think of where I could find my wife. I needed to apologize and convince her to move back to our home.

My phone was still blowing up. I ignored the buzzing while with Fred, but now I pulled it out, hoping I'd get a message from Hads. There were twenty-two from Wanda, but one was from my buddy Jeff.

Jeff: I saw your truck at the rodeo grounds. Would you be free to swing by my office?

I quickly responded: I can go there now.

Jeff: See you in a few.

Ten minutes later, I walked into Jeff's home office. His assistant, Vera, waved me in and told me to go right back.

Jeff was sitting behind his big wooden desk, which was full of law books. His brown hair was neat and his wire-rimmed glasses perfectly framed his nose. "Have a seat."

I took the leather chair across from him. He rubbed at his temples. "Why do I feel like you didn't call me here for a social visit?"

He tapped on some papers on his desk. "I was going to call a process server for this, but we've been friends too long. I wanted to do this in person. I've held onto these for as long as I could." He used his index finger to push the papers toward me.

I glanced halfway across the desk and saw that it was a divorce decree. If I didn't pick it up and look at it, it wouldn't exist. I shook my head, crossed my arms over my chest and put my hands in my armpits.

"How long have you known?"

"A month. She sent me a message right before she disappeared."

Hope unfurled in my chest. "Then you know where she is. Tell me, and I'll go to her and fix this."

"I don't know where she is. We only communicate by email, and those are sporadic from her." He let out a heavy sigh. "Plus, I believe it's too late."

"It's never too late and I'm not signing it."

"If you don't sign, we'll go to court. She claimed abandonment of the marriage."

I scrunched up my face, trying to figure out what that meant. "I didn't abandon her. I'm here. She's the one who left me."

"Did you or did you not move in with Shawanda?"

"Yes, but ..."

"But nothing. That's all the proof we need." He handed me more papers.

"What's this?"

"They're all the social media posts Shawanda tagged your wife in."

I flipped through the pages. One picture showed my truck sitting in Wanda's driveway, with a little step stool by the passenger side door. The caption read, "When he knows you need help getting in his truck for date nights, he makes sure you're always taken care of."

There was one with a table set with candles. "Still romantic after all these years."

There were many pictures of wedding dresses and flowers. "Stay tuned, my friends. It's going to be the wedding of the decade."

There was one where her legs were on a man's legs, his left hand on her calf. There was no mistaking the wedding ring on his finger. That one read, "Foot rubs after a long day are the best when they're done by the one who loves you the most. #strongerthanever #moreinlovenow #distancemakestheheartgrowstronger." In each picture, all the likes were shown, and Hadley's name was highlighted with every like and comment.

The last photo had a comment from Hads that read, "I'm so glad Dakota is happy."

I threw the pictures back on the desk. "That's bullshit! Why didn't I see any of these? If I had, I would have put an end to this nonsense."

"My guess is that when she posts these, she will only allow a certain audience to see them." He pulled up the one with the legs. "Hadley said she knew this was your hand and it was your wedding ring."

"It is. Wanda and I were engrossed in a movie, and she put her feet in my lap. Without thinking, I rested my hand on her legs. Why are those printed out?"

"Evidence."

"Is there any way you can hold this off for a bit more?"

"I've held off too long already, telling Hadley I was busy with a case, but I might be able to tell her you can't sign anything, until the doctor has cleared you. You shouldn't be signing anything when you're not in your right mind, and you leaving Hadley proves that you, my friend, are not in your right mind." I glared at my friend. "I'd say the same thing to her if she was sitting where you are."

Jeff stood up, turning to a small safe on the wall and placing his thumb on the pad. It beeped and opened. It was full of keys. He took one out and tossed it on the desk, then sat back down. "I know you don't remember much about Hadley, but you do know she used to live with her grandma in Deadwood Canyon, right?"

"Vaguely, why?"

He picked up the key from the desk and swung it from the keyring around his finger. "When you and Hadley got married, she put her grandma's cabin on one of those rental sites. She's made you guys a nice sum of money. We manage everything for her."

"Okay?" I wasn't sure where he was going with this.

"Sometimes, she would stop the rental if you two had family or friends coming into town and needed a place to stay. She took the cabin off the site about a month ago and recently asked us to put it back up. I need to send someone over there to clean it." I stared at him, wondering where the hell he was going with this. "I believe that's where your wife has been for the last month."

My heart rate increased. "Do you think she's still there?"

He shook his head. "No, but it needs to be cleaned. If you go there, you might find clues about where she is now."

I took the key from him. "I need to go back to work at the ranch for a bit, talk to Wanda, and then I'll go there. You have no idea how much this means to me."

"You two are meant to be. I'm doing this for love. Now go find your girl, and don't make me regret putting my license in jeopardy."

8

DAKOTA

I got back to the ranch to finish working and usually, I don't mind rounding up cows as I ride Orion through the hills, but today, I could only think of Hads, praying she was okay. Dreams and memories assaulted me at all times of the day and night, and I let them wash over me.

~

We were in bed after making love. She had her hand on my chest over my heart. "I never knew I could be this happy. You've created heaven for me." She kissed me.

"You're my angel, and if you are lucky enough to have an angel by your side, then one must give her heaven so she will never want to leave."

She straddled me, kissing me so lovingly that she got a rise out of me, and then she rode me into oblivion.

~

In every memory or dream, she was always there, ready and willing whenever I wanted her. I knew I missed holding her in my arms at night and having dinner with her. I may not remember everything, but I knew without a doubt I missed her, and I fucked things up by staying with Wanda.

When the day at the ranch was over, my mom told me Wanda was the right person for me. My dad told me to remember my vows and follow my heart, because those two things were the same.

I went right over to Wanda's and the closer I got, the more pissed off I became, seeing those damn posts she made and tagged my fucking wife in.

I pounded on the door as if I had a search warrant. She pulled open the door in a silky robe. "Baby, I'm so glad you're here, but you don't have to knock. This is just as much your home as it is mine." She flung her arms around my neck. I walked with her into the house before pulling her arms away.

"I have a home."

"Once you sell it and move in here, it will be yours. When are you putting your house on the market?"

"Sit down, Wanda." She sat tentatively in the chair by the fireplace.

"This sounds serious."

"It is."

"Yes!" she screamed, clapping her hands.

"What exactly are you agreeing to?"

"I'll marry you! A thousand times, yes!" When she stood, I put a hand up to stop her from advancing and shook my head. She sat back down with her bottom lip sticking out.

"I'm married, and I don't have any plans to change who my wife is. I'm not living with you. You and I were over the moment I saw Hadley." She opened her mouth to speak, but I went on. "She didn't poison me against you. You will delete all those posts on your social media accounts that you tagged Hadley in, and if you don't, I'll sue you. I should have never moved in with you or given you hope. I don't want to be lovers, and I don't want to be friends with you."

"Think about how huge we would be if we combined our family businesses. We would be unstoppable."

"No. It's not happening. Even if Hadley hadn't shown up, you and I would have ended. I'm going to find my wife and grovel for her forgiveness. I will be blocking you on everything. If you see me walking down the street, walk on the other side. I don't want you." I knew it was cruel, but with Wanda, that was the only way she would understand. I turned on my heel, leaving her as she fell to the ground, screaming and crying.

On my way to the canyon, I replayed the ride that caused this mess so many times, but once I got to the accident, nothing—everything—was black. I knew I needed to give Hads and me a chance. My actions were unfair to her.

I pulled up to the cabin and looked around. I remembered Hadley and me on the back deck watching the river. We sat, holding hands, content with only the sounds of nature and one another.

In my head, I heard a blood-curdling scream filled with so much pain and heartache that it had me clutching my chest. With that scream, every memory I've ever had with my wife came rushing back so fast, I got a throbbing headache. It was her scream when I had been kicked in the head.

It was a scream so painful, it had the power to unblock everything. With the memories came the pain of what I had done to my wife, my angel, my everything. I chose another woman over her.

I wasn't much of a crier and never had been, but now I felt the hot tears streaming down my face, not at my pain, but at Hadley's pain. The hurt I caused her was crushing me, after promising always to follow her and to create heaven for her. She would always be my angel. I failed her and us.

My thoughts turned toward what I would have done had the tables been reversed and she forgotten me, then moved in with an ex of hers. At that thought, cold, hard rage took over the pain.

We lost months together. Months of me causing her so much pain.

How could I ever make things up to her?

There was no gesture big enough to warrant her forgiveness. I prayed once she knew I remembered her, she'd accept me again. I remember the love we shared. There was no one I loved more than my Hads ... no one.

I may have lost my memories, but there was no excuse I could give for not staying with her in our house—the place where we worked side by side to make a home. The home where we thought we would raise our children and grow old together. I left that life, because Wanda was what was familiar at the time, even though Hads told me I needed to stay with her while recovering.

A traumatic head injury was no excuse to shun my wife. I should have stayed in our home by her side, trying to relearn everything about her and our relationship. There was a reason I asked her to marry me and if I pulled my head out of my ass, I would have understood how much I needed her. I may have gotten my memories back sooner by staying where I spent the last few years of my life, but I was an ass to the one person who mattered most to me.

I shook my head out of my memories and stared closely at the property. Looking at the little cabin, I knew she wasn't there. Her car wasn't in the driveway. It didn't stop me from hoping. I couldn't believe she wanted a divorce. There was no way I was giving her one. If it went to court, I could see her again and beg her to take me back.

She wouldn't want to leave me now that my memories were back. At least I can hope this is true. I needed to find her and remind her of how much we love each other, because there's no way I would want to live in a world without my Hads. You can't live without a heart, and she is mine. I'll promise her anything—counseling, a vacation, moving someplace else—anything to bring her back to me.

With my head pounding and my heart aching, I made my way to the door of the cabin. I needed her to be here, but I knew she wasn't. Deadwood was too small and she would have never wanted to run into Shawanda and me. She'd leave here so as not to see us together. I couldn't fault her for leaving, but I hoped she wouldn't.

Once I opened the door, the scent of the cabin, which was all hers, made my heart soar.

The place was clean, but I could tell someone had been staying there. However, there was no Hadley, other than her smell.

The trash cans needed emptying and the dishes were in the drying rack by the sink. Most of the small trash cans contained tissues, making it seem like whoever was there had been sick with a cold. But I knew she had been crying her heart out ... because of me.

After searching for clues about where she had gone and finding nothing, I kicked the trash can in the bathroom, scattering the contents all over the floor. I was going to leave it there, because the cleaners were coming, but I heard Hadley's voice in my mind: *"Don't make someone else's life harder if you don't have to."* She said those words after we had dinner out and she started cleaning up the table. I told her to leave it, because they had people to clean it up.

I didn't want to disappoint her more than I already had. I bent down to start putting the trash back in the can when not one, but three white sticks caught my attention.

Pregnant.

All three tests were positive.

Hads was pregnant.

I knew the baby was mine.

I also knew she was out there all alone.

I needed to find her. If I had more hair, I'd be pulling it out right now.

I would find my wife and bring her home, or stay with her no matter where she was. But I hope she wants to raise our child in Deadwood with me.

HADLEY

Three months later

I could not stay in Deadwood and watch Dakota and Shawanda rekindle their love. I needed to forget about Dakota.

My hands went to my stomach. I blocked everyone from Deadwood, because there were no secrets in a town that small. Everyone was too close. I didn't want Dakota to feel obligated to care for a child he had with a woman he didn't know.

The plan was to stay away until he regained his memories. I would check in with Jeff periodically to see if and when that would happen.

The hurt from leaving was still so intense that, on certain days, it brought me to my knees. However, having a piece of Dakota inside me was beginning to heal me.

Jeff told me Dakota couldn't sign the divorce papers until his memories came back, which meant if I wanted to proceed, we'd have no choice but to go to court. I was at a crossroads in my thinking, because on the one hand, I left him to allow him to move on, and on the other, if I showed up, he'd know I was pregnant with his child.

After leaving Deadwood, I traveled to Colorado, where my uncle lived. He had an apartment above his garage, which he let me move into, until I could find a place for myself and the baby. However, the cost of living in Colorado is insane.

To supplement my virtual assistant job, I had to take a part-time job at a coffee shop within walking distance of my place. Being a single mom would not be easy, but I'd do it for as long as Dakota's memories are gone.

Thankfully, the scent of coffee didn't make me want to puke anymore. I had to breathe through my mouth for the first month after I started working in the shop. Today was just going to be another day of working and waiting for my love to remember me. I rubbed my belly as I took out the coffee grounds and replaced them to make another pot before the mid-morning rush.

"Hadley, I'm taking my break. Will you stay up front?" Shelly asked as she grabbed her vape and headed out back.

"No problem." I had been in the back taking out some scones before changing the coffee. I began placing them on the cooling rack when I heard the bell over the door.

I wiped my hands on a white towel while approaching the cash register rubbing my growing belly.

"Are you ready to come back to Deadwood, Hads?" He looked as sexy as ever ... tired, but sexy.

Dakota found me. The emotions flooded both of us. Tears were in our eyes as we slowly gravitated toward each other, unaware of the world around us.

It looked like there would be no forgetting Dakota.

If you enjoyed Forgetting Dakota, follow me so you don't miss the upcoming full-length novel. Find out what happens next.

This is dedicated to anyone trying to forget their true love. I hope you find what you're looking for in love. To my husband Mark, the best husband ever, I love you most!

Thank you to all the authors and organizers of Wild Deadwood Reads for letting me participate in this incredible event and share my story with you. Also, thank you to my excellent editor, Hillary Crawford, my Alpha reader, Monica Bird, and my beta readers, Shana Colbert and Deanne Fenton. You guys are the best.

ABOUT THE AUTHOR

Vicky Wahl, writing as VJ Lee, writes the Glowing series, a paranormal romance, sci-fi, and action series with steamy content and characters you will love but also want to punch in the face. She also writes contemporary/light fantasy/murder mystery romances. Vicky lives in Colorado with the best husband (Mark) in the world and, besides writing, stays home to care for her 200-pound Furbaby. She has two sons, Nick and Larry. The entire family loves the mountains and hiking, but Vicky also enjoys shopping for shoes and reading. Find out more on her website: https://www.facebook.-com/VJLeeauthor

Blog: vjleeauthor.wordpress.com

THE WOLF'S GAMBLE

AMANDA REID

1

JOSEPHINE

Deadwood, South Dakota, 1908

I searched for my quarry through a gap between the swinging door and the jamb. The position allowed me to see only a bare sliver of the Franklin Hotel's luxurious lobby. Air seemed impossible to draw into my lungs. I pulled away, my heart thudding with both anticipation and fear.

With a tug to straighten my apron's lacy shoulder strap, I gave myself a stern admonishment, ending with, *The plan* will *work.*

I shoved aside the gnawing anxiety and took a settling breath. In a whisper I asked, "Which one is he?"

Milo, a tall, gangly porter who stood on the other side of the door facing the patrons, murmured back, "The tall one in the gray, striped suit with the dark red tie."

Since the position limited my view to a tiny fraction, I strained for several seconds to see the fancily clad visitors and high-profile Deadwood residents. No fat, old bankers loitered in the lobby. "You sure?"

"Yes." Milo's tone turned snappish. "He's in the governor's suite. Now leave me alone, witch."

His sour, hissing whisper struck like a rattlesnake. A momentary twinge of guilt stabbed me. I shoved away the misgiving. Unless I had a sincere need, I tried not to read someone's mind. And I never black-mailed anyone with the information I found...well...usually. I had reason enough this time, though card cheat Milo Fenster would never learn how I discovered his secret or why I'd targeted him. "I will. Thank you."

No response came from him because while I was busy feeling guilty, the porter had moved from his position, drat him.

I plied my gaze through the gap, once more in search of my target. A woman wearing a wide-brimmed hat moved away, and my gaze snagged on a man, one who wasn't the corpulent, wealthy busi-nessman I'd envisioned when I wrote my letter. This one, clad in the gray, striped suit with a maroon tie, made my heart jump against my ribs and my mouth go dry.

This was Aaron Monaghan, president of the Emerald Hill Corporation, owner of a bank and a very profitable mining company?

Perhaps sensing my perusal, he lifted his head. His piercing hazel gaze connected with mine carrying all the impact of Zeus's thund-erbolt. Voices and movement seemed to slow, yet time remained curi-ously the same between him and me. My cheeks flooded with heat when he widened his lids and intensified his focus until electricity seemed to arc between the two of us.

In a panic, I pulled away and slid around to the narrow employ-ees' hallway, heart pounding heavier than the thuds of a mule train carting ore.

While I frantically sucked for moisture in order to swallow once more, I tried to convince myself that Milo had been incorrect. The whipcord-muscled man who stood a head taller than anyone in the lobby was no rotund, ancient banker. I'd be tempted to discount the man as my target, yet his features seemed familiar. The thick auburn hair with a widow's peak, dimple in his chin, and a prominent nose were all similar enough for me to consider he might be the cousin Sean asked me to find.

At least the handsome man would never be able to identify me.

"What are you doing here?"

The sharp voice brought me out of my reverie to the short man standing right inside the door. He stared at me with bug eyes, while his dark hair and handlebar mustache fairly dripped with Macassar oil.

Oh no. The front desk manager, Jim Nicholson. *Hades bells.*

I dropped my chin, trying to hide from his prying scrutiny. After a small curtsy, I said, "Sorry, sir. I saw...a pretty hat and wanted to study it."

"Aren't you Josephine Lukas? What's a schoolteacher doing working as a maid?"

Hera's toga. The Deadwood area might have a population in the three thousands but the number who stayed in this old boomtown even a year remained small. I'd been here for four full years, and though teachers were generally considered old maids, in this part of the world, a woman was a woman whether attractive or a dried-up schoolmarm. Like my instructors at the Indiana Normal School suggested, I'd arrived in town with my hair pulled back into a knot severe enough no one would've guessed I had a wild mass of corkscrew curls.

Mr. Nicholson shifted his position, and I realized I needed to answer his question, both stated and implied. I adopted my most marm-ish tone. "Yes. I am *Miss* Lukas. I thought I could earn some money while the children are out of school."

When I'd started at the hotel last week, I came ready with my reason, though a flat lie. I could earn more giving piano, drama, and art lessons to the children of the more well-to-do in Deadwood and Lead during summer recess. He wouldn't know otherwise.

Heat poured into my cheeks once more when his beady eyes swept down my body and lingered on my bodice. Furious, I tried to shut out his thoughts. They battered my mind. A picture of him grabbing my quite large bosom and the words *"great titties"* in the most lustful tone imaginable slid past my mental wall. I bit the inside of my lips to keep from making a snappy comment to the same unwanted attention I'd been subjected to since fourteen years old.

He stepped closer. While not a tall man, he loomed over my petite frame. The spice-scented Macassar oil he used couldn't cover his body's stench, and I wanted to retch from the acrid combination. His small, ogling eyes grew speculative. "If you need more money, I know how you could make more...a lot more."

This was a mining town. Even the Franklin Hotel, the nicest accommodation in Deadwood, happily provided carnal services to their male travelers. Discreetly, of course. My palm itched with the urge to reach up and slap him for the presumption. Unfortunately, I needed this job, at least until I could determine Mr. Monaghan's intentions. Then I could leave and never look back.

I dipped my chin to hide my rage at the manager's insinuation and squeaked out, "No, thank you." I slid by and hurried down the short hallway.

The weight of his leer landed on my back like a brand.

"Let me know if you change your mind." His greasy pompousness made me curl my hands into fists.

I turned the corner, grateful when I didn't detect the awful man pursuing me. Avoiding him had, and would continue to be, a priority. I sped toward the stairs leading to the third floor and that much closer to fulfilling my promise. Along the way, I grabbed bed linens and bath sheets as an excuse should I be waylaid.

The stairs were busy during midafternoon hours. Happily, I dodged the matron who rode herd on the maids. With a nod to those I didn't know and a hushed greeting to those I'd encountered in town before, I finally stopped in front of the door to the suite where Governor Crawford had stayed. I'd heard the furnishings were as fine as could be found for hundreds of miles. A large parlor paired with an equally opulent bedroom. The hotel provided a telephone and steam heat for the winter, not to mention a private water closet and bathroom.

Luck must've been with me—the long hallway stood empty. My fingers shook when from my pocket I pulled the master key I'd filched earlier. I taught school, not burgled people's possessions. *Not being nervous would only indicate you're comfortable poking around in Mr. Monaghan's possessions.*

With that assurance, I let down my mental wall and allowed the thoughts around me to filter in, wincing at some of the stray images and silent comments around me. Though my radius was only about thirty feet, I could often reach for certain people with concentration.

The picture of him formed in my mind. Thick auburn hair with hints of bright copper, surprisingly tanned skin, a square jaw. Broad shoulders under his jacket came to a narrow waist, which could've been added padding at the top, yet I suspected not. Gorgeous, gleaming hazel eyes came fringed with the thickest lashes. I focused hard, since I might discern his whereabouts if I could sense his thoughts.

Just when I thought I'd come up with nothing, my senses tingled.

My stomach wobbled when a picture of Aaron Monaghan flashed into my mind, his arms lining either side of the tub, his head leaned back against the rolled porcelain rim, fingers idly brushing against the smooth, white surface. His knees tented above the water, and his shoulders...goodness. They were hard, muscled, and quite pale compared to his tanned face, hands, and neck.

I hastily pulled my senses back. A trickle of sweat slid down my cleavage, my cheeks blazed with the warmth of a smelter furnace, and my breaths came in swift puffs. The vision had been in third person, not from his viewpoint. Unlike my mother, I'd never experienced visions, let alone anything this...this sensual before.

Voices echoed in the stairwell over my right shoulder and the whirring from the elevator over my left shoulder said I shouldn't be wasting time on silly fantasies. I hadn't received any of his thoughts. He must not be inside. I knocked briskly and announced, "Hotel maid, sir. I have towels."

I didn't wait for an answer. The trembling in my hand made the key rattle in the lock. Heartbeats pounded in my ears when I slipped into the room, then applied the deadbolt.

With a sigh of relief, I leaned back against the door and took stock of the room. A trunk and a travelling case sat next to the bedroom's entrance to my right. Perhaps they held clues. My choice might not be the Sisyphean challenge I imagined.

At some point, I must get close enough to read his thoughts. Until then, a quick examination of his personal effects would give me a better idea of his moral quality. Now began my task to determine whether he possessed the worth to claim his cousin's legacy.

2

AARON

From my position in the tub, my keen wolf's hearing picked up the quick knock on the door, followed by a woman's quiet voice saying, "Hotel maid, sir. I have towels."

I glanced to the bars, and indeed, no towels were hanging. Since I'd shut the bathroom door out of habit, I didn't bother to rise from my position in the tub. She wouldn't see anything upsetting to a woman's delicate sensibilities. Up until recently, I'd shared my one-bathroom house with others, including an ornery, quite capable cook. Modesty wasn't a routine practice in in my world, but the presence of Cookie meant nudity went by the wayside. I liked my meals edible, thank you.

The door had no lock. Though I suspected the maid would knock, since the tub I currently lounged in sat next to the door, I put my palm flat against the thick oak panel to stop her from barging inside. The obsequious front desk manager told me upon check-in that he could provide me assistance in obtaining whatever entertainments I desired during my stay. His arch tone suggested he would be happy to arrange female companionship for the night. I had no need of one of the maids for the evening, nor of giving one an eyeful.

I leaned my head against the tub's rim once more and stared at the patterns in the painted tin ceiling. The reason I'd made the trip from Denver returned to my thoughts. Dated three weeks ago, the letter claimed my cousin and his wife were killed for their mining claim not far outside Deadwood. The word "murdered" had seemed to leap from the page, and the allegation written in an elegant hand still stole my breath.

When Sean came into adulthood ten years ago, he'd withdrawn from the pack structure and our friendship, eventually leaving the family mining business to seek his own fortune. He'd refused to keep in touch, and as soon as he realized I'd hired people to watch him, attempts to monitor his activities were as impossible as following a wolf in the forest.

I hadn't believed—hadn't *wanted* to believe—the anonymous letter. Via telegram, I confirmed Sean had indeed died. The response concerned me since the sheriff said my cousin and his wife, Anne, had died in a fire caused by his stove. The conflagration had burned his home to the ground in the middle of the night. He added he would be happy to have someone pack up what effects could be recovered and send them on. On the face, this explanation seemed innocent enough. Except, we weren't affected by drink or drug. He should've woken—unless he couldn't.

More importantly, Sheriff Plunkett hadn't mentioned the mining claim in the telegram I'd received after his death.

These two facts had added to my instinct, which said I needed to obey the author who commanded my immediate attention. I hadn't informed the sheriff of my arrival in Deadwood to investigate. Discreet inquiry said he was an honorable man. I would have to trust fortune in that matter. Unfortunately, I had business to conduct in Chicago, which delayed me for the better part of the week.

I'd become impatient and irritable by the time I'd concluded the meetings. For the nearly one-thousand-mile trip, I'd had no time to arrange for a private car, which left me on a hard bench for the two-day jaunt to Rapid City, with an additional half-day to Deadwood.

The town reminded me of Walsenburg, Colorado—a community trying to grow beyond its start as a rough and tumble mining town. Here, respectable stores and two reputable hotels lined the upper part of the main street, sitting next to gambling saloons. Pull back the curtains on the main thoroughfare, and you'd find the seedy backstreets teeming with every manner of society's worst villains. A lone wolf must be careful without the safety of his family's pack. Even an

Ossory wolf could be overcome, as our ancestor king Laignech Fáelad well knew.

My thoughts jumped to Sean's burning need to escape our close-knit pack. We'd practically grown up together, only in his teen years to inexplicably drift apart. I never knew where he'd come to live or discovered he'd married. My sorrow grew until a wolf's pain with the loss of a pack brother howled in my head.

A trembling in my arm's muscles pulled me from the dark thoughts to the recognition the maid hadn't knocked or tried to open the door. Surely at least a minute, if not more, had passed. Suspicion flared, and I opened the hearing I normally kept suppressed in town.

Rustles met my ears, then a *click*. One sounding like the latch on my business case.

A case I kept locked because of bank business and the money I typically kept inside.

Though my clothing hung from hooks in the bathroom, I'd left my keys on the dresser, along with my watch, stickpin, ring, and wallet.

Dammit. I'd been in the room only long enough to draw a bath and had already been targeted by a thief. I rose from the warm water, seeking both silence and speed before I lost all my valuables. Corralling my anger, I cracked open the door, grateful the hinges didn't squeak, then I channeled my feral half to swiftly cross through the bedroom to the suite's parlor.

The growl in my head turned into a snarl when a petite figure in a black dress and white apron dug through my case.

She snapped the metal lock shut and turned the small key. When she pivoted toward me, the growls in my head immediately ceased.

Petite and generously curved in all the best places, she let out a squeak of surprise. Her gaze darted below my waist, then back up. Her wide eyes were blue, and her face carried an unnatural pallor. "S-Sir. I didn't know you were in here."

"Obviously." I crossed my arms, uncaring of my nudity. This thief undoubtedly had plied her body to the trade as well, possibly even been sent up by the greasy front desk manager. "What did you steal?"

She stood straighter and threw back her shoulders, an action that emphasized her magnificent chest, an action my wolf found inordinately desirable.

Shit.

I lunged for the towels on the desk before my animalistic side betrayed me, somehow snagging the fabric square while keeping the little thief firmly pinned with my gaze. While I often used my feral senses to assist me when assessing new people, I shut down my wolf, which had begun to pace at the periphery of my conscious mind. I didn't need the acrid, tell-tale scent of fear—her constant plucking at her apron hem and licking her lips under my scrutiny said enough.

"I didn't steal anything," she finally blurted out.

With a firm tuck, I finished wrapping the towel around my waist while I affixed her with my most intimidating glare. I wanted to believe her innocent act. The unusual impulse immediately made me reexamine her, my senses alert. There were far more than Ossory wolves in the wild, such as Russian bears, coyotes native to America, jaguars from the south. Then there were psychics, though I'd only met those who could read minds or emotions. And those were merely the beings known to me.

She made a slight movement, inching closer to the door.

The little sneak. "Stop."

Her face paled even more, and she nodded with jerky motions. "Sir, I can ex—"

"Shut up." I swiftly crossed the short distance until I stood not two feet away.

Her gaze riveted on my chest, then her lids fluttered, and she swayed.

"Don't you faint." I added the hint of a growl to the end of the order.

After a hard swallow, she whispered, "No sir."

"What's your name?" Her pause prompted me to add, "And don't lie."

"Jo-Josephine. Josephine Lukas."

"Okay, Miss Lukas." She didn't controvert the fact she was unmarried, a guess I made from the lack of a ring on her finger. "I'm going to search you now."

She craned her head back, and her generous lips formed an O. "Suh-search me?"

"For what you stole. Stay still."

I began with her hair. The sheer volume of the knot she'd fashioned could hide small items like coins and jewelry, even if the mass didn't contain my property. Except for the keys, my money clip, stickpin, and ring remained on the dresser. I squeezed the large bun she'd figured on the top of her head. Soft and springy with nothing hard inside. My hands itched to tunnel through and test the strands' texture, maybe to pull pins from—

My wolf howled his approval, and I shut down that tempting thought. I'd been in charge of my family gold mine's security, as well as the bank's, prior to assuming the presidency of both under the Emerald Hill Corporation. I needed to at least act like I could search a criminal, starting with where she could easily conceal a stolen item.

Once again, my wolf lunged to the fore, wanting to search the ample breasts under her apron's bib and the lacy black shirtwaist. Annoyed, I told my feral half, *Not practical.* With the collar tight against her throat, she couldn't have dropped important papers or the money from the case into her cleavage. I stared at her fluttering pulse for several moments before I shook myself free. The manager must have an uncanny ability to read his customers if he could send such a woman who shook my concentration and tempted me to undress her.

I finally regained reason. She would've had to untie her white apron, untuck the dark fabric from her skirt, push the items in, then reassemble her clothing, all in the short time between entry and when I encountered her. Not likely.

I stepped to her side. *Where else?* I checked the most likely place, a pocket on her apron, earning me a gasp upon contact, though no protest.

Good. She understood her predicament.

My palm met hardness and delved inside. I pulled a set of keys on a large ring from her pocket plus an additional key, well-used and with an attached charm. I held up both in front of her face.

"H-hotel keys and my house key."

"You have a house?"

She compressed her lips and jerked her chin a couple of times but avoided my gaze.

Interesting. Not many maids or even chippies could afford a house. She must be good then...

Back to the search.

I placed the keys next to mine on the desk where she'd dropped them. Her skirt pockets came next. I crushed the fabric at her hips with my hands. Damn, her curves fit my palms perfectly, though nothing else felt to be within those pockets.

I swore. My unquenchable attraction to this woman fired an impatience surging through me like lightning. She must have stolen from me. Perhaps she had a hidden pocket in her skirts or petticoats. Now I would have to go methodically down her person to be sure.

Starting at her waist, I crushed and patted my way along the black cotton, all the while pretending I was unmoved by both her softness and the muted rose and lavender scent she wore that mixed with the razor-sharp tang of her fear. My cock under the towel proved me a liar, though, and I willed my rampaging libido to melt away.

Focus. Where had she hidden her loot?

I lifted her skirt hem. She had to have a pouch on her garter facing inside her legs.

"Stop."

The panic-y tremble in her harsh whisper caused my protective nature to come to the surface. I ceased my search and glanced up.

She bit her lip, her cheeks red and her jaw clenched. "I know why you're here."

"I'm here to investigate local investment opportunities."

"No, you're here because your cousin and his wife were murdered."

I rose rapidly and grasped her upper arms, not caring about her muffled cry. My wolf beat at me to shift, the hairs prickling along my spine. I forced back my feral self yet prepared to allow the wolf's growl to enter my voice.

"How do *you* know they were murdered, Miss Lukas?"

3

JOSEPHINE

Mr. Monaghan's accusing stare froze me in place, where I stood most inappropriately in his hotel room. I could almost forget that he wore naught but a towel to cover his classically masculine perfection. Assuming Greek sculptors had been correct in their portrayal of the masculine form, of course.

"You. You wrote the letter." With his teeth bared and nostrils flaring, Cerberus couldn't have been more intimidating, and I snapped out of my scandalous assessment of his naked person.

"Yes," I whispered, apprehension clogging my throat. I dared not even breathe lest I enrage further the man who loomed over me, still clutching my skirt. Why had I not considered that he could he be like Sean and able to turn into a wolf? For too many beats of my racing heart, my life seemed to hang in the balance like the proverbial Sword of Damocles. Would he change and tear me to shreds for what he thought I knew?

Harsh braying laughter from the hotel's hallway broke the tense moment. He dropped my hem and stepped back. Crimson spread across the planes of his cheeks while his lips flattened to join the "V" furrowed in his brow.

"I asked how you knew he was murdered." His words, harsh, low, and mean, matched his demeanor.

Sean had said I needed to contact this man if aught happened to him or his family. His wish meant Aaron Monaghan might be trusted. Yet, Sean did not automatically confide his most precious secret. I'd tell the man standing before me the truth, or at least as much of the truth as I could afford. "I heard it from someone who was present when the murder happened."

"Who?"

Still unsure of his intentions, a spurt of gumption nonetheless prodded me to speak. "I'm not at liberty to say who at this time."

"What?" He'd pulled his upper lip into a snarl.

Though my heart galloped faster than Phaethon's horses, I lifted my chin and added my sternest stare. "I said I am not able to tell you at this time."

For a moment he blinked his gorgeous hazel eyes, then his features smoothed. He backed up to the bedroom's entryway and reached behind the door's jamb, all without taking his eyes off me. Curse him. I wanted to flee but certainly wouldn't reach the door before he would pounce on me.

What did he intend? *Read his mind, you dolt.*

Duh. I'd been shocked enough that I'd totally forgotten I could at least get an idea of his intent. I tried to ignore the wild, curling heat in my body stemming from the way my earlier fantasy of him had come exactly to life. Tried not to see the water drops still clinging to the planes of his taut skin. Tried to erase the unsettling curiosity of how his lips against mine might feel. Instead, I focused my senses on him, searching for his thoughts.

He came forward with something in his hand. I concentrated harder. Nothing—no thoughts, no words, no images—came to me. How could this be?

"I assume you were looking for this." He held up a gold clip containing a thick stack of bills folded in half. He pulled two pieces of rectangular paper from the grouping. "You don't get it all, of course. How about twenty?"

Like Koalemos himself had struck me witless, I stared at him, uncomprehending both his meaning and the possible reasons behind not being able to read his thoughts. Either he possessed abnormal mental abilities like me, or...

Or fate had deemed him the perfect man for me, a person foretold by my mother. Chaos reigned within me, making my thoughts reel.

"Twenty's not enough? You greedy girl." His words brought me back to this room and this nearly naked man in time to witness him pulling another set of bills from the stack and adding them to the first bundle. He held them out to me. "A hundred is as far as I can go. The name, please. Or should I call the sheriff?"

The casual manner he composed his question sent shivers through me, as if he cared less for me than the hundred dollars he held in his hand. Definitely not the love sent by the fates Mother promised. Fury lit within my heart. I was no thief, only attempting to make the best of a vow made to another.

"I want nothing." I pitched my tone low and with as much venom as possible. "I have taken nothing. Unlike the ones who stole from you and your family."

His head canted slightly, then he dropped his faux blasé demeanor in favor of a scowl. "Tell me who the murderers were then."

"Charles Williams, Robert Farley, and a third unknown man. They killed Sean and Anne."

"How?" The word shot from his mouth like a crack of a whip.

"They told Sean they wanted to buy the claim and said they had the money. Then they attacked. Hit him over the head until they cracked his skull, demanding the claim title. When Anne told them she didn't have it, they raped and killed her. Then they set fire to the cabin." The words I had repeated had been told to me in a quivering, lisping voice. The information still chilled me to my marrow. The last decade had brought much justice to this often lawless area of the county, yet much evil still persisted.

I shook off the dark thoughts and stared at the man oppose me. Mr. Monaghan's hands were bunched into fists, while a muscle feathered in his cheek. Violence seemed to roll off of him in waves, and I had to suppress the urge to flee what could only be Nemesis personified. After several tense seconds that kept my breath hung in my lungs, he asked, "You won't tell me who told you this?"

"No." The word came out on a croak because my mouth had become drier than the Badlands. I forced myself to gather moisture and swallow before I continued, "I neither want nor require your money. All I can say is I didn't witness this abomination."

"Why did you contact me?"

"I promised Sean and Anne I would if something happened to

them." A small pang of guilt lodged in my heart for the omission I'd made. I had to be sure. From a small pocket in the back of my skirt's waistband that I sewed into all my clothing, I withdrew an envelope I'd folded in two. I held the crumpled item to him. "From Sean."

He plucked the paper from my fingers, then opened the single fold to expose the seal used to close the flap. For several moments he stared at the emerald-green wax, brushing his thumb back and forth over the embossed, stylized wolf's head.

The anguish that flitted across his face lessened my fear. This was a hard country. No doubt he was a hard man, but one capable of feelings...unlike many in this town. I placed this fact into a column in his favor.

After popping the seal from the paper, he unfolded the letter and began to read. For several moments I watched him while his eyes followed what had to be script. If Anne had told me the truth, Mr. Monaghan would be reading Sean's will, where he left all of his possessions, including the Golden Shamrock mining claim, to his mother, controverting the bogus will filed with the county clerk leaving the mine to his supposed partners, Charles Williams and Robert Farley.

The version Mr. Monaghan currently read contained no mention of Sean and Anne's two boys, Patrick and Thomas.

Sean and Anne told me the decision would be mine. If I felt Aaron Monaghan would treat his and Anne's children and their inheritance with respect, I would deliver the children to him along with the second letter, which contained a newer will.

But, if I believed him to be covetous and unworthy, I should take them, along with the third letter, and escape to San Francisco. I'd already secured employment as Mrs. Lukas, a widow teaching classical Greek literature at a private girls' school. Luckily, my grandmother's gold ring fit on my left hand's third finger, and my classics professor at Indiana Normal School agreed to write me a recommendation including the small lie of my marriage status. After all, widows received far more leeway in society. A doctorate could be within my grasp soon, though not if I didn't get to San Francisco.

My chest squeezed hard, and I forced my lungs to expand while panic began to surge through me once more. I dropped my gaze to where my fingers twisted together, and I clasped them tightly to stop them from giving away my anxiety. This must be what Odysseus felt when having to decide between Scylla and Charybdis. The two choices weighed like titans on my shoulders—deny Mr. Monaghan his cousins or give them over to someone who might exploit them.

While I likened my dilemma to Greek myths, I might as well compare the challenge of raising the two boys. My stomach cramped when the urge buffeted me to hand over Patrick and Thomas and run away to my new job.

A prickling awareness rose, and I glanced up to where Mr. Monaghan surveyed me, this time with a keen eye. He tapped the now refolded letter against one of his palms, suggesting deep thought.

I must get more information soon. I taught children. I didn't know how to raise...werewolves. At least Sean said they would start transforming around time the boys turned thirteen.

"Show me their house."

I tried to hide my flinch and obviously failed by how his keen gaze narrowed on me. Sean and Anne had built their cabin on the claim. I had no desire to be anywhere near the scene of their murder. "It's burned to the ground. I could show you their graves."

He shook his head from side to side. "Not good enough. I will see the claim...*and* where they died."

I had no other option but to tell him, and I sucked for moisture to wet my arid mouth. "I believe the men responsible are already working the mine. I dare not go there. I'm not married and have nothing and no one to protect me."

He dipped his head in a brusque acknowledgement. "Show me the way. There is no need to get you involved with killers. You must stay in the area. I will return home and have vastly more resources to protect myself."

Another stroke in his favor. I almost told him about the teaching arrangement I had already secured. *The less he knows about me the better.* When—if—I told him about the boys, he might not appreciate my duplicity, not to mention if I determined I couldn't trust him, he'd know where to find his cousins should he learn about them from other people.

Despite him not hurting me or reporting me to Jim Nicholson when he caught me snooping, I couldn't trust Mr. Monaghan wouldn't seek revenge. Best to keep the plans to myself.

"Very well." His acceptance of my assistance gave me the gumption to make a suggestion. Or three. "Use the staff stairs at the end of the hall, down to the basement, and leave through the employees' entrance. Turn left to the end of the alley, then right. I'll meet you three blocks down. Got it?" After his quick agreement and before continuing, I dared a sweep down his magnificent body, a virtual Greek statue come to life. "Please dress. The clothing in the secret compartment in the top of your trunk would work best. You'll attract too much interest otherwise."

I continued my perusal back up, past the freckles dusting his nose and cheeks, until I connected my gaze with his. "And bring the strange-looking gun you have too. It may well save your life."

4

AARON

I tucked the Browning semi-automatic pistol into my back waistband, then deposited a second magazine into my jacket's pocket. The sleek new gun had been a last-minute addition, one that I'd stored in my trunk's hidden compartment.

How had she found the false panel so quickly, and without disturbing the surrounding clothing? She must be a very good burglar. I shouldn't have been surprised. The unexpected pocket in the back of her skirt meant she had intelligence.

That Sean would take up with a very pretty petty criminal when he'd been married did surprise me. Perhaps *he* had become a petty criminal and no longer protected the weak. My heart stuttered to contemplate his fall into lawlessness, the antithesis of our reason for being Ossory wolves. Many changes can happen to a person in a decade.

Fortunately, his handwriting hadn't changed. He could write logically and legibly, something that would provide his stern mother cold comfort.

I hadn't wanted to crush her hopes of being reunited with her son when I'd received Miss Lukas's letter. Now, I had no choice. His will, one I recognized as in his own hand, left everything to his closest living blood relative exclusively outside of marriage. No problem there, since his mother's second husband, a man I'd never trusted, had died two years prior. She would inherit the Golden Shamrock Claim where Sean and his wife, Anne, died.

Correction. Where they'd been murdered.

Fury lit my blood to flame. If Miss Lukas's accusation was true, I would locate the ones responsible. The sheriff might be involved or merely delinquent in his duties. No matter the case, I would deliver justice.

I checked myself in the wardrobe's mirror, satisfied with the way my threadbare cap hid my red hair. My current clothing had also been in the trunk's false bottom. As the president of the Emerald Hill Corporation, many might think the well-worn getup I wore would never have been in my possession.

Many would be wrong.

I frequented the mine to ensure the safety of our workers and deal with any thieves, plus my previous security position within the pack meant I often required anonymity. Not everything could be handled in wolf form. Some activities needed two-legged stealth, usually things generally not achievable in my finer suits.

My wolf howled his approval, in my mind showing his canines with a growl. He intended to mete his own justice.

I urged the beast to simmer down. First, we must scout the area. And that meant meeting Josephine Lukas as soon as possible. The wolf sat with perked ears at the idea of encountering the beautiful little thief once more.

After I tucked my valuables into the trunk's hidden compartment and secured the lock, I pocketed the key. A quick glimpse outside the door showed a clear hallway. Swiftly, I locked my room's door and hustled to the stairs, pulling my brim low when I encountered a maid. In the basement, I spied the exit and had almost left the building when I heard a man bellow, "Hey, you there!"

I sprinted out the door into the bright sunshine. The clatter of boot heels indicated pursuit. I didn't turn around to gauge the extent, but after two blocks their volume indicated they had slowed. Next, I turned a corner and another, then spotted a saloon suiting my purpose. I ducked inside and strode to the back of the bar, not even out of breath. To blend into the crowd, I leaned my elbows on the stained, worn wood surface. From the corner of my eye, a man jogged by, his head swiveling from side to side. The front desk manager from the hotel.

Interesting.

I slipped out the back of the saloon and retraced my path, my strides long. I needed to find Miss Lukas. Several blocks later, I spied her standing on the corner under a tree. She no longer wore the apron, and she'd perched a modest, unadorned black hat on her golden hair. She shook her head slightly, perhaps disappointed I had showed.

"I was about to leave." She turned abruptly and hurried down the street, south toward the creek, Whitewood, if my memory served. She'd ducked her head, probably to avoid recognition by others. "Hurry. You'll want to get out there before nightfall, and it's more than a mile to the road to the claim between here and Pluma, then yet another two miles into the mountains."

I fell in step next to her, adjusting my pace to match her much shorter stride. "I had to escape the front desk manager. He followed me out of the hotel and chased me down the street."

"Jim Nicholson?" She glanced up at me with her features screwed up as if she'd sucked on the bitterest of lemons. "He's awful. Did he catch you? Dressed as you are, he probably thought you were stealing from someone."

"Didn't catch me, and mostly likely he thought that. I'll have to be careful going back." I pulled the room key from my pocket and offered it to her. "While I'm at the claim, you go to the hotel and get a change of clothing for me so I can enter from the front as Aaron Monaghan and not a casual laborer."

She pulled her hand across her body and away from the key, then tucked her chin even lower. "I can't. I quit the position after I left your room. I have no way to get your clothing out without Mr. Nicholson thinking I'm stealing. Besides, I'm doing enough even being seen with you."

Guilt smacked me in the chest. If we had to travel for more than a mile, then she had to walk back... "You're going to be okay walking back alone, right?"

"I'll continue to Pluma, then take the last train back to Deadwood." Her words were clipped.

"No. I'll walk with you, out of sight if you want me to, until you reach the train." Around us the housing—shacks, really—had become less frequent. "If I lag far enough behind, people won't put us together."

"Would you?" Relief lightened her previously tight tone. "Behind me a bit is better. The terrain shortly becomes even more rocky and steep. You wouldn't be able to keep up if you were off the road."

I could easily pace her in my wolf form. She didn't need to know that information, and the beast didn't need an excuse to get near her. His size would likely only scare her. Then there was the problem of where to put my clothing after I shifted.

"I'll be behind you. Stop when we reach the turnoff to the claim."

"Very well." She hurried along, her skirt twitching with the movement of her hips. I forced myself to ignore the way my pulse jumped each time I looked at her. Rather, I should mull over the stupid move of not asking one of my cousins to join me here.

I let her gain a distance of several hundred yards before I started again. Further beyond her, my keen wolf's sight picked out a cart and team of horses rounding a bend in the distance. I shuffled along, adding a limp to my gait, affecting a man who could walk only as quickly as the woman now ahead of me.

Several minutes later, the team slowed, and the driver addressed Miss Lukas. She glanced over her shoulder and nodded her head, then both continued their original directions, her toward Pluma, the cart toward me and Deadwood.

The older man driving, his thick brown mustache already shot with gray, pulled the team to a stop next to me. A hard glint shone in his eyes from the shade of his hat's wide brim. Crates and boxes piled in the cargo area, while another man, this one young and armed with a shotgun, also sat on the plain board-cum-seat.

The driver said, "Mister. I don't know if you have any intentions on Miss Lukas. I'm here to tell you, we have both seen you."

They wanted to defend a thief? I played dumb. "Who?"

"Miss Lukas." He hooked a thumb behind him and narrowed his gaze even more.

"Don't know her. Who's she to you anyway?" The logo for a general store had been painted on the side of the cart, the gold flourishes crisp. His clothing spoke of a prosperous merchant, while the man next to him wore clothing of slightly lesser value. Why either would know a common thief confused me.

"My girl is going to have her next year, and I won't have you messing it up." He rested his hand on an old Colt he had strapped to his hip, his threat clear.

Have her next year? Regardless of my questions, I held up my hands at chest level. "Just missed the train and decided to walk to Pluma." I added a shrug to indicate my indifference, then pointed to the dark figure in the distance. "I have no intentions toward whoever she is."

"Better not." The man's voice fairly snarled. "Or I'll find you, hear?"

The younger man beside him tapped his hand on the barrel of the shotgun.

Already this had gone on too long. Miss Lukas would turn the bend in the road in seconds. I touched my cap's brim. "Yessir."

"Remember what I said." He slapped the reins on the stout horses' backs and the cart moved on. Despite the violence simmering in his words, I was thankful men such as these still existed on the edges of the world. While much had been accomplished to bring order to an often chaotic frontier, too many scofflaws remained.

With Miss Lukas already out of my sight, I chafed with the delay, waiting until the men in the cart could no longer see me. I could pick up my pace finally, and I rounded the corner to the long stretch of road visible.

My heart jolted in my chest—Miss Lukas had disappeared. I raced ahead. When I came level with a rough bridge spanning the creek with a cart track leading into the trees, a hiss-like whisper on my right said, "Up here."

I turned away from the creek toward the tree line and spied Miss Lukas about twenty yards from the road, up a small slope pocked with summer-browned grass. She peered around a pine's thick trunk, her lower lip tucked in her teeth.

"Come up." She added jerky, urging hand gestures, then ducked back behind her cover.

No one occupied the road. Why would she give the directions there? I climbed the rise, my muscles tight, wary of attack.

When I rounded the brush sitting at the base of the tree, she pulled hard at my sleeve, and I crouched down next to her.

"You could have just shown me the track."

She looked to the heavens as if for deliverance then hit me with a deadpan look. "If the murderers are around, they might get the idea

I'm helping you. Charles Williams is a tall man, a couple inches shorter than you, thin but with a big belly. Wears a black derby hat. Robert Farley is shorter by about half a foot, brown hair, no mustache, almost mousy looking."

"Duly noted. Thank you." *Impressive.* I hadn't thought to ask for their descriptions.

She pointed and then said, "The road to the claim. It makes several switchbacks. After you crest the hill, about a mile later, you'll see the 'no trespassing' signs with the claim listed on the bottom. Be..."

I glanced to her, curious why she didn't finish her sentence. Fear swam in her wide, blue eyes. Softly she said, "Be careful, please. These men are dangerous."

She laid a hand on mine where it rested on my thigh. Tingling rose from the connection, and my wolf leapt forward. For several seconds, I pushed back the shift, trying to shut out the wild howls in my brain. Why would my feral side react to—

Oh no.

Oh, yes, my wolf seemed to say within me.

This woman was my mate. Blood pounded through me, hot and needy. My wolf eagerly sought to claim her lush body, while I struggled to maintain my human form.

"Are you okay?"

I pulled myself from the maelstrom within me and focused once more on the woman, the thief with whom my wolf would demand I spend the rest of my life.

"I appreciate your concern for me with your warning." I added sarcasm to my tone in order to mask my disorientation and lack of focus.

"You have no idea how much your welfare does concern me." Her words were muttered under her breath, low enough so a regular human probably wouldn't have caught them.

My wolf took this as a sign of her acceptance and surged once more. The skin on my forearms prickled. A sheen of sweat broke out over me as I struggled with the other half of me, the one that wanted Josephine Lukas like no other. Finally, I shoved him back. *Dammit. Not now.*

When? A whine came with the word.

I will call you soon.

With a huff, the animal circled and laid down, his tail over his nose, eyes watchful.

The wolf's mischief managed for now, I concentrated once more on my mate. "I'll continue following you to Pluma, then I'll double back here. Where can I find you?"

She examined me, her gaze sharp and intelligent. During her pause, I could almost see the conversation in her head. *Give him the information or not?*

The furrow between her brow eased. "Mount Moriah Cemetery. Eight o'clock tomorrow morning."

"Very well." I tried to shield my reluctance to accept her delay. Not like I could threaten my mate. My constant companion didn't like my answer either. Fortunately, the beast didn't make another attempt at changing my skin to fur.

Sensing she wished to move on, I rose, and she accepted my hand to assist her to standing.

Though reticent to release her, I peeled my fingers away, then watched her pick her way down the hill and continue on toward Pluma. While I trailed her, my wolf kept sniffing for her essence carried to me on the breeze, interrupting my planning.

Approximately twenty minutes later, I reached the rough and tumble crossroad between Deadwood and Lead. Once I had passed the first large mill and could see the small train depot in the distance, I forced my feet to stop, though my desire to follow her nearly won out. She'd be safe enough until tomorrow morning.

I retraced my steps, this time jogging along until I reached the bridge across the creek. After a quick glance both ahead of and behind me to ensure no one would spot my deviation, I sprinted across the bridge, then again across the train tracks that followed the creek back to Deadwood. With swift feet, I climbed, keeping an ear out for a wagon or pedestrian. After about fifteen minutes, I found the claim signs and their warnings to keep out. They were the mass-produced "no trespassing" signs with the claim's name and number stenciled at the bottom.

I must focus. Any misstep I made here could mean the difference between justice for my cousin and potential death for me. Though I should've had another pack member meet me in Deadwood, an urgency gripped me, one saying I needed to do this *now*, then return to Miss Lukas.

After vaulting the barbed-wire fence, I loped off to a small copse of scrubby trees, the ground around them obscured by thick, thorny brush, a perfect hiding place. I set aside the images of the beautiful little thief, and I started shedding my clothing.

The work here would be best done on four legs.

5

JOSEPHINE

With a breath of relief, I unlocked the door and stepped inside my small clapboard house. Fear surged through me like a wave. I had to make sure the children were okay, but not yet.

The inset window rattled when I quickly shut the door behind me, and my fingers trembled while I threw the deadbolt. I strained my hearing for any sign of an intruder—a creaking rafter, a hushed whisper...even the footfall of an enemy who'd figured out my secret. Nothing.

I scanned my small parlor. No one could hide here, not even behind the small sofa whose cushions barely had room for one posterior. Two walls had windows, and they remained intact, latches still applied, curtains drawn. I placed the house's key in my pocket, careful to make no sound. From the desk next to me, I retrieved the small derringer I'd placed there from behind a stack of my favorite Greek literature. I curled my fingers around the cold metal and palmed the mother-of-pearl handle. Though the tiny gun comforted me, a great shudder wracked my frame at the thought of pulling the trigger. I didn't want to hurt anyone.

"This probably won't kill them, though it may keep them occupied for a time." Sean's words floated back to me. To save the kids, though, I knew I could use what some might call a peashooter if required.

I took a calming breath before resuming my search. On my

tiptoes, I continued into the dining room in case an intruder lurked within. Walking silently on wood floors in leather-soled boots wasn't easy, and I winced with every slight sound my steps made. Between the pulse pounding in my ears and the breath sawing in and out of my chest, I probably wouldn't hear an attacker before they struck anyway. I continued through the kitchen at the back of the house and checked the back door.

Locked. Next, I crept into the adjacent bedroom, through the washroom, then onto my bedroom at the front of the house and entered back into the parlor, completing the circle. All window latches were intact. I rubbed my chest, trying to assuage my hammering heart, which seemed to want to break free of my ribcage.

Two more days. Two more days until the train would take me, possibly with the children, to the anonymity of San Francisco. Two more days until all of this fear would end.

Two more days until you'll never see Aaron Monaghan and his classically sculpted body again.

Now why had that thought popped in my head? I shoved the idea aside since my future plans didn't include him.

I pocketed the derringer, stepped back to the small washroom's door, and looked up to the panel built seamlessly into the beadboard-clad ceiling. In a low tone, I said, "Okay, boys, you can come out now."

No movement came from above. Half of me feared they'd snuck out and been found. The other half rejoiced in their discipline.

"Lahnee fahlad." My tongue slipped around the unfamiliar Irish words Patrick had suggested as a safe phrase, though I had no idea of their meaning. "You can come down."

Light footfalls shifted on the attic's rough floorboards. Then the beadboard lifted revealing a dark square, which two pale faces quickly filled.

"We were beginning to worry." Patrick's face screwed up into a scowl. In another ten years, he'd be the spitting image of his father with his dark auburn hair and widow's peak, plus the ruddy complexion. The dusting of freckles similar to his older cousin's made his hazel eyes seem to gleam. *Zeus's thunderbolts. Stop thinking about that man.*

I glanced down to the watch pinned to my bodice, startled to find the hour's lateness, nearly seven o'clock. "My apologies. I met your cousin Aaron today, and he delayed me."

"You did?" Patrick's features disappeared from the access, as did his brother's, replaced by a ladder, which I helped to guide to the floor.

The boys scrambled down the rungs as nimbly as the monkeys I'd seen in the traveling circus cages.

Patrick rounded on me and slid past the ladder in the narrow space. "What is he like? Do you think he's a good man?"

I gazed down to his eager features, then took in the pinched expression on the face of his younger brother, Thomas, who stood at his shoulder. My heart squeezed hard, like Dionysus tried to wrangle the last drop of a grape's juice.

"Shh. Let's sit at the table, and I'll tell you everything." *Well, not the part where I thought he has a form that would make a Greek god envious, of course.*

My kitchen had scant room for a table, which I'd pushed against the wall. Thomas didn't join Patrick and me in one of the three small chairs. Instead, he stood next to his brother, one of his hands wrapped around the ladder-back chair's top rail in a white-knuckled grip. Undoubtedly, the poor child's eyes were haunted with the ghosts of the acts he'd witnessed. His whimpers in the night often left me sobbing silently. I worried if what the two had seen could ever be overcome.

"What did he say?"

Patrick's question pulled me from my ruminations.

I told them of the encounter and how I followed his parents' wishes—I had delivered the first letter. I added that he appeared to be an honorable person, but I would know more in the morning, after I met him at his parents' graves.

"Will I never get to see them again?"

Thomas's forlorn tone caused the tip of my nose to buzz, and I pushed away the tears pricking my lids. The danger of their discovery had meant the boys hadn't attended Sean and Anne's funeral. Or seen anyone other than me, for that matter. How they'd withstood their isolation after such trauma amazed me.

I enfolded his small hand with mine and gave what I hoped was a comforting squeeze, adding a warm, encouraging smile. "If you come to San Francisco, we'll come back every summer to see them. We'll figure out a way. Promise." I should have enough left from what Sean and Anne left me. Even if I didn't, by Hades's hounds, I'd find a way to afford visits and mask their identities.

"If you go with your cousin, you can ask him to come back. Perhaps he might have them sent to Colorado." Lord knew the Monaghan family would give Croesus a run for his riches. They could afford a disinterment and reburial if they chose.

He searched my eyes and nodded, possibly satisfied with what he saw there. "Thank you."

The boy's solemn gratitude humbled me. I'd met many eleven-year-olds. None exhibited this maturity. He might as well be an adult.

I lightly slapped my thighs, giving both a smile. "You're welcome. Now, how about a little dinner? I'm sure your stomachs have forgotten lunch long ago. It'll be dark in a while, and I'll have to get you two settled in the bedroom. Why don't you both wash up?"

"Yes ma'am," Patrick said, while his brother merely followed behind his older sibling. What I wouldn't give to see Thomas laugh once more. He took after Anne and had received her infectious joy for life. Now his shoulders hung limp, and his movements were both stilted and rushed while he tried to keep up, as if afraid Patrick would leave him too.

The door to the bathroom shut behind them, and I turned to the icebox, pushing back the tears once more. Luckily, I had half of a chicken left over from last night, and another whole bread loaf, a sizable cheese wedge, and dried figs to round out the meal. Not the most nutritious, but I could clean out my pantry since I wouldn't be here in two days.

I tried to focus on what might lie ahead, not on what I'd leave behind—my books. I'd pared down to the essentials, those I would need to teach my classes. Though easily five percent of my library, they were still heavy. I'd arranged for the general store's owner I passed today to come pick up the small crate I'd ship to my new school and bring it to the train station on Friday morning. He thought I would be sending them to my "brother" John. Initials came in handy on address labels.

The boys returned, their faces scrubbed and hands meticulously clean. I finished laying out the food while the two set the table with plates and silverware. Possibly due to the day's events, my stomach didn't want to cooperate, and I pushed my meager morsels around the china. The boys didn't have any compunction about wolfing down their generous portions. I did not begrudge their consumption since their needs seemed far greater than normal children. They got oatmeal with raisins before I left, then I provided three ham sandwiches for each during the day. I encouraged them to take more of the simple fare now on the table and heartened to see that, despite Thomas's withdrawn nature, his appetite remained intact.

I silently blessed Sean and Anne. They'd both provided their children manners *and* included five hundred dollars with the letter I'd opened only after the boys came to my house in the dead of night. I pushed the picture from my mind of the two broken and quietly sobbing.

Once they'd finished their milk, they went off to prepare for bed. I washed their dishes, leaving them in the drainboard to dry. At this time of year, sufficient light remained at eight in the evening, and their day's inactivity meant they weren't tired. I gave Patrick a book to read to his brother, Kingsley's *Greek Heroes*. Patrick had sworn they could hide quietly during the day, and though I came by a couple of times early on, I'd not heard as much as a mouse's scurry.

For what had to be the thousandth time in the span of nearly three weeks, I wondered at their fortitude while I sat in my parlor's wingback chair and perused a copy of White's translation of Plutarch's *Lives* one more time before I left the book behind. Though I tried to concentrate, I was familiar enough with the work that I could automatically scan the lines and turn the pages yet contemplate a completely different line of thought.

Like how I would be leaving almost all of this behind. My books, my dishes, my quilt, my world. Sure, the money Sean and Anne gave me would more than provide for new belongings, but I'd built a life here. Friends. Community.

Yet, the dream of teaching Greek literature had been with me for as long as I could remember. I could now achieve my goal as a "widow." Hah. One who had never felt a lover's touch, though I'd had tantalizing hints of the ecstasy between a woman and a man.

A man like Aaron Monaghan.

The weight of my promises pressed on my chest. I'd always thought I would never marry. Enough men told me I "thought too much" and I'd long become comfortable in my path's solitude. Now, despite my denials, I greatly suspected he was the match fated to me. I couldn't read him, the surest sign. How could we possibly mesh— the schoolmarm living in a humble cottage who spent her days in a book and the wealthy banker who undoubtedly lived in a mansion and mingled with only the elite.

Yet, he *had* transformed into a humble laborer.

And virtually a Greek master's statue. Muscled shoulders, chest, abdomen...

Horrified at the direction of the small voice drifting through my mind, I had to shut out the image of Aaron Monaghan in all of his glory. Nothing could come of lingering on the fact I could not explore the possibility of joining with him. The boys needed me to keep them alive, not lust after a man like Zeus did with...well, pretty much any beautiful woman.

I shut my book, and my sight fell on the list of things I had yet to do sitting on the desk next to me. At the top of the list, writing a letter to my friend, a librarian who I would miss dearly, apologizing for leaving unexpectedly, and that she could do what she wished with what I left in the house. Over the last couple of weeks, I'd been slowly selling off the more valuable items due to a lack of room in my carpet bag, but many useful things remained, like my flatware, glassware, curtains, and quilt. My friend made little money, so what I left would help with her finances. The librarian in her would make sure the books would add to what Andrew Carnegie had generously endowed Deadwood.

Endowed.

The events of the afternoon, the part I'd left out of my recitation to the boys, returned to my thoughts, and this time I couldn't shut them out. *Fine.* This one time, I could give in to the temptation of what might've been in different circumstances.

I lapsed into the luxury and the images replayed in my head, more vital, more enticing, and far more carnal than any of the moving pictures I'd seen in the opera house. I leaned my head back and closed my eyes, gliding my fingers across the deckled edges of the book's pages seeking sensory relief from the urge to sample his skin, to discover for myself if his muscles were as hard as they appeared. To learn if his lips provided mine pleasure in the way I'd seen my parents act in my younger years.

Now I desired to experience the full spectrum of the senses I'd read about in my books, not to mention the actions and talk I'd witnessed while on the streets here in Deadwood.

My belly—and parts below—turned hot and liquid with the recall of his anatomy. I squeezed my thighs together at the fullness there and my breathing shortened with the pressure's tingling promise of pleasure. I allowed my memory to leisurely review his body, hard chest, strong arms, the trail of auburn hair down to the apex of his thighs where his...I sucked a swift breath, yet, strangely, my arousal increased, my breasts now straining against my corset with each pant. He appeared much larger than those Greek sculptors had indicated. Though I had rudimentary knowledge of the sexual act's mechanics, how he'd fit—

A scuff of what seemed like a boot met my ears and jolted me from my fantasy. I bolted upright in my chair. The book fell to the floor with a hard *thunk*. Another hard heel met my ears. The sound had come from my front porch on the other side of the wall from me. I had no reason for callers this late, even if dusk only just approached.

I rose to warn the children, but the faintest of scrapings through the door to my bedroom made me think the children were pulling up the ladder.

The knock rattled the whole house, and I slapped a hand over my mouth to stifle a scream with the force used.

"Huh—" I had to swallow hard to moisten my mouth enough to talk. "Who is it?"

"Aaron Monaghan. Open the door, Miss Lukas."

6

AARON

The blood-stained proof I'd found at the mine fled my mind, along with the images of Williams and Farley, both of whose wounds still were no more than half an hour old. Also shoved from top of mind was the question of who killed them.

Fury wanted to burn everything else away.

Having tracked her here, I stood on this porch in a quiet Deadwood neighborhood with her sweet arousal teasing my nose.

Mingled with the clear scent of another wolf. The stench mocked me, pushing me toward frenzy.

My wolf snarled and demanded vengeance.

I barely restrained myself from tearing down Miss Lukas's door. To my left along the short porch, curtains obscured the window most likely to the parlor. The window to my right had drawn curtains as well, probably for a bedroom. A thick ruffled swath of fabric obscured the inset glass on the door. I could see nothing inside, adding to my agitation. Only the dim recognition that the neighbors on this quiet street might come with guns or a sheriff's deputy kept me from shifting, bursting through the door, and tearing apart the other wolf inside the house.

Over the last couple of hours, I'd practically talked myself out of the whole idea, convinced myself I'd mistaken attraction for a much more serious situation. *You're really sure?*

Yes, the beast snarled. *Mate.* He launched himself against my momentarily distracted resolve. The sharp prickles of fur sprouting along my skin put me into a panic lest he gain control. I frantically shoved him back with all of my will.

The lock clicked, and I swung my arms behind me. She couldn't witness the long claws and furry paws my hands had become.

Then the door opened, revealing Miss Lukas.

Revealing my *mate.* This time I was prepared for my wolf to try to force the shift to root out the interloper in her house.

I barreled inside, snatching the door from her hand when I swung it closed. I'd guessed correctly that she'd set up the room as a parlor. There. The book on the floor next to a footstool must've been the *thump* I'd heard moments ago.

I turned to her. "Where is he?"

"Who?" Puzzlement creased her forehead.

The sweet smell of her desire rose to me once more. Fury nearly blinded me, and I hung onto my control by a razor-edged claw. "The other wol—man. Where is he?"

Rosy spots practically leapt into her cheeks. "There is no other man here. How did you find me?"

I tracked her from the train station but remained mum since my rage threatened to turn my veins to cinders. She lied like a professional. With her acting skills, she should be on the stage rather than stealing. If she didn't have a man here and her arousal... Despair turned my blood to ice. Certainly, Laignech Fáelad wouldn't do *that* to me? "Woman then. Where is she?" I nearly choked on the words.

She crossed her arms across her magnificent bosom. "No women other than me. Did you follow me home?"

My sense of smell said she lied to me about others in the house. I followed my nose. To the right stood a door, where the other shifter's odor grew stronger. I stepped around her, not caring if she thought me an ass. The lack of control over my anger, though galling, was better than shifting into my giant, red wolf alter-ego.

Once through the door, I recognized this as her bedroom. An iron bed with a thick patchwork quilt in bright yellows and blues sat against an interior wall. The covers had been thrown back.

The scent of wolf lingered.

I yanked open the closest door, revealing a closet, one empty of clothing except for a couple of women's garments. Nowhere to hide in there. I hastily rounded the bed and crossed through the bathroom door. With a claw-foot tub and utilitarian sink, hiding would be impossible here too. I raced into the adjoining second bedroom, then into the kitchen at the back of the house where she'd recently finished dinner, if the dishes drying in the drainboard were any indication.

Wait. The odor had lessened here. In full tracking mode, I retraced my steps to the bathroom, where Miss Lukas stood in the doorframe, her lower lip snagged between her teeth and her hands in the pockets of the same black skirt she'd been wearing earlier today.

The wolf had to be here. My roving gaze stopped on three wash-cloths carefully folded on the rail next to the sink. I turned to the towel bar next to the tub. Three arranged neatly there as well.

I ran my fingers across the small squares of fabric. Two were wet, as if they had recently been wrung out and hung to dry.

"You shouldn't be here. You need to leave." Her voice had taken on a tough tone, one I'd heard before when she'd tried to mask a tremor of fear.

My focus shifted to Miss Lukas. She stood in her bedroom with her finger pointing toward the front door.

Three washcloths. Three towels.

And three plates and glasses in the drainboard.

Three.

My wolf howled with his frustration making my brain matter vibrate like aspic.

Silence, I commanded.

The wolf acceded to my command and calmed himself. Finally, I could think once more.

I stared at Miss Lukas, who'd put both fists on her hips. I wanted to grasp her arms and shake the truth from her, yet I'd never harm a woman unless she tried to harm me or a loved one.

The keen hearing abilities given to an Ossory wolf allowed me to divine her frantic heartbeat. Wait. There were more. I pushed my senses as hard as I could.

Two more.

My resolve hardened to solve this mystery. There must be a trap door. Even my sharp sight couldn't make out the pattern. I stomped on the floor, planting my heel, but the solid nature led me to believe there no secret hiding place existed there. Not in the wall either.

Then...

I looked up to the beadboard-clad ceiling. There. The faintest outline of a panel big enough for someone to enter. Though the ceilings were at least ten feet high, if I could jump, grab the edge, and pull myself up, another wolf could as well.

Miss Lukas's pulse raced now.

I'd found the hiding place, and likely, with this single-story house, there would be no escape for whoever hid in the attic.

"Tell them to come down." I pinned her with the force of my anger, and she grew pale enough I feared she might faint. "Stay with me. They can come down, or I'll go up and get them."

"Don't you hurt her." A young man's voice came from above at the same time wood scraped against wood.

I stepped back at the right moment for the descending ladder to miss hitting me while my mind grappled with the knowledge she had children in her attic. "I'm not going to hurt her."

Rustling and light footsteps heralded their descent. The odor of wolf grew even heavier in my nose. My thoughts raced with the possibilities.

Not a wolf lover. Ossory wolf offspring.

Were they hers, or had she come across lone cubs?

The first child reached the floor and turned to me, his expression fierce and pugnacious. The air rushed from my lungs.

Not lone cubs.

This youngster was the spitting image of Sean at that age. The second joined the first to stand half a step back at his brother's shoulder. This one was more slight, younger, and his freckles stood out against the pallor of his skin. His hair also matched the deep auburn color of mine and my cousin's.

Another of Sean's cubs. Miss Lukas and he...

Every bit of fury and anger that she had a secret lover in her bower shifted. She'd hidden these two from me. Had she intended to blackmail me to get them back to the pack? "How dare you."

She gasped and her hand went to her throat, probably not mistaking the growl in my tone as one of fury and menace. She had no idea what she'd awakened.

"You're *not* going to hurt her." The older boy took a step forward, his fists at the ready.

The cub's statement shook me from my rage, and I glanced down to find his eyes narrowed on me. Even his brother, one I'd make for less aggressive, had stepped up next to him, his teeth bared, ready to attack.

Their defense caused me to pause, and I grabbed for my logic. I had yet to fully assemble this puzzle. With my hands held at chest level, I said, "Whoa. Not going to hurt her."

The eldest eyed me for several moments, his nostrils quivering, as if he tried to scent deception from me. Perhaps satisfied I told the truth, he relaxed his fists and shoulders, but not the mean look in his eyes. "Better not."

"Yeah. Better not."

The younger child's echoed warning lacked his brother's snarl, and I was impressed enough with their gumption that I suppressed my amusement. I took a moment to take in the duo, who were in blue-striped pajamas and barefoot.

My cousin's offspring, certainly. With supreme effort, I put aside my roiling thoughts and emotions. "Now who do we have here?"

The two scooted around the ladder, which took up much of the floor space in the small bathroom, stopping next to Miss Lukas. They said not a word.

She sighed, her features a sad combination of wariness and weariness, then she pulled back farther into the room. "Come in here," she said to me.

I thought she'd continue on to the parlor. Instead, she paused to light an oil lamp on a nightstand, then turned to the cubs who kept even with her. Whether the two were intent on protecting her or being protected I couldn't ascertain.

"Alright, you two. Introduce yourselves."

The eldest stepped forward with a maturity that belied his age—possibly ten or eleven. He offered his hand and said, "I'm Patrick Seamus Monaghan."

Monaghan. Not Lukas. Had I been wrong about her and Sean? I took the small hand in mine with as much dignity as I could muster. "I'm glad to meet you. I'm your cousin, Aaron Matthew Monaghan."

"Cousin Aaron, I'm Thomas Padraig Monaghan." The younger stepped forward and offered his small hand, which I accepted. "Pleasure to make your acquaintance."

My gaze flashed to Miss Lukas. "Care to explain?"

"I have something for you." She bustled from the room.

I stepped around the bed to make sure she didn't escape out the front door. I needn't have bothered. She upended a basket next to her chair. Spools and a needle case spilled onto the chair's seat. What was she doing?

She dug around in the basket and pulled out a fabric liner. More digging ensued. She'd turned and I couldn't see what she'd extracted until she pivoted back to me and had in her hand...

A letter.

She returned to the bedroom and handed me the envelope, one appearing much like the missive she'd given me earlier, with an embossed, green wax seal, one identical to the gold ring I often wore on my pinkie.

"From Sean and Anne." She stepped back, her eyes downcast, hands clasped in front of her.

I tapped the envelope against my palm. The delay in her explanation began to rub my patience thin. "You gave me their letter earlier. Explain what is going on. Why do you have these children?"

The boys rushed past me, bumping against my side in their haste, and took up positions in front of her. Pleading in his eyes, Patrick said, "Please read the letter, Cousin Aaron."

Despite my irritation with the delay, I lifted the green wax seal with its embossed wolf's head from the paper and set my gaze to Sean's script.

Aaron, my pack brother,

If you are reading this, Anne and I are no longer part of this earth and have gone to join Laignech Fáelad in his great halls among the emerald hills. I am happy Jo, our name for Miss Josephine Lucas, has found you worthy of taking care of our sons.

My stomach plummeted. I had indeed been wrong about her. A quick glance showed she worried her lower lip between her teeth. Of what would she find me worthy? I returned to the letter.

Please forgive me the misdirection of my plan, and do not find blame with our dear friend. As you know, mining is a dangerous game. I took a chance on finding a financier and now metaphorical wolves have begun to circle, having heard rumors of what is a true gold strike —a wide vein that I predict won't exceed Emerald Hill's output but will be quite a producer in the end. Whether by the hand of another or by cave-in, my wife and I are no longer here. We asked Miss Lukas to be our children's guardian. For this she has my and Anne's undying gratitude, as she should have yours, for we may have put her in great danger. She has unexpected talents. Of this I will say no more.

For a long while I have missed you. I now know that I should have told you why I abandoned the family. Abandoned you.

My hand trembles to write this, but you deserve the truth. Mother's husband used me in the worst manner and threatened to kill her should I tell anyone. Once I reached seventeen, he told me to leave or, again, he would kill her. There. I have written the truth.

And now I must ask once more for forgiveness. I asked Miss Lukas to evaluate whether she could trust you to take the children. If you are reading this, I assume she has.

Despair joined the black horror blooming in my heart, the jagged tendrils like wicked claws trying to emerge from my chest. I could barely breathe. My knees began to shake, and I sat heavily on the bed.

I reread the last two paragraphs again.

Tears sprung to my eyes, and I rubbed them away. The horror morphed to anger. By the Kings of Ossory, why hadn't he told me? I would have done everything to protect his mother and him. If I could now, I would reanimate the bastard and kill him all over again. Now Sean's stepfather's death two years ago made sense. A young wolf, only fifteen years, had murdered him, then disappeared into the wild. We'd never understood the act.

Until now.

Intending to read the rest of Sean's letter, I glanced down at the page. The scrawl swam in front of my eyes. I should have seen this abomination.

I should have known something caused him to withdraw, to become alienated from his pack. A howl grew within me, one so great I could not contain the emotion.

Hair sprouted from my skin. Bone and sinew scraped, contorted. I pitched forward to the floor.

With this change I bore the agonizing shift as a penance. My muzzle lifted to the ceiling, I allowed the howl that burst forth to convey all my sadness, pain...and rage.

7
JOSEPHINE

An enormous, red-furred wolf stood before me, half garbed in the ripped clothing Mr. Monaghan had worn as a man, back paws still in the rough work boots. The terrible sight snatched the air from my lungs. Yet, his plaintive howl nearly broke my heart with the sadness and anger the sound contained.

His cry knocked me from my frozen state. I snatched at the boys' shoulders and pulled them behind me while I scrambled backward into the corner, as far as I could be from him, as well as to use the walls to supplement my quaking knees. If I hadn't seen the transformation with my own eyes, I never would've believed this could be true. Even with Anne and Sean telling me he and the boys could turn into werewolves—Irish Ossory wolves they'd corrected me—I now knew I had never truly comprehended this to be possible.

Yet the prosperous banker who made the shift from man to beast in mere seconds stood in *my* bedroom. He'd ended his lament and now stood with his head hung low, his flanks heaving with each breath.

What had prompted this reaction? The letter?

Though I desired to learn of his reason, I dared not cross to where the page had fallen and leave the boys without protection. For a fleeting moment, I inched my hand to my pocket where I'd stashed the derringer, then pulled away. Instinct said I would not need to use the gun on him.

Besides, what would a peashooter do against his monstrous size, one taking up most of the available floorspace in the tiny room? Though wolves had largely been culled from this land, I'd seen their pelts. Aaron Monaghan or whatever he'd become was easily twice their size. His back must come to my chest.

Contradicting my earlier fear, laughter bubbled in my throat at the sight of his odd outfit of garments rent at the seams and back legs still shod in the boots like a man.

He turned and his hazel eyes, irises glowing with a faint emerald light, bored into mine.

"Forgive me."

I gasped. He could speak. Dogs—and wolves would be no different, I assumed—couldn't chew, let alone speak, because of their tongues, at least according to an article I'd once read. "How..."

When the wolf—Mr. Monaghan—moved his front paws, tiny ripping sounds came from his clothing, as well as a heavy *thunk*. The strange gun he'd stored in the bottom of his trunk lay on the floor. In little more than a couple of seconds, he returned to his human form, stooped, retrieved the firearm and his cousin's letter, then returned to his full height. Relief lightened my shoulders a little when he shoved the gun into the back of his trousers' waistband and the letter into his breast pocket.

I might have stared at him in frozen wonder like an unlucky soul who'd sighted Medusa, but the rag-tag nature of his garments with their popped buttons and torn seams affording peeks of skin added a dose of humor.

He glanced down to the clothing hanging from his person. The only things appearing to be unaltered were his waistband, where he'd worn a sturdy leather belt, and his boots. Otherwise, he appeared like he'd donned clothing that had been through an ore crusher.

"Dammit." His tone carried the heavy weight of self-disgust. He widened his stance and crossed his arms, then stared pointedly at his cousins where I'd corralled them. "This is what happens when you don't control your wolf."

His gaze then turned to me, and I processed only enough to comprehend his eye had lost their glow. Finally, he said, "You don't seem upset by my transformation."

"Sean and Anne told me about the...his ability to become a werewolf." I clutched at my skirts and stared at the length of wool jacket sleeve hanging from Mr. Monaghan's elbow to his hip. "Said the boys would be able to become wolves too."

"We aren't werewolves." Patrick stepped out from behind me. "Right, Cousin Aaron?"

He ruffled the boy's hair in an affectionate manner, like he'd done this with many youngsters. "That's right. We're Ossory wolves. Descendants of King Laignech Fáelad."

"*Lahneh fahlad.*" Mr. Monaghan must've caught my indrawn breath because his gaze flew to mine, and he narrowed his lids. "You recognize the name?"

I stood my ground against the examination. "I didn't know the meaning. Patrick had me use it as a safe word, well, phrase."

His grin revealed a blindingly white smile. "Smart boy. Only the family would know."

A knock from the front door derailed my intent to ask more about their history and this king. I drew farther back against the corner as if I could seep into the wood to escape. Who would come calling at this late hour?

A weight fell on my shoulder, and I slapped a hand over my mouth to stifle my scream. I turned to find Mr. Monaghan had crept quietly to my side.

He leaned close and on a bare breath he said, "Are you expecting anyone?"

I shook my head negatively while I tried to quiet the fear drumming through my body with each beat of my heart.

"Ask who it is," he mouthed.

With effort, I laced my trembling fingers together and summoned my courage, then did as he requested. I was pleased with my tone—loud enough to be heard through the door and with barely a tremor.

"Open the door, Miss Lukas."

The voice, though slightly muffled by the thick cloth covering the window, seemed familiar...

Jim Nicholson, the hotel's front desk manager.

A spiky shiver crept down my spine. I wished for the Helm of Hades so I could disappear. Mr. Monaghan gently squeezed my shoulder, and I drew resolve from his presence. Plus, I had the children to think about. I turned my focus to the person lurking outside and what I must do next—delay him in order to read his thoughts. I formed a picture of the oily man in my mind while I asked, "What do you want?"

"I want you to open the damn door."

There. I had reached him. I closed my eyes, striving for his thoughts. A picture formed. Mr. Williams and Mr. Farley dead in the dirt, sightless eyes still glistening in the sun, bloodstains blossoming across their shirts, the barrel of a smoking revolver hovering in the foreground. Then I received his inner monologue. "...*screwing up my plan. I'll tell the sheriff I followed him here. Thought he had a gun. I shot and the only one left standing was me. Sad the bitch will die. Nice tits.*"

The smug emotion I received from him made my blood leap to boiling. I placed my hand in my pocket and gripped the derringer. At least he hadn't mentioned the boys. Perhaps he'd not learned they'd escaped the cabin alive. To the man next to me, I mouthed, "He has a gun and wants to kill us."

Mr. Monaghan quirked a brow, then nodded, apparently understanding my mimed actions along with my mouthed words. Thankfully, he didn't question how I knew this information. He pointed to the boys' boots, then his own, and the youngsters scrambled to the small cedar chest and pulled out theirs without a noise. When they faced me, both were extremely pale.

"That's the man—"

After I held a finger to cut off Thomas's high-pitched comment, I said, "I'm coming."

A bang against the door suggested my singsong tone hadn't delayed him in the least, and he now tried to break into the house.

Fear squeezed my gut. *Escape.*

I shooed the boys through the bathroom and toward the kitchen at the house's rear, wincing with every creaky footfall. Mr. Monaghan followed me. Though I heard nothing of his boots on the floor, I could *feel* him, like a connection now existed between us. I couldn't stop and examine this because escape took top priority.

The boys threw open the back door, and I managed to keep the panel from banging on the wall. The tinkling sound of shattering glass came from the front of the house. He must've not been able to break the lock and chose the easier path.

I continued after the boys, down the stairs and into the deep twilight toward the neighbors behind my cottage. If only night had fully descended. Hopefully they wouldn't note Patrick and Thomas or me as we fled past. I had nearly reached the apple tree at the back of the small lot and though I probably shouldn't have, I glanced over my shoulder. Mr. Monaghan waited to the side of my house's open back door, pressing himself flat against the clapboard siding.

My foot caught a rock, and I flew forward with a cry I tried to stifle. I landed on my hands and knees. Rocks savagely bit into my bare palms, dazing me for a moment and causing me to whimper with the agony.

"Got you."

Terror spiked my heart. I rolled over, scrambling back to escape Mr. Nicholson's dark silhouette in the door's jamb, gun in hand. The revolver's metal glinted in the gathering gloom, and he aimed it directly at me. Though he still stood inside the house, at only about fifteen yards away, he wouldn't miss. What I *could* see of him frightened me more —the glittering lust in his eyes and the satisfied grin gleaming under his mustache—for me or for killing, I couldn't tell.

The derringer! None of my limbs obeyed. Dread froze me where I sat on the ground.

"Where is he?" He used the weapon to emphasize his demand, pushing the handgun toward me and through the doorframe.

Mr. Monaghan grabbed the barrel and yanked the gun from the other man's hands, the action like lightning. The violent movement caused Mr. Nicholson to jerk forward through the door, and the taller man's pistol came down on the hotel manager's head like a club. Mr. Nicholson crumpled into a pile of black clothing on the ground and became still.

For several hyperventilated breaths I remained where I lay. I both knew and yet couldn't comprehend what had happened. Jim Nicholson almost killed me.

A hand shook my shoulder. "Miss Lukas—Josephine."

I glanced up to the man now crouching next to me. "How... What..." My wits had flown, and I couldn't form a coherent sentence. A part of me stood apart almost as if an observer.

Mr. Monaghan said quietly, "Time to get up. We've got to get moving."

A fine trembling in my body turned to violent shaking, and my teeth started to chatter. I searched for my ability to speak.

He scooped me in his arms and continued in the direction the boys had fled, toward the neighbor's house and the street beyond. Somehow, I wound my arms around his neck. His warmth and bergamot-leather scent comforted me. I buried my face in his shoulder while I recovered my wits.

"Patrick. Thomas." His words were low. "Laignech Fáelad. You are safe."

From behind a bush the brothers emerged, and I gasped, believing they'd be halfway to Pluma by now.

"We wasn't going to leave you, Miss. Lukas," Thomas said.

"Weren't," I managed in a croaky voice, my correction practically a reflex. With a gurgle, I cleared my throat. "Thank you for not running off." To the one who still held me, I said a little more breathlessly than I would've liked, "You can let me down now, Mr. Monaghan."

His eyes seemed to gleam emerald in the waning dusk while he released his arm holding my legs aloft. He let me slide down slowly, like he savored the connection of my softest parts against his hard body. Once my feet reached the ground, he said, "Aaron, please. We must get back to the hotel quickly."

My heart felt like fire in my breast. No time now to examine those feelings either. I turned back toward the house, with its door an even blacker silhouette against the white house paint. A pile of darkness lay on the stoop. "What about Mr. Nicholson?" I whispered. "Is he dead?"

"When I checked moments ago, his heart still beat," Mr. Monaghan—Aaron—said. His features turned hard, though his hand was surprisingly gentle when he took mine. "I have a plan, but the boys must be safe first. I need to change clothing and get them in my hotel room without being seen."

"I think I can help." The ordeal for them would end, and the justice for their parents seemed to be in hand.

For the first time since the boys had come to me, I felt like smiling.

8

AARON

"The staff is limited after eight, and they keep the employee door locked after dark," Jo whispered into my ear while she, the children, and I waited behind shrubbery for a pedestrian to pass.

I already thought of her in the less formal manner similar to my cousin's reference. I desperately wanted to hear my given name from her lips, preferably when in the throes of passion.

The tempting thought had to wait. "If the door's locked, how will we get in?"

"There's a night watchman, Mr. Baker. He's an old Pinkerton agent, a very nice man. Deaf in one ear. He walked me home a couple of nights when I had to work late. He goes on rounds at nine-thirty, perimeter first, starting at the employee entrance. Then he goes floor by floor through the hotel. I can meet him when he comes outside, ask him to let me in and then let you in when he leaves. We should be able to get back in time."

A distant church's bell had chimed the quarter hour moments ago, and I estimated we were about ten minutes from the hotel. While her plan seemed sound, a Pinkerton, even if a former agent, couldn't be discounted. Some of them were honest. Some, not at all. The general populace often thought of them as merely private detectives they could employ when needing discretion or when a police investigation failed. I knew better. They were also the go-to union-busting company who employed thugs to break strikes where men, women, and children were often hurt or killed.

I'd long suspected Pinkerton created problems within the overall industry in order to drum up business for themselves. In fact, Emerald Hill Corporation's mining side had been the focus of union agitators in years past. We'd been able to avoid trouble other mines faced by treating our employees with respect. Both fair wages and safety practices went a long way with workers.

Though I'd like to think Jo's assessment of the Pinkerton was correct, based on my dealings, I couldn't trust him. I tucked a springy wisp of hair behind her ear, then whispered, "Yell if you have trouble. I *will* be listening. Can you whistle for an all clear when we can't see you?"

She patted her hair back into the topknot, then puckered her lips in a way that might've distracted me in less fraught moments. The sound mimicked a bird call well enough, though one wouldn't typically trill this late at night. "I'll whistle if I have to but would prefer to wave you in, so watch for me."

"Will do." I took Thomas's hand in mine. "Let's go."

Less than ten minutes later, I spied the back of the Franklin Hotel. We'd stuck to back streets, alleyways, and gardens, moving quickly in the relative darkness. Only three times did passersby force us to hide in the deep shadows.

The bloodstained, folded paper I carried, the one I'd found in one of the dead men's pockets, wanted to burn a hole in my plans. I longed to go back and kill Jim Nicholson outright. The knowledge the children's safety stood paramount quenched the malevolent desire.

Once I got them into the hotel room and could change from my tattered laborer's clothing and back to Aaron Monaghan, I'd be in a better position to launch my quest for justice against the hotel employee. The president of Emerald Hill Corporation, wealthy banker and mining company owner, would hold more weight with the law.

While we paused a block away in the shadow of a rubbish pile to let a wagon depart from a delivery at the hotel, I leaned toward her once again to ask quietly, "How'd you know Nicholson had a gun?"

She paused, then murmured over the clatter of shod hooves and wooden wheels on the bricks, "I can often read people's thoughts if I concentrate."

Despite her clipped words, elation filled my heart, and not merely from her warm breath in my ear. Within my world, our wolves often chose a psychic woman. According to all of my pack members' wives, they were not able to use their talents on their mates. Now wasn't the time to ask if she could read my mind or explain why her abilities thrilled me.

Instead, I said, "I can turn into a wolf. Not like I wouldn't believe you."

Her gaze sought mine in the murky shadows. While the dray and wagon turned the corner toward Main Street, she took her hand in mine. Hope sprang fresh within me. Yet, the desire to protect her gripped my gut even more with her revelation, doubling my worry. The possibility existed that the hotel manager would awaken and return to the hotel before us. The awareness of the time taken traversing the town seemed to weigh on me like the boulders I'd passed on the way to my cousin's mining claim.

A wave of unease buffeted me. Putting my mate in harm's way was a gamble I preferred not to take. "You sure you can do this?"

She paused in taking off the simple silver watch pinned to her shirtwaist. Only the slightest quiver at the corner of her smile indicated her nerves. "I can."

Since I didn't have a better plan to enter the hotel unnoticed, I quelled my conscience. "Good. I'll go get ready."

A concrete retaining wall had been built behind the hotel, and at the top, brush had been allowed to gather, a perfect place to hide in the shadows. Clasping my cousins' hands tightly in mine, I scampered into the bushes.

From my perspective, about ten feet above the alley, I could view the working area behind the hotel.

Over the employee's entrance, a light provided enough illumination to show no one loitered. I opened my wolf's senses, aiming them for anyone behind the hotel's door, while trying to exclude the aural clutter from surrounding businesses. Nothing seemed to come from there—no voices, no noises. Perhaps The Morrigan would be kind when she wove my fate and allowed us to protect the children.

The church's carillon chimed the half-hour. Like he was

controlled by the same clockworks, a tall, whipcord-thin man stepped outside and scanned the area, exactly as Jo had said he would. His gray, drooping mustache gleamed in the light above him, until he settled his hat atop his pomaded silver hair. The man swept back the left side of his coat and pulled something from his vest's pocket, a watch by the size and metallic glint. With his thumb, he popped the case, glanced at the face, then snapped the metal shut once more and tucked the item whence it came. A bulge on his right side under his jacket when he straightened the garment spoke of a gun.

With a final tug on the doorknob, he turned toward the north side of the building.

Light booted heels on the brick paving caught my ears coming from the opposite direction of the Pinkerton's travel. From the corner of my eye, I caught Jo's figure as she bustled toward the employee entrance. "Mr. Baker."

The watchman pivoted and started toward her. He stopped a respectable distance from her and touched his finger to his derby's brim, his features inscrutable in the shadow of his hat. "Miss Lukas. What are you doing out this late at night?"

"I must've dropped my watch. My mother gave it to me when I graduated. I hoped someone has turned it in."

"The one you wear on...uh...on your..." His question trailed off, and he cleared his throat.

"Right," Jo said brightly. "The one I pin to my shirtwaist."

"Yes." His brim dipped. Did he dare glance to her chest? "Ah, your shirtwaist."

A low growl began in my head. *Quiet you.* Though I didn't blame the man for admiring my mate's generous breasts, I didn't care for the sentiment. Her bosom, as well as the rest of her, belonged to *me*.

"Can you let me in?" Jo seemed oblivious to the man's admiration.

"Sure. Look for me before you leave. I'll check in with Milton and walk you home."

"Absolutely." Jo nodded her head in an earnest manner that might have annoyed me, yet I understood she merely acted. "Thank you."

He pulled a jingling key ring from his pants' pocket, selected a key, and inserted it into the lock. After a turn of his wrist, he pushed the door open. "You're welcome. Can't be too careful. Be sure to lock the door."

Baker shut the door behind her, and the lock's metallic slide met my ears. With a whistled tune suggesting his good mood, he walked away from me, down the rear side of building.

The growl in my head deepened. *Will keep her safe.*

I couldn't agree with my wolf more. The man was more than "nice." He had eyes for my mate.

When he'd turned the corner, a quick survey assured me no one would observe. With a glance to either cousin, I asked, "Ready?"

"Yes, sir." Their hushed voices came in unison.

"Quieter than a wolf hunting," I whispered, then leapt down from my perch to the pavement, my boots making a bare scrape upon landing. Patrick and Thomas landed next to me as silently as if they were already able to shift. They might as well not have been wearing the well-worn boots they'd quickly donned before we made our mad dash to the hotel. Pride wanted to burst from my chest. My cousin had raised some fine boys.

Like we'd discussed, the door cracked open, and Jo gave a quick, urgent wave.

Careful to minimize noise, I raced with my cousins across the short distance, maybe ten yards. Jo opened the door, and we hurried inside. With the barest snick, she threw the deadbolt.

A woman's laughter echoed from the hallway to our right.

"Hurry," Jo whispered.

She dashed to the stairway on the left, followed by the children, with me at the rear. Though our boots were muffled by a carpet, every step creaked. I couldn't care now. On the first flight we encountered no one, gaining the second floor without incident. I couldn't believe our luck. Jo rounded to the stairs' next flight.

"...where Nicholson is." The gruff male voice echoed from above. "No one has seen him."

Damnation.

Jo's brow creased, and she pivoted swiftly to glance around the corner into the second-floor hallway. She grabbed Thomas's hand right when a jumble of footfalls hit the first riser on their way down.

I followed with Patrick. While no customers were in the hallway, this way carried risk, though less so than encountering the men descending from the third floor on the employee stairs.

The hotel was small, not like The Grand Pacific where I'd stayed in Chicago, and soon Jo turned the corner to the patron's stairway. Patrick kept pace, but Thomas began to lag while we stormed up the flight. I scooped him into my arms.

"Who was that?" A different man this time. His voice echoed from below us in the second floor's corridor.

"Dunno. His clothing looked ragged," the first man said. "They're goin' up."

I turned the corner on the flight. "Faster. We've been spotted."

Jo picked up even more speed, like a fleeing deer. I dug in my vest's pocket for the room's key and had it in hand when I gained the third floor. My suite stood across the hallway from the stairs. I jammed the key in the lock, twisted my wrist, threw open the door, ushered Jo and Patrick inside, then shut the panel with as much delicacy as possible owing to the circumstances. With care, I slid Thomas to the floor.

"Where'd he go?" one of the men asked moments later. Footsteps thumped on the thick carpet.

Wincing against the possibility the lock would give me away, I turned the deadbolt with care. If they tried doorknobs, I didn't want them to barge in or think anything other than the lock denied them entry.

"I don't see him. He must've gone downstairs. Let's find Baker."

The men's footsteps receded, and I released my pent-up breath. Safe. For now.

Jo moved to the windows and began to draw the parlor's curtains.

"Where are the boys?"

She pivoted to face me, her cheeks ruddy from exertion, her hands balled into fists, like she readied to fight. My admiration for her skyrocketed. She motioned to the door leading to the bedroom. "I sent them to get into bed. Let's get you dressed before someone comes calling."

Crafty and valiant. Exactly what I would want in a mate. At that moment, I desired to take her into my arms and kiss her because my regard seemed to know no bounds.

Rather than give into my emotions, I followed her into the adjacent bedroom where a side table's lamp glowed softly. The boys had already climbed into the large bed with its ornate headboard, their boots lined up neatly on the floor, covers pulled up to their chins.

While Jo pulled the curtains closed here, too, they watched with wide eyes while I approached them, already shedding my tattered coat and vest.

"We may have visitors. I'd appreciate you staying quiet until I call for you." I pulled the shirt off me, not bothering with the remaining buttons, then added them to the ruined garments on the bed. "If anyone asks about where you've been since your mother and father were killed, tell them Jo—Miss Lukas—has been taking care of you. The truth, right?"

My cousins' heads nodded in unison, their eyes wide.

"Keys?" Jo stood next to my trunk, my shirt in her hand. "I'll get your clothing hidden while you dress."

Bless her. Quickly, I fished into my jacket's breast pocket and handed off the keys. I'd moved my trunk in here and locked my case inside before I left. She knew the one she needed since she'd been into the compartment before.

While she accessed the hiding place, I continued removing my clothing and handing the garments to Jo.

"Are you and Miss Lukas married?" Thomas's voice held an especially high, squeaky edge.

What...? I glanced down to where my cousin's eyes were pinned.

I halted my hand, which had been about to pull down my underwear. Shifting my gaze to Jo, I noted she'd averted her head yet peeked from the corner of her eyes. Were her cheeks rosy because of the question or the fact she would see me nude for the second time that day?

My pulse jumped, along with the wolf within me. I shook away my alter-ego, who was being entirely too invested in the mating ritual and not interested at all in getting dressed quickly.

Shedding my underwear had been largely automatic, as well as unneeded. I left them in place, then strode to the closet to retrieve the banker's costume.

I glanced over my shoulder at Jo, who worked at folding my shredded garments and packing them in the false compartment built into the top of my steamer trunk. The woman who'd protected these boys at great risk to herself. The smart, capable, loyal woman. Kind. Even if a thief, she was everything I wanted. I had no qualms in giving up the bank's presidency. I'd been in the position only a couple of months after another cousin stepped back for his mate.

The gray striped suit I wore earlier would do. I flicked a glance to the boys. "No, we're not married."

I selected, then pulled on the pants. While I buttoned the flap, I eyed the woman across from me who stood still as a hare in a wolf's sights.

"Not married *yet*."

9
JOSEPHINE

As if Poseidon himself shook my world, I froze while the room spun around me.

"Not married yet."

Aaron's single word had changed the statement's meaning completely and challenged a long-held belief. Marriage? Men didn't want smart women. I'd been told repeatedly I should play dumb to attract a man.

"You two are going to get married?" Thomas's voice rose, high and excited.

I forced myself to move. While I finished folding Aaron's pants and placing them carefully in the compartment, I struggled to form a response. Both denial and acceptance stuck in my throat. I'd never believed I would one day willingly tie myself to another, yet I couldn't read his thoughts, which should mean fate decreed him to be my perfect match.

What a conundrum.

Like an automaton, I added the work boots, situating them so the heels wouldn't knock against the wood with rough handling. All of his laborer-class clothing was packed inside, save one thing—his gun. I spied the firearm on the top of the dresser, next to the final letter I'd provided him, as well as another folded scrap of paper.

I can address his "yet" later without the audience. I must have time to think. After a deep breath, I turned toward Aaron, intent on asking if he wanted to add the gun before I closed up the compartment.

"Well, are you?"

The hope in Patrick's question caused me pause, and I glanced toward the bed. Both boys seemed so solemn, and my heart lurched to think I would part from them. Their perseverance and intelligence to comprehend quite adult topics earned them a place in my heart. I agonized on how to answer, finally sending a glance to Aaron, one he should clearly interpret as, *"You started this, you need to fix it."*

Rather than assisting, he said nothing, merely curling his lips into a satisfied smile while he applied his cufflinks to the stiff folds he'd gathered at his wrists.

Annoyance flared within me. I tamped down the emotion and focused on the youngsters, whose features shone bright with expectation. Rustling said Aaron had moved toward the door to the parlor. With a glance over my shoulder, I caught his exit. He left the door a bit ajar and had taken the gun with him.

Drat him.

I summoned my best teacher façade to answer Patrick's marriage question. "That's for your cousin and I to discuss." I added a bright smile and moderated my brusque tone when I said, "Remember, I have a teaching position to get to in San Francisco."

Tears gathered in Thomas's eyes, and his lower lip wobbled. In a small voice he said, "But you can't go."

His brother made a better attempt at a brave face, though by his pallor, I knew my answer disappointed him too.

Well, Hades. They'd lost both of their parents not a month ago. The boys would need to settle into their new home with a person they trusted before they felt comfortable. I'd have to have Eris's dark heart to abandon them now.

I did quick mental math with the day the school would start instruction and determined I should be able to swing a diversion to my plans. After crossing the short distance, I sat on the bed. This time I added compassion to my words, which should've been there in the first place. "If you really want, I'll accompany you to Denver."

I had been about to add, "Then I'll be on my way to San Francisco." Their enthusiastic *whoops* the two let out kept me from dashing their excitement.

Or did I stay my addition because I might not want to go to San Francisco after all?

From over my shoulder and just inside the room, Aaron asked, "May I speak with you, Miss Lukas?"

"Certainly." I rose and kissed both their heads. While I left the room, my nose prickled and caught me unawares. I would really miss them. Miss watching them grow and learn. Miss them becoming men like their cousin.

Behind me, Aaron murmured to the boys.

I continued into the parlor to the sofa, my thoughts awhirl. Being this close to my planned date to flee Deadwood with no response from the Monaghans, I'd come to expect Patrick and Thomas to be with me. I'd probably never see them again.

Or Aaron for that matter. Any sense of happiness deserted me, sucking any strength from my knees. I sat heavily on the cushion.

Aaron crossed the room and knelt before me, yet with his height, his head came almost even with mine. He took my hands in his. "What's wrong?"

If I tried to speak, I'd become a watering pot. While I tried to compose myself, I searched his gaze, finding his hazel eyes filled with concern. How could this man, one who turned into a wolf, one who owned both a bank and a gold mine for Hera's sake, be this tender?

He pressed my hands between his in a comforting manner, then said in a low tone, "A lot has gone on today. Too much to make any decisions." His eyes began to shine as if lit from within. "If you can bear with me and the boys through this evening, I have a question for you."

Time seemed to slow between us, and my heart hung in my chest as if suspended by a thread. I understood his question. He would give me time to consider without pressure. Could I love him? Perhaps I already carried a small admiration for him in my heart. Finally, I was able to say, "Of course, I'll take your question."

A brisk knock came to the door, and dread dropped into my stomach like Sisyphus's boulder.

"At last." Relief flitted across his features, and he abruptly rose, taking quick strides to the door. From over his shoulder, he said, "I called the sheriff a couple of minutes ago."

I stood too. Before I could set my mind to the person on the other side, Aaron pulled the panel open.

Jim Nicholson stood, the gun in his hand pointing directly at Aaron, then quickly shifted his aim to me. With an evil look in his eyes, the desk manager said, "Step back or she's dead."

Aaron complied, a fine muscle feathering in his jaw.

The other man stepped inside the parlor, then swiftly shut the door. A smirk tilted his waxed mustache, and he gestured with the revolver. "You thought you killed me."

"I thought nothing of the sort." Aaron's tone held strain.

I pushed my thoughts toward the other man, gaining entry to his mind more quickly since I'd been there all too recently.

...them together. I'll kill them both and say he drew a gun on me. Him first.

No! I had to occupy the desk manager's attention for Aaron's and the boys' sake.

Another knock on the door interrupted any play I might've made and sent my already wildly skittering pulse to frantic.

"Don't answer it," Mr. Nicholson said quietly, and he motioned threateningly toward me with his gun.

"Do you need any help, Mr. Nicholson?" Mr. Baker, the night watchman, inquired.

The desk manager swore under his breath.

Before the he could even speak, I used my abilities to dive into Mr. Baker's thoughts.

"...damn odd lately. Don't trust him."

Keys jingled on the other side of the door. Of course, the guard would have skeleton keys to ensure patrons' safety. Could he actually help us?

"Don't say anything to him." Mr. Nicholson tucked the gun behind his back, pivoted, and cracked open the door.

Aaron moved silently to shield me from the desk manager, but I peeped around him.

"I have no problems. You are dismissed." He used his most supercilious tone.

Aaron said with a more commanding voice, "Mr. Baker. Please come in."

A war of wills seemed to be going on between the hotel employees, until Mr. Nicholson caved. He brought the door with him when he backed up, an obvious strategy to hide the fact he had a weapon behind him. The red dappling the man's cheekbones spoke of his fury.

Mr. Baker barely moved into the room, then took a couple of sideways steps to his right such that he remained next to the door with his back against the wall. His position reminded me of Wild Bill Hickok's untimely fate thirty odd years ago in this very town. Even if merely a watchman in the most prestigious hotel in town, people charged with keeping the peace didn't live long in a rough and tumble community like Deadwood without being cautious.

His focus danced between the other two men, perhaps sensing the tension. Then his gaze met mine and surprise lifted his brow. "Miss Lukas?"

I scooted out from behind Aaron with a patently fake smile pasted on my features. "Hello, Mr. Baker. Happy to see you again."

"You found your...watch?"

"Oh yes." I nodded vigorously and stared pointedly at him, willing him to understand the danger manifested in this room. I scooted closer to Aaron, hoping Mr. Baker understood who posed the real threat. "I found it on the floor in the linen press."

He brought his hands together at waist level, fingers touching, his gaze on the man next to me. "I'm afraid I don't know you, sir."

"Aaron Monaghan." His calm tone seemed incongruous with the veritable cloud of danger swirling in the room. "Emerald Hill Bank, Denver. Miss Lukas told me what a good man you are. Retired Pinkerton, is that correct?"

From the corner of my eye, Mr. Nicholson's face grew more florid, most likely his loss of control. The tension in the room seemed like a thunderhead about to break at any moment. An icy trickle slid down my spine, and I put my hand in my pocket to grip the derringer.

"Miss Lukas?"

My stomach plummeted with Thomas's voice coming from my left. Without taking my gaze from the desk manager, I leapt toward where the boy stood framed by the jamb, while at the same time pulling the gun from my pocket and pointing the tiny pistol in Mr. Nicholson's direction. Before I could get inside, the bedroom door slammed behind me like a crack of thunder, something I dimly registered over my pulse hammering in my ears.

Mr. Nicholson swung his arm, aiming his gun directly at me, his eyes narrowed and mean. I had no doubt he would pull the trigger, and I bent my thoughts to his.

"Hey now," Mr. Baker said. "Let's put the gun down, Jim."

In the desk manager's thoughts, I caught a desperate, *"Bastards told me the kids died in the fire. All of this will be for nothing if I don't kill those kids!"* Through tight lips he said in a vicious manner, "I'll shoot her if all three of you don't put your guns down."

Then I noticed Aaron and the Pinkerton both aimed pistols at the desk manager.

Sharp raps at the hallway door startled me enough that my sweaty palms lost their grip on the derringer. The weapon fell to the floor and skittered under the couch. I backed up to the bedroom door. He could shoot me, but like Artemis, I'd defend those children to my dying breath.

"Sheriff Plunkett?" Aaron's tone carried none of the moment's strain. The satisfaction on his features directed at Mr. Nicholson might as well have said, "Checkmate."

"Yes, Mr. Monaghan. I came as fast as I could." The deep voice came from the hallway.

Not nearly fast enough.

Aaron's gaze didn't waver from the desk manager when he said quietly, "I called as soon as I got dressed. Mr. Baker, please open the door for the sheriff."

While he moved his hand toward the doorknob, the guard kept his gaze planted on Mr. Nicholson. Time seemed to slow. Everyone's movement became exaggerated yet crystal clear. Noises distorted and stretched. Nicholson's mouth pulled into a sneer and his grip tightened on the gun, index finger pulling the trigger.

I squeezed my eyes shut, ducking my head, tightening every muscle in anticipation of the bullet's tortuous path through my flesh. I wished for more time. More time to discover what might've been with Aaron.

Two nearly simultaneous explosions rang in my ears, yet I felt none of the pain.

I opened my lids and found no harm had come to me. My clothing remained unmarred. No blood seeped from my body. How could this be? Surely, he stood too close to miss.

The regular march of time resumed, and I glanced up.

Mr. Nicholson wavered, the gun hanging from his one index

finger by the trigger guard, while the other hand spread across his chest. His grimace spoke of his agony.

With what sounded like a well-placed boot strike, the door sprung open, and Sheriff Plunkett surged in, gun in hand. His gaze swept me, then focused on Aaron. "What's going on in here, Monaghan?"

The desk manager's revolver fell to the floor and landed on the carpet with a muffled *thunk*, apparently drawing the lawman's attention. Sheriff Plunkett pivoted to the man he hadn't seemed to realize stood behind him. "Nicholson?"

The desk manager's mouth opened as if to speak. Only crimson froth emerged.

The man who'd organized Sean's and Anne's murders, then killed his own confederates, fell to the floor in a heap.

10

AARON

Electric energy still buzzed within me. I had gambled and almost lost her.

The vermin, the one responsible for the murders of my cousins, lay in a pile on the floor. Blood seeped from his chest and dribbled from his lips.

He'd almost murdered my mate.

I stared at the man on the ground, trying to drum up sympathy for the last of the three in the conspiracy. Those men would've added my young cousins to their murderous spree's total if they'd had a chance. My wolf howled his fury within me.

I glanced to my right, where Jo stood barring the bedroom door, her hand at her throat, seemingly all eyes and round mouth.

The urge to race to her, to soothe her until her fear subsided, rode me hard, but the sheriff might take exception to any sudden movements. I needed his goodwill to ensure the boys and Jo walked away from this with their lives whole.

Sheriff Plunkett's stony features brooked no argument. "Monaghan, put the gun down."

With reluctance, I set the Browning on a side table next to me, then held my hands up at my chest. "Thank you for coming so quickly, I—"

"Why did you shoot Jim Nicholson?"

"We both shot him, Matt," Baker said.

The sheriff whipped his head to where the watchman stood next to the door, gun still in hand, only now, Baker held his revolver with the cylinder open. "He intended to shoot Miss Lukas, who was unarmed."

With deliberation, Baker tilted the weapon, dumping five rounds and one casing on the ground. He handed the pistol by the barrel to the lawman standing before him.

Sheriff Plunkett glanced at the revolver before snapping the cylinder back into place with a flick of his wrist. He tucked the gun into the front of his waistband. He motioned with his hand to me. "Back up."

Unease scuttled through me while I took several steps toward the windows and farther away from my weapon, though closer to Jo. What if he was involved too? I gathered my wolf close to shift in case I needed to defend my mate.

The lawman picked up my Browning and added it next to the pistol he'd confiscated from Baker. I relaxed when he shoved his own weapon into a holster he wore at his waist and turned to Jo. "Miss Lukas, please go into the bedroom for a moment. I need to speak with Mr. Monaghan."

I glanced to her, and she seemed ready to protest. When she connected her gaze with mine, I nodded minutely, and she opened the door and then slid inside.

My wolf protested the separation. I calmed him and directed my attention to Sheriff Plunkett.

"Why would he want to shoot Miss Lukas? What does he have to do with a schoolteacher?"

A schoolteacher? The merchant's comment earlier in the day returned to me, and I wanted to kick myself for how stupid I'd been. I'd treated her poorly, thought no better of her than a common thief, or worse, a prostitute, and even my cousin's paramour. I'd apologize, but now I needed to answer the sheriff's question. "Sean and Anne tasked her to watch over their children."

The sheriff shot a glance to Baker, who shook his head in answer to what must've been a silent question. Plunkett turned back to me. "Sean and Anne's children? We thought those two died in the fire."

"I think they're in the bedroom, Matt," Baker offered.

The retired Pinkerton seemed to be on familiar terms with the sheriff. I tucked the information away.

"They are," I said, confirming Baker's statement. "If you don't mind me reaching into my breast pocket, I have a letter to me from Sean explaining the matter." I wasn't excited about the Sheriff knowing how my cousin had been abused, yet the letter seemed the most logical way to clear up the matter since nowhere did he mention the pack.

"Nice and slow, Mr. Monaghan."

After following Sheriff Plunkett's order, I handed the envelope to him. He examined the wax seal, then took a moment to read the letter. Soon he folded the missive and tapped the paper against his palm. "Your cousin suspected something might happen. Why didn't he come to you?"

"You read the letter." I cocked my brow. "Would you contact your family?"

"If it meant I could save my sons, yes."

"Even if they might be molested?"

The sheriff's lips twisted under his thick, graying mustache. Finally, he said, "No. Okay, what does Jim Nicholson have to do with this? Why would he want to kill Miss Lukas?"

"A second bit of information might help shed light." I held up my right hand to show him I hadn't palmed anything. "It's also in my breast pocket."

Once the lawman had nodded his assent to my implied question, I pulled out the bloody scrap of paper. "When I first met Miss Lukas this morning, she said a witness saw the men who killed Sean and Anne, naming two as Charles Williams and Robert Farley, the third unknown. I believe now that she protected the children who'd witnessed the murder. She provided me directions to the claim. When I went up there, I found two men recently dead from gunshot wounds. Their blood had barely congealed. I assumed they were Williams and Farley since they matched her description, plus one had a watch on him with "R. Farley" engraved into the case." I waved the piece of paper I held. "I poked around the place, and I found this. The note says he wanted to meet today and at the bottom are the initials "J.N.""

The sheriff held out his hand, and I gave him the paper. While he read, I said, "I believe the third conspirator beyond Williams and Farley was Nicholson, with possibly a fourth, since the author of that note says the clerk wants more money. Sounds like the three were possibly being extorted by the county clerk and were going to meet to discuss what they should do. The more probable situation, since both are now dead, is I suspect by the gun you removed from the floor, Nicholson lied and intended to eliminate his partners and take the mining claim for himself."

The sheriff again glanced to Baker, who gave the barest nod.

I then shared my purpose in Deadwood, the events of the day, and the flight back to the hotel, minus the ideas he wouldn't comprehend, like transforming into wolves and reading minds. "I'm sure she'll apologize for her prevarication, Mr. Baker. She had to think of a reason to get back inside, and while she trusts you, she had the boys to think of."

The watchman dipped his chin, a silent acknowledgement she'd made the correct decision.

"You think he followed you to her house?" Sheriff Plunkett crossed his arms "Why didn't he just kill you?"

"I'm not sure. Perhaps he sensed there was more to me nosing around." I pointed to the dead man on the floor.

"Makes sense." He seemed deep in thought for a moment, then flashed a glance to the guard. "Keep an eye on him. I need to speak with Miss Lukas and the two boys."

Though I understood his continued caution, I expended every ounce of my willpower not to follow Plunkett to the bedroom. Instead, I turned to Baker. "What's going on?"

"I'd prefer the sheriff tell you at his discretion." Baker's tone carried a firmness, though no confrontation.

He seemed content with silence, and I humored him because I could open my hearing to the voices from the next room. Jo explained what Sean and Anne had asked, and that if she'd deemed me unworthy, she would've taken the boys with her when she fled.

The shock caused my heart to stutter. I might never have known about Patrick and Thomas. She could've easily kept them from the family, then come back and claimed the boys' inheritance before they reached their majority. The money from the claim would've been hers.

Instead, she'd stuck to the plan. At least until I forced her hand by showing up at her home.

After the sheriff asked why she trusted me after not even a day, Jo said, "I saw his grief when he read the letter. How he treated me as an equal. How he protected the children. He's a good man."

She'd seen my worth. I managed not to smile with the praise, though my wolf chuffed with pleasure.

"And I've agreed to go with the children to Denver. They've had a lot of...upheaval lately. They deserve a little continuity."

I barely had time to register the elation that I wouldn't have to convince her to come with me, when Thomas said, "Sir, can I tell you something?"

"Sure, young man. You're Thomas, right?"

"Yessir. I-I wanted you and Miss Lukas to know the man in the other room, the one who came to Miss Lukas's house, is one of the men who killed my poppa and momma."

My reality stuttered, then resumed. He'd been trying to tell me about Nicholson, both when he opened the door minutes ago and also when we left the house. Poor child—

"You saw him?"

"I did. And heard them talk." His voice cracked. I heard light footsteps cross the room, a bed creak, then vague *shh*-ing, Jo, most likely. At least someone in there could comfort the children.

"That's enough, son," the sheriff said kindly. "I think it's best we shouldn't talk about what you saw now. I believe your cousin and Miss Lukas. I need to go talk to them now for a bit. Will you boys be okay for a little while?"

"Yessir," both boys answered in unison, though Thomas's voice carried a hint of tears.

Heavy boot steps on the carpeted floor mixed with lighter ones. The door opened. Jo proceeded the sheriff, her gaze downcast and features somber. She crossed to me and stood at my shoulder near the couch. A quick peek from the corner of her eyes and her watery smile signaled the effort she made not to break down from the boys' trauma and the events of this single day.

She couldn't comprehend the emotions her earlier praise had given me, nor those she invoked now by standing shoulder to shoulder with me. She sought me out for comfort. My chest wanted to swell with pride.

"Ahem," the sheriff said. "Deputy Baker and I have been investigating a group of claim jumpers, the very ones we'll probably find dead at your cousin's mine."

My gaze flashed to the man still standing next to the door, who sent me a tight nod. Not a night watchman. A deputized officer of the law.

"I needed eyes and ears not associated with my office. I asked Deputy Baker to poke around town." Plunkett tugged on one end of his mustache. "The Franklin is in the unique situation to see all classes of people—working class, trades, businessmen. I'd received information that the clerk was filing fraudulent documents and confronted him yesterday. He wouldn't give up the brains of the operation. I believe your speculation is correct. Nicholson intended to eliminate witnesses. Sheer luck put Deputy Baker in the right spot at this hotel."

The sheriff paused to take in the woman at my left, then continued, "Mr. Monaghan, I think we all should thank you for coming and saving Miss Lukas and those boys from this nefarious plot. Without you, we might've had a very different outcome today."

My actions were woefully inadequate in comparison. "She hid these children at great personal risk for almost a month. I swooped in at the last moment. While I appreciate your gratitude, it's best given to her."

The Ossory tradition believed everyone had value. "Most men think females are the weaker sex in both body and mind. Josephine Lukas might be a lovely, petite woman. She also has intelligence. Loyalty. Courage. Honor. I would take one of her above the strength of one hundred men."

She sought out my hand. Her fingers were trembling, and she gripped mine hard.

"Oh, ahem. Of course," the sheriff blustered. "Miss Lukas, I know we can all agree you did an amazing job protecting those boys and getting them reunited with their family. You said you would be traveling to Denver to get them settled. Will you be returning to Deadwood? My sister was looking forward to you teaching her son next year."

My wolf huffed, already secure in the knowledge she would go with me.

"No, Sheriff. I won't be back. I have already accepted a teaching position in San Francisco."

11

JOSEPHINE

The *click-clack* swaying of the private train carriage might've made my lids want to close, just like the slumbering children on the sofa across from me. Except I couldn't stop my thoughts whirling like Charybdis himself swirled them in my head.

Beyond Patrick and Thomas, the train streamed by the Badlands' dun-colored landscape with its narrow channels and rugged peaks, summer burnt prairie, and stratified rock layers. I tried to pay attention to the desolate, yet strangely beautiful vistas, though I couldn't stop sneaking glances at Aaron, who sat in the comfortably stuffed chair next to me.

Other than to ascertain my comfort and confirm the travel arrangements, he hadn't said much to me since we boarded hours ago, seemingly content to keep to his own thoughts.

Not that I would ordinarily complain about another's silence. Most people described me as more of a bookworm than a chatterbox, though I possessed social graces. Yet, with his question—or lack thereof—hanging between us, my ability to make small talk vanished with my certainty of what choice I would make.

This decision might change everything I'd ever thought about myself. Though my mother said the man destined for me would be impervious to my psychic skills, I resolved never to marry. Or more accurately, I determined this mythical man would never really want *me.* Who would want an intellectual woman, one determined to teach college? No one of my acquaintance.

Yet the very man I never thought to encounter might be right next to me. Or would he want me to give up those dreams?

The drawn-out expectation of his question had me more on edge than I'd ever been...well, except for two days ago when I thought Jim Nicholson would shoot me twice in the span of less than an hour.

Before I'd fallen into an exhausted sleep that night, Aaron had said we'd talk in the morning. The emerald fire in his eyes, the exact shade of the wolf's, seemed a promise. Instead, I went to my house yesterday to pack what remained of my possessions and arrange for my abrupt departure, meeting with my landlord, librarian friend, and finally, the school's principal to tender my resignation. Aaron and the boys went to arrange for travel, clothing for them, and visiting their parent's graves. While excited my possessions—my mother's tea set, Plutarch's *Lives*, the quilt my cousin made for my graduation from college, and more—would travel with me, there had been no time to visit the cemetery with the Monaghans, let alone have a moment for a private discussion with Aaron.

I snuck another glance at him, taking in the way his gaze seemed to stretch into the distance, like he was half a world away rather than on this train to Denver.

My dilemma stretched between him and me, even if he had no knowledge.

Abruptly, he leaned his forearms on his thighs. He studied my features for a moment, then said in a low tone, "Jo—may I call you that?"

Too stunned by the intensity in his features, I merely nodded my acquiescence.

"Thank you. I have been loath to ask you the question from the other night. I nearly blurted it out with the emotion of the evening. Still not sure how I managed to keep my counsel." He shook his head with a wry expression on his features. "One day's acquaintance is far too early for most to know if they would want to bind themselves to another for the rest of their lives."

"Bind?" What odd phrasing.

"I am not like regular humans. Of course we would marry, but the relationship with an Ossory wolf brings a much deeper passion." He searched my features, perhaps sensing my relief with his honorable intentions. "I want you to know that you may take as long as you need to tell me yes."

His arrogance made my temper rise, then I saw the teasing quirk in his grin. Instead of outrage, I asked with genuine curiosity, "What if I say no?"

A spasm crossed his face. He sat back and his hands clasped the chair's arms until his knuckles turned white. "Then your answer is no. I won't lie and say it will be easy for me to accept. My wolf does not like this—you may walk away at any time."

"No tricks?" Despite my heart knowing his response, my head needed assurances.

"No tricks," he said with grave solemnity. "You may leave if you wish. All I ask is you talk to me before you go."

His generosity spurred my conscience. My conundrum was unknown to him. I licked my lips and admitted, "This will not be an easy decision."

"I will endeavor to make your choice easy." He reached out slowly enough for me to have avoided his hand, then took mine in his. "How can I help?"

The comforting warmth of his fingers strangely left me more miserable. I disengaged, then threaded my fingers together in my lap, praying he would understand my situation. My ambitions burned like the sacred fire in Hestia's temples. His failure to comprehend this would give me a quick answer, before I grew too fond of him. For I knew in my heart, I was far too fond of him already.

"My move to San Francisco is to a private boarding school to teach Greek history and literature."

He merely nodded, then opened his mouth as if to say something before closing his lips, so I forged on. "I don't want to stop at secondary education. I want to be a college professor. I planned to save money to get my master's degree and then my doctorate."

"That's an admirable goal," he said with a bob of his chin and no hint of disdain or condescension. "I have no doubt you'll achieve it."

He obviously didn't understand.

"Where will I find such an opportunity in Denver?"

"If you want to teach, I'll go wherever you want." He spread his hands. "If you still want to go to San Francisco, I will go with you for the position. If you'd prefer to start college instead, I hear Stanford's

University is top-notch. Or Yale or Harvard, maybe Vanderbilt, would suit your needs."

His equanimity flustered me. He should be mocking me—a "little woman"—for daring to enter a man's world. "You're the president of the Emerald Hill Corporation. Why should I believe you'd give that up? Why should I believe these aren't pretty promises you'll forget when convenient or I need to host your parties?"

"I don't need all of this." He swept his hand out to encompass the train carriage's posh amenities. "Being with my wife and my wolf's mate is truly all I need. I know this probably doesn't mean much to you right now, but I give you my word as an Ossory wolf."

With his oath, his eyes once again had taken on his wolf's verdant hue. He fisted his right hand and placed it across his heart.

The magnitude of the decision threatened to rip me in two. Everything I'd ever experienced taught me men had no respect for women like me. If I started the education path now, within the next decade women should have the vote, opening up more opportunities, like academia.

Dare I take the leap of trust? If I chose my heart's desire right now, there'd be no going back. I would fall in love with this man, one who'd shown such bravery and consideration, such devotion to his family, only to have my dreams wither away. Without examining his thoughts, I would have to trust his word. The chasm I must span between my lived experience with men and this man seemed as far as from America to France.

Yet, according to my mother, fate had chosen him for me. Surely the Moirai counted for something.

"Miss Lukas?" Hesitation colored Patrick's tone. I'd been so focused on Aaron that I hadn't realized the boys had risen from the sofa and stood at my left.

I struggled to regain a teacher's demeanor, neutral features, patient curve to my lips. "I'm sorry we woke you up."

"It's okay," the young man said. "I wanted to let you know that Papa told us when an Ossory wolf speaks an oath, he must keep the promise, or it'll be bad."

Thomas nodded vigorously. "A wolf must keep his promise in his heart."

My father's words from some ten years ago came to me when I asked if I would ever find a man who would believe in me. *"You will, kochanie.*" With the endearment, he'd wiped away the tears on my cheeks. "*Settle for no less than one who fights for you with the heart of the wilk.*"

Gooseflesh broke out across my body. *Wilk.* "Wolf" in Polish. Could my father have been prescient?

Aaron reached into his vest's pocket, then held up two silver dollars to his cousins. "Why don't you two go to the dining car and ask the porter for ice cream?" When the boys both grabbed for the coins, he whisked them out of reach. "Two ice creams each, and the rest to the porter. Then you come directly back. Watch out after each other. No shenanigans. Honor Laignech Fáelad." He leveled a stern gaze upon the two. "I need your oaths as Ossory wolves."

"Promise!" came from both of the boys with enough gusto and chest thumps with their fists to make me smile. Patrick palmed the coins, then took his brother's hand and led him to the exit. "Come on. They want to be alone."

Amusement tinged with embarrassment burst from me and Aaron. Once our merriment died away, I couldn't tear myself from his gaze. The moment grew charged, and my pulse began to accelerate. Aaron took my fingers with his, and his thumb brushed my knuckles. My lips were dry, and I licked them, my breath hanging in my lungs...waiting, hoping...

He leaned forward, the slightest smile curling the edges of his lips. "I want to apologize to you."

Confusion reigned within me. "Apologize for what?"

"For thinking you were a thief...and worse." His rueful smile tilted to one side in a charming manner.

The idea was so preposterous I straightened in my chair, unable to form words. Me? A criminal?

He braced his forearms on his legs. "You went through my possessions efficiently, not to mention found my trunk's hidden compartment. I jumped to the wrong conclusion. And then for a couple of minutes, I thought the boys were yours and Sean's."

The silence stretched for several moments while I struggled with his honesty, something I didn't experience often, especially from men. Finally, I said, "I can see how you might've come to those conclusions, but no harm was done. You didn't even need to tell me."

"I know. It's been weighing on my mind. I want no secrets between us." I didn't need my mind reading talents to decipher his straightforward words. He told the truth. "How *did* you find the trunk's compartment so quickly?"

I relaxed back against the chair. "When my father came to America, accounting work was hard to find for a man with the last name Lukaszewicz and a heavy Polish accent."

The cant to Aaron's lips suggested he understood the discrimination against new immigrants. How many generations ago had the ship brought his people from Ireland?

Instead of the question, I went on with my story. "He needed money for his wife who was about to give birth to me, and he relied on his father's trade, cabinetry. Eventually, Papa started helping people repair their furniture. After a couple of years, he started a business buying and selling used furniture. I'd often help, particularly with locked pieces. My job was to figure them out, though I'm fairly certain he wanted to keep me busy in the shop after school."

"My father had a similar theory," Aaron said with a chuckle. "Please, continue with your story."

His encouragement was all I needed to warm to my subject. "I love puzzles, and particularly enjoyed the challenge of figuring out which keys worked for sideboards and cabinets, then traveling cases and trunks, though if needed, I could often open them with special tools a locksmith gave me. Then I discovered a hidden compartment in one of the desks, and a trunk next. After that, he had me check all of the furniture coming in."

He cocked his head, almost as if a wolf hearing an intriguing noise. "How do you know if there's a compartment?"

"There's a difference in the dimensions, like in the Sherlock Holmes story, *The Adventure of the Empty House*." I couldn't have been more surprised when Aaron said the title with me. For a moment I gaped at him. "You know Sherlock Holmes?"

"The stories are quite fun to decipher. Though I've read almost all of them, admittedly, I have only deciphered a couple before the reveal." His confession came with a self-deprecating smile and rueful shake of his head.

For a moment I sat nonplussed, unable to believe he revealed not solving them all, unlike most men I'd talked to about the stories. Something within me clicked, like yet another piece of me fit seamlessly with him.

The dam breached, releasing the longing I'd denied my entire life, the yearning for a connection with a man who would believe in me. The emotion swelled until my heart nearly burst in my chest. If I dared, I might have the love of a man who supported my dreams.

I could fight this no longer, this attraction to this handsome *wilkolak,* this werewolf who would capture my heart. Tears gathered in my eyes, and I quickly blinked them back. Before I lost my courage, I stood and took a step toward him.

He rose and met me halfway, yet made no move, merely tangled his gaze with mine until my breath came in short bursts with the anticipation of his lips against mine.

The world around me disappeared, and we were close enough that I could feel the heat of his body. Treacherous memories of his naked form, all taut skin over tempting muscles rose in my mind, making my fingers itch to touch him. Why didn't he touch me? Kiss me?

He seemed to be waiting. Soon, I recognized he'd declared his intentions, and the moment belonged to me to take the next step.

Could I?

"You really don't have to choose now." He brought his hand to cup my cheek and gazed tenderly into my eyes. "You will know when you have your answer. Pressure is unfair when your considerations are this weighty."

After a deep breath, I slid my hand up his chest and around to his nape, pulling his head toward mine. I met his mouth with a sigh, confident in my decision.

I would make the leap right into the arms of my handsome *wilkolak*...my werewolf.

ABOUT THE AUTHOR

Amanda Reid is the author of *The Flannigan Sisters Psychic Mysteries* and is a participating author in *The Enchanted Rock Immortals* world of paranormal romance novellas. She began writing after careers as a globe-trotting Army brat then as a federal agent. Now she's settled in Texas and enjoys traveling with her husband and two gonzo Australian Shepherds.

If your sweet spot is smack in the middle of Romantic Suspense and Urban Fantasy, you'll love Amanda's action-packed paranormal romances, and those who love a small-town, paranormal mystery with a sister vibe will adore her cozies. Be sure to check out her website for new releases, free books, and fun giveaways! https://amandareidau thor.com

GRACE.

A LADIES OF THE LINKS NOVELLA

HALEY RHOADES

A LADIES OF THE LINKS NOVELLA

ABOUT *LADIES OF THE LINKS*

Life at the country club entails much more than golf. The Ladies of the Links are a tight-knit group, but when a rumor blog posts, drama ensues.

1

SHATTERED REFLECTIONS

Morgan

I lean against the closed door, my back sliding down until my butt hits the floor. Like never before, I feel alone; I feel dead inside. My walls crumble, and my facade falls as I no longer need to fake it. Alone in my empty house, I have no need to pretend.

My children, the lights of my life, walked through this door moments ago, climbing into their father's car. Excited for their first visitation weekend, I played my part as their mother. I didn't make him out to be the bad guy of our separation. I did not comment on Brock's fling with a woman 12 years our junior. I did not let on that he cheated repeatedly on me. I chose to take the high road, and now my children continue to see their father as the man they idolize.

Quieter than it's been in the 13 years since their births, my house feels like a cold, medieval stone castle. Alone without my babies, I dread the next 48 hours.

For over six months, I put the needs of my children above my own; I put my husband's selfish wants above my own. I did my best to hide my hurt until I climbed into bed each night. The floodgates are open, and my strength is gone. I plan to sit right here until I must move to open my door on Sunday night when my children return.

When my cell phone vibrates on the tile floor of the entryway beside me, I glance at its illuminated screen.

GIBSON:

on my way to your house

u r staying with me

pack a bag

Ty & Aaron are with me

no arguing

dinner on our deck

girls' movie night

only us

I attempt to grab for the phone; I try to text her not to come. I don't have the strength. Silent tears slip down my cheeks, dripping off my chin.

This is my new life; this is my new reality. For years to come, I'll hand over my children to my ex-husband every other weekend. Each time, my house will become my prison, and I will be watching the clock, counting down the minutes until my stint in solitary confinement ends.

The doorbell rings twenty minutes later. I haven't moved from my spot on the floor. My legs have gone numb, and my tears have dried into salty tracks on my cheeks. The sound of Gibson's key turning in the lock—the emergency key I gave her last month when our separation was finalized—echoes through the foyer.

"Morgan?" Her voice cuts through the silence as the door pushes against my shoulder. "Jesus, are you sitting against the door?"

I scoot forward just enough to let her in. Gibson squeezes through the gap, her designer handbag clutched to her chest. Behind her, I catch glimpses of her husband, Aaron, and his friend, Ty, leaning on Ty's truck.

"Oh, honey." Gibson crouches beside me, tucking a strand of hair behind my ear. Her manicured nails brush against my cheek. "First drop-off is always the hardest."

"I don't think I can do this," I whisper, my voice cracking. "Bryce looked so excited to go. What if they like it better there? What if that... hussy... makes them forget me?"

Gibson snorts, settling onto the tile beside me. "No one could replace you. Besides, Bryce texted Ty already. Apparently, Brock's new girlfriend can't cook for shit. Made them frozen pizza." She squeezes my hand. "Trust me, they'll be begging to come home by tomorrow. Bryce never complains to Ty about your cooking."

I'm eternally grateful that Ty invited my boys over to help with renovation projects and learn about construction. For a few hours every weekend, they have undivided attention of a strong male figure. It's more than Brock's interested in sharing with them.

I manage a weak smile as Ty appears in the doorway. "Aaron's threatening to pack a bag for you if you don't."

"I don't feel like going anywhere," I protest, but there's no real resistance in my voice.

"Yeah, and when have we ever listened to you?" Ty extends his hand to pull me up. "Remember when you said that lime green was a terrible choice for the ladies' golf tournament shirts?"

"They were terrible," I mumble.

"And we wore them anyway," Gibson finishes, standing up beside me. "We looked fabulous, we came in second place, and the world didn't end."

I let them pull me to my feet, my legs tingling as blood returns to them. The house suddenly feels less empty with their presence filling the spaces.

"Pack a bag," Gibson instructs, guiding me toward the stairs. "You're not spending tonight alone in this mausoleum."

"The boys—"

"—will know exactly where to find you when they get back," Ty interjects. "Besides, it's forty-eight hours, not forty-eight years. You get to have a life too, you know."

I pause at the foot of the stairs, looking back at the three of them —Gibson in her cute black and white tennis outfit, Ty in his tight blue t-shirt and ripped jeans. My group of friends. My lifeline. One by one, these women show up over and over. Sandy and Paige were first at my door with wine and tissues the night I discovered the texts on Brock's phone, Gibson sat with me through mediation, Gwynn helped me find the perfect lawyer when Brock announced he's not returning.

"What would I do without you?" I ask softly.

Gibson gives me a gentle shove toward the stairs. "Let's hope you never have to find out. Now go. Pack pajamas and something cute. Just because your heart is broken doesn't mean you can't look hot while you heal."

As I climb the stairs to my bedroom—our bedroom, once—I hear Aaron and Ty vow to help Gibson keep me occupied this weekend, the familiar sound of ice clinking in a shaker. For the first time since watching Bryce and Greg climb into Brock's new Lexus (bought with the bonus he'd been hiding from me), I feel something other than despair.

It's not happiness, not yet. But it might be the first faint glimmer of possibility—that maybe, just maybe, there's a version of me waiting on the other side of all this pain. A Morgan who isn't defined by being Brock's wife or even just Bryce and Greg's mom.

A Morgan I haven't met yet, but who might be worth knowing.

2

GHOSTS OF THE PAST

Derek

I close my email tab, the words of my... I guess she's tryng to be my new manager's email swirling in my head like a persistent fog that refuses to lift. The blue light of my computer screen casts an eerie glow across my home office as evening approaches. Outside my window, the manicured fairway of Tryst Falls' nineth hole stretches into the distance, golfers wrapping up their rounds as shadows lengthen.

I knew better than to open it. I wish I would have walked away when my fingers hovered over my mouse, that momentary hesitation a warning I should have heeded. The subject line had been innocuous enough: "Opportunity Worth Considering." But I knew what it meant. The same thing it always meant.

"I didn't put out feelers. The venues are faunching at the bit to be among the first to book the band. Your fans haven't forgotten you. You're wasting your prime years putting around with rich housewives."

Her email brings my past to the front of my mind, dragging me back to a life I deliberately left behind, like the platinum records I keep hidden on my locked office wall, the magazine covers I've stuffed into storage, and the fame that felt increasingly hollow with each concert we played. I plan not to respond, as I have with all her attempts to contact me over the past eighteen months. If I do not respond, eventually she will get the hint—though Turner's persistence suggests otherwise.

I close my laptop with more force than necessary, the sharp snap echoing through the quiet room. Placing it back on my desk, I run my hands through waves of my long hair, feeling a tension headache building at my temples. The frames on my wall—album covers and multi-platinum records—mock me.

I shut and lock my office door as I exit, leaving the ghosts of my former career behind it. Unable to stand the silence of my house that is far from the raucous life I once lived—hotel parties, sponsor events, the constant chatter of fans online—I picked up a Harlequin Great Dane puppy last month. The local breeder raised an eyebrow when I listed my occupation as retired, clearly questioning my young age. Above all else, the anonymity remains refreshing.

I named the rambunctious pup Frank, after Frank Zappa whose music pumped through my headphones before I even picked up a guitar. Now he gives me someone to talk to and adds life to my large, empty home on the course of the country club property. As if summoned by my thoughts, I hear the clicking of his nails on the hardwood floor before he rounds the corner, tennis ball in mouth, tail wagging with unrestrained enthusiasm.

"Not now, buddy," I murmur, bending to scratch behind his ears. His brown eyes looking up at me with adoration I'm not sure I deserve. "We'll go for a walk later tonight."

At the word 'walk', his ears perk up. He drops the slobbery ball at my feet, hopeful, but I shake my head. "Later, I promise." The unconditional love of a dog—something else I never made time for during my years on tour.

I pull out my cell phone, scrolling past notifications from music sites I keep meaning to delete. The headlines still occasionally feature my name: "Whatever Happened To...?" and "The Mysterious Disappearance of Rock's Heart Throb."

I've never regretted walking away from that life, despite Turner's persistent emails suggesting otherwise. The constant travel, the pressure, the scrutiny—it all became too much after losing my bandmate. No one understood why I'd walk away at the peak of my career. No one except maybe my bandmates, who'd seen firsthand how the spotlight had changed me, hollowed me out until the person at the mic strumming the six strings.

I head to my master bathroom, Frank trailing behind me. I pause at my reflection in the vanity mirror. The lines on my face softened since leaving the tour, the perpetual tension in my shoulders gradually eased. I look... happier. More like the kid who fell in love with music for the pure joy of placing pen to paper then sharing my music with the world, before gigs then concerts, managers, obsessive fans, groupies, music charts and critics complicated everything.

The hot water of the shower pounds against my back, easing the tightness that always follows one of Turner's messages. As steam fills the bathroom, I let my mind drift to Morgan—her laugh, the freckles across her nose that become more pronounced in sunlight, the way she looks at me like I'm just a man, not a former rockstar, a disappointment, or a cautionary tale.

At the Lynks at Tryst Falls Country Club, I'm just Derek Fox, the new member, not Chipper Wade the multi-platinum, Grammy Award winning singer-songwriter who walked away from it all after the pandemic changed the world forever. I've been careful to keep it that way, appreciating the small-town anonymity of the club life where most members care more about my handicap than the fake back story I created.

As I step out of the shower, wrapping a towel around my waist, I feel lighter. Turner's email, the new siren to the ghosts of my former life, recedes a little further into the background.

Eighteen months ago, I couldn't imagine feeling hopeful about the future and consider possibilities beyond the next city, venue, and set list.

But here I am. And for the first time in a long time, the path ahead feels like something to look forward to rather than something to dread.

3

ON THE ROAD

Morgan

"If I have to hear one more true crime podcast, I'm going to create a crime scene of my own," Sandy announces, reaching between the front seats to turn down Paige's carefully curated playlist. "Two hours of murder porn is my limit."

"It's not porn!" Paige protests, taking offense.

Mere hours into our road trip I begin to reconsider my decision to come. The Kansas City skyline long behind us as Paige's Tahoe cruises north on I-29. June's afternoon sun glints off the Missouri River to our left, the landscape gradually shifting from small towns.

"Driver picks the entertainment," Paige responds primly, her hands at a perfect ten and two on the steering wheel. Her French-tipped nails matching her white knuckles as Sandy continues to fiddle with the stereo system.

"Don't distract the driver," Kirby chides from the front seat, swatting Sandy's hands away.

"Then let someone else drive," Sandy counters, settling back into her seat beside me. "I vote for something that doesn't involve dismembered body parts. My bladder can't handle both coffee and anxiety."

Scoffs fill the vehicle, as we all know it's not coffee in her travel mug.

From the third row, Gibson and Kirby chime in with agreement while Brooks remains suspiciously silent, I suspect she dozes behind her oversized sunglasses.

I catch Paige's gaze in the rearview mirror and offer a sympathetic smile. As the planner of this whole expedition, she's already fielding complaints before we've even crossed the Iowa border. This doesn't bode well for our two-day journey to Deadwood.

"I have the perfect playlist," I volunteer, connecting my phone to the Bluetooth. The opening notes of Cyndi Lauper's "Girls Just Want to Have Fun" fill the SUV, and Sandy immediately perks up.

"Now we're talking!" she exclaims, performing an impressive seated dance move that threatens to spill her travel mug of what I suspect to be some vodka drink—because of course Sandy brought alcohol on a five-hour road trip.

"We've got a long drive ahead," I remind everyone. "Let's pace ourselves."

"That's rich coming from the woman who nearly backed out last night," Gibson teases from the back.

She's not wrong. With Bryce and Greg spending the week at Brock's parents' lake house—a visit I forced when brock backed out on me twenty-four hours before our trip—I'd briefly considered using the time to work on my latest secret manuscript. My self-imposed deadline is looming, and my editor's emails are growing increasingly frantic.

But the promise of four days away from the country club, away from pretending I'm not struggling financially, away from the constant reminder of my failed marriage, ultimately won out. My alter ego Tris Holiday would just have to wait.

"Earth to Morgan," Sandy waves her hand in front of my face. "Where'd you go?"

"Sorry, just thinking about the boys," I lie. "This is my first trip without them since the divorce."

The car falls momentarily silent, the unspoken understanding hanging in the air. Then gently Sandy squeezes my knee.

"All the more reason to make this count," she declares. "Wild Bill Days in Deadwood! Four days of drinking, dancing, and—if we're lucky—some handsome bikers or cowboys."

"Oh! I read about that," Kirby adds from the back. "Deadwood's crawling with motorcycles this time of year. I think Deadwood's close to a biker's heaven called Sturgis."

"I'm just excited about the history," Gibson says. "The HBO show made me want to see the real thing."

"You do realize the show was filmed in California, right?" Brooks murmurs, apparently not as asleep as she appeared. "And that the real Deadwood burned down multiple times?"

"Always the optimist," Sandy rolls her eyes. "Can someone please check if her seatbelt is too tight? I think cutting off blood flow to her personality."

"Ladies," Paige interjects in her most authoritative tone—the same one she uses when scolding her children. "We have a schedule to maintain. The next rest stop is in forty-five minutes."

"Or sooner if Sandy drinks anymore," I quip, earning a playful swat from my seatmate.

In between Sandy's multiple potty breaks, the miles roll by, Missouri gives way to Iowa, the landscape flattening into an endless horizon broken only by occasional home and billboards. We fall into a rhythm of frequent stops, driver changes, and increasingly absurd car games.

"Fuck, marry, kill, club edition." Sandy announces somewhere past Omaha. "Tennis pro Frank, kill Dr. Soto from the board, and fuck Ty, Gibson's construction guy."

"Sandy!" Paige gasps from the driver's seat.

"Our men are off limits," Christy states.

"Ty's not Gibson's man. He's just a live-in friend, so he's fair game," Sandy argues.

While she may be fooling the others, I believe Ty is much more to Aaron and Gibson than a live-in friend.

"Kill Palmer so we get a new head golf pro and sleep with Maddux," I blurt.

"And..." Sandy prompts. "Who would you marry?"

I shake my head. "I haven't been divorced two months yet, I'm not ready to even joke about marrying again."

"Maddox, my sixteen-year-old lifeguard?" Christy asks in disbelief.

"Oh god no!" I cough. "Maddux as in Ryan's older brother."

"Ooo..." Gibson croons. "He's perfect for you."

"Brooks, it's your turn," I encourage, changing the subject.

"Marry Blake from maintenance, sleep with Frank the tennis pro for his thighs and arms, and..."

She pauses looking back at Sandy.

"Poor Dr. Soto," Gibson finishes with mock solemnity. "Death by country club ladies."

"He'd die the happiest any members have ever seen him," Sandy assures us.

By the time we reach our hotel in Sioux Falls, tension and fatigue set in. Brooks and Kirby's constant bickering about the air conditioning settings, Sandy's requesting way too many bathroom breaks, and Paige's carefully planned itinerary is already more than two hours behind schedule.

As the sun begins to set, The Canopy by Hilton is a welcome sight as the sun begins to set. We tumble out of the Tahoe like survivors of a shipwreck, stretching cramped limbs and retrieving entirely too much luggage for an overnight stay.

I'm dumping my luggage in the room and heading straight to the first bar I find in the Steel District.

"Remember, brunch and out the door by noon tomorrow," Paige reminds us as she hands out room keys in the lobby. "Gibson and I are in 212, Sandy and Kirby in 214, Morgan, Christy, and Brooks in 216."

Sandy's groan is audible. "Why are we leaving so late? Wild Bill Days waits for no woman!"

"Switch with me," Gibson whispers as we head toward the elevators. "You take Paige, and I'll take Brooks and Christy."

I squeeze her arm gratefully. "Be nice. Drop off your bag and meet me back in the lobby in five minutes. I looked up the surrounding area after the second potty break. Bars are nearby."

~

"This is our last stop until Deadwood, so make sure you wait," Brooks states, climbing from the third row of the SUV at Wall Drug.

When we climb back in the vehicle, excited discussions about our Deadwood accommodations begin.

"A restored brothel," Sandy sighs dreamily, from the front passenger seat. "Do you think they kept any of the original features?"

"Like what, the STD collection?" Brooks scoffs. "It's just marketing. Probably a regular apartment with some old-timey wallpaper."

"Actually," Gibson chimes in, scrolling through her phone,

"Aggie's was originally a hardware store in 1876. It was one of the few buildings that refused to become a casino when gambling was legalized back in 1989."

"Trust Gibson to have done her research," Brooks teases.

"And trust Brooks to be a buzzkill," Sandy adds, earning a glare from our resident tattoo artist.

"Let's draw our room assignments," Paige announces, ever the organizer even while driving. "The AirBnB has three bedrooms—two with full beds and one with bunk beds."

"Dibs on not bunk beds," Sandy and Brooks say simultaneously, then glare at each other.

"We'll draw names," Paige reminds, pulling a plastic bag from her purse. "Fair is fair."

Ten minutes and several disputed draws later, the arrangement is set: Gibson and I in bunk beds, Paige and Sandy sharing one full bed, with Brooks and Kirby sharing the other.

"This is going to be a disaster," Kirby whispers to me as Sandy celebrates avoiding the bunks with an improvised victory dance in her seat.

"Or the best weekend ever," I counter, feeling optimistic despite myself. "When was the last time any of us did something this adventurous and low key?"

"Golf retreat in Scottsdale last year," Gibson offers.

"That was a Four Seasons with a spa," I remind her. "This is different. This is..."

"Wild!" Sandy finishes with a wicked grin. "Just like us."

The second leg of our journey takes us west across South Dakota, the landscape growing more dramatic as we approach the Black Hills. Sandy has taken over the music, treating us to a cycle of 80s hits in preparation for our rockstar and Eighties themed nights out.

"I still can't believe we're doing theme nights," Brooks grumbles from the back seat. "We're grown women, not sorority girls."

"That's exactly why we need theme nights," Sandy counters. "When was the last time any of us had actual fun? Not charity-gala fun or country-club-approved fun. Real, let-your-hair-down, act like single women with no responsibilities fun."

"Three of us are single," Brooks states.

"I'm proud to be a married woman and refuse to act single," Paige declares.

"I wasn't suggesting you sleep with anyone this weekend," Sandy explains. "However... if you wanted to, I would not try to stop you."

"Sandy! Please stop." Paige uses her serious mom tone.

Our conversation ceases and we gaze at our phones while music plays over the stereo.

As we near Deadwood, the landscape transforms dramatically. The flat prairie gives way to pine-covered mountains, winding roads, and glimpses of rugged terrain that make the hills and bluffs of Missouri look like mere wrinkles in the earth.

"It's beautiful," Brooks breathes, pressing her face against the window like an excited child.

"And historic," Gibson adds, consulting a guidebook on her cellphone. "Deadwood was founded illegally in the 1870s on land that had been granted to the Lakota Tribe. Gold miners just moved in and set up camp."

"Sounds like some of our club members with their new builds," Sandy quips. "Changing rules to suit themselves."

"Dr. Soto," I say under my breath.

The town appears suddenly as we round a curve.

"Welcome to Deadwood, ladies, our home for the next three nights," Paige announces as the historic Deadwood sign comes into view.

The street is blocked off street is already crowded with tourists and motorcycles for the Wild Bill Days festival.

"Oh no!"

"Oh no what?" I ask.

"Um..." Paige pulls into the Deadwood Welcome Center parking lot. "Directions to the Air BnB tell me to drive on Main Street."

"And Main Street's closed for Wild Bill Days," Gibson finishes for her.

In the rearview mirror, I witness Paige's frustration skyrocket. The ultimate over planner can't stand it that her plans were lacking.

"I'll drop a pin on the road behind the Air BnB," Brooks offers.

"You can't access it from that street," Paige huffs. "We'll have to park here and walk. Or try to find a side street further down and walk from there."

"How far are we talking?" Sandy inquires.

"One block over then about three more," Paige answers, turning toward the rear seats for our response.

Sandy makes a production of checking her travel mug. Pleased with the beverage level, she nods okay.

"Paige and Sandy have the most luggage," Gibson states. "They should decide where we part."

"I say we park here for now," Paige suggests and Sandy concurs.

Decision made, amid a few grumbles and groans, we climb from the vehicle.

"Finally," Brooks sighs as we exit the vehicle on stiff legs. "If I had to spend one more minute listening to Bon Jovi, I might have opened the door at highway speed."

"Hater," Sandy accuses, stretching dramatically. "I had six more hours of 80s gold queued up."

Ever thankful I'm a savvy packer, I stack my duffle on my carry-on rolling bag and offer to roll one of Sandy's two large bags.

Paige's guidance and Sandy's colorful commentary about the sidewalks, eventually leads us to our door and stairway. Aggie's 1895 Saloon & Brothel sits proudly on Main Street, its brick exterior reminiscent of centuries past.

"Dibs on testing out all the beds!" Sandy announces, already heading up the stairs with her suitcase bumping behind her.

"For historical research purposes," Gibson adds with a wink, perpetuating Sandy's fixation on the brothel history of the building.

The interior of the Air BnB surprises all of us—even Brooks seems impressed by the blend of historic charm and modern amenities. Large windows and original hardwood floors contrast with updated appliances and tasteful furnishings. The hardware store's history remains visible in the high ceilings and large front windows.

"This is amazing," I breathe, bending down to run my hand along the wooden floors that's been smoothed by a century and a half of use.

"Not what I expected," Brooks admits.

As the women scatter to find their assigned beds and explore our temporary home, I linger at the window, taking in the busy view of Main Street through the tall window. The energy of Deadwood pulses visibly—motorcycles rumble nearby and tourists wandering in and out of shops.

For the first time in months—maybe years—I feel a weight lifting.

Here, no one knows me as the woman whose husband left her for someone barely out of college. No one cares about my financial struggles or my secret. For four days, I can just be Morgan—not ex-Mrs. Merrifield, not new author Tris Holiday, not the mother barely holding it together.

"What are you thinking about?" Gibson asks, appearing beside me with that intuitive sense she often displays.

"That I needed this more than I realized," I admit.

She bumps my shoulder with hers. "We all did. Even Brooks, though she'd rather die than admit it."

"I heard that!" Brooks calls from her room.

Gibson and I dissolve into laughter, the kind of unguarded moment that's become rare in my carefully constructed post-divorce life.

"Come on roomie," she urges, signaling to our room.

"Paige!" Sandy bellows from down the hall. "Get in here and pick your drawer before I claim them all! And fair warning—I brought enough outfits for a week-long stay!"

"We know!" many of us retort.

With a deep breath of anticipation, I head toward our small room, ready to embrace whatever wild adventure awaits us in this historic town. For once, I'm not writing the story—I'm living it.

4

IT'S NOT CHEATING

Derek

In the hallway, I lean against my closed hotel door. A glance at the watch on my right wrist tells me it's one forty-five. Each tick of the second hand amplifies my nerves. Although I've performed hundreds of times for crowds much larger than this, we're starting over. When we step on the stage tonight, it's the end of an era. It will mark the end of Sugary Pick Me Up and the beginning of Grace..

Across from me the door opens, and Turner pops out.

"Good. At least one of you follows directions," she states tapping the screen of her iPad while her cell phone sounds in her bag.

"Fifteen minutes," Turner shouts, silencing her alarm, as she knocks on the two hotel doors next to mine.

"I'll deny it if you tell anyone, I love that my job allows me to boss my father around," she snickers. "He's the worst one of all of you."

"You can't claim you didn't know what you were getting yourself into," I remind her.

"Ba ha ha," she mocks, her fingers flying on one screen then the other. "We will not be late for our first gig." She tucks her devices in her bag before banging on each door again. "Was it like this with Sugary Pick Me Up?"

"Worse. You'd be chasing them down in the bar or pulling them away from hookers in their rooms." I chuckle. "You had to witness some of that on our final tour. You were old enough to know what was up."

Turner rolls her eyes, her hand swiping that thought away. Our heads turn with the opening door. Corbin enters the hallway, a large duffle over his shoulder, wearing a Girls Gone Wild tattered tank top and paint-stained cargo shorts.

"Uh huh!" she protests, pointing from him to his hotel door. "Not on my watch. Go change."

Corbin looks to me for back up, but I simply shake my head, looking at my black motorcycle boots to hide my smile.

"Where does it say you get to dictate our wardrobe?" he growls like a petulant child.

"Trust me; it's in the contract," she warns.

He looks to me once more. Biting my lips, I nod.

"What's all the racket?" Cruz grumbles joining us.

"So help me Kershaw if you make us late for our first..."

Corbin cuts Turner off. "My clothes are in my bag." He pats his duffle. "It's 85 degrees. I'll change before we take the stage tonight."

"You could have told me that before my blood pressure skyrocketed," she grumbles. "Damn talent..." Her words trail barely above a whisper.

"Alright, you two," Cruz chides. "Don't jinx us. We're all a bit on edge for our first performance in five years."

"Our ride's out front," Turner states with a roll of her eyes after vibrations in her bag called her attention to her cell phone.

"After you," I gesture.

Corbin doesn't subscribe to my ladies first chivalry, striding toward the front desk. I swing my arm, urging Turner and her father to go ahead of me. Let Corbin go first; he'll be forced to sit in the back of the Tahoe.

I barely take my seat and shut the door, when Turner directs the driver to go.

"The setup crew claims their running thirty minutes behind," she informs as she texts a response.

"That means they're about an hour behind," Cruz chuckles. "I could still be napping."

"Damn your old," Corbin laughs. "Try not to let the fact that you nap daily come up during the set tonight. We can't have the babes thinking we're too old to rock and lack stamina in the sheets."

"Chipper's doing all the talking tonight," Turner reminds the band at the same time her father flips Corbin off over his right shoulder. She turns to look at us from the front seat, pointing at Corbin and Cruz. "The two of you can't be trusted."

Now her father flips Turner and I the bird.

"What would Mom say if she saw you making rude gestures?" she asks.

"She'd ask if it was an invitation," Corbin deadpans.

While I laugh, Cruz agrees, "That's exactly what my old lady would say."

"If a man ever refers to me as an 'old lady'..."

"You'll be lucky if you ever find a man willing to hang around long enough to call you anything," Corbin quips at the same time Cruz and I vow to kick any guy's ass that calls Turner his old lady.

Corbin places his hands on our seat backs, leaning between us in the center row. "Let me get this straight. You call your woman your old lady in front of Turner but you won't allow her to be someone's old lady?"

"She's not old enough to date," Cruz growls.

"Turner deserves better than the likes of us," I add.

Turner stares daggers in her father's direction.

"She does deserve better than Corbin and me," Cruz agrees. "But I'd be okay with a country club guy like you Chipper."

As Turner's eyes bug out in the mirror on the visor, I scoff at her father's words.

"You mean you'd be okay with an emo, golfer banging your daughter?" Corbin asks.

"Corbin!" Turner shrieks mortified as her cheeks turn pink.

"She brought home a lot worse than a millionaire, musically-inclined, golfer," Cruz mumbles. "If you weren't 22 years older than her, I'd marry her off to you in a heartbeat."

"He's not my type," Turner states.

"What's not to love?" Corbin laughs, turning his attention toward me. "According to him the married ladies at the club lust after him day and night."

"Imagine what they'd do if they knew Derek Fox is actually Chipper Wade of their favorite band Sugary Pick Me UP," Cruz joins in.

In the mirror, Turner mouths 'sorry.'

"We're not buying the fact that you haven't slept with any of the country club women," Corbin scoffs. "Not buying it for a minute."

"I believe it," Cruz argues. "Chipper writes his best when he's off pussy."

I close my eyes tight, cringing at this conversation in Turner's presence. Although she grew up with a rockstar dad, she's no where near as crude as her father.

"He has written a fuck-ton of lyrics in the five years he's hidden at the club. Hmm..." Corbin exaggerates his thinking. "No offense, man, I make money off your celibacy."

"Knock it off," I mumble, focusing on the route our driver takes to drop us off backstage in the middle of Main Street.

"Should we give the poor guy a weekend off from writing to get his dick sucked?" Corbin chortles.

"Leave him alone," Cruz orders. "All he has to do if focus those green eyes and he'll have three times the pussy we will."

"I think I'll call Mom," Turner says out loud, hoping to put her dad in place.

"Go ahead. Put her on speaker phone. She'll agree with every word," Cruz states.

"I'll never understand how she's put up with you for nearly thirty years," she grumbles.

"Spending time apart makes us appreciate each other more when we're together," Cruz answers.

"I meant the cheating." She glares at her father over her shoulder.

As soon as the Tahoe parks inside a barricade, Turner opens her door.

Before she makes her escape, Cruz adds, "It's not cheating if it's an open relationship."

While I close my eyes tight, drawing I two long deep breaths, I attempt to center myself in preparation. I told myself I didn't miss life on the road and the guys in the band, but truthfully I've been a bit lost without them. I created a new identity and persona at the club-one polar opposite of my band life. It's going to take me a while to adjust to the bold and very different personalities in our new band.

5

GIRLS GONE WILD BILL

Morgan

I park my suitcase in the corner before flopping onto the bottom bunk in our tiny room. The cheap mattress groans in protest, a sound I echo as I turn my head toward Gibson, my body attempting to starfish over the entire surface of the twin bed. My muscles ache from twelve hours in Paige's Tahoe, and the lumpy mattress of last night's hotel.

"What are you doing?" Gibson laughs, her hand rocking my ankle where it dangles off the edge. Her country club facade wilts during our journey—designer capris wrinkled, sweater vest swapped for a comfortable band t-shirt when we stopped at the iconic Wall Drug.

"With all of Sandy's bathroom stops, I never thought we'd get out of that Tahoe," I mutter, eyes closed against the sunshine streaming through the tiny window. "I counted five stops between Paige's driveway and here, not counting the hotel last night. Five stops for a ten-hour drive!"

Laughter continuing, Gibson agrees, "I'm glad we limited her liquid intake after leaving Sioux Falls this morning. It would've taken us two more hours if we hadn't." She pauses to stretch, her spine crackling audibly. "Sandy nearly caused a riot when Paige refused to stop at that sketchy gas station an hour into our journey because it wasn't on her precious itinerary."

"Funny, on the course and around the club, I never noticed her frequently using the restroom." I roll onto my side, watching Gibson methodically hang items in the tiny closet that smells vaguely of mothballs from decades past.

I quirk my head as the walls around us come alive with the sounds of our friends. Through the paper-thin barrier to our right, Sandy's unmistakable cackle rings out as she argues with Brooks about closet space. From the left, Paige's precise, slightly bossy tone lectures Kirby on the virtues of maintaining the schedule.

Gibson catches my eye and leans close, whispering conspiratorially, "We hit the roommate jackpot."

"Yep, I'll take twin bunks over sharing a bed with Sandy any day," I agree with conviction. "If Brooks isn't happy, then she should've put her foot down to room with Christy. None of us would dare stand up to her." I remember the look of horror on Sandy's face when she drew Brooks' name from the bag. Something tells me neither of them will emerge from this weekend as friends.

I return my focus to the task at hand. "What time is it?"

She checks Hermés Apple Watch—a gift from her husband. "3:30. Paige says we're out the door at five."

Covering my face, I groan into my pillow, which smells strongly of bleach. After the divorce, I'd fantasized about a wild weekend away with the girls—cocktails by a pool, lazy brunches, maybe a spa day. Instead, Paige orchestrated a military campaign disguised as a fun getaway in a historic town.

"It's just enough time to unpack and freshen up," she urges, already hanging her collection of theme night outfits in the tiny closet.

"I just want to relax," I grumble, flipping to my back and staring at the underside of the top bunk, where someone has carved their initials inside a heart. "Paige's minute-by-minute itinerary is not what I envisioned when I agreed to this girls' trip."

"How long have you known Paige? You know this is what she does." Gibson's voice carries affectionate exasperation. "Remember the charity gala she chaired and the fifteen-page instruction manual she created for the volunteer committee?"

I begrudgingly slide my body to the side of the bottom bunk. Twelve hours cooped up in an SUV with six women for two days took a toll on me. The soundtrack of our journey—Sandy's dirty jokes, Brooks' complaints about the snack options, Christy's phone calls to check on her kids, and Paige's constant schedule updates—still echoes in my head.

Phone in hand, I start my party playlist. With Pink's "Get the Party Started" blasting, I find my second wind and join Gibson, unpacking my suitcase into the drawers, the closet, and the surfaces of the kitchen now turned grooming station. The dated kitchenette with its two-burner stove and small fridge won't be used for cooking, but the countertop quickly transforms into prime real estate for our collective beauty products.

With the seven of us unpacked, it looks like Sephora puked on the counter around the sink—highlighting palettes, eye and lip pencils, curling irons, and enough hairs products to puncture another hole in the ozone layer compete for space with Paige's impressive collection of MAC lipsticks.

"Reminder," Paige hollers like a drill sergeant, hands on the hips of her crisp white capri pants as she stands in front of pedestal sink of the lone bathroom, which we'll all be fighting over for the next three days. "Tonight's theme is rockstar. If you're voted the lamest attempt at rockstar attire, you'll buy our drinks all night."

"Whoa, that could get expensive," I say under my breath, calculating the cost of Sandy's notoriously bottomless thirst.

"Game on!" Sandy yells from next door, her voice penetrating the wall with ease. "Be warned, I plan to drink like a fish tonight."

"Do fish drink?" Gibson asks me, her forehead wrinkling in genuine scientific curiosity.

I answer with a shrug.

"How do I look?" I spin in place, my arms out wide for Gibson to assess.

I feel over-dressed compared to my roommate in my faux-leather, skin-tight, red and black striped pants, my black leather vest with only a black bra beneath, and black biker boots.

"Very rock-n-roll," she laughs, strumming her air guitar. "You look like a kick-ass lead singer for a female only rock band. Let's send a pic to Aaron and Ty."

Gibson quickly snaps a full-length selfie of the two of us, texting it to her husband and Ty. I take a sip from my Bud Light, and before I can set it back down on the table, her phone vibrates.

"Ty says we look hot," she informs, a wide smile upon her face as her fingers tap out her reply.

I smirk to myself. My friend doesn't know I suspect Ty is more than just a live friend of hers. Someday, she'll open up to us, until then, I'll keep my thoughts on what really happens inside her villa to myself.

"And you look like a fan girl." I appraise her grey vintage tee from Sugary Pick Me Up, one of my favorite bands. Her faded denim shorts with frayed hem and matching grey high-top Converse complete her look.

She groans. "I was going for a groupie."

"Groupie or fan girl there's no difference."

"Sure there is," she argues. "Groupies follow a band on tour. A fangirl is over the top and border-line fanatical."

"Then groupie it is," I state.

Time for hair and makeup, we enter the kitchen. Each at a free-standing mirror on the table, we apply heavy black eyeliner. Finished, I check my phone.

"Fifteen minutes," I warn my friends, raising my voice to reach through the walls. "Last one buys dinner tonight!"

"No fair!" Brooks complains from next door, panic evident in her voice. "No one told us to hurry."

"It's called an itinerary," Paige reminds, her type-A personality clearly enjoying this moment. "It's on every one of your phones."

Despite my initial reluctance, I'm starting to feel the excitement of the weekend—my first real escape since I finalized my divorce.

"Paige won't be yelling at us," I state proudly.

Unlike the polished country club wives who normally sip cock-tails on the patio after nine holes in their designer golf gear. Gibson is playful, comfortable, and completely at home with her own style. Neither one of us fit the hoity toity country club mold.

I stifle my laughter when Sandy enters the kitchen in a short black pleated catholic school skirt, knee-high socks, white much-too-tight tank top and grey short-sleeved cardigan.

"Oh. My. God!" Gibson laughs.

"Avril Lavigne has arrived!" Sandy announces proudly spinning.

"Uh... hate to break it to you," Gibson struggles to speak through her laughter. "You look like Britney Spears in her "Hit Me Baby One More Time" video, not Avril Lavigne. She wore plaid miniskirts and fishnets."

"Trust me, Gibson would know," Christy defends. "This girl is a music guru. Heck, her parents even named her after a famous guitar."

"Sooo... Britney Spears has arrived," Sandy amends without missing a beat.

"You should braid your hair to finish the look," I suggest, passing her my cellphone with the image on display.

I bite my lips between my teeth, stifling my laughter as I glance in Gibson's direction. Sandy looks like a slutty version of Britney Spears.

"I must admit, when Morgan and I entered the kitchen alone, I worried the theme nights were a joke you were playing on the two of us," Gibson confesses, adjusting the tongue of her high-tops.

"Oh trust me, we're going all out both nights," Sandy assures, claiming a spot at the mirror to braid her pigtails.

"We look hot. We need to be careful not to hook up with a biker tonight."

Gibson's eyes bug out, causing me to laugh. After years of living next door to Sandy, I would have thought nothing could shock Gibson anymore.

"She's teasing," I assure, though with Sandy, one never knows for certain. "No one's hooking up with anyone tonight. Well... maybe Sandy, but not the rest of us."

"Speak for yourself," Sandy winks. "Deadwood during Wild Bill Days is crawling with men on bikes or wearing cowboy hats and boots. I plan to make at least three bad decisions this weekend."

Christy enters resembling Axl Rose with a crimson bandana around her head and a matching one tied around her thigh over her zebra-striped pants. A black skull face t-shirt and black motorcycle boots finish the look.

"Let me guess... Axl Rose," Gibson chuckles. "You look awesome!"

Paige joins us in faded black skinny jeans, black Misfits tee, black Converse, and a black leather jacket thrown over her shoulder. Behind her, Brooks strolls in low-slung camouflage cargo pants, a white see-through tee over a black bra, a necktie loose around her neck and a plethora of bracelets and bands adorning both wrists.

"That's how you do it. She's the epitome of Avril Lavigne," Gibson informs Sandy with a nudge.

"I thought you looked like Britney Spears," Paige claims with a furrowed brow.

"I wanted to channel Avril, but instead I mimicked Britney," Sandy states still proud of her look.

Last to enter, Kirby's tricked out head to toe as an 80s rocker, complete with a long-haired black wig, leather pants so tight they might qualify as medical compression wear, and enough chains and studs to set off every metal detector in South Dakota.

"Kirby," Gibson drawls appreciatively. "Tomorrow's Eighties night, not tonight." She motions to the rest of us in our rockstar gear.

"I know," Kirby informs with a smug smile. "I brought a better costume for tomorrow."

Better?

"How does it get any better than you looking like Nikki Sixx on the cover of Motley Crüe's *Girls, Girls, Girls* album?" Gibson scoffs, hands on her hips.

Sandy pulls Gibson into a side hug. "Yet again you prove you were born in the wrong generation. This child knows more about 80s rock than people who lived through it."

While I know the band and song Gibson referenced, I'm not completely culturally illiterate. I have no idea who Nikki Sixx is. Taking my phone in hand, I quickly search the internet for the album cover she mentioned.

"Whoa! You do look like this Motley Crüe guy," I state, pointing to my phone screen where a leather-clad, wild-haired rocker poses with a motorcycle.

"I can't believe you had to look that up," Sandy mocks as Paige looks at my screen over my shoulder. "Did any of you know who Nikki Sixx is?"

Only Brooks and Gibson raise their hands.

"Why do I hang around with you infants?" Sandy grumbles, spinning her braid around her finger.

"Because we are the only ones that can tolerate you," I quip, earning approving laughter from everyone except Sandy, who pretends to be offended but can't hide her smile.

I watch as Christy whispers conspiratorially to Sandy, before the latter darts toward her room. When she returns, a small black gift bag hangs from her fingers.

"I almost forgot. I brought a gift for you." She grins slyly.

Warily, I take the proffered bag, remove the red tissue paper, and slowly withdraw a bright orange t-shirt. Pinching my fingers at its shoulders, I hold it up to inspect it. The fabric is soft, high-quality cotton—at least they splurged on the material if they were going to force me into something embarrassing.

Unfolding it, I find "5-6-24" on the front pocket and "Just Released" in bold letters on the back. The date of my divorce finalization stares back at me, immortalized in screen-printed permanence.

"Uh-huh," I protest, hands on my hips, though a small part of me appreciates the humor. Months of tedious paperwork, lawyer meetings, and emotional rollercoasters reduced to a prison-release joke on a t-shirt.

"Yes," Sandy argues, her perfectly glossed lips curving into a mischievous smile.

"No way am I wearing this tonight," I state firmly, though my resolve is already crumbling. The shirt represents something I've been trying to embrace—the end of a chapter that should have closed years ago.

"The only people you know are in this Air BnB," Sandy reminds me, gesturing around the rustic-chic rental we secured on for our girls' weekend.

"It'll be a fun little story we'll laugh about for years," Gibson adds.

"We want you to wear it tonight," Sandy announces proudly.

"Um...I can't wear it tonight. It's not rockstar attire."

"We're making an exception for you," Christy chuckles.

Shaking my head, I make my way to the small bathroom, extricate myself from my black vest and slip on the t-shirt. Not many can pull off the color, but it actually looks great with my warm skin, natural hair color, and light green eyes.

"I can't wear these pants with it," I call to my friends, in the other room. "I refuse to look like a clown in red and black striped pants and an orange shirt."

"She'll wear it," Gibson announces with authority. "And we'll purchase every drink she wants all night."

"Uh-huh," I protest, feigning my red-headed stubbornness. "This has Sandy written all over it, so she'll purchase all my drinks for the entire weekend." I knew exactly who plotted this little scheme.

Approval slides upon Sandy's features. She believes she's won, but I planned to wear the shirt all along. She doesn't need to know that. It feels good to be celebrated, even if it's for something as uncomfortable as a divorce.

"Here you go." Kirby hands me a pair of black skinny jeans through the bathroom door. "We're the same size."

It never occurred to me that Kirby's height and curves resemble mine. I take it as a compliment that I look as good as my much younger 21-year-old friend. While I'm no where a size zero like brock's new fling, I do look damn good for a thirty-four-year-old mother of two.

I take a deep breath and slowly exhale. I love my group of friends. They only want to celebrate my fresh start and mean this shirt to be funny. I can handle funny, especially in a town where I don't know anyone.

I glance one more time in the mirror. On the front pocket area is the date my divorce was finalized. On the back... That's the part of the shirt that gives me pause. It reads 'Just Released' in large, bold, black letters. Exiting the restroom, I decide to have a little fun of my own.

With the new shirt in place, I spin my arms out, modeling for them.

"She's wearing the shirt!" Sandy cheers.

"Chop, chop, ladies. It's time to go," Paige orders, consulting her watch. "Wild Bill Days is here, open container law started at noon, and we need to grab dinner before the bands start at eight."

"Let's head next door," Gibson urges our group.

I tuck one piece of my shirt into the waist of my jeans while Gibson read from her phone about the Winery Tasting Room I clocked as we lugged our luggage along the sidewalk.

As we file out of the Air BnB, I catch a glimpse of our motley crew in the full-length mirror by the door. Seven grown women, professionals and mothers, dressed like refugees from a MTV rock-star reunion and one felon headed out to paint the town in a cloud of perfume and laughter. The weight of my divorce, my financial worries, and my secret writing career were left in Missouri, their weight not pressing down on my shoulders at least for the night.

Whatever happens this weekend—Sandy's inevitable inappropriate behavior, Paige's schedule tyranny, and the distinct possibility of public humiliation in our themed outfits—I'm suddenly, fiercely glad to be here, 700 miles from the country club and all its judgments.

For three days, I can just be Morgan—not Morgan-the-divorcée, not Morgan-struggling-to-make-ends-meet, and certainly not Morgan-the-secret-romance-author. Just Morgan, in orange, ready for an adventure.

"How perfect is this place? It has a wine tasting room next door," I murmur as Gibson pulls two cast iron tables for four together for our clan, their feet scratching in loud protest against the concrete. The late-afternoon sun casts a golden glow over the historic buildings, and the mountains surrounding the town to form a dramatic backdrop.

"It's like it was meant to be," she agrees, settling into her chair. "A weekend out with the girls before you re-enter the dating world."

I roll my eyes but can't suppress my smile. "Who says I'm entering the dating world? Maybe I'll become a nun."

Gibson snorts, flagging down a server. "A nun with a 'Just Released' t-shirt. Very believable."

The server approaches--a young man with kind eyes who does a double-take at my shirt as he passes out menu and claims he'll return to take our drink orders. The ladies discuss the menu as I busy myself people watching the multitude of visitors heading downtown for Wild Bill Days and the free concerts tonight.

When the young man returns with our wine, I raise my wine glass, allowing myself to embrace the moment. "To freedom and to friends who make it worth celebrating."

6

THIS CAN'T BE HAPPENING

Derek

I can't believe my eyes. I tip the front brim of my Stetson El Presidente down to shield more of my face but no so low I can't keep my eyes on her.

Near the sidewalk, a group of women from the country club position 2 small tables together and snag empty chairs for their group of seven.

I'd recognize her anywhere. Morgan, my red-headed siren along with her friends from our club claim their space amid their conversations.

One row of round cast iron tables separate me from acquaintances that know me as Derek Fox the golfer not Chipper Wade the rockstar. Heart palpitations feel they might bust through my chest wall. These women threaten my carefully constructed disguise. Concrete settles deep in my gut as my two worlds might collide at any moment.

I gulp down the next varietal in my flight of wines, not tasting it, equal parts fearful and beguiled by Morgan's presence.

While I attempt to hide alone at my table near a the small white building, these ladies of the links are loud and proud, drawing much attention. In their rock-n-roll attire, I wonder what the club's gossip columnist would place in *The Back 9 Talks* with the image of the women before me.

I'm familiar with each of the women through the guys I golf with upon occasion. Maddux Harper, a real estate genius, dates Brook an edgy tattoo artist that owns her own business. She's dressed like Avril Lavigne circa early 2000s. His younger brother, Ryan Harper, is an outstanding NFL tight-end and recently married Christy, who looks likes the frontman of Guns 'N Roses. Trainer of KC's elite athletes, Bill Bellinger, is married to Paige. Usually prim, proper, and neat as pin, today she's dressed in all black. I don't golf with her husband, but everyone knows loud-mouth Sandy Anderson, dressed today as a slutty Britney Spears in her early years in the music industry. The woman dressed as member of Mötley Crüe is the only one I don't recognize.

Most inspired by eighties hairbands and female rock vixens, it's Gibson's Sugary Pick Me Up t-shirt from our second tour that I stare at. The shirt features my unmistakable pink tongue lapping at a large red lollipop.

Shit.

If anyone is going to make the connection between Derek Fox and Chpper Wade, it would be a fan dedicated enough to still wear merch from a defunct band. Gibson scans the rest of the tables, and I quickly look away, fiddling with the stem of the next wine before me. I swirl the red liquid in its glass as I count slowly to ten before I chance a glance in their direction.

Trying to distract myself from that line of thought, I focus on Morgan. Her shirt vexes me. Her friends clearly dressed like rock-stars, but she wears a simple orange t-shirt and black jeans with boots. My eyes squint desperately attempting to make out the small numbers on her shirt. The first number is a five, and the last two are a two and a four.

Could they be a date?

May...2024...?

What could a date mean?

I search my memory for any singer in an orange shirt with numbers on it, but for the life of me, nothing comes to mind.

"Find one you like?" The waitress asks, standing between me and the women.

I tap my forefinger on the second empty glass of the flight.

"I liked the crisp light taste here." I motion to the glasses I have yet to taste. "But I've mot had a chance to sample these yet."

"I'll check back with you in a bit."

I bet she makes a mint in tips with her sweet girl-next-door looks. She steps away, allowing me once again to gaze at Morgan. Next to her, Sandy prattles on about drama at the club's pool, as Morgan looks disinterested.

My brow furrows when she stands, steps around the table, and moves in my direction. I release a breath I didn't realize I held when she exchanges seats with Brooks.

Her back now to me, I read "Just Released" in bold black lettering.

Like a light bulb flickering on, it comes to me. "Just Released" refers to her divorce and the date on the front must be the day the divorce was official in May.

I waited month after month to hear of a change in her marital status, while I vowed not to interact with her until she was truly available. Month after month, I fantasized about Morgan in my life. She's always there, lurking, waiting to take over my thoughts, distracting me everywhere. A welcome distraction that I'm ready to see come to fruition.

On a girls' trip over a long weekend, wearing a bright orange shirt proclaiming her freedom is surely a sign. I'll take it as a sign the waiting as a gentleman is over.

Slowly, careful not to draw any attention, I rise, cringing as the metal chair scrapes the concrete beneath. I don't chance a glance in her direction, setting my steps for the stage area.

I'm not sure what the proper grace period is after a divorce before you ask a woman out.

The grace period is over.

I'm proclaiming it.

It's time to make my move.

7

GRACE. = GRACE PERIOD

Morgan

The roadies make final adjustments as we claim our spots in the second row. Our gracious Air BnB host placed lawn chairs out early today for us. Main Street Deadwood transformed into an impromptu concert venue, the historic buildings serving as a dramatic backdrop for tonight's performance. The crowd buzzes with anticipation—a mix of tourists, bikers, and locals, all drawn by the promise of free music and the legendary country band headlining tonight.

"I still can't believe you made me wear this," I grumble to Sandy, pointing to the t-shirt she'd forced on me earlier. The garish shirt, emblazoned with "RECENTLY RELEASED" in black letters, has been drawing stares all evening.

"It's your divorce celebration weekend!" Sandy declares, already on her third plastic cup of beer. "Embrace it!"

"It looks like I just got out of prison," I protest.

"Same thing, honey," Sandy winks. "Brock was a life sentence with no possibility of parole."

The women laugh, even Brooks, who's loosened up considerably since our arrival in Deadwood. Gibson hands me a fresh beer, her expression sympathetic beneath her dark eyeliner.

"Ignore the shirt," she advises. "Focus on the fact that we have prime spots for the show."

She's right about that. Paige's militant insistence on dining and arriving at our seats early—"It's on the itinerary, ladies!"—paid off. Only one row of lawn chairs separates us from the stage, close enough to see the musicians' sweat clearly when they perform.

"I'm just here for main act," Kirby announces, referring to the country band headlining tonight. "My parents played their albums constantly when I was growing up."

"What about the opening act?" Paige asks, consulting her phone. "Grace? Anyone heard of them?"

"It's Grace period," Brooks corrects, surprisingly knowledgeable. "They're new—formed from the ashes of one of Gibson's favorite rock band that lost a member to COVID. They've been getting buzz for their return and new sound."

"How do you know this?" Sandy demands.

Brooks shrugs. "I read things other than Tris Halladay books occasionally."

Before anyone can respond, the stage lights dim, then flash brightly as the MC takes the stage.

"Deadwood! Are you ready for some music?" He waits for the obligatory cheers before continuing. "Wild Bill Days is proud to present a band making waves with their unique sound. Formerly known as Sugary Pick Me Up, please welcome... GRACE PERIOD!"

The crowd's response is mixed—polite applause interspersed with genuine enthusiasm from those who recognize the previous band name. I clap along, curious about this opening act I've never heard of.

Four men take the stage, bathed in blue light that gradually brightens as they take their positions. The drummer settles behind his kit while two guitarists strap on their instruments. But it's the lead singer who catches my attention—tall and lean, with an easy confidence as he approaches the microphone. Something about him tugs at my memory, a vague familiarity I can't quite place.

8

TAKE IT OFF

Derek

"Hello Deadwood!" I greet center stage with my guitar in front of me and mic in hand. I pause for the crowd to calm before continuing. "We're Grace Period." Again I pause for the crowd noise, forcing my eyes not to lock on the friendly female faces center stage, two rows back. "You may recognize us from our previous band, Sugary Pick Me Up."

The crowd goes wild, now that they know who we are. I gather my strength, forcing myself to focus on the performance and not on Morgan and her gang.

"We have a new sound, but we're not sure if Deadwood is ready for it... "

This causes the crowd to protest.

Corbin leans into my side, his mouth moving to the mic in left hand. "I think they can handle it."

In their lawn chairs, filling Main Street, they cheer, encouraging us to entertain them. Not waiting any longer, I start the show.

"Okay if you think you can handle country metal, here we go. 1!... 2!... 3!"

I lose myself in my guitar and focus on the lyrics. The energy of the horde fuels my performance.

After strumming the final notes, I take a sip of water from my bottle on the drum platform, worrying one of the six women from Missouri will unveil my secret. In the second row, any one of them could put two and two together and demolish the safe world I've created at the Lynks at Tryst Falls Country Club. Covering my tattoos and wearing contacts isn't much of a disguise.

How deluded am I?

Unbeknownst to me, Corbin stands center stage stealing my mic. "You look ridiculous in that hat," our bassist declares.

I spin, brow raised. Turner specifically stated that I would be the only band member speaking to the crowd tonight.

"I can pull off the look, you my friend can not," he taunts.

My brow furrows. I'm wearing one of our band's trucker hats Turner ordered us to promote tonight.

Corbin shakes his head at me a wicked smirk upon his face, then turns to face our crowd. "What do you say ladies should he take it off?"

"Take it off! Take it Off!" the crowd taunts at Corbin's prompting. Slowly the chant turns to "Shirt off! Shirt off!"

Cruz joins the conversation from his drum kit. "Seems our fans have a mind of their own."

"If Chipper removes his hat, he'll let down his long locks, but if he removes his shirt, his tattoos will be on display. Let's vote," Corbin suggests. "Who wants our man to take off his hat?"

Members of the crowd shout in approval.

"Who wants him to take off his shirt?"

They boom in response.

"Shirt it is," he announces, gesturing to me.

Roadies magically appear as if this entire production were premeditated. They hold up a blanket, offering me privacy, but I wave them off.

Quickly, I contemplate whether to only remove the t-shirt I wear beneath my unbuttoned plaid shirt or go entirely shirtless. It's been too long since we've performed, and I'm not sure I'm comfortable wearing only my jeans for the remainder of the performance.

While I make a production of stripping off my outer shirt, twirling it above my head as I gyrate my pelvis, Cruz pounds a seductive drum beat that the crowd gobbles up. Spinning around, I raise one hand over my head, fisting my black t-shirt near my neck. In many of the romance books I read while on previous tours, I learned women love this one-handed shirt removal move. Slowly, I pull, tugging it up my back and over my head.

When I spin, the women erupt. Much to their disproval, I slip on my plaid shirt, leaving it unbuttoned, and roll the cuff once at the sleeve.

"Ladies, ladies," Corbin soothes. "Have some respect. Act like you've seen finely defined abs paired with low slung jeans before."

That's enough of Corbin's antics.

I sling my guitar in place and return to the microphone, blocking out the crude suggestions from the female voices of the crowd. I cling to the security my Les Paul provides.

"Okay, how about we slow it down a little bit," I suggest, my smoldering gaze locking on the women I recognize from my country club.

Fuck!

Quickly, I look anywhere but the second row center stage.

"Here's an oldie from our Sugary Pick Me Up days."

Cruz counts us off with his drum sticks beating the rims of his snares. While I strum my trusty Les Paul and Corbin lays down a bass line, I silently curse Turner's insistence that we play one previous hit during the set. When we lost our keyboardist to the Covid-19 pandemic, I vowed to never play Sugary Pick Me Up hits again.

"If ever I leave... if ever I go... you need to believe... I want you to know... You. Take. My breath away." I detest the pain in my voice now that the lyrics no longer call to mind a lost lover. "On my death bed... remembering the life we shared... my last thought will be... You. Take. My breath away."

Loving the emotion in my lyrics, the throng awards us a standing ovation. My dry throat and stinging eyes hint I need to take a break while Corbin walks the front edge of the stage, shaking hands with screaming fans, and kissing a few cheeks.

Staff members offer me a dry towel, water bottles, and my favorite whiskey. Snagging water I pour one over my head then drink half of a second bottle. With my nod, the towel sails towards me, and I return to the stage as I pat myself dry.

That was the one and only time we'll perform a Sugary Pick Me Up song without Chapman.

Cruz shows off his talent, utilizing every inch of his drum kit, while Corbin encourages the crowd to applaud. Josh returns my Les

Paul, and I take comfort once more with it between me and the crowd. I avoid Corbin's concerned gaze as he extends the mic.

"If you don't stop encouraging him, Cruz will hog the spotlight all night." The crowd chuckles with Corbin.

Sensing my need for a few moments before I return to the music, Josh draws his bow across the strings of his fiddle. As his fingers fly, he strides to the front of the stage. I ground myself in this moment, pushing back the painful memories of my past life. After a minute, I signal to Josh I'm ready to move on.

"Next up is a cover of a song written by a friend of ours. The first time we shared it with Adam Levine, he stated Maroon 5 might perform our version from time to time on tour. So here we go..."

I strum the opening chords of our country metal version of *Girls Like You*. When I scan the crowd, I fight my smile at Gibson and Morgan banging their heads in time with our beat. Clearly this is not their first metal concert. By the end of the song, every woman dances in time with the beat, belting the lyrics with us.

~

Morgan

Three songs in, and even the skeptics in the crowd are won over. The band is tight, professional, clearly seasoned performers despite their new incarnation. The singer—Chipper, I hear someone call him —works the stage with charismatic ease, occasionally bantering with his bandmates between songs.

During a brief break while the guitarist chooses a new guitar, Chipper steps to the edge of the stage, scanning the crowd. For a split second, his gaze seems to land directly on me, a flash of recognition in his eyes that's gone so quickly I must have imagined it.

"Beautiful night in Deadwood," he says into the microphone. "We spotted some of you earlier today while we were grabbing lunch. This town knows how to party, doesn't it?"

Cheers erupt from the audience.

"Couldn't help but notice a redhead with a very interesting shirt," he continues, and my stomach drops as several heads turn in my direction. "Orange, 'Recently Released' written on it." He turns to his guitarist. "What do you think that means, Corbin?"

The guitarist leans into his own mic. "Released from jail, obviously."

The crowd erupts in laughter, and my face burns hotter than the stage lights. I sink lower in my seat as Sandy howls with delight beside me.

"What's that?" Chipper cups his ear as someone in the front row shouts up at him. "Ah, divorce. Recently divorced." He nods thoughtfully, a smile playing at the corners of his mouth. "Well, to the lady in the prison orange shirt congratulations on your freedom-whatever it may be."

The crowd cheers, and Sandy elbows me hard in the ribs. "He's talking about you!"

"I'm aware," I mutter, wishing the earth would open up and swallow me whole. Public attention is the last thing I want—it's why I write under a pen name, why I've kept my blog anonymous, why I've worked so hard to keep my struggles private at the club.

"He's totally checking you out," Gibson whispers from my other side.

"He is not," I insist, though I can't help noticing that his gaze does seem to drift to our section with unusual frequency.

The band launches into another song, this one slower, more introspective. The lyrics catch my attention—a story about masks and identities, about presenting one face to the world while hiding another. There's unexpected depth to the writing, a poetic quality I wouldn't have anticipated from a country-metal fusion band.

As the concert continues, I find myself increasingly drawn to Chipper's performance. There's something compelling about him beyond the obvious physical appeal—a hint of mystery, of hidden complexity beneath the confident stage persona. The way he phrases certain lines, the subtle emotion he brings to the quieter moments... it reminds me of something I can't quite identify.

~

Derek

The last three songs of our set fly by. Before I know it, Turner joins me center stage, stealing the microphone. That's our cue, waving to the crowd, we exit stage left. I can't help but glance over my shoulder to Morgan once more.

"Hi, I'm Turner Cruz, manager of Grace Period. If you enjoyed the performance tonight, find our swag table behind the staging area. We offer shirts, cds, and you can find their songs are available anywhere you download your music." Turner returns the mic to its stand, before joining us back stage.

~

Morgan

The band's final song brings the house down—an anthemic piece about redemption that has the crowd on their feet. As they take their bows, Chipper once again scans the audience, and this time I'm certain his eyes linger on me momentarily before he tips his hat to the crowd.

"That. Was. Amazing," Brooks declares as we retake our seats. "I'm downloading their album as soon as it's out."

"The singer was staring at you," Paige informs me, always observant. "Multiple times."

"He was working the crowd," I dismiss, though a flutter of something—interest? excitement?—stirs in my chest.

"No, Morgan, he was definitely looking at you specifically," Brooks insists. "Trust me, I recognize that look. It's the same way Ryan looks at Christy."

"Oh my god," Sandy gasps with theatrical realization. "You've been chosen! The universe is sending you a hot musician after releasing you from Brock's prison!"

"The universe did no such thing," I counter. "And even if he was looking at me, which he wasn't, he's a touring musician. He'll be gone tomorrow."

But as the headliner takes the stage to enthusiastic applause, I find my thoughts drifting back to Chipper and his intense gaze. For a brief moment, I allow myself to imagine a different life—one where I might be the kind of woman who catches a musician's eye, who inspires songs about second chances and new beginnings.

It's a fantasy, of course. Just like the romances I write. Entertaining, but ultimately not my reality.

Still, I can't help glancing toward the side of the stage, wondering if he's watching from the wings. For the first time since the divorce, I feel a spark of something I'd thought long extinguished—possibility.

9

DOUBLE LIFE

Derek

The morning sun filters through the hotel blinds, waking me earlier than I'd like after our late-night post-show celebration. I roll onto my back, staring at the ceiling, and allow myself a moment to replay last night's performance.

Grace.'s official debut exceeded all expectations. The crowd's energy, the seamless performance despite minimal rehearsal time, Cruz and Corbin nailing their parts—it all come together perfectly. But what keeps replaying in my mind isn't the performance itself, but the flash of red hair in the second row and that bright orange shirt.

Morgan Merrifield. Here in Deadwood, seven hundred miles from the carefully constructed life I've built at Lynks at Tryst Falls Country Club.

I swing my legs over the side of the bed and reach for my phone. No messages from Turner yet, which means I'm still free. Today is ours to kill in this historic tourist town, and I should focus on relaxing, on bonding again with the guys, on anything but the divorced redhead I've been watching from afar for months.

A sharp knock at my door interrupts my thoughts.

"Rise and shine, princess!" Corbin calls through the door. "Turner says breakfast in twenty or she's ordering without us."

"Got it," I call back, dragging myself to the shower.

Under the lukewarm spray, I try to sort through my conflicting instincts. The smart move would be to avoid Main Street entirely today, to minimize any chance of running into fans that recognize me or Morgan and her friends. One of them might recognize me, might connect Derek Fox, the reserved golfer from the club with his long naturally brown hair and brown contacts, to Chipper Wade, the tattooed, green-eyed frontman of our new band.

But the thought of potentially seeing Morgan again sends an embarrassing thrill through me. It's pathetic, really—this schoolboy crush I've been nursing while pretending to be someone else entirely, while rooting for the end of her marriage.

Thirty minutes later, the four of us plus Turner sit around a table in a restaurant on Main Street. I chose a seat facing the wall, with a cowboy hat low over my eyes, and my sunglasses on despite being indoors.

"You look like you're in witness protection," Cruz observes, shoveling eggs into his mouth. "Relax, man. No one's going to recognize you here."

"You don't know that," I mutter, scanning the restaurant for the fifth time since we sat down. "Those women from the club could walk in any minute."

Corbin looks up from his pancake stack. "What women from the club?"

"The ones he was eyeballing during our set," Turner supplies, not looking up from her schedule-planning on her iPad. "Particularly the redhead in the orange shirt."

"You spotted them too?" I ask, surprised by Turner's observation skills.

"My job is to notice everything," she shrugs. "Including when our frontman keeps singing to the same section of the audience even when he struggles to keep his eyes off them."

"I wasn't singing to her," I protest weakly.

"Her?" Cruz pounces on my slip. "So there is a specific 'her'?"

I stab at my breakfast, avoiding eye contact. "Just someone from the club back home. She doesn't know I'm... this." I gesture vaguely to encompass my current appearance.

"Wait," Corbin leans forward, eyes lighting with mischief. "Is this the mysterious woman you've been writing all those songs about? The recently divorced hottie who doesn't know you're secretly a rock star?"

"Country-metal lead singer," I correct automatically. "And keep your damn voice down."

"Holy shit," Cruz laughs. "It is her!"

Turner sighs heavily. "As the only responsible adult at this table, I feel obligated to remind you that we have a career to revive, an album to finish, and a tour to plan. We don't have time for your Clark Kent/Superman romantic drama."

"It's not a drama," I insist. "I'm just... being cautious."

"Cautious would be avoiding her entirely," Turner points out. "What you're doing borders on creepy stalker territory."

She's right, of course. I've spent months watching Morgan from a distance, learning her habits, her friends, her preferences—all while hiding my true identity. It sounds worse than it is.

"I'm not stalking her," I clarify. "I just... want to make sure my cover doesn't get blown before I'm ready to tell my friends the truth."

"And when exactly where you planning to do that?" Cruz asks, suddenly serious. His paternal instincts—normally reserved for Turner—occasionally extend to the rest of us.

I don't have a good answer. The truth is, I don't plan to confess my true identity. I've been waiting to approach her, giving her time to fully heal from her divorce, and for my own life to settle into this new reality of balancing Derek Fox with Chipper Wade. I'm not sure the right moment will ever arrive.

"Let's focus on today," I redirect. "What's the plan?"

Turner accepts the subject change, detailing our schedule—free time until meeting during the opening act of tonight's concert, then dinner between sets, and hanging backstage with the headliner an eighties country band.

After breakfast, we split up—Corbin and Turner heading to the historical brothel museum, Cruz making a beeline for the nearest casino. I wander Main Street alone, ostensibly shopping for souvenirs but really hoping for, while simultaneously dreading, a glimpse of Morgan in equal measure.

I spot them about noon, outside Madam Peacock's—all seven women clustered around a display window, Sandy gesturing dramatically about something that has the others laughing. Morgan stands slightly apart, her attention caught by something to her left, across the street. She's traded last night's orange shirt for khaki shorts and a green tank that makes her hair look even more vibrant in the midday sun.

I duck into the nearest doorway, which turns out to be Happy Days Gift Shop, and pretend to browse while keeping them in my peripheral vision. I pull my hat lower and turn away as they enter a store. Only when I'm safely down the block do I exhale.

The rest of the afternoon passes in a similar pattern of near-misses and strategic retreats. I spot them having late lunch on the restaurant patio at Mustang Sally's and take a detour back the way I came. I glimpse Morgan on a park bench, thumbs rapidly tapping on her phone screen and quickly cross the street. Each time, I feel equally relieved and disappointed to avoid detection.

Bored out of my mind, I find myself playing black jack for several hours.

That evening, we're seated in the reserved section near the stage for the show. Under normal circumstances, I'd be fully engaged, studying their stage presence, their crowd work, and marveling at their musical arrangements.

Instead, I'm distracted by Morgan and her friends, seated one row back to our right. They've dressed for tonight's apparent theme— the eighties, and Morgan went all out with her . Her hair falls in loose waves around her shoulders, catching the stage lights when she throws her head back laughing at something Sandy says.

"You're staring again," Turner murmurs beside me.

"I'm watching the show," I lie.

"Sure," she nods toward the stage. "What song are they playing right now?"

I have no idea. "Something about trucks or beer."

"That narrows it down to approximately every country song ever written," she snorts. "Just go talk to her."

"I can't." (Better transition to leaving deadwood)

Not yet but soon. Very soon.

10

IT'S TEE TIME

Derek

I park my golf cart near the short wooden fence lining the edge of the course. I see her on her knees, working in a flower bed along the side of her house. This is where I spotted her for the first time over a year ago. That day, she caught my eye and has haunted my thoughts ever since. I swing my nine-iron through the tall grass as I approach the white out-of-bounds stakes near her fence line.

While I pretend to search the ground and tall weeds for a lost ball, I keep glancing in her direction with the hope she will notice me. My eyes watching her, I slip a golf ball from my pocket and toss it into her yard without her noticing.

"Excuse me," I call to her, raising my voice.

She looks up from her gardening, her hand shielding her eyes in the bright afternoon sun. I point in the direction of the ball I tossed into her yard.

"I lost my ball." I lie. "Could you help me?"

She rises, brushes off her knees, removes her gardening gloves, then walks in my direction.

"You lost your balls?" she asks, smirking as her auburn hair shimmers in the sun.

"Ball. Singular," I correct.

"You know, those white stakes are out of bounds." She nods her chin in their direction, pausing with her hands upon her hips.

"I think I see it right there," I state, pointing.

Her emerald green eyes follow my index finger.

"How do I know that is your ball?" she challenges.

The wind blows stray tendrils across her warm cheek.

"My balls have a big D on them," I deadpan.

"What?" she sputters, drawing my attention to her full pink lips.

I replay my words in my head and smirk as if I meant the double entendre.

"A big D?" she teases.

Her melodious laugh tickles my ears and causes my heart to speed up.

I wet my lips before speaking again. "A big D. Yes."

She chuckles, and it is the finest music I've ever heard.

"My name is Derek," I share, extending my hand across the fence toward her.

"Ah-ha!" She grins, waving instead of shaking my proffered hand. "The big D is for Derek."

"Among other things." I smirk playfully.

She bends, scooping up my white ball from her manicured lawn. She rolls it in the palm of her hand, turning it this way and that.

"Oh, now I see it," she claims. "Although, the D is not as big as I expected it to be."

That little minx. She steps up to the fence opposite me. She hands over the ball, with a coy smile.

"Trust me when I say it is a big D."

For an instant, her eyes grow wide, and her pouty lips form an O. As quick as it appears, she schools her features, but the tinge of pink on her cheeks cannot be erased as easily.

"Well, Derek, you have your ball. Shouldn't you return to your round of golf?" she urges, swinging her hand towards the fairway behind me.

"I've lost interest in tiny balls and skinny sticks." I wink.

"Surely you have better things to do than..."

I don't let her finish what is sure to be a self-deprecating sentence. Reaching across the fence, I take her hand in mine.

"I'm rather distracted by you, Red," I profess before placing a kiss to the back of her hand.

I watch her pupils dilate in reaction.

"I...I'm...MMMoor..." she stammers as my thumb rubs circles into her palm.

"Morgan. I know," I state, assuming she was trying to spit her name out.

Shock floods her expression.

"We have mutual friends, and I asked for your name," I confess, unashamed. "I've seen you around and made it my goal to meet you."

Morgan clears her throat.

"Me?" she squeaks.

"Do I have your permission to jump this fence?"

It's forward, and I know it. I am taking a risk that Red will take the bait and let me in. One little opening is all I need. *Please. Please. Please take a chance on me.* I dart my tongue out to wet my lips as I anxiously await her answer.

"And..." she drawls. "If I allow you to hop over my fence, what would happen next?"

My eyes scan from her red hair to her bare feet with fire-engine red toe polish.

"I will follow you inside, you will strip, and I will worship every inch..."

I stop speaking when Morgan's wet lips plaster to cover mine. Leaning towards her, my erection collides with the hard boards. I stifle a groan, focusing instead upon her kiss as I allow her to lead. She sucks my lower lip firmly between her own, holding it for a long moment before releasing.

"Get your ass over here," she urges, hands tugging my collar.

I waste no time, placing my hands on the top of the fence and hopping. I'm thankful it's a four-foot fence, which allows me to vault over it in a show of strength instead of bumbling like a fool. Walking backward, an ornery smirk upon her face, I follow Morgan into her house. On her patio, she halts me with her palm flat upon my chest.

"My house, my rules," she states.

I raise one eyebrow, attempting to take my next step.

"Uh-uh," she reprimands. "I need to hear that you agree. What I say goes," Morgan clarifies.

I nod as I speak. "You are in charge."

I wonder if this means she is into kink or is OCD? Her yard and landscaping are tidy, but she is barefoot; I don't think it is OCD. Her hand presses harder to my chest.

Sensing she is rethinking her invitation, I assure her, "I'm not usually this forward. I hope... I mean...I am excited to see what might happen between us, but I can be a patient man. Spending some time getting to know you is the reason I stopped by today."

She drops her hand, spins on her heels, and leads me through the patio doors without a word. I find myself in a seating area facing the glass patio doors where most would position a dining set. On the ottoman rests a hard-cover book and a light blanket. Perhaps she likes to read with the natural light and watch the sunsets over the course here.

She clears her throat, calling my attention to her position on the other side of the open living area, near the mouth of the hallway. Her index finger beckons me to approach. I pause three feet from her.

"We don't have to..." I jut my chin down the hallway.

"Don't lose your nerve now," she taunts.

Taking her upper arms in hand, and pulling her chest to mine, I gently place my lips upon hers, needing to assess her intentions. I hoped to talk to her and set up a time to get together. I had no intention of making my way into her house, let alone her bedroom. Something about this woman bends my willpower. She is recently divorced, and her kiddos are visiting their father for the weekend. I figured I would need to spend more time up front to earn her trust.

Again, she tugs my lip, sucking it hard. Without releasing each other, we slowly take one step then another until she places her hand on a door frame.

"I hope you brought your A game because I am in need..."

Not letting her finish, I kiss without restraint. My kiss promises her all she can expect from me in her bedroom. It is slow, sensual, and builds in anticipation. Pleased with my promise, she slowly backs into the room. My hands rest on her hips as hers start exploring my shoulders, arms, and chest. When she lifts the hem of my golf shirt skyward, I suddenly remember I played fifteen holes in 90-degree heat.

"I need a shower," I state, hoping my sweat hasn't already turned her off.

Shrugging, she leans in, caressing my abs and pecs.

"So do I." She shows me small clippings and seeds clinging to her sweat-covered forearms.

In the blink of an eye she proceeds to slip out of her tank top and shorts, standing before me in a royal blue bra and panties set. The color pops brightly in contrast to her fair skin. Uncomfortable, I reach down to adjust my cock, which strains against the zipper of my golf slacks. Morgan's eyes track the movement.

"Condom," she murmurs breathily.

FUCK! I came here to meet her and talk; I didn't plan for sex. Needless to say, I am ill-prepared. Eyes closed, I shake my head, fearing our play time is over.

"I have some." She smirks, patting my chest. "Make yourself comfy. I will be back in a minute."

She passes me, exiting the bedroom.

I should make myself comfortable on her bed as she suggested. Instead, I choose to help myself to a shower. Given this unprecedented opportunity, I need to be at my best.

The cool water feels heavenly on my over-heated skin. I enjoy it for a moment before turning the dial to a warmer temperature. A thought enters my mind: it's been a long time since I've enjoyed the company of a woman. I fist my cock, setting a rapid pace, seeking release. Rubbing one out in the shower will ensure I please her before I seek my own orgasm. As my breath steadies and the final spurts of semen wash down the drain with the water, I hear Morgan enter the bathroom.

"Opted for a shower?" she calls.

I peek my head through a small opening in the shower door. "Join me," I urge.

She squints in my direction for a moment before her expression morphs into a smile. I return to lathering my hair with her fruit-scented shampoo while I watch through the glass door as she unfastens her blue bra, letting it fall to the tile floor. Then she shimmies out of the matching panties. I tilt my head back into the spray, rinsing my hair, as she steps in. Not wanting our first time to be in the shower, I rub conditioner through my hair to keep my hands from joining the water droplets caressing her skin. I conjure up all my willpower not to slather her glorious breasts in slick, soapy bubbles before my hands explore every inch of her.

"Turn around," I instruct.

I squirt shampoo into the palms of my hands and massage it into her scalp. She moans in pleasure as my fingertips work up a lather, I repeat the motion when I apply the conditioner.

I'm eager to hear these little moans grow when we move to her bedroom.

We take turns rinsing off under the shower spray before I exit.

"For a guy, you are surprisingly knowledgeable about conditioner," she states as I pass her the Terry cloth robe on a nearby hook.

I chuckle, wrapping a grey towel around my waist. "My hair used to be almost as long as yours. I had to take care of it." I shrug.

In the large mirror over the vanity, she scrutinizes me.

"What?"

"I am imagining you with longer hair," she admits.

Snagging the brush from her grip, I lay it on the vanity. Painstakingly slow, I raise the hem of her robe until my hands find her hips. When I hoist her onto the marble counter, she hisses as the cold stone connects with her skin. I slide my hands to her knees, spreading her. Slowly, I slide my palms up as my thumbs caress the soft flesh of her inner thighs. My eyes remain on hers as I crouch in front of her. My cock twitches as a small whimper escapes when I place my lips on the delicate skin of her inner thigh. She leans back, her shoulders connecting with the mirror, her eyes watching my every move.

11

BLISS

Morgan

Head between my thighs, his soulful brown eyes look up through his dark lashes. When a whimper escapes, Derek darts his tongue towards me. The sensation of his hot, wet tongue connecting with my swollen clit catapults me toward release. The bathroom's bright lights illuminate every plane of his face as he works, his five o'clock shadow brushing against my inner thighs with a delicious friction that only heightens every sensation. I've missed sex. Toys are okay, but nothing compares to a hot-blooded man between my thighs. This man I barely know but who somehow makes me feel more alive than I've ever felt.

My fingers tangle in his long thick hair, feeling the softness against my skin as I fight to maintain control. It grows harder and harder to keep my eyes focused on his dark brown ones looking up at me. Those eyes are so intense, they watch my every reaction with a hunger that makes my stomach flip. I'm perched precariously on the marble vanity, the cool stone a stark contrast to the heat building between my legs. Losing the battle, my eyes close, and my head falls against the mirror behind me, the glass cool against my flushed skin.

Derek sucks hard once more on my clit before depriving me of his mouth. I groan my protest; I am too close for him to stop. The bathroom's acoustics amplify my neediness, making me sound desperate even to my own ears. I open my eyes to find his mouth moving towards mine as his fingertips connect with my core. My arousal glistens on his mouth, as he rises up to capture my lips. His mouth tastes like me, a reminder of where he's been, and the thought sends another pulse of desire through my body. My eyelids grow heavy once more as his calloused fingertips strum against my greedy bud.

"Holy fuck!" I groan, my voice echoing off the tile walls. The bathroom fan hums steadily in the background, a mundane counterpoint to the extraordinary sensations coursing through me. "Close... So...damn...close," my breathy voice communicates, hoping he won't take another break before I cum, fucking his fingers.

How is he playing me so perfectly when we only just met?

My thoughts scatter like leaves in a windstorm as his rhythm increases. "Yes!" I proclaim as lightning shoots through my veins, and pleasure sweeps over me.

My legs tremble uncontrollably, thighs clamping around his wrist as waves of pleasure ripple outward from my center. The chandelier lights above seem to pulse with my heartbeat as I ride out the most intense orgasm I've experienced. Brock never worked me like this.

He continues to work his fingers, drawing out my pleasure. His eyes never leave my face, studying every twitch, every gasp, cataloging my responses like he's memorizing a map. Unsure if I can take any more, I slap my hand against the marble in surrender, the sharp sound cracking through the humid air. Taking pity on me, his fingers cease moving and rest upon my bare thighs. This allows me to catch my breath. His long damp hair curls slightly over his ears, calling my fingers to tangle within. A wicked smirk on his sun-tanned face, he picks me up as if I weigh nothing.

His arms, corded with muscle, cradle me against his bare, damp chest. I can feel his heart hammering beneath his ribs. My skin feels hypersensitive, every flutter of air, every brush of his hard chest against my nipples, every touch magnified a thousand times.

The absurdity of the situation hits me. I'm a 34-year-old divorced mother of two, being carried half naked through my master bathroom by a man I just met.

. . .

"Put me down; I can walk," I demand while swatting his chest, I need to slip out of my robe and remove his towel.

To my surprise, he lowers me slowly to the floor. My body slides down his in blessed friction. The cool tile sends a shiver up my spine, bringing me back to the reality of what we're doing. What I'm doing. My first encounter since the divorce, and it's with a stranger. It's like a plot in one of my books. A one-night stand that rocks the main character to her core. The irony that he's a member at the very place where my ex-husband holds court every weekend, flaunting his new, younger girlfriend in the restaurant.

His eyes roam appreciatively over my body, making me resist the urge to cover myself. Thirteen years of motherhood have left their marks—the silvery stretch marks across my hips, the slight softness of my belly and the sag of my breasts, but the hunger in his gaze makes me feel beautiful for the first time in years.

∼

Derek

Morgan lies naked on the bed in front of me, propped up on her elbows while her folds glisten with her desire. Her auburn hair spills across the pale green sheets, framing her like a halo of red. The afternoon sun filters through the plantation shutters, painting golden stripes across her pale skin, highlighting the freckles scattered across her shoulders like constellations I can't wait to trace.

I watch her eyes study my actions, and I decide to play with her a bit. Tugging on the corner of my towel, I drop it beside me. With my left hand, I grip my cock, stroking my shaft slowly, deliberately. The anticipation builds between us, a tangible heated thing in the air-conditioned bedroom. My smirk grows; I know I'm blessed, and she's about to be very pleased.

She bites her lower lip, leaving teeth marks in the soft flesh. Her chest rises and falls with quickened breaths, her nipples pebble as if reaching for me. There's something deliciously taboo about this. I'm a stranger to her although I've learned much about her this past year.

"C'mon," she protests, voice husky with need. Her foot nudges my thigh impatiently. "Let me play with your manaconda."

I laugh out loud at her terminology, the tension breaking momentarily. This is what drew me to her. Like me she doesn't fit the country club mold. She's feisty, vocal, with an her unexpected humor, the way her eyes crinkle when she smiles. I'm drawn to her the sharp wit beneath the country club polish.

"I'm not sure you are ready," I tease, continuing to stroke myself. The head of my cock glistens with pre-cum, my body as eager as hers despite my attempt to maintain control.

"Fine. I don't need you. I have a drawer full of toys..." she threatens, her voice playful yet determined. The mental image of her pleasuring herself makes my cock twitch in my hand. He wants her, he needs her.

I grab her ankle as she attempts to roll to the drawer of her nightstand. Her skin is soft beneath my fingers, tanned from afternoons on the golf course. I can smell the scent of her arousal upon my chin.

"Where do you think you are going?"

"Afraid of toys, are you?" she smiles coyly.

"Red, I like toys, but I don't think we'll need them this time," my voice rumbles from my chest. The nickname—inspired by the fiery highlights in her hair when the sun hits it just right—slips out naturally, though we've known each other less than an hour.

I love her fiery side, thrill me, and I'm relieved it carries over to sex. The contrast between her country club persona—polite, reserved, the perfect ex-wife of a successful businessman—and this passionate woman before me is intoxicating. I find nothing hotter than a woman that says what she wants and takes control from time to time.

Morgan breaks free of my hold crawling toward the edge of the bed, looking over her shoulder, eyes cast below my waist. Her appreciative gaze is hungry. I'm not mammoth, but I am above average. While I'm out of practice, I have not forgotten what women like. The sheets rustle beneath her as she shifts position, anticipation evident in every movement.

"Nope. No toys," she agrees, rubbing her hands together in playful anticipation. Her wedding ring is gone, but the pale band of skin where it used to be serves as a reminder of her recent loss.

As I climb onto her bed, the mattress dips beneath my weight. She reaches for a condom on the nightstand, the gold foil packet catching the light. The sheets are cool against my knees, a stark contrast to the heat radiating from her body. Remembering her little detour to fetch one earlier, I must ask.

"So, where do you keep your condoms?"

Morgan's cheeks turn red, and she groans, covering her face with her hands, the gesture unexpectedly adorable for a woman in her thirties. "I'm a new divorcée, so I wasn't prepared for your... Well, for all of this." She points up and down my body before her hand returns to her face. "I bought a box for my son, figuring soon I'll need to have the safe sex talk with him, and I placed the box on the top shelf of the pantry."

She peeks through her fingers, looking toward me once again. The confession makes her seem vulnerable, reminding me that beneath the confidence and desire, she's navigating new territory—a woman finding herself again after the end of a marriage.

"So, these are your son's condoms?" I chortle, amused by her resourcefulness and the slight absurdity of the situation.

She wobbles her head from side to side, her embarrassment fading as she smiles. In that moment, with her guard down, she's even more beautiful than during her perfect golf swing when out with the ladies.

"Since he isn't active, they're fair game in my book." She smiles, cheeks still flaming. "Besides, better me than him using them since he's only thirteen."

"We'll need to replace his and stock our own," I inform her, kissing my way up her arm. My words suggest a future—more encounters, more afternoons like this—and I mean it. This isn't just a one-time thing for me. Soon she'll know it, too.

"We'll need that many?" she inquires, wide-eyed, her surprise genuine and flattering.

I nod. "Yes. I plan to need..."

Her hands fly to the back of my head, and she plasters her mouth to mine, halting my sentence. Her lips are soft but demanding as she kisses me deeply, her tongue twirling with mine. Controlling the kiss, she maneuvers me to roll. Pushing my back to the bed, she straddles my hips, aligning our bodies, providing perfect contact and friction. Too perfect. The weight of her, the heat of her core against me, nearly undoes me.

"Condom," I growl. She eagerly rolls the rubber down my shaft eagerness alight on her face.

I ease my hand between us, guiding the head of my cock to her entrance. She wastes no time, impaling herself to the hilt.

With her heat enveloping me, it catapults me closer to the edge. I close my eyes, attempting to tamp down my next orgasm. The sensation is overwhelming—her slick heat gripping me, her soft moans filling the room, the scent of sex heavy in the air.

Hands on her waist, I flip us over, planting her back to the mattress. The sheets rustle beneath us, already damp from our shower. Still connected, I lift her left leg over my shoulder. Her calf rests on my back, skin smooth against mine. As I thrust, Morgan's back arches off the mattress, her breasts on display. She's a vision—hair splayed across the pillow, lips parted, eyes half-closed in pleasure.

I'm close enough that when I dart my tongue out I lick her pebbled nipple. The taste of her skin, hard yet soft, fuels my desire. She arches closer on the next thrust, and my balls tighten in that telltale sign. The headboard knocks gently against the wall, creating a rhythm to match our movements.

Needing to service her first, I slow my thrusts, press circles into her swollen clit with the pad of my thumb. Her breathing hitches, her inner walls clench around me. The knowledge that I can give her this pleasure—this moment of pure release and freedom—fills me with unexpected satisfaction. This isn't just sex; it's liberation for both of us, a new beginning in the most primal way possible.

This is a beautiful beginning for us.

THE END FOR NOW.

Read all of Morgan and Derek's story in *Ladies of the Links #5*.

ABOUT THE AUTHOR

Haley Rhoades's writing is another bucket-list item coming to fruition, just like meeting Stephen Tyler and Ozzie Smith, and skydiving. As she continues to write contemporary romance, she also writes closed-door romance and young adult books under the name Brooklyn Bailey, as well as children's books under the name Gretchen Stephens.

Haley's under five-foot, fun-size stature houses a full-size attitude. Her uber-competitiveness in all things entertains, frustrates, and challenges family and friends.

Haley's guilty pleasures are Lifetime and Hallmark movies. Her other loves include all things peanut butter, *Star Wars*, mathematics, and travel. Past day jobs vary tremendously from a radio station DJ, to an elementary special-education para-professional, to a YMCA sports director, to a retail store accounting department, and finally a high school mathematics teacher.

Haley resides with her husband and fur-baby in the Des Moines area. A new grandma known as "Gigi", she spend many evenings on video calls with her grandson Murphy or traveling to spend time with her latest obsession. This Missouri-born girl enjoys the diversity the Midwest offers.

http://www.haleyrhoades.com/

ADRIFT AND OUT OF TIME IN DEADWOOD

A JARVIS MANN DETECTIVE SHORT STORY

R. WEIR

FOREWORD

There are some cases for a private eye you don't quickly forget. For good reason or bad, they latch onto your memory for an eternity. One such case took me, Jarvis Mann, to Deadwood, South Dakota. The strange and unfathomable events to this day, ones I still can't explain or completely match what history books tell us. And it all started when I was hired by a husband and wife to find their runaway daughter. My journey began as I ventured out of the Mile High city of Denver, on the winding road north, to the wild, wild west of Deadwood. The town being wilder than I bargained for or ever imagined.

1

Bart and Winona had hired me to find their daughter, Cassidy. She had run away from home two years ago at the age of sixteen. Bart being a strict, overbearing parent, had forbidden his daughter from dating an older man when he had learned of their romantic involvement. This created many hostile confrontations between them. Which led to the threat of grounding and restricting her to her room, making for tense moments at home.

Cassidy stood firm and defied her father at every turn. Determined and in love, she fought until she couldn't take the conflict anymore. A secret plan she soon concocted. Late one night, she stealthily slipped out of the house and ran off with the nineteen-year-old man. A note left behind proclaiming she wouldn't be returning home. Fairy tale dreams of starting their life together shared between them with no more interference from her father.

When he learned of her departure, Bart with a dismissive wave, was happy his daughter had left. The stressful conflict between them had ceased. But when Cassidy left, her mother Winona was heartbroken. Her baby and only child had left the nest too soon. Winona's fiery rage now directed at Bart. Subtle reminders around the house of her daughter setting off her fury. Photos, her bedroom and possessions she had left behind, being triggers. A verbal domestic battle was waged on and off between the spouses for two years. When Cassidy's eighteenth birthday came and went, Winona's constant pressure eventually wore Bart down to the point where he was willing to extend an olive branch and welcome Cassidy back, though with conditions. The only problem was they had no idea where she had run off to. All contact between them had been broken during those two years.

Winona asked around, and a friend of a friend passed on my card. A gold embossed font, which read: *Private Eye Jarvis Mann.* After a couple of phone calls, a data gathering interview with the parents and a cash deposit, I began my work. Doing what I do best, which was to find people who didn't want to be found. My investigation took a month of personal interviews, web research, and phone calls, until I finally learned that Cassidy was living and working in Deadwood, South Dakota. Armed with this knowledge, I made arrangements in June for a commercial airline flight to Rapid City and a rental car for transport. After landing, a forty-five-minute drive west on I-90 to US Highway 14A took me to my destination.

When I entered Deadwood, I found Main Street had been closed to vehicle traffic. A yearly celebration for Wild Bill Days was in full swing. A large stage erected for concerts at the north end, with a huge screen in the middle for those farther away to clearly see the entertainers. At the south end, a huge pool and stands for spectators to watch Dock Diving dogs and their owners competing against each other. The crowds of people had come from all over the country to enjoy the multi-days of festivities. Which made finding parking a challenge. A long uphill walk for myself was required from the lot on the outskirts of town. The establishment I was searching for was on Main Street, in an old, multi-story, red brick building known as: The Wild Bill Bar.

On my way, I passed buildings which had stood for over a hundred years. Many had been rebuilt thanks to several fires that had ravaged parts of the town throughout its lifetime. My feet walked over the red brick road which once was traveled by horse and buggy. The never-ending search for gold and dreams of striking it rich, which many failed to obtain. The ebbs and flows which nearly led Deadwood to be a footnote in history and another Old West ghost town.

From quick research on my phone, I learned in 1961 Deadwood was designated a National Historical Landmark with the hopes of preserving the town's history well into the future. Then in 1989 gambling was legalized and stimulated the economy of this old mining town. Its survival was fueled by the digital sounds of electronic machines which echoed up and down the main strip. Additional revenue from restaurants, bars, and shops for souvenir-searching tourists. I admired the modern touches mixed in with the past. I could have dropped a few bills and coins of my own as I passed each building, but I had a job to do.

I made it to the front doors of 624 Main Street. A wooden sign hanging from the front facing claiming the historical significance of the building. I glanced inside but couldn't see much, because the windows were darkly tinted, no light visible from my vantage point. I trusted my skills and was certain my long journey would be fruitful and I would find Cassidy. I pulled the door open and stepped in. I immediately felt a rush of wind wrenching me forward. I struggled and fought to keep my balance and soon felt dizzy. Popping and ringing filling my eardrums which created the sensation of vertigo. My eyes now closed, I steadied myself, carefully stepping onward, until I came to a stop. I opened my eyes and regained my balance, stunned by the surroundings. I closed my eyes once more, shook my head, and opened them again. The scene before me, one I couldn't comprehend.

2

Everywhere I looked, every sound I heard, every aroma I smelled, told me I was now standing in the past. The setting, the people, all of it, screamed of the wild west. Tables with men in western gear and packing sidearms playing poker. Women cinched tightly with corsets under gowns and bustled skirts of lace and ribbons designed by men to tempt the male libido. Ragtime music filled the airwaves as a piano player tickled the ivories. I had no idea what had happened. It was like everyone in the bar had come dressed for a costume party. All of it from the late 1800's. No modern amenities were evident, like electricity. Besides sunlight cascading through windows, illuminance was provided by oil lamps from the walls, ceiling and tables. Not a television or gambling machine in sight.

I found a wall mirror and checked myself out, shocked at what I was wearing. I had on a brown western shirt, leather chaps over jeans, and boots. My Colorado baseball cap had been replaced with a well-worn, black cowboy hat. On my hip was a belt and holster loaded with a western colt revolver. I slapped my scruffy face and looked again, but nothing changed. I had no explanation for whatever had happened.

I stood there dumfounded when I realized a disgusting taste in my mouth. I had been chewing gum worried about my breath after the long flight. The gum now gone and replaced with a hideous hot and bitter flavor. I glanced around and saw a large container one of the men had spat into. I ran over and discharged every ounce of chewing tobacco nastiness which had somehow replaced the gum. The taste one I wasn't certain I'd ever be free of. I went to the bar and ordered a glass of ice water. The bartender squinted his eyes and snorted at me. He dropped a shot glass on the counter and poured a dark colored liquid until it overflowed. I swore the concoction was burning the wood counter as steam rose from the excess.

"Water will get you shot in here," he bellowed. "Drink this. It will put hair on your chest."

I picked up the wet glass. It smelled of pure alcohol. Mixing it with the tobacco would likely cause a fire in my mouth. I sat the glass down and started to walk away.

"Hey, you need to pay for the drink." The bartender pulled out a pistol and waved it at me.

A female voice spoke firmly. "It's okay Lance. I'll handle it."

Lance seemed displeased. "Damn, it's been a while since I had the opportunity to kill someone." He tucked the pistol back behind the counter. "No need for this to go to waste." He grabbed the shot glass and drank it down in one swig to prove his cast iron stomach could handle the firewater.

"Hello sheriff." A woman, several inches shorter than me, approached with a smile on her heavily made-up face. "What brings you in today?"

My face scrunched in confusion. "Sheriff?"

She put her hand on my chest and rubbed a shiny silver star. "That is what it says. Though you ain't a sheriff from these parts. I know them all, and I've never seen you before. Where are you from?"

I wanted to say Kansas, for I thought myself and Dorothy might have something in common.

"Denver."

She kept her hand on the star. "Wow. You've traveled a long distance. Did you ride a horse all this way or take the stagecoach?"

I could have said Mustang, for that is what I drove back home. Though it had more horsepower than what I believed she was referring to.

"I flew on a jet to Rapid City and then I drove here."

She pulled her hand back. "Flew?" She started to laugh. "Honey, I don't see no wings for you to fly with."

It appeared she had no idea what I was talking about. Hell, I was confused, too.

"I'm here looking for a woman."

Her eyes lit up. "Honey, you're in the right place." She put out her hand. "I'm Dirty Em, the owner of this establishment. Well, at least the female entertainment part of the bar."

I shook her hand, finding it rough but warm. Her blue eyes and long eyelashes gazed at me lovingly. Her long dark hair pulled tightly into a bun. She wore a bright colored dress which accentuated her breasts and hips while squeezing her waist. I wanted to ask her if she could breathe with the constraints of her outfit but decided now was not the time for my snarky attitude.

"Dirty Em?" It was a question, for I had no idea who she was. "Quite an unusual name."

"A name given to me because of my profession. I'm the Madam of this bar, in charge of the girls who provide pleasurable entertainment for the rowdy men of this town."

"Dirty Em, I think you misunderstood what I'm looking for."

She came to my side and put her arm through mine. "Oh sweety, don't play coy with me. After such a long trip I bet you could use a little company. My girls will show you a good time and give you a happy ending. And we give discounts to law enforcement, no matter where you're from." She tugged on my arm to direct me forward. "Do you like blondes, brunettes, or redheads? Or maybe your tastes run more exotic, like from the oriental Far East."

The picture I'd been given of Cassidy meant I was searching for a redhead, but for a different reason than what Dirty Em assumed. I was about to tell her Cassidy's name, when there was a disturbance at one of the tables. A loud argument, one man yelling at another.

The first man stood and knocked over his chair. He couldn't have been much older than eighteen. "You're a cheat, mister! Show me the cards you have up your sleeve."

The other man leaned back in his chair. "Son, you need to take your seat before you get hurt."

The young man started to go for his gun, but the other man was faster, his Colt pointed and ready to fire.

"Like I said, best you sit down. I don't want to kill you, but I won't sit still and let you fire first."

Dirty Em tugged at my arm. "Do something sheriff!"

I looked down at the shield wondering if I should get involved. I knew I wasn't a sheriff, only a private eye. Though at this point I wasn't certain of anything.

"I might be a sheriff, but not a sheriff of Deadwood."

"I guess it's up to me then."

She started to walk over but I stopped her. My male bravado couldn't allow her to step into the middle of a skirmish.

"Young man." I spoke with a deep, forceful timbre. "He is right. Best you sit down or leave. You have a long life ahead of you but it will end quickly at this man's hand."

"How is it your business?" he asked.

I pointed at the silver star, hoping it was enough to get him to stop his aggression.

The young man looked around the room, seeing all eyes on him. Backing down was never easy, especially when you don't want to look like a coward. Reputation was important even when you were young, but there was little doubt his life would be over if he didn't walk away. He threw out his chest and huffed in a final act of defiance, finished off his drink, then stormed off to the other side of the bar.

The man who had been accused of cheating turned on his chair and looked at me. His winning hand on the table of two aces and two eights, with the fifth card hidden under one of the eights. He stood and put out his leathery hand.

"Thanks. I'm glad I didn't have to kill the young man. I have done enough killing in my day."

I grabbed his quivering hand which was rough like a day laborer. The hulk of a man was about my height, with wavy long coal black hair and a bushy mustache. He was wearing a dark tight-fitting jacket over a white shirt and a crooked bow tie. He smelled as if he hadn't bathed in a week. The body odor mixed in with the smell of booze and cigars. His face was familiar, one I'd seen sketched on several posters plastered around Deadwood.

"Sheriff, I'm William. Though most call me Wild Bill."

3

I was flabbergasted, for a famous western legend stood before me. Wild Bill Hickok in the flesh it would seem. I wanted to reach out to see if the upper lip mustache and hair on his head was real or was Hollywood magic. I started to wonder if this was a dream or if someone had spiked my drink, not that I'd had a drink. Maybe it was from the horrible chewing tobacco which mysteriously replaced the gum in my mouth. *Could it have been laced with a hallucinogenic?* If I were truly tripping, it was the most lucid of trips a man could have. There were no rainbow unicorns or talking animals. Maybe they were hiding in a backroom or upstairs waiting to spring on me.

"It's nice to meet you." Once I said the words, I knew I sounded like a star struck teenager.

"I did time as a sheriff back in the day." Wild Bill took a puff of his cigar. "A Deputy US Marshal and then a city marshal in Kansas. Are you a sheriff here in town?"

"Denver," was all I said.

"Are you on the hunt for someone, sheriff? I'm sorry what was your name?"

"Jarvis Mann."

He looked cross-eyed at me. "Jarvis. What type of name is that?"

It appeared even in this timeframe, the name Jarvis was unusual.

"It was my grandfather's name. Given to me by my parents."

Boisterous laughter filled the background. A few of the men in the bar had heard me say my name. One stood, walked over, and started to look me up and down. His foul stench nearly knocked me over. His day must have been spent shoveling manure.

"What a sissy name." He slapped me on the back. "For someone who came all the way from Denver, you look and smell awful pretty. Are you wearing women's underwear under them chaps?"

He laughed even harder. I wanted to punch him in his filthy snout. Instead, I turned toward him and glared him in the eye.

"Better than smelling like an overused stable!" I was pleased I'd not lost my razor-sharp wit in this fantasy world I was trapped within.

The man's joy turned to rage. "It seems you have a backbone after all. Care to step outside and see who can draw the fastest!"

This couldn't be real. A duel in the streets of Deadwood. I'd heard of actors recreating the duels from days gone by. *Had I stumbled into a movie set? Would the director be stepping into the room soon and yelling cut!* I had no idea, but I knew I wasn't about to jump out into the streets with this man and learn the hard way.

"You aren't worth my time." I turned my back on the man, which was stupid.

"You coward!"

The bar went deathly quiet after he yelled. I heard him unholster his gun and the audible sound of the hammer being pulled. It seemed in this lawless town, I was about to get shot in the back.

"Drop the gun," a coarse voice declared. "Or I'll drop you."

"This is none of your business," the man replied.

"I made it my business. Now put the gun away before I shoot you."

Bill added his two cents. "I'd do as you've been told. That rifle will leave a huge hole in you."

There was a long pause. The second armed showdown of the day. Probably not the last. I turned around and saw the angry man slowly holstering his gun. There, a few feet away was a tall, plain-looking, short haired man, from head to toe wearing what looked like buffalo skin. Jacket, pants, and boots. A rifle in his hand, a belt of bullets around his waist. He stepped up and waved for the man to leave, which he promptly did. Though he cussed all the way out the front door.

"Damn, what the hell did I walk into today?" I asked.

485

"Just another day in Deadwood," Dirty Em replied. "We normally have a dead body or two on the floor by now."

"And what about the law?"

"There is no law here. Justice is carried out with a gun."

"I thought you said the law came into the bar frequently."

"They do. They normally are from other nearby towns. If we had a sheriff here in Deadwood, I imagine he wouldn't live too long. He'd have to be tough and smart. And not stupid enough to turn his back on someone. You're lucky Jane came along and intervened."

"Jane. I thought..."

"That she was a man? No surprise, for she dresses like one. Hates wearing traditional women's clothing. But yes, she is a woman. A damn tough one. There are many tales about Calamity and what all she has done."

"You mean, that rifle toting person is Calamity Jane?"

Even saying her name, I couldn't believe it.

4

It wasn't long before I was left alone in this crowded room of people. I was seemingly adrift and out of time in Deadwood. I started to wander around looking for anything to explain where I was. A green screen, camera, or movie set lighting. Even a modern device like a cellphone, which would tell me I was still standing in the 21st century. But nothing came into view. All the evidence told me I was back in the late 1800's. *How the hell was this possible?* No answer coming to fruition. I pinched my arm, thinking it was all a dream. No luck. I was truly awake and alive in the madness.

I turned around. The sounds and smells of the room had returned. Wild Bill was back playing cards. Calamity Jane sitting nearby drinking, her eyes fixed on Bill. Dirty Em working the room, sending men upstairs to be serviced by her girls. Money exchanged for those services. I shook my head, for I needed to get back to the reason why I was there. I was searching for a runaway girl, and I needed to find her and escape from this time travel adventure, or whatever the hell this was.

I walked over to the bar and called the bartender over to me.

"Are you wanting another water?" Lance chuckled at his cynical snide.

I ignored the shot. "Is there a girl working here named Cassidy?"

Lance grabbed a couple of empty glasses and tossed them into a bin of soapy water. "Maybe. Why are you asking?"

"Her parents hired me to find her. I was hoping to talk with her."

He started to rub down the counter. "The only way you talk with any of the girls around here is to pay Dirty Em. She is in charge of the ladies of the evening."

"And who owns the bar?"

"Mister Swearengen. He owns a couple of buildings here in town, including The Cricket."

I had no idea what or where the Cricket was. I'd not seen it when I walked Main Street. I wondered if it was a building of the past, lost in one of the Deadwood town fires. Or maybe I hadn't looked hard enough.

"Is Mister Swearengen available to talk?"

"I don't think he'll talk with a man wearing a badge. He isn't the most upstanding citizen. He enjoys the lawlessness of Deadwood. When the town folk talk of hiring a sheriff, he jumps in and kills those discussions. He likes the fact he can do anything he wants. And I mean anything."

Swearengen sounded like the type of character I needed to avoid. My best option was to approach Dirty Em. And it would cost me. I checked my pockets to see if I had any money. I pulled out a few coins, which included silver dollars. I looked at the date and most were stamped in the 1870's. Whatever had sent me back in time had provided me with money to survive on. Though I had no idea what a few dollars would get me. Maybe enough time to talk with Cassidy. I waded through the crowd to get her answer.

"Dirty Em, I wonder if you have a woman working here named Cassidy. She is a redhead. I was hoping to talk with her."

She put her hands on her hips and grinned. "A good-looking man like yourself; I doubt there will be much talking. Are you sure Cassidy is who you want? She is new to us. Not experienced if you know what I mean."

"She is who I want. What will it cost me?"

Dirty Em mulled over her answer. "Since you're a lawman and she is new to us, how about the bargain price of five dollars." She held out her hand. "Paid upfront."

I checked my pocket again. I found five silver dollars and handed them over. She took the money, pulled up the hem of her dress and stashed it in a cowhide coin purse tied to her ankle.

"I'll have you escorted to her room. You have one hour. If you need longer, then you'll need to pay more."

"One hour is plenty of time."

"It normally is for the men around here." She leaned forward and whispered. "Hell, ten minutes is all most of these horny males need." She laughed at her humor.

I was led up to the second floor and down a narrow dark hallway. A knock on the door and soon I was inside. The room, dimly lit with a couple of oil lanterns. The single bed neatly adorned, covered with a dingy comforter and two pillows. A small wooden dresser with a mirror on the opposite wall. No windows and only one other door which must have been a closet. Sitting in a rocking chair was a woman dressed in a wrinkled, white, lacey shirt and long flowing black skirt. Her long red hair pulled up and tied into a bundle on top. She rocked in the chair, without a smile on her makeup-laden face. From the pictures I'd seen, this was definitely Cassidy. And she didn't appear to be thrilled with the predicament she was facing. An emotion I understood all too well!

5

My first thought was: did Cassidy understand why we both were in this crazy timeframe. Could she explain to me what this was all about? Before I could ask, she stood with a sneer on her face and fumbled with the buttons on her blouse.

"Let's get this over with." Her words had no jolt to them.

I put out a hand and waved for her to stop. "I'm not here for sex. I'm here to take you home."

One button was undone and then she stopped. "What do you mean, take me home?"

I needed to come out and tell her the truth. Give her all the details as I knew them. Details I hoped translated in this timeline.

"Back to Denver. I'm Private Eye Jarvis Mann. Your parents hired me. Bart and Winona. They want you to come home."

"This makes no sense. I left home two years ago and now they *send* someone to find me. There is no way my father would let me come back."

I felt relief she understood the circumstances I had spelled out.

"Your mother was persistent and wore your father down. They both want you to come home." I left out the part about Bart's conditions. I knew this would only make Cassidy balk at returning.

"Even if I wanted to leave, they wouldn't let me."

"Who is they?"

"Dirty Em and her boss, Mister Swearengen. He is a brutal man, with enforcers to keep us in line."

"Dirty Em told me you are new. Is this your first day?"

"For working here, yes. I had a job at The Cricket, waiting tables. Mister Swearengen bullied me into moving here. He said I would make a better living lying on my back and letting men have their way with me."

"And you agreed?"

"He didn't give me much choice." A couple of tears stained her makeup. "Said he would sell me to some mining prospector who would put me to work digging for gold and then rape me each night. At least that is how he colorfully explained it. Here I at least have a bed to sleep in, instead of living in a musty tent."

I glanced around for a box of tissues, then realized there was no such invention during this time. I found a drab piece of cloth and tossed it to her.

"What happened to the man you ran off with?"

Cassidy wiped her tears and made a fist. "All was great for a while and then, without notice, he ran off with someone else, leaving me with nothing but the clothes on my back and little money."

"Why did he bring you to Deadwood?"

"We moved around at first trying to find our way. After a year we came to Deadwood. He met a man working in one of the bars here. Told him he could make a good living as a professional gambler and even worked with him to sharpen his skills. It wasn't long before he was winning a lot. Unfortunately, it brought wanton women in his direction as temptation. Men with money are like magnets around here."

"And he ran off with one of these women?"

"It was the only explanation I could muster. One day he was gone without a word. I had to find a way to support myself."

"Why didn't you give your parents a call?"

Her darkened brow furrowed. "What do you mean by *a call*?"

I should have known better. If I truly was in the 1870's timeline, phones were still in the process of being invented and not available for public use. "Sorry, I meant to say why didn't you try to contact them?"

"My only option was to write them a letter, which would take months to arrive. And after our blowout, how could I? All I would have heard was 'I told you so' from my father. Being lectured non-stop by him is why I left in the first place." She blew her nose. "Even if I could go home, I had no money. I was trapped here."

If I could discover a way out of this past world we've been transported to, I knew taking her back to her parents would give her a chance at a better life. Clearly preferable to having men screw her for money she would never receive. All of it likely ending up in Dirty Em and Mister Swearengen's pockets.

"What if I told you I could get you out of here and fly you back home?"

The creased brow returned. "What do you mean by fly?"

Like Dirty Em, it appeared she didn't understand the term either. "It's just an expression. Time will fly by and you'll soon be back home with people who love you."

"Even if I agreed, there is no way they'll let you take me. They own me. If I walk out, they'll stop me and you, violently."

I pointed at the badge on my shirt. "I'm a sheriff. They wouldn't dare challenge my authority."

Cassidy chuckled halfheartedly. "You do know you're in Deadwood. Right? There is no law here. The only law is at the end of a gun. They'll shoot you in the back, or face to face out on the street. I've seen it often enough."

I reached for my gun and pulled it out of the worn brown holster. It was an old Colt with six shots. I was used to a Beretta with seventeen rounds. And this was a weapon I'd never fired before. At least as far as I knew. I was at a disadvantage. I could kill six people and reload. By that time, I'd be long dead. Still, I didn't have a whole lot of options. I was paid to bring Cassidy back. If she wanted to go home, I owed it to my clients to complete the job.

"If I can guarantee to get you out of here, without you getting hurt, would you be willing to go with me?"

She crumpled up the piece of fabric in her hand and thought it over for a minute. "You speak like a confident man. If you can provide a guarantee, then I will go. Though I don't know how you'll get me past everyone downstairs and out the front door. Our lives are limited to these rooms on the second floor and nowhere else."

I hoped there might be a back way out, but I didn't see any when I surveyed the bar. I had a longshot of an idea I thought would work if I could get one person to help me out.

"Pack only the essentials in a small, easy to carry bag. We have a flight to catch."

She glared at me like I was from another planet, which wasn't all that farfetched.

"I mean stagecoach." I corrected myself and reached for the door-knob. "I'll be right back."

I walked into the hallway with an out-of-this-world plan forming. But what else would work in this out-of-the-world setting?

6

Once I was downstairs, I went to the poker table where Wild Bill was still playing cards. Off to the side I saw Calamity Jane watching the game, her drink glass nearly empty. I confidently sauntered over to her and said hello.

"Thanks for saving my neck earlier." I pointed at her glass. "It appears you could use another. Let me buy you a drink as a thank you."

She grabbed her glass and finished what was inside. A premonition had told me strong drink was Calamity Jane's biggest failing. Her big heart helping those in need, her strongest conviction. I needed to make an ally, and she was my best bet.

"What do you say we go to the bar counter," I said. "This card game has to be boring to watch as a bystander."

Without a word, Jane stood and walked with me to the bar. I found an open space where we leaned up against the edge. Lance placed a glass down and filled it with a dark liquor and then asked for money. I reached into my pocket and found more change and handed it to him.

"It appears he knows what you like to drink," I said.

She grabbed the glass and took a sip. "I'm a regular. Whiskey and beer are the only options for drink around here. And the beer tastes like piss water."

I had debated on ordering a beer earlier but I was glad I didn't!

"It appears drinking, gambling, and dueling rule this town."

She nodded and took another sip. Her eyes were on me, sizing me up or so I thought. I needed to get her trust. The drink was a beginning.

"You appear to spend a lot of time hanging with Wild Bill. Are you two close friends?"

She shrugged. "In a manner of speaking. We came into town together on the same wagon train."

"Married?"

Jane let out a puff of frustration. "No. He loves someone else."

Out of nervousness, I drummed my fingers on the counter. "The way you look at him, I figured differently."

Her eyes directed downward. "Then, you would be wrong."

"How did you get the nickname Calamity?" I was trying to build a bond with the woman.

Jane finished the drink. I waved to the bartender to pour again, after throwing down another coin.

"I rode into a group of fighting hostiles and saved a wounded captain. He is the one who gave me the name."

I grinned ear to ear and slapped the bar at her valor. "An amazing story."

"Not to many here. There are those who think I made it all up."

"Why?"

She gave a nod in Wild Bill's direction.

"I'm guessing the story didn't sway him any."

She took the newly filled glass and downed it all in one gulp. "Nope."

"I've heard tales of your humanitarian efforts to help people." I wasn't certain how I knew this. It was part of the premonition which came to me out of the blue while I was forming my plan. "I was wondering if you'd be interested in helping me."

She put the glass back down and tapped the bar to get it filled again. I hoped I had enough money to keep the whiskey flowing.

"I'm listening."

"I was hired by the parents of a young woman to find her. She is upstairs. I need a way to get her out of here. She is worried those who run this place will stop her."

Jane snickered. "She isn't lying."

"Those here," I leaned in and whispered, "especially Swearengen, bullied her into becoming a prostitute. A life she doesn't want. I was hoping I could borrow you to assist me."

"How?"

I pointed at her clothing.

"You mean have her dress up like this? It's not like I carry spares around."

"I want you to loan her what you're wearing. Once she is out, I'll return it to you."

"What do I wear in the meantime?"

"One of her dresses?"

Jane sneered. "I hate wearing a whore's clothes."

"You can hang out in her room until I can return them." I knew it was a long shot I would even make it back. "She has a nice room, with a bed. It will give you a chance to take a nap away from all this noise."

Jane twirled the glass around in her hands. She looked and saw another man being escorted up the stairs for his paid liaison. She swallowed down the rest of the drink and smiled.

"Why the hell not. I'm feeling bold thanks to the whiskey. Lead the way."

I stood and headed for the stairs when Dirty Em stopped me.

"See, I knew you'd be quick. All men are."

I promptly made up an excuse. "All I did was talk with her. I needed to come down here and have a couple of drinks to get up the nerve to complete the deed. Jane stopped by to give me some pointers. I believe I still have thirty minutes left on the hour I paid for."

"Yes you do. Now get to it. I may have another man who'll want a crack at Cassidy after you break her in."

I nodded but shivered internally at the thought. I turned and saw Jane had already gone up the stairs and down the hall, apparently with no one the wiser. People didn't seem to pay her any mind, which I knew would work in my favor. I hustled up the steps, found her and took her into Cassidy's room. It was there I introduced them.

"The sheriff tells me you want out of here. Is this correct?"

Cassidy nodded. "Yes. I don't want these smelly, creepy men lying on top and violating me."

"I understand. I've had a few try through the years without my permission and each one ended up dead."

"Let's hope we can avoid killing," I declared. "Jane is going to lend you her clothing. Then we'll walk you out of here and hope everyone thinks it's her leaving."

Cassidy looked at Jane, seeing the height difference. "I'm probably four inches shorter than her. Her clothing will be huge on me."

"Do you have some shoes with a tall heel?" I asked.

Cassidy nodded. "I have some boots with a good-sized heel."

"Good. Wear the boots and put Jane's clothes on over some other clothing you can strip down to, once we're out of sight. With her hat on, if you look down, I doubt anyone will be the wiser."

I didn't want to say out loud the part about the men not paying Calamity Jane much attention. Hurting her feelings or worse, pissing her off at this moment in time wouldn't help us.

"I'll step out of the room so you can swap clothing. Jane you keep your rifle and any other weapons you have. Once I get Cassidy somewhere safe, I'll return with your clothes. You have my word." I began to open the door and then thought of something. "Cassidy, please remove the makeup and lipstick on your face. Jane doesn't use any and we don't want people to get suspicious."

I stepped out and it took about fifteen minutes before I was called back in. Jane was lying on the bed, with the covers pulled over her body. Apparently, she didn't want me to see her in her undergarments. Cassidy was dressed in the buffalo skin clothing, the white scarf and hat. I went to her and rolled up the sleeves on the coat for they extended over her hands. I then pulled the bill of the hat down to make her face difficult to see. If you didn't look too closely, you couldn't tell the difference.

"Good luck," Jane said. "I'll remain here and have a snooze."

With all the whiskey consumed, this was no surprise and had been worth the silver dollars spent.

I glared at Cassidy. "Are you ready to do this?"

Along with more tears in her eyes, she shuddered. I used a finger to wipe them off her pale cheeks.

"It will be fine. Keep your head down and walk quickly. Once we get outside, we'll be in good shape." I saw a small bag at her feet. "We're taking this?"

She nodded.

I picked it up with my left hand and handed it to her. I needed to keep my hands free just in case. "It will all be over soon and we'll have you back home with your parents in no time."

Once we were in the hallway, I had my eyes peeled and ready for whatever phantasmal occurrence the past would present me.

7

We took the steps one by one. I wanted to rush, but didn't want to appear to be in a hurry. We made it to the ground floor, and I surveyed the room. Dirty Em was working a table, trying to drum up business. Cards and chips were going back and forth. The noise as loud as ever. The smoke as thick as fog. The piano man still playing what sounded like the same song over and over again. I wanted to ask him if he knew any Elton John songs, but I knew I'd only get a blank stare in return.

There was a partially clear pathway to the front door. Though the constant movement in the room meant it might not remain clear for long. I put my arm through Cassidy's and started to guide her. We got past a couple of poker tables and were a third of the way to our goal. We had to make a slight detour which added to our walk time, as a couple of drunk men had sprung up from their cards and were arguing. I got us around them but we got hit by the liquid of a thrown drink, the two men now on the floor wrestling.

At the halfway mark, I heard a male voice call out, yelling for Jane. I picked up the pace for I didn't want to be discovered. We got to within twenty feet of the exit when a hand grabbed Cassidy and spun her around.

"You bitch, don't try to ignore me!"

I moved in between Cassidy and the man to protect her. I saw his face and immediately knew it was the man who thought my first name was humorous until I pointed out his stench. Jane interceding to prevent him from shooting me in the back.

"Back off mister!" I pushed him backward. He still smelled like a distillery that brewed swill next door to a manure pile.

"I ain't talking to you Jarrrvis!" He strung out my name in distain. "I want Calamity to feel my wrath!"

From behind the man, Wild Bill approached. "McCall, you need to come back to the table and play poker. Leave old Jane alone."

"You stay out of this too Bill, before I plug you full of holes."

"Come on Jack, you know you aren't a killer. Return to the table. I know you've lost most of your money, but I'm willing to spot you some cash, even buy you a meal if you take it down a notch."

While they were talking, I started to walk backward while pushing Cassidy closer to the door. I had my right hand at the ready to pull out my gun if necessary. All I needed was a couple more minutes and we'd be out of there.

"Bill, I don't want or need your charity. Hell, I know you don't give two craps about Jane by the way you talk when she isn't around." McCall's hand inched down to his gun. "Go back to your table and leave me to my business."

Wild Bill held up his hands, turned and sat down at the table, his back to the man and picked up his cards. McCall pulled his gun, snarled and fired, shooting Bill in the back of the neck, his body jolting forward, what was left of his bloody head now resting on the table.

The shot echoed through the entire bar, followed by his shout of defiance. "I bet you think I'm a killer now!" McCall turned and aimed his pistol in my direction, smoke still coming from the barrel. "Now it's your turn! I doubt Jane can save you this time!"

We were at the door, and I pushed Cassidy through and out into the street. I had my gun in hand, uncertain of my ability to shoot the weapon. I aimed and fired, while falling backward toward the door. The power of the shot wrenched my wrist and hoisted me in the air and out onto the sidewalk. I had no idea if I hit McCall or anyone else with my wild shot. My eyes had gone blurry, and I felt a rush of air all around me.

It took a minute to find my faculties. I needed a while for my entire body to stop shaking. When my eyes opened, the modern world of Deadwood had returned. People walked the streets in shorts and T-shirts. Most strolled around me, assuming I was a drunk man lying on the sidewalk from their comments. I pulled myself up and looked to see if Cassidy was there. A few feet away she stood in shorts and a Deadwood 1876 T-shirt with two aces and eights, the very hand Wild Bill had left earlier on the table. I looked down at myself. I was back in the clothes and Colorado baseball cap I was wearing before I had been yanked into the bar. It appeared we had returned in time to where I had started.

"Wow, that was strange," I said. "What the hell just happened?"

Cassidy put her hands on her hips. "You're telling me! We were walking out the door and you suddenly pushed me. What was that all about?"

"I was trying to protect you from Jack McCall shooting you."

Cassidy drew her head back in surprise. "Who the hell is Jack McCall?"

"He had just shot Wild Bill Hickok and was about to shoot you as he thought you were Calamity Jane."

"Damn Jarvis, you must have bumped your head. I have no idea what you're talking about."

I glanced around and shook my head, for it hurt like hell. Then all of a sudden, I heard yelling and then gunfire out on the streets. I went to reach for the Colt, but there was no longer a holster or gun on my hip. I moved to protect Cassidy when I heard applause from people lining the street.

"It's only a performance," Cassidy said. "They do these reenactments several times a day. They are actors. I've been here so long, I hardly even notice the gunfire anymore."

I recalled my earlier notion about one of the main Deadwood attractions people came to witness. "A reenactment like Wild Bill Hickok getting shot by Jack McCall?"

"I suppose so. I never paid much attention. Is that why you freaked out and tossed me out the door?"

I thought about it for a minute and then shrugged. At this point, I had no idea what the hell had happened. All I knew was I'd had my fill of Deadwood, both the modern version and the wild west one. I put my hand on Cassidy's shoulder.

"We have a jet to catch in Rapid City to take you home."

Cassidy hesitated and then nodded. "Okay, I'm ready to face them."

I was pleased I didn't need to explain to her what a jet was, for I was no longer adrift and out of time in Deadwood.

8

I was sitting in my first-class seat on the flight back to Denver. Cassidy breathing softly next to me, a pillow around her neck, asleep. Sleep something I could use but was too worked up about the day's events. I had even stopped in a souvenir shop and picked up a book on the history of Deadwood. Trying to fill in the blanks and maybe give me answers about what happened. I thumbed through the pages reading all about the famous names which had made Deadwood the wild west town it was. A few names I had encountered or heard about, like Wild Bill Hickok, Calamity Jane, Al Swearengen, Jack McCall, and Dirty Em. And then a few others I hadn't run across. E.B. Farnum, Poker Face Alice Tubbs, Potato Creek Johnny, Seth Bullock, Solomon Star, and W.E. Adams. All with their own stories, each making their mark in one manner or another in the history books. Both good and evil. Portions of the facts not lining up to what I had experienced after I walked through those bar doors. Or at least thought I had experienced, for I really wasn't certain.

One difference was Al Swearengen. From the book, Swearengen did have the gambling and fighting establishment called The Cricket and a year later would open The Gem Theater. The doors I walked through with no apparent connection to the brutal man. Though Swearengen's reputation of luring women was well documented, which made Cassidy's story, at least the one from the past, accurate.

The book told me Wild Bill Hickok had been shot in the back of the head on August 2nd, 1876, by Jack McCall in the Nuttal & Mann's Saloon, later known as Saloon No. 10. The Wild Bill Bar now claiming to be the Historic Site of the shooting, even though the original structure had burned down. The infamous day still talked about, the facts still in debate. Was it over a disagreement playing poker? Or did Jack kill Wild Bill as revenge for his brother's death, which he blamed Wild Bill for perpetrating? Much like many stories of the wild west, the legend would live on and be debated for eternity.

Was this the time and place I had been transported to? Who the hell knows!

It was then I came across a name which shook me. One I knew, or at least I knew the surname. Colorado Charlie Utter. He was a trapper, guide, and prospector in the gold fields of Colorado before organizing a thirty-wagon wagon train to Deadwood in the Dakota Territory. The train had stopped in Wyoming to pick up passengers which included Wild Bill Hickok, Calamity Jane, Madam Mustache, Dirty Em, and her working girls.

None of this was the surprising part. The shock had been the surname of Utter, which was rare and unusual. And in this case the surname of Bart, Winona, and Cassidy. Could it be they were related to the man who had brought several of those famous characters to Deadwood? And now brought me there too, to witness history. The events of the last day were fresh and burned in my psyche. *Had it all been a dream or a hallucination?* No matter what, it was a wild memory I won't soon forget. A tall tale I might share with others, while I'm spending my final days in a rocking chair spinning yarns of old west legends for those who will listen.

ABOUT THE AUTHOR
R. WEIR

Award-winning Author R Weir lives in the Mile-High City with his family, where the Rocky Mountain High isn't always achieved with an herbal substance. When not glued to the computer, he relaxes by enjoying the outdoors and traveling in his motorhome. His writing delves into genres with gritty investigators exploring mystery, crime, suspense, and thrills, with involved plots and unexpected twists. Featuring former US Marshal Hunter Divine, a dire, determined man searching for salvation in his broken life. Private eye Jarvis Mann is tough and snarky, with as many faults as virtues. And his newest series featuring retired police officer Donnie Steel and his K-9 companion, Kogel. Characters exhibiting traces of his sense of humor, though he's not nearly as tough and fearless. Though no evil stands a chance against his written word!

A NOTE FROM R WEIR

Thanks for reading my fun Jarvis Mann Private Eye short story, **Adrift and Out of Time in Deadwood**. I hope you enjoy the adventure, as much as I did, creating the tale. The story is included in the 2025 Wild Deadwood Reads Anthology, **Wild in Deadwood Vol 2,** featuring many other great fictional stories across all genres about Deadwood South Dakota.

Be sure you check out all my Jarvis Mann Private Eye novels, of which there are ten books to read. Starting with, **The Case of the Missing Bubble Gum Card, Tracking a Shadow, Twice as Fatal, Blood Brothers, Dead Man Code, The Case of the Invisible Souls, The Front Range Butcher, Mann in the Crossfire, Lethal Blues and Murder by a Hundred Cuts**. All are available on Amazon in eBook, Paperback and Kindle Unlimited.

Plus check out my award-winning **Divine Devils** Suspense/Thriller series. Read the entire series in this order: **The Divine Devils, Fallen Star: The Divine Devils Book 2, Sold Souls: The Divine Devils Book 3, and Divine Retribution: The Divine Devils Final Chapter.** All are available in eBook, paperback, and on Kindle Unlimited.

And finally, the first book in my new series, **Justice For The**

Forgotten: A Steel Wheels Cold Mystery. Available in eBook, paperback and on Kindle Unlimited.

Find all my books via this link: https://www.amazon.com/R-Weir/e/B00JH2Y5US

If you want to reach out, please email me at: author@rweir.net

Receive two free eBooks of my Jarvis Mann PI series, ***The Case of the Missing Bubble Gum Card and Tracking A Shadow.*** All you need to do is sign up for my newsletter on my website. https://rweir.net

Follow R Weir, Jarvis Mann, Hunter Divine and Donnie Steel on these social sites as I appreciate hearing from those who've read my books:

https://www.facebook.com/randy.weir.524

https://www.facebook.com/JarvisMannPI

https://www.instagram.com/rweir720/

Thanks for reading. Stay Safe, Happy, and Healthy!!

AFTERWORD

Thanks for reading our anthology!

If you haven't already, be sure to read the first ten stories in Wild in Deadwood, Wild Deadwood Reads Anthology Volume 1 featuring ten stories set in Deadwood.